PAYMENT IN BLOOD

PAYMENT IN BLOOD

ELIZABETH GEORGE

BANTAM BOOKS
NEW YORK · TORONTO · LONDON · SYDNEY · AUCKLAND

PAYMENT IN BLOOD
A Bantam Book / September 1989

*Grateful acknowledgment is made for permission to reprint the following
excerpts: THE THREE SISTERS of Chekhov: THE MAJOR PLAYS translated
by Ann Dunnigan on pages 248–249. Reprinted by permission from NAL
BOOKS. SUMMER AND SMOKE by Tennessee Williams on page 227.
Copyright 1948 by Tennessee Williams. Reprinted by permission of New
Directions Publishing Corporation.*

Library of Congress Cataloging-in-Publication Data
George, Elizabeth.
  Payment in blood / Elizabeth George.
    p. cm.
  ISBN 0-553-05701-4
  I. Title.
PS3557.E478P39 1989   89-426
813′.54—dc19   CIP

Published simultaneously in the United States and Canada

In fond memory of
John Biere

When lovely woman stoops to folly
And finds too late that men betray,
What charm can soothe her melancholy,
What art can wash her guilt away?

The only art her guilt to cover,
To hide her shame from every eye,
To give repentance to her lover
And wring his bosom—is to die.

Oliver Goldsmith

1

GOWAN KILBRIDE, aged sixteen, had never been much for early rising. While still living on his parents' farm, he had grumbled his way out of bed each morning, letting everyone within hearing distance know, through a variety of groans and creative complaints, how little to his liking the life of husbandry was. So when Francesca Gerrard, the recently widowed owner of the largest estate in the area, decided to convert her Scottish great house into a country hotel in order to recoup upon the death duties, Gowan presented himself to her, the very man she would need to wait on tables, officiate behind the bar, and oversee a score of nubile young ladies who no doubt would eventually apply to work as serving girls or maids.

So much for fantasy, as Gowan soon discovered. For he had not been employed at Westerbrae a week before he realised that the workings of that immense granite house were to be orchestrated solely by a contingent of four: Mrs. Gerrard herself, a middle-aged cook with too much growth of hair on her upper lip, Gowan, and a seventeen-year-old girl newly arrived from Inverness, Mary Agnes Campbell.

Gowan's work possessed all the glamour commensurate with his position in the hotel hierarchy, which is to say that there was virtually none. He was a factotum, a man for all seasons of travail, be it working the grounds of the rambling estate, sweeping the floors, painting the walls, repairing the ancient boiler on a biweekly basis, or hanging fresh wallpaper to prepare the bedrooms for their

1

future guests. A humbling experience for a boy who had always seen himself as the next James Bond, the irritations of life at Westerbrae were mitigated solely by the delicious presence of Mary Agnes Campbell, who had come to the estate to help put the house in order prior to its receiving its first paying customers.

After less than a month of working at Mary Agnes' side, even getting up in the morning was no longer a chore, since the sooner Gowan bounded out of his room, the sooner he would have his first opportunity of seeing Mary Agnes, talking to her, catching her intoxicating scent on the air as she passed by. Indeed, in a mere three months, all his former dreams of drinking vodka martinis (shaken, not stirred) and showing a marked preference for Italian handguns with skeleton grips had been quite forgotten. In their place was the hope of being favoured with one of Mary Agnes' sunny smiles, with the sight of her pretty legs, with the agonising, tantalising, adolescent hope of brushing up against the swell of her lovely breasts in one corridor or another.

All that had seemed quite possible, quite reasonable in fact, until the arrival yesterday of Westerbrae's very first bona fide guests: a group of actors from London who had come with their producer, their director, and several other hangers-on to work the wrinkles out of a new production. Combined with what Gowan had found in the library this morning, the presence of these London luminaries was making his dream of bliss with Mary Agnes look more remote every moment. So when he pulled the crumpled piece of Westerbrae stationery out of the rubbish in the library, he went in search of Mary Agnes and found her alone in the cavernous kitchen, assembling trays of early morning tea to be carried up to the rooms.

The kitchen had long been a favourite haunt of Gowan's, mostly because, unlike the rest of the house, it had not been invaded, altered, or spoiled. There was no need to suit it to the tastes and predilections of future guests. They would hardly come wandering through to sample a sauce or talk about the turn of the meat.

So the kitchen had been left alone, just as Gowan remembered it from his childhood. The old tile floor of dull red and muted cream still made a pattern like an enormous draughtboard. Lines of coruscating brass pans hung from oak stringers against one wall where iron fixtures were like smudgy shadows on the cracked ceramic surface. A four-tiered pine rack atop one of the counters held the everyday dishes of the household, and beneath it a tricornered drying stand wobbled under its burden of tea towels and cloths. Pottery urns stood on the windowsills, holding oddly tropical plants with large, palmate leaves—plants that by rights should have withered under the icy adversities of a Scottish winter, but nonetheless thrived in the room's warmth.

It was, however, far from warm now. When Gowan entered, it was nearly seven, and the frigid morning air had not yet been cut by the huge stove heating against one wall. A large kettle steamed on one of the burners. Through the transomed windows, Gowan could see that the previous night's heavy snowfall had smoothly sculpted the lawns rolling down to Loch Achiemore. At another time, he might have admired the sight. But right now, righteous indignation prevented him from seeing anything but the fair-skinned sylph who stood at the worktable in the centre of the kitchen, covering trays with linen.

"Explain this tae me, Mary Agnes Campbell." Gowan's face flushed nearly to the colour of his hair and his freckles darkened perceptibly. He held out a discarded piece of stationery, his broad, callused thumb covering the Westerbrae estate crest upon it.

Mary Agnes directed guileless blue eyes towards the paper and gave it a cursory glance. Unembarrassed, she went into the china room and began pulling teapots, cups, and saucers from the shelves. It was every bit as if someone other than herself had written *Mrs. Jeremy Irons, Mary Agnes Irons, Mary Irons, Mary and Jeremy Irons, Mary and Jeremy Irons and family* in an unpractised script up and down the page.

"Wha' aboot?" she replied, tossing back her mass of ebony hair. The movement, designed to be coy, caused the white cap perched rakishly over her curls to fall askew, over one eye. She looked like a charming pirate.

Which was part of the problem. Gowan's blood had never burned for a single female in his entire life as it burned for Mary Agnes Campbell. He had grown up on Hillview Farm, one of the Westerbrae tenant holdings, and nothing in his wholesome life of fresh air, sheep, five brothers and sisters, and boating on the loch had prepared him for the effect Mary Agnes had upon him every time he was with her. Only the dream of someday making her his own had allowed him to keep hold of his reason.

That dream had never seemed entirely out of the range of possibility, in spite of the existence of Jeremy Irons, whose handsome face and soulful eyes, torn from the pages of countless movie magazines, graced the walls of Mary Agnes' room in the lower northwest corridor of the great house. After all, girlish adulation of the unreachable was typical, wasn't it? Or so Mrs. Gerrard tried to tell Gowan when he daily unburdened his heavy heart to her as she supervised his advancing skill at pouring wine without sloshing most of it onto the tablecloth.

That was all fine and good, so long as the unreachable remained unreachable. But now, with a houseful of London actors to mingle among, Gowan knew very well that Mary Agnes was beginning to see Jeremy Irons within her grasp. Surely one of these people was acquainted with him, would introduce her to him, would let nature take its course from there. This belief was attested to by the paper Gowan held in his hand, a clear indication of what Mary Agnes felt the future had in store for her.

"Wha' aboot?" he repeated incredulously. "Ye left this lyin' in the lib'ry, tha's wha' aboot!"

Mary Agnes plucked it from his hand and shoved it into her apron pocket. "Ye're kind tae retairn it, laddie," she replied.

Her placidity was infuriating. "Ye gie me no explanation?"

" 'Tis practice, Gowan."

"*Practice?*" The fire inside him was heating his blood to a boil. "Wha' kind of practice d'ye need tha' *Jeremy Irons*'ll help you with? All over the blessit paper. And him a marrit man!"

Mary Agnes' face paled. "Marrit?" She set one saucer down upon another. China jarred together unpleasantly.

Gowan at once regretted his impulsive words. He had no idea whether Jeremy Irons was married, but he felt driven to despair by the thought of Mary Agnes dreaming of the actor nightly as she lay in her bed while right next door Gowan sweated for the right to touch his lips to hers. It was ungodly. It was unfair. She ought well to suffer for it.

But when he saw her lips tremble, he berated himself for being such a fool. She'd hate *him*, not Jeremy Irons, if he wasn't careful. And that couldn't be borne.

"Ah, Mary, I canna say faer sairtin if he's marrit," Gowan admitted.

Mary Agnes sniffed, gathered up her china, and returned to the kitchen. Puppy-like, Gowan followed. She lined up the teapots on the trays and began spooning tea into them, straightening linen, arranging silver as she went, studiously ignoring him. Thoroughly chastened, Gowan searched for something to say that would get him back into her good graces. He watched her lean forward for the milk and sugar. Her full breasts strained against her soft wool dress.

Gowan's mouth went dry. "Hae I tol' ye aboot my row to Tomb's Isle?"

It was not the most inspired conversational gambit. Tomb's Isle was a tree-studded mound of land a quarter of a mile into Loch Achiemore. Capped by a curious structure that looked from a distance like a Victorian folly, it was the final resting place of

Phillip Gerrard, the recently departed husband of Westerbrae's present owner. Rowing out to it was certainly no feat of athletic prowess for a boy like Gowan, well used to labour. Certainly it was nothing that was going to impress Mary Agnes, who probably could have done the same herself. So he sought a way to make the story more interesting for her.

"Ye dinna know aboot the isle, Mary?"

Mary Agnes shrugged, setting teacups upon saucers. But her bright eyes danced to him briefly, and that was sufficient encouragement for Gowan to wax eloquent upon his tale.

"Ye havena haird? Why, Mary, all the villagers know tha' when the mune is full, Missus Francesca Gerrard stands buck nakit a' the windae of her bedroom and beckons Mister Phillip to coom back to her. From Tomb's Isle. Whair he's buried."

That certainly got Mary Agnes' attention. She stopped working on the trays, leaned against the table, and folded her arms, prepared to hear more.

"I dinna believe a word of this," she warned as preamble to his tale. But her tone suggested otherwise, and she didn't bother to hide a mischievous smile.

"Nar did I, lass. So las' full mune, I rowed out myself." Gowan anxiously awaited her reaction. The smile broadened. The eyes sparkled. Encouraged, he went on. "Ach, what a sicht Missus Gerrard was, Mary. Nakit at the windae! Her arms outstretched! An' glory, those dugs hanging claer tae her waist! Wha' an awful sicht!" He shuddered dramatically. " 'Tis na wunner to *me* tha' auld Mister Phillip be lying so still!" Gowan cast a longing glance at Mary Agnes' fine endowments. "Coorse, 'tis true tha' the sicht of a *luvely* breast cuid make a man do anything."

Mary Agnes ignored the less-than-subtle implication and went back to the tea trays, dismissing his narrative effort with, "Gae on wi' yere work, Gowan. Weren't ye supposed tae see tae the biler this mornin'? It wus fozling like my grannam last nicht."

At the girl's cool response, Gowan's heart sank. Surely the story about Mrs. Gerrard should have engaged Mary Agnes' imagination more than this, perhaps even encouraging her to request a row on the loch herself next full moon. With drooping shoulders, he shuffled towards the scullery and the creaking boiler within.

As if taking pity on him, however, Mary Agnes spoke again. "But aiven if Missus Gerrard wants, Mister Phillip winna coom back to her, laddie."

Gowan stopped in his tracks. "Why?"

" 'That my body shinna lie on this cursit ground of Westerbrae,' "
Mary Agnes quoted smartly. "That's what Mister Phillip Gerrard's
will said. Mrs. Gerrard told me that herself. So, if yere story is true,
she'll be at the windae forever if she hopes tae hae him back that
way. He isna aboot to walk across th' water like Jesus. Dugs or no
dugs, Gowan Kilbride."

Finishing her remarks with a restrained giggle, she went for the
kettle to begin making the morning tea. And when she came back
to the table to pour the water, she brushed so near him that his
blood began to heat all over again.

COUNTING MRS. GERRARD'S, there were ten trays of morning tea
to be delivered. Mary Agnes was determined to do them all without
stumbling, spilling a drop, or embarrassing herself by walking in on
one of the gentlemen while he was dressing. Or worse.

She had rehearsed her entry often enough for her debut as hotel
maid. "Guid mornin'. Luvely day," and a quick walk to the table to
set down the tea tray, careful to keep her eyes averted from the bed.
"Juist in case," Gowan would laugh.

She went through the china room, through the curtain-shrouded
dining room, and out into the massive entry hall of Westerbrae. Like
the stairway at its far side, the hall was uncarpeted, and its walls
were panelled in smoke-stained oak. An eighteenth-century chandelier hung from its ceiling, its prisms catching and diffracting a
soft beam of light from the lamp Gowan always switched on early
every morning on the reception desk. Oil, a bit of sawdust, and a
residual trace of turpentine scented the air, speaking of the efforts
Mrs. Gerrard was making to redecorate and turn her old home into
an hotel.

Overpowering these odours, however, was a more peculiar smell,
the product of last night's sudden, inexplicable flare of passion.
Gowan had just come into the great hall with a tray of glasses and
five bottles of liqueurs to serve to their guests when Mrs. Gerrard
tore wildly out of her little sitting room, sobbing like a baby. The
resulting blind collision between them had thrown Gowan to the
floor, creating a mess of shattered Waterford crystal and a pool of
alcohol a good quarter-inch deep from the sitting-room door stretching all the way to the reception desk beneath the stairs. It had taken
nearly an hour for Gowan to clean the mess up—cursing dramatically whenever Mary Agnes walked by—and all that time people

had been coming and going, shouting and crying, pounding up the stairs and down every corridor.

What all the excitement had been about was something that Mary Agnes had never quite determined. She knew only that the company of actors had gone into the sitting room with Mrs. Gerrard to read through a script, but within fifteen minutes their meeting had dissolved into little better than a furious brawl, with a broken curio cabinet, not to mention the disaster with the liqueurs and crystal, as evidence of it.

Mary Agnes crossed the hall to the stairs, mounting them carefully, trying to keep her feet from thundering against the bare wood. A set of house keys, bouncing importantly against her right hip, buoyed her confidence.

"Knock quietly first," Mrs. Gerrard had instructed. "If there's no answer, open the door—use the master key if you must—and leave the tray on the table. Open the curtains and say what a lovely day it is."

"And if 'tisna a luvely day?" Mary Agnes had asked impishly.

"Then pretend that it is."

Mary Agnes reached the top of the stairs, took a deep breath to steady herself, and eyed the row of closed doors. The first belonged to Lady Helen Clyde, and although Mary Agnes had seen Lady Helen help Gowan last night in the friendliest fashion with the spilled mess of liqueurs in the great hall, she wasn't confident enough to have her first-ever tray of early morning tea go to the daughter of an earl. There was too much chance of making a mistake. So she moved on, choosing the second room, whose occupant was far less likely to notice if a few drops of tea spilled onto her linen napkin.

There was no answer to her knock. The door was locked. Frowning, Mary Agnes balanced her tray on her left hip, and fumbled about with the keys until she found the master to the bedroom doors. This done, she unlocked the door, pushed it open, and entered, trying to keep all her rehearsed comments in mind.

The room, she discovered, was terribly cold, very dark, and completely soundless, where one would have expected at least the gentle hiss of the radiator at work. But perhaps the room's sole occupant had decided to pop into bed without turning it on. Or perhaps, Mary Agnes smiled to herself, she wasn't in the bed alone, but was snuggling up to one of the gentlemen under the eiderdown. Or more than snuggling. Mary Agnes stifled a giggle.

She walked to the table beneath the window, set down the tray, and pulled open the curtains as Mrs. Gerrard had instructed. It was not much after dawn, the sun only an incandescent sliver above the misty hills beyond Loch Achiemore. The loch itself shone silver, its surface a silky sheen upon which hills, sky, and the nearby forest were duplicated exactly. There were few clouds, just shredded bits like wisps of smoke. It promised to be a beautiful day, quite unlike yesterday with its bluster and storm.

"Luvely," Mary Agnes commented airily. "Guid mornin' tae ye."

She swung around from the curtains, straightened her shoulders to head back towards the door, and paused.

Something was wrong. Perhaps it was the air, too hushed as if the room itself had drawn in a quick breath. Or the odour it carried, rich and cloying, vaguely reminiscent of the scent that flew up when her mother pounded meat. Or the mounding of the bedcovers, as if pulled up in a hurry and left undisturbed. Or the absolute lack of movement beneath them. As if no one stirred. As if no one breathed . . .

Mary Agnes felt the bristling of hairs on the back of her neck. She felt rooted to the spot.

"Miss?" she whispered faintly. And then a second time, a bit louder, for indeed the woman might be sleeping very soundly. *"Miss?"*

There was no response.

Mary Agnes took a hesitant step. Her hands were cold, her fingers stiff, but she forced her arm forward. She jiggled the edge of the bed.

"Miss?" This third invocation brought no more reply than the previous two.

Seemingly on their own, her fingers curled round the eiderdown and began pulling it away from the figure beneath it. The blanket, feeling damp with that kind of bone-chilling cold that comes with a heavy winter storm, snagged, then slid away. And then Mary Agnes saw that horror had a life all its own.

The woman lay on her right side as if frozen, her mouth a rictus in the blood that pooled crimson about her head and shoulders. One arm was extended, palm up, as if in supplication. The other was tucked between her legs as if for warmth. Her long black hair was everywhere. Like the wings of ravens, it spread across the pillow; it curled against her arm; it soaked itself to a pulpy mass in her blood. This had begun to coagulate, so the crimson globules edged in black looked like petrified bubbles in a hell-broth. And in the centre of this, the woman was held immobilised, like an insect on a display board, impaled by the horn-handled dirk that plunged through the left side of her neck right into the mattress beneath her.

2

DETECTIVE INSPECTOR Thomas Lynley received the message shortly before ten that morning. He had gone out to Castle Sennen Farm for a look at their new livestock and was on his way back in the estate Land Rover when his brother intercepted him, hailing him from horseback as he reined in a heaving bay whose breath steamed from flaring nostrils. It was bitterly cold, far more so than was normal in Cornwall even at this time of year, and Lynley's eyes narrowed against it defensively as he lowered the Rover's window.

"You've a message from London," Peter Lynley shouted, wrapping the reins expertly round his hand. The mare tossed her head, sidestepping deliberately close to the dry-stone wall that served as border between field and road. "Superintendent Webberly. Something about Strathclyde CID. He wants you to phone him as soon as you can."

"That's all?"

The bay danced in a circle as if trying to rid herself of the burden on her back, and Peter laughed at the challenge to his authority. They battled for a moment, each determined to dominate the other, but Peter controlled the reins with a hand that knew instinctively when to let the horse feel the bit and when it would be an infringement on the animal's spirit to do so. He whipped her round in the fallow field, as if to circle had been an agreed-upon idea between them, and brought her chest forward to the frost-rimed wall.

"Hodge took the call." Peter grinned. "You know the sort of

thing. 'Scotland Yard for his lordship. Shall I go or you?' Oozing disapproval from every pore as he spoke."

"Nothing's changed there," was Lynley's response. Having been in his family's employ for over thirty years, the old butler had for the last twelve refused to come to terms with what he stubbornly referred to as "his lordship's whimsy," as if at any moment Lynley might come to his senses, see the light, and begin to live in its radiance in a manner to which Hodge fervently hoped he would become accustomed—in Cornwall, at Howenstow, as far as possible from New Scotland Yard. "What did Hodge tell him?"

"Probably that you were engaged in receiving obsequious servilities from your tenants. You know. 'His lordship is out on the land at the moment.' " Peter did a fair imitation of the butler's funereal tones. Both brothers laughed. "Do you want to ride back? It's faster than the Rover."

"Thanks, no. I'm afraid I've grown far too attached to my neck." Lynley put the car noisily in gear. Startled, the horse reared and plunged to one side, ignoring bit, rein, and heels in her desire to be off. Hooves clashed against rocks, whinny changed to a rolling-eyed call of fear. Lynley said nothing as he watched his brother struggle with the animal, knowing it was useless to ask him to be careful. The immediacy of danger and the fact that a wrong move could mean a broken bone were what attracted Peter to the horse in the first place.

As it was, Peter flung back his head in exhilaration. He'd come without a hat, and his hair shone in the winter sunlight, close-cropped to his skull like a golden cap. His hands were work-hardened, and even in winter his skin retained its tan, coloured by the months that he spent toiling in the southwestern sun. He was vibrantly alive, inordinately youthful. Watching him, Lynley felt decades more than ten years his senior.

"Hey, Saffron!" Peter shouted, wheeled the horse away from the wall, and, with a wave, shot off across the field. He would indeed reach Howenstow long before his brother.

When horse and rider had disappeared through a windbreak of sycamores at the far side of the field, Lynley pressed down on the accelerator, muttered in exasperation as the old car slipped momentarily out of gear, and hobbled his way back down the narrow lane.

LYNLEY PLACED his call to London from the small alcove off the drawing room. It was his personal sanctuary, built directly over the entrance porch of his family's home and furnished at the turn of the century by his grandfather, a man with an acute understanding of what made life bearable. An undersized mahogany desk sat beneath two narrow mullioned windows. Bookshelves held a variety of entertaining volumes and several bound decades of *Punch*. An ormolu clock ticked on the overmantel of the fireplace, near which a comfortable reading chair was drawn. It had always been an altogether welcoming site at the end of a tiring day.

Waiting for Webberly's secretary to track down the superintendent and wondering what both of them were doing at New Scotland Yard on a winter weekend, Lynley gazed out the window at the expansive garden below. His mother was there, a tall slim figure buttoned into a heavy pea jacket with an American baseball cap covering her sandy hair. She was involved in a discussion with one of the gardeners, a fact which prevented her from noticing that her retriever had fallen upon a glove she had dropped and was treating it as a midmorning snack. Lynley smiled as his mother caught sight of the dog. She shrieked and wrestled the glove away.

When Webberly's voice crackled over the line, it sounded as if he had come to the phone on a run. "We've a dicey situation," the superintendent announced with no prefatory remarks. "Some Drury Laners, a corpse, and the local police acting as if it's an outbreak of the bubonic plague. They put in a call to their local CID, Strathclyde. Strathclyde won't touch it. It's ours."

"Strathclyde?" Lynley repeated blankly. "But that's in Scotland."

He was stating the obvious to his commanding officer. Scotland had its own police force. Rarely did they call for assistance from the Yard. Even when they did so, the complexities of Scottish law made it difficult for the London police to work there effectively and impossible for them to take part in any subsequent court prosecutions. Something wasn't right. Lynley felt suspicion nag, but he temporised with:

"Isn't there someone else on call this weekend?" He knew that Webberly would supply the rest of the details attendant to that remark: it was the fourth time in five months that he had called Lynley back to duty in the middle of his time off.

"I know, I know," Webberly responded brusquely. "But this can't be helped. We'll sort it all out when it's over."

"When *what's* over?"

"It's one hell of a mess." Webberly's voice faded as someone else in his London office began to speak, tersely and at considerable length.

Lynley recognised that rumbling baritone. It belonged to Sir David Hillier, chief superintendent. Something *was* in the wind, indeed. As he listened, straining to catch Hillier's words, the two men apparently reached some sort of decision, for Webberly went on in a more confidential tone, as if he were speaking on an unsafe line and were wary of listeners.

"As I said, it's dicey. Stuart Rintoul, Lord Stinhurst, is involved. Do you know him?"

"Stinhurst. The producer?"

"The same. Midas of the Stage."

Lynley smiled at the epithet. It was very apt. Lord Stinhurst had made his reputation in London theatre by financing one successful show after another. A man with a keen sense of what the public would love and a willingness to take enormous risks with his money, he had a singular ability to recognise new talent, to cull prize-winning scripts from the chaff of mundanity that passed across his desk every day. His latest challenge, as anyone who read *The Times* could report, had been the acquisition and renovation of London's derelict Agincourt Theatre, a project into which Lord Stinhurst had invested well over a million pounds. The new Agincourt was scheduled to open in purported triumph in just two months. With that hovering so near in the future, it seemed inconceivable to Lynley that Stinhurst would leave London for even a short holiday. He was a single-minded perfectionist, a man in his seventies who had not taken any time off in years. It was part of his legend. So what was he doing in Scotland?

Webberly went on, as if answering Lynley's unasked question. "Apparently Stinhurst took a group up there to do some work on a script that was supposed to take the city by storm when the Agincourt opens. And they've a newspaperman with them—some chap from *The Times*. Drama critic, I think. Apparently he's been reporting on the Agincourt story from day one. But from what I was told this morning, right now he's frothing at the mouth to get to a telephone before we can get up there and muzzle him."

"Why?" Lynley asked and in a moment knew that Webberly had been saving the juiciest item for last.

"Because Joanna Ellacourt and Robert Gabriel are to be the stars of Lord Stinhurst's new production. And they're in Scotland as well."

Lynley could not suppress a low whistle of surprise. Joanna Ellacourt and Robert Gabriel. These were nobility of the theatre indeed, the two most sought-after actors in the country at the moment. In their years of partnership, Ellacourt and Gabriel had electrified the stage in everything from Shakespeare to Stoppard to O'Neill. Although they worked apart as often as they appeared together, it was when they took the stage as a couple that the magic occurred. And then the newspaper notices were always the same. *Chemistry, wit, hot-wired sexual tension that an audience can feel.* Most recently, Lynley recalled, in *Othello*, a Haymarket production that had run to sell-out crowds for months before finally closing just three weeks ago.

"Who's been killed?" Lynley asked.

"The author of the new play. Some up-and-comer, evidently. A woman. Name of . . ." There was a rustle of paper. "Joy Sinclair." Webberly *harrumphed*, always prelude to an unpleasant piece of news. It came with his next statement. "They've moved the body, I'm afraid."

"Damn and blast!" Lynley muttered. It would contaminate the murder scene, making his job more difficult.

"I know. I know. But it can't be helped now, can it? At any rate, Sergeant Havers will meet you at Heathrow. I've put you both on the one o'clock to Edinburgh."

"Havers won't work for this, sir. I'll need St. James if they've moved the body."

"St. James isn't Yard any longer, Inspector. I can't push that through on such short notice. If you want to take a forensic specialist, use one of our own men, not St. James."

Lynley was quite ready to parry the finality of that decision, intuitively comprehending why he had been called in on the case rather than any other DI who would be on duty this weekend. Stuart Rintoul, the Earl of Stinhurst, was obviously under suspicion for this murder, but they wanted the kind of kid-glove handling that would be guaranteed by the presence of the eighth Earl of Asherton, Lynley himself. Peer speaking to peer in just-one-of-us-boys fashion, probing delicately for the truth. That was all well and good, but as far as Lynley was concerned, if Webberly was going to play fast and loose with the duty roster in order to orchestrate a meeting between Lords Stinhurst and Asherton, he was not about to make his own job more difficult by having Detective Sergeant Barbara Havers along, chomping at the bit to be the first from her grammar school to slap handcuffs on an earl.

To Sergeant Havers, life's central problems—from the crisis in the economy to the rise in sexual diseases—all sprang from the class system, fully blown and developed, a bit like Athena from the head of Zeus. The entire subject of class, in fact, was the sorest of tender spots between them and it had proved to be the foundation, the structure, and the finial of every verbal battle Lynley had engaged in with her during the fifteen months that Havers had been assigned as his partner.

"This case doesn't speak to Havers' particular strengths," Lynley said reasonably. "Any objectivity she has will be shot to hell the minute she learns that Lord Stinhurst might be involved."

"She's grown past that. And if she hasn't, it's time she did if she wants to get anywhere with you."

Lynley shuddered at the thought that the superintendent might be implying that he and Sergeant Havers were about to become a permanent team, joined in a wedlock of careers he would never be able to escape. He looked for a way to use his superior's decision about Havers as part of a compromise that would meet his own needs. He found it by playing to a previous comment.

"If that's your decision, sir," he said equably. "But as to the complications attached to the removal of the body, St. James has more crime-scene experience than anyone currently on staff. You know better than I that he was our best crime-scene man then and . . ."

"Our best crime-scene man now. I know the standard line, Inspector. But we've a time problem here. St. James can't possibly be given—" A short bark of conversation from Chief Superintendent Hillier interrupted in the background. It was immediately muffled, no doubt by Webberly's hand over the mouthpiece. After a moment, the superintendent said, "All right. St. James has approval. Just get going, get up there and see to the mess." He coughed, cleared his throat, and finished with, "I'm not any happier than you are about this, Tommy."

Webberly rang off at once, allowing no time for either further discussion or questions. It was only when he was holding the dead telephone in his hand that Lynley had a moment to consider two curious details inherent to the conversation. He had been told virtually nothing about the crime, and for the first time in their twelve years of association, the superintendent had called Lynley by his Christian name. An odd cause for unease, to be sure. Yet he found himself wondering for the briefest of moments what was really at the root of this murder in Scotland.

*   *   *

WHEN HE left both alcove and drawing room—on his way to his own suite of rooms in Howenstow's east wing—the name finally struck Lynley. *Joy Sinclair*. He had seen it somewhere. And not all that long ago. He paused in the corridor next to a fruitwood mule chest and gazed, unfocussed, at the porcelain bowl on its top. *Sinclair. Sinclair.* It seemed so familiar, so within his grasp. The bowl's delicate pattern of blue against white blurred in his vision, the figures overlapping, crossing, inverting. . . .

Inverting. Back to front. Playing with words. It hadn't been *Joy Sinclair* he had seen, but *Sinclair's Joy*, a headline in the newspaper's Sunday magazine. It had been an obvious aren't-we-clever inversion that was followed by the teasing phrase: "A score with *Darkness* and on to bigger things."

He remembered thinking that the headline made her sound like a blind athlete on her way to the Olympics. And aside from the fact that he'd read far enough into the article to discover that she was no athlete but rather an author whose first play had been well received by critics and audiences seeking respite from London's usual glitzy fare, and whose second play would open the Agincourt Theatre, he had learned nothing else. For a call from Scotland Yard had sent him to Hyde Park and a five-year-old girl's naked body, shoved in among the bushes beneath the Serpentine Bridge.

Little wonder he'd not remembered Sinclair's name until this moment. The devastating sight of Megan Walsham, the knowledge of what she'd suffered before she died, had driven every other thought from his mind for weeks. He'd moved through time in a fury, sleeping, eating, and drinking his need to find Megan's killer . . . and then arresting the child's maternal uncle . . . and then having to tell her distraught mother who was responsible for the rape and mutilation and murder of her youngest child.

He had just come off that case, in fact. Bone-weary from long days and longer nights, yearning for rest, for a spiritual ablution to wash the filth of murder and inhumanity from his soul.

It was not to be. At least neither here nor now. He sighed, rapped his fingers sharply against the chest, and went to pack.

DETECTIVE CONSTABLE Kevin Lonan loathed drinking his tea from a flask. It always developed a repulsive film that reminded him of bath scum. For that reason, when circumstances required him to pour his longed-for afternoon cuppa from a dented Thermos resurrected from a cobwebbed corner of the Strathclyde CID office, he gagged down only a mouthful before dumping the rest out onto the meagre strip of tarmac that comprised the local airfield. Grimacing, wiping his mouth on the back of his gloved hand, he beat his arms to improve his circulation. Unlike yesterday, the sun was out, glittering like a false promise of spring against the plump drifts of snow, but still the temperature was well below freezing. And the thick bank of clouds riding down from the north promised another storm. If the party from Scotland Yard was to put in an appearance, they had better be flaming quick about it, Lonan thought morosely.

As if in response, the steady throb of rotor blades cut through the air from the east. A moment later, a Royal Scottish Police helicopter came into view. It circled Ardmucknish Bay in a tentative survey of what the ground afforded as a landing site, then slowly touched down on a square in the tarmac that a wheezing snow-plough had cleared for it thirty minutes earlier. Its rotor blades kept spinning, sending up minor snow flurries from the drifts that bordered the airfield. The noise was teeth-jarring.

The helicopter's passenger door was shoved open by a short, plump figure, muffled like a mummy from head to toe in what looked like someone's old brown carpeting. Detective Sergeant Barbara Havers, Lonan decided. She threw down the steps the way one would fling a rope ladder over the side of a tree house, pitched out three pieces of luggage, which hit the ground with a thud, and plopped herself after them. A man followed her. He was very tall, very blond, his head bare to the cold, a well-cut cashmere overcoat, a muffler, and gloves his only capitulation to the subfreezing temperature. He would be Inspector Lynley, Lonan thought, the object of Strathclyde CID's particular interest at the moment, considering how his arrival had been manipulated by London from beginning to end. Lonan watched him exchanging a few words with the other officer. She gestured towards the van, and Lonan expected them at that point to join him. Instead, however, they both turned to the helicopter's steps where a third person was slowly negotiating his descent, one made awkward and difficult by the heavy brace he wore upon his left leg. Like the blond, he also had no hat, and his black hair—curly, far too long, and wildly ungovernable—blew about his pale face. His features were sharp, excessively angular. He had the look of a man who never missed a detail.

At this unexpected arrival, Constable Lonan mouthed unspoken words of awe and wondered if Detective Inspector Macaskin had been given the news. London was sending in the heavy artillery: forensic scientist Simon Allcourt-St. James. The constable pushed himself off the side of the van and marched eagerly to the helicopter, where the arrivals were folding the steps back inside and gathering their belongings.

"Have you ever given thought to the fact that there might be something breakable in *my* suitcase, Havers?" Lynley was asking.

"Packing on-the-job drinks?" was her tart reply. "If you've brought your own whisky, more the fool you. That's a bit like taking coals to Newcastle, wouldn't you say?"

"That has the sound of a line you've been waiting to use for months." Lynley gave a wave and a nod of thanks to the helicopter's pilot as Lonan joined them.

When the introductions were made, Lonan blurted out, "I heard you speak once in Glasgow," as he shook St. James' hand. Even inside the glove, Lonan could sense how thin it was, yet it gripped his own with surprising strength. "It was the lecture on the Cradley murders."

"Ah, yes. Putting a man behind bars on the strength of his pubic hair," Sergeant Havers murmured.

"Which is, if nothing else, metaphorically unsound," Lynley added.

It was obvious that St. James was accustomed to the verbal sparring of his two companions, for he merely smiled and said, "We were lucky to have it. God knows we had nothing else but a set of teeth prints gone bad on the corpse."

Lonan itched to discuss all the quixotic convolutions of that case with the man who four years ago had unravelled them before an astounded jury. However, as he was winding himself up to hurl a dagger-like insight, he remembered Detective Inspector Macaskin, who was awaiting their arrival at the police station, no doubt with his usual brand of tense, hall-pacing impatience.

"Van's over here" replaced his scintillating observation about the distortion of teeth marks kept preserved on flesh in formaldehyde. He jerked his head towards the police vehicle, and, as they gave their attention to it, his features settled into a non-verbal apology. He hadn't thought there would be three of them. Nor had he thought they would bring St. James. Had he known, he would have insisted upon driving something more suitable in which to fetch them, perhaps Inspector Macaskin's new Volvo which, if nothing else, had a front and rear seat and a heater that worked. The vehicle he was leading them towards had only two front seats—both belching forth stuffing and springs—and a single folding chair that was wedged in the back among two crime-scene kits, three lengths of rope, several folded tarpaulins, a ladder, a tool-box, and a pile of greasy rags. It was an embarrassment. Yet, if the trio from London noticed, they didn't comment. They merely arranged themselves logically with St. James in the front and the two others riding in the rear, Lynley taking the chair at Sergeant Havers' insistence.

"Wouldn't want you to get your pretty topcoat dirty," she said, before flopping down on the tarpaulins, where she unwound a good thirty inches of muffler from her face.

Lonan took the opportunity of getting a better look at Sergeant Havers when she did so. *Homely sort*, he thought, surveying her snubby features, heavy brows, and round cheeks. She certainly hadn't got herself into this kind of exalted company on her looks. He decided that she had to be some sort of criminological *wunderkind*, and he gave serious consideration to watching her every move.

"Thank you, Havers," Lynley was responding placidly. "God knows a spot of grease would reduce me to uselessness in less than a minute."

Havers snorted. "Let's have a fag on it, then."

Lynley obliged by producing a gold cigarette case, which he handed to her, following it with a silver lighter. Lonan's heart sank. *Smokers*, he thought, and resigned himself to a bout of stinging eyes and clogged sinuses. Havers did not light up, however, because hearing their conversation, St. James opened his window and let in a sharp waft of freezing air, which struck her right in the face.

"Enough. I get the picture," Havers groused. She pocketed six cigarettes unashamedly and gave the case back to Lynley. "Has St. James always been this subtle?"

"Since the day he was born," Lynley replied.

Lonan started the van with a lurch, and they headed towards the CID office in Oban.

DETECTIVE INSPECTOR Ian Macaskin of Strathclyde CID was driven in life by a single fuel: pride. It took a number of distinct and unrelated forms, the first being familial. He liked people to know that he had beaten the odds. Married at twenty to a seventeen-year-old girl, he had stayed married to her for the next twenty-seven years, had raised two sons, had seen them through university and on to careers, one a veterinarian and the other a marine biologist. Then there was physical pride. At five feet nine inches tall, he weighed no more than he had as a twenty-one-year-old constable. His body was trim and fit from rowing back and forth across the

Sound of Kerrera every night in the summer and doing much the same on a rowing machine he kept in his sitting room all winter long. Although his hair was completely grey and had been for the last ten years, it was still thick, shining like silver in the fluorescent lights of the police station. And that same police station was his last source of pride. In his career, he had never once closed a case without making an arrest, and he expended considerable energy making certain that his men could say the same about themselves. He operated a tight investigations unit in which his officers ran every detail to ground like hounds after a fox. He saw to that. As a result, he was omnipresent in the office. Nervous energy personified, he bit his fingernails down to the quick, sucking on breath mints or chewing gum or eating sacks of potato crisps in an effort to break himself of this single bad habit.

Inspector Macaskin met the London party not in his office but in a conference room, a ten-by-fifteen-foot cubicle with uncomfortable furniture, inadequate lighting, and poor ventilation. He had chosen it deliberately.

He was not at all happy with the way this case was beginning. Macaskin liked to pigeonhole, liked to have everything put in its proper place with no muss and no fuss. Each person involved was supposed to act out his appropriate role. Victims die, police question, suspects answer, and crime-scene men collect. But right from the beginning, aside from the victim, who was cooperatively inanimate, the suspects had been doing the questioning and the police had been answering. As for the evidence, that was something else entirely.

"Explain that to me again." Inspector Lynley's voice was even, but it carried a deadly tone that told Macaskin that Lynley had not been made party to the peculiar circumstances that surrounded his assignment to this case. That was good. It made Macaskin decide to like the Scotland Yard detective right on the spot.

They had shed their outer garments and were sitting round the pine conference table, all save Lynley, who was on his feet, his hands in his pockets and something dangerous simmering behind his eyes.

Macaskin was only too happy to go over the story again. "Hadn't been at Westerbrae thirty minutes this morning before there was a message to phone my people at CID. Chief Constable informed me that Scotland Yard would be handling the case. That's all. Couldn't get another word out of him. Just instructions to leave men at the house, come back here and wait for you. Way I see it is that some highbrow at *your* end made the decision that this would be a Yard operation. He gave our chief constable the word and, to keep things on the up and up, we cooperatively put in a 'call for help.' You're it."

Lynley and St. James exchanged unreadable glances. The latter spoke. "But why did you move the body?"

"Part of the order," Macaskin answered. "Blasted strange, if you ask me. Seal the rooms, pick up the package and bring her in for autopsy after our medical examiner did us his usual honour of proclaiming her dead on the scene."

"A bit of divide and conquer," Sergeant Havers remarked.

"It looks that way, doesn't it?" Lynley replied. "Strathclyde deals with the physical evidence, London deals with the suspects. And if someone somewhere gets lucky and we fail to communicate properly, everything gets swept under the nearest rug."

"But whose rug?"

"Yes. That *is* the question, isn't it?" Lynley stared down at the conference table, at the stains created by myriad coffee rings that looped across its surface. "What exactly happened?" he asked Macaskin.

"The girl, Mary Agnes Campbell, found the body at six-fifty this morning. We were called at seven-ten. We got out there at nine."

"Nearly two hours?"

Lonan answered. "Storm last night closed the roads down, Inspector. Westerbrae's five miles from the nearest village, and none of the roads were ploughed yet."

"Why in God's name did a group from London come to such a remote location?"

"Francesca Gerrard—widowed lady, the owner of Westerbrae—is Lord Stinhurst's sister," Macaskin explained. "Evidently she's had some big plans of turning her estate into a posh country hotel. It sits right on Loch Achiemore, and I suppose she envisaged it as quite the romantic holiday destination. Place for newlyweds. You know the sort of thing." Macaskin grimaced, decided that he sounded more like an advertising agent than a policeman, and finished hastily with, "She's done a bit of redecorating and, from what I could gather this morning, Stinhurst brought his people up here to give her a chance to work out the kinks in her operation before she actually opened to the public."

"What about the victim, Joy Sinclair? Do you have anything much on her?"

Macaskin folded his arms, scowled, and wished he had been able to wrest more information from the group at Westerbrae before he had been ordered to leave. "Little enough. Author of the play they'd come to work on this weekend. A lady of some letters, from what I could gather from Vinney."

"Vinney?"

"Newspaperman. Jeremy Vinney, drama critic for the *Times*. Seems to have been fairly thick with Sinclair. And more broken up about her death than anyone else, from what I could tell. Odd, too, when you think about it."

"Why?"

"Because her sister's there as well. But while Vinney was demanding an arrest that very minute, Irene Sinclair had absolutely nothing to say. Didn't even ask how her sister had been done in. Didn't care, if you ask me."

"Odd indeed," Lynley remarked.

St. James stirred. "Did you say there's more than one room involved?"

Macaskin nodded. He went over to a second table which abutted the wall and picked up several folders and a roll of paper. This latter he smoothed out on the tabletop, revealing a more than adequate floor plan of the house. It was extraordinarily detailed, considering the time constraints that had been put upon him at Westerbrae this morning, and Macaskin smiled at his finished work with real pleasure. Weighing it down at either end with the folders, he gestured to the right.

"Victim's room is on the east side of the house." He opened one of the folders and glanced at his notes before continuing. "One side of her was the room belonging to Joanna Ellacourt and her husband . . . David Sydeham. Other side was a young woman . . . here it is. Lady Helen Clyde. It's this second room that's been sealed off." He looked up in time to see the surprise on all three of the London faces. "You know these people?"

"Just Lady Helen Clyde. She works with me," St. James replied. He looked at Lynley. "Did you know Helen was coming to Scotland, Tommy? I thought she'd planned to go to Cornwall with you."

"She begged off the trip last Monday night, so I went alone." Lynley looked at the floor plan, touching his fingers meditatively to it. "Why has Helen's room been sealed?"

"It adjoins the victim's room," Macaskin answered.

"Now there's a piece of luck," St. James said with a smile. "Leave it to our Helen to get herself booked right next door to a murder. We'll want to talk to her at once."

Macaskin frowned at this and leaned forward, placing himself squarely between the two men to get their attention with a physical intrusion before he went on with a verbal one. "Inspector," he said, "about Lady Helen Clyde." Something in his voice arrested the other two men's conversation. Warily, they looked at each other as Macaskin added grimly, "About her room."

"What about it?"

"It appears to be the means of access."

LYNLEY WAS STILL trying to understand what Helen was doing with a group of actors in Scotland when Inspector Macaskin imparted this new piece of information.

"What makes you think that?" he asked at last, although his mind was taken up mostly with his last conversation with Helen, less than a week ago in his library in London. She'd been wearing the loveliest jade-coloured wool, had tasted his new Spanish sherry—laughing and chatting in that light-hearted way of hers—and had rushed off promptly to meet someone for dinner. *Who?* he wondered now. She hadn't said. He hadn't asked.

Macaskin, he noted, was watching him like a man who had things on his mind and was merely waiting for the right opportunity to trot them all out.

"Because the victim's hall door was locked," Macaskin replied. "When Mary Agnes tried to rouse her without success this morning, she had to use the master keys—"

"Where are they kept?"

"In the office." Macaskin pointed to the map. "Lower floor, northwest wing." He continued. "She unlocked the door and found the body."

"Who has access to these master keys? Is there another set of them?"

"Only one set. Just Francesca Gerrard and the girl, Mary Agnes, use them. They were kept locked in the bottom drawer of Mrs. Gerrard's desk. Only she and the Campbell girl have keys to get into it."

"No one else?" Lynley asked.

Macaskin looked thoughtfully down at the plan, moving his eyes along the lower northwest corridor of the house. It was part of a quadrangle, possibly an addition to the original building, and it grew out of the great hall not far from the stairway. He pointed to the first room in the corridor.

"There's Gowan Kilbride," he said pensively. "A kind of jack-of-all-trades. He could have got to the keys had he known they were there."

"Did he know?"

"It's possible. I gather that Gowan's duties don't generally range to the upper floors of the house, so he'd have no need of the master keys. But he might have known about them had Mary Agnes told him where they were."

"And might she have done so?"

Macaskin shrugged. "Perhaps. They're teenagers, aren't they? Teenagers sometimes try to impress each other all sorts of silly ways. Especially if there's an attraction between them."

"Did Mary Agnes say if the master keys were in their normal place this morning? Had they been disturbed?"

"Apparently not, since the desk was locked as usual. But it's not the kind of thing the girl is likely to have noticed. She unlocked the desk, reached into the drawer for the keys. Whether they were in the exact spot she had last left them, she doesn't know, since the last time she put them in the desk she merely dropped them inside without a second thought."

Lynley marvelled at the amount of information Macaskin had been able to gather in his restricted time at the house. He eyed the man with growing respect. "These people all knew each other, didn't they? So why was Joy Sinclair's door locked?"

"Argie-bargie last nicht," Lonan put in from his chair in the corner.

"An argument? What sort?"

Macaskin shot the constable an aggrieved look, apparently for lapsing into colloquialism, something that his men were obviously not supposed to do. He said, apologetically, "That's all we managed to get from Gowan Kilbride this morning before Mrs. Gerrard strong-armed him away with the order to wait for Scotland Yard. Just that there was some sort of row involving the lot of them. Seems some china was broken in the midst of it, and there was an accident in the great hall with liquor. One of my men found bits and pieces of broken porcelain and glass thrown into the rubbish. Some Waterford also. It looks like quite a set-to."

"Involving Helen as well?" St. James didn't wait for an answer. "How well does she know these people, Tommy?"

Lynley shook his head slowly. "I didn't know she knew them at all."

"She didn't tell you—"

"She begged off Cornwall with other plans, St. James. She didn't tell me what they were. And I didn't ask." Lynley looked up to see the change in Macaskin's expression, a sudden movement of his eyes and lips, nearly imperceptible. "What is it?"

Macaskin seemed to give pause to think before he reached for a folder, flipped it open, and drew out a slip of paper. It was not a report but a message, the kind that gives information in "eyes only" fashion from one professional to another. "Fingerprints," he explained. "On the key that locked the door adjoining Helen Clyde's and the victim's rooms." As if in the knowledge that he was dancing his way down a very fine line between disobeying his own chief constable's orders to leave everything to the Yard and giving a brother officer what assistance he could, Macaskin added, "Appreciate it if you'd make no mention of hearing this from me when you write your report, but once we saw that the door between those two rooms was our access route, we brought its key back here for testing on the sly and compared the prints on it with some we lifted from water glasses in the other rooms."

"The other rooms?" Lynley asked. "So they're not Helen's prints on the key?"

Macaskin shook his head. When he spoke, his voice was tellingly noncommittal. "No. They belong to the director of the play. A Welshman, bloke called Rhys Davies-Jones."

Lynley did not respond immediately. Rather, after a moment, he said, "Then Helen and Davies-Jones must have exchanged rooms last night."

Across from him, he saw Sergeant Havers wince, but she didn't look at him. Instead, she ran one stubby finger along the edge of the table and kept her eyes on St. James. "Inspector—" she began in a careful voice, but Macaskin interrupted her.

"No. According to Mary Agnes Campbell, no one at all spent the night in Davies-Jones' room."

"Then where on earth did Helen—" Lynley stopped, feeling the grip of something awful take him, like the onslaught of an illness that swept right through his skin. "Oh," he said, and then, "Sorry. Don't know what I was thinking about." He fixed his eyes on the floor plan intently.

As he did so, he heard Sergeant Havers mutter a brooding oath. She reached into her pocket and pulled out the six cigarettes she had taken from him in the van. One was broken, so she tossed it in the rubbish and picked another. "Have a smoke, sir," she sighed.

ONE CIGARETTE, Lynley found, did not do much to ameliorate the situation. *You have no hold on Helen*, he told himself roughly. *Just friendship, just history, just years of shared laughter. And nothing else.* She was his amusing companion, his confidante, his friend. But never his lover. They had both been too careful, too wary for that, too much on guard ever to become entangled with each other.

"Have you started the autopsy?" he asked Macaskin.

Clearly, this was the question the Scot had been awaiting ever since their arrival. With the kind of undisguised flourish typical of magicians on the stage, he removed several copies of a perfectly assembled report from one of his folders and passed them out, indicating the most pertinent piece of information: the victim had been stabbed with an eighteen-inch-long Highland dagger that had pierced her neck and severed her carotid artery. She had bled to death.

"We've not done the complete postmortem, however," Macaskin added regretfully.

Lynley turned to St. James. "Would she have been able to make any noise?"

"Not from this kind of wound. Burbles at best, I should guess. Nothing that anyone could have heard in another room." His eyes went down the page. "Have you managed a drug screen?" he asked Macaskin.

The inspector was ready. "Page three. Negative. She was clean. No barbiturates, no amphetamines, no toxins."

"You've set the time of death between two and six?"

"That's the preliminary. We've not analysed the intestines yet. But our man's given us fibres in the wound. Leather and rabbit fur."

"The killer was wearing gloves?"

"That's our guess. But they've not been found and we had no time to search for much of anything before we got the message to come back here. All we can say is that the fur and leather didn't come from the weapon. Nothing came from the weapon, in fact, save the victim's blood. The handle was wiped clean."

Sergeant Havers flipped through her copy of the report and tossed it on to the table. "Eighteen-inch dagger," she said slowly. "Where does one find something like that?"

"In Scotland?" Macaskin seemed surprised by her ignorance. "In every house, I should say. There was a time when no Scotsman ever went out without a dirk strapped to his hip. In this particular house," he pointed to the dining room on the floor plan, "there's a display of them on the wall. Hand-carved hilts, tips like rapiers. Real museum pieces. Murder weapon appears to have been taken from there."

"According to your plan, where does Mary Agnes sleep?"

"A room in the northwest corridor, between Gowan's room and Mrs. Gerrard's office."

St. James was making notes in the margin of his report as the inspector talked. "What about movement on the victim's part?" he asked. "The wound isn't immediately fatal. Was there any evidence that she tried to seek help?"

Macaskin pursed his lips and shook his head. "Couldn't have happened. Impossible."

"Why?"

Macaskin opened his last folder and took out a stack of photographs. "The knife impaled her to the mattress," he said bluntly. "She couldn't go anywhere, I'm afraid." He dropped the pictures on to the table. They were large, eight by ten, and in glossy colour. Lynley picked them up.

He was used to looking at death. He had seen it manifested in every way imaginable throughout his years with the Yard. But never had he seen it brought about with such studied brutality.

The killer had driven the dirk in right up to its hilt, as if propelled by an atavistic rage that had wanted more than the mere obliteration of Joy Sinclair. She lay with her eyes open, but their colour was changed and obscured by the settled stare of death. As he looked at the woman, Lynley wondered how long she had lived once the knife was driven into her throat. He wondered if she had known at all what had happened to her in the instant it took the killer to plunge the knife home. Had shock overcome her at once with its blessing of oblivion? Or had she lain, helpless, waiting for both unconsciousness and death?

It was a horrible crime, a crime whose enormity delineated itself in the saturated mattress that drank the woman's blood, in her outstretched hand that reached for assistance that would never come, in her parted lips and soundless cry. There is, Lynley thought, no crime so execrable as murder. It contaminates and pollutes, and no life it touches, no matter how tangentially, can ever be the same.

He passed the photographs to St. James and looked at Macaskin. "Now," he said, "shall we consider the intriguing question of what happened at Westerbrae between six-fifty when Mary Agnes Campbell found the body and seven-ten when someone finally managed to get round to phoning the police?"

3

THE ROAD TO Westerbrae was poorly maintained. In the summer, negotiating its switchbacks, its potholes, its steep climbs to moors and quick descents to dales would be difficult enough. In the winter, it was hell. Even with Constable Lonan at the wheel of Strathclyde CID's Land Rover, well equipped to handle the perilous conditions, they did not arrive at the house until nearly dusk, emerging from the woods and swinging through the final curve on a sheet of ice that caused Lonan and Macaskin to curse fervently in unison. As a result, the constable took the final forty yards at a respectable crawl and switched off the ignition at last with undisguised relief.

In front of them, the building loomed like a gothic nightmare on the landscape, completely unilluminated and deadly quiet. Constructed entirely of grey granite in the fashion of a pre-Victorian hunting lodge, it shot out wings, sprouted chimneys, and managed to look menacing in spite of the snow that mounded like fresh clotted cream on its roof. It had peculiar crow-stepped gables shaped from smaller granite blocks stacked in a staggered fashion. Behind one of these, the curious architectural appendage of a slate-roofed tower was tucked into the abutment of two wings of the house, its deeply recessed windows bare of covering and without light. A white Doric-columned portico sheltered the front door, and over it trailing wisps of a now leafless vine made an heroic effort to climb to the roof. The entire structure combined the fancies of three periods of architecture and at least as many cultures. And as Lynley evaluated it, he thought that it hardly had the potential to be Macaskin's romantic spot for newlyweds.

The drive they parked on was well channelled and gouged, evidence of the number of vehicles that had come and gone during the day. But at this hour, Westerbrae may well have been deserted. Even the snow surrounding it was pristine and untouched across the lawn and down the slope to the loch.

For a moment no one stirred. Then Macaskin, casting a glance over his shoulder at the London group, shoved open the door, and fresh air assaulted them. It was glacial. They climbed out reluctantly.

A nasty wind was gusting off the water a short distance away, an unforgiving reminder of how far north Loch Achiemore and Westerbrae really were. It blew numbingly from the Arctic, stinging cheeks and piercing lungs and carrying with it the flavour of nearby pines and the faint musk of peat fires burning in the surrounding countryside. Huddling into themselves for protection against it, they crossed the drive quickly. Macaskin pounded on the door.

Two of his men had been left behind that morning, and one admitted them into the house. He was a freckled constable with monstrously large hands and a bulky, muscled body that strained against the buttons of his uniform. Carrying a tray covered by the sort of insubstantial sandwiches that usually decorate plates at tea, he was chewing ravenously, like an overlarge waif who has not seen food in many days and may very well not see it again for days more. He beckoned them into the great hall and thudded the door closed behind them, swallowing.

"Cuik arrived thirty minutes back," he explained hurriedly to Macaskin, who was eying him with a disapproval that thinned his lips. "I was juist takin' this in tae them. Dinna seem they should gae much longer wi'out fude."

Macaskin's expression withered the man to silence. Dismay stained his cheeks, and he shifted from one foot to the other, as if unsure about what he should do to explain himself further to his superior.

"Where are they?" Lynley's glance took in the hall, noting its hand-moulded panelling and its immense, unlit chandelier. The floor was bare, recently refinished, and even more recently marred by a wide stain that pooled across it and dripped like treacle down one of the walls. All the doors leading off the hall were closed, and the only light came from the reception desk tucked under the stairs.

Apparently the constable had made this his duty post that day, for it was littered with teacups and magazines.

"Library," Macaskin answered. His eyes darted suspiciously to his man, as if the courtesy of supplying the suspects with food may well have led to other courtesies which he would live to regret. "They've been in there since we left this morning, Euan?"

At this the young constable grinned. "Aye. Wi' brief visits tae the toilet down the northe'st corridor. Two minutes, unlocked door, maiself or Will'am richt awside." He went on as Macaskin led the others across the hall. "Th' one is still in a fair rage, Inspector. Not used tae spendin' the day 'n her nichtgawn, I should guess."

It was, Lynley quickly discovered, a more than accurate description of Lady Helen Clyde's state of mind. When Inspector Macaskin unlocked and pushed open the library door, she was the first one on her feet, and whatever had been simmering on the back burner of her self-control was clearly about to boil over. She took three steps forward, her slippers moving soundlessly on what looked like—but could not possibly have been—an Aubusson carpet.

"Now you listen to me. I absolutely *insist* . . ." Her words were hot with fury, but they iced over into mute astonishment when she saw the new arrivals.

Whatever Lynley might have thought he would feel at this first sight of Lady Helen, he was not prepared for tenderness. Yet it overcame him in an unexpected rush. She looked so pathetic. She was wearing a man's greatcoat over her dressing gown and slippers. The cuffs had been folded back, but there was nothing at all to be done about the garment's length or about its wide shoulders, so it hung on her baggily, dangling to her ankles. Her usually smooth, chestnut hair was dishevelled, she wore absolutely no make-up, and in the half-light of the room she looked like one of Fagin's boys, all of twelve years old and badly in need of rescue.

It passed through Lynley's mind that this was probably the first time he had ever seen Helen at a loss for words, and he said to her drily, "You always did know how to dress for an occasion."

"Tommy," Lady Helen replied. A hand went to her hair in a gesture that was born more of confusion than self-consciousness. She added, inanely, "You're not in Cornwall."

"Indeed. I'm not in Cornwall."

That brief exchange charged those assembled in the library into furious action. They had been fairly spread out across the room, seated near the fire, standing by the bar, gathered in a collection of chairs under the glass-fronted bookshelves. But now nearly everyone began to move—and to shout—at once. Voices came from all directions with no desire for answer, merely a need to give vent to wrath. It was instantaneous pandemonium.

"My solicitor *shall* hear—"

"Bloody police kept us locked—"

". . . the most outrageous behaviour I've ever seen!"

"We're supposed to be living in a civilised—"

". . . no wonder to *me* that the country's gone to hell!"

Unmoved by their anger, Lynley passed his eyes over them and made a quick survey of the room. The heavy rose curtains were drawn and only two lamps had been lit, but there was quite enough light for him to study the company as they continued to make vociferous demands, which he continued to ignore.

He recognised the principal players in the drama, mostly by their relative proximity to what was clearly the main attraction and dominant force in the room: Britain's foremost actress, Joanna Ellacourt. She was standing by the bar, a wintry blonde beauty whose white angora sweater and matching wool trousers seemed to emphasise the temperature of disdain with which she greeted the arrival of the police. As if in the expectation of meeting some need of hers, at Joanna's elbow stood a brawny, older man, with heavy-lidded eyes and coarse, greying hair—no doubt her husband, David Sydeham. Only two steps away on Joanna's other side, her leading man turned abruptly back to a drink that he was nursing at the bar. Robert Gabriel was either not interested in the newcomers or eager not to be seen until properly fortified for the encounter. And in front of Gabriel, having risen quickly from the couch on which he had been sitting, Stuart Rintoul, Lord Stinhurst, studied Lynley intently as if with the purpose of casting him in some future production.

There were others in the room whose identities Lynley could only guess at for the moment: two older women near the fire, most likely Lord Stinhurst's wife and his sister, Francesca Gerrard; an angry-faced, pudgy man somewhere in his thirties who smoked a pipe, wore newish tweeds, and seemed to be the journalist Jeremy Vinney; sharing a settee with him, an exceedingly ill-dressed, unattractive middle-aged spinster type whose extreme lankiness if not her resemblance to Lord Stinhurst indicated that she had to be his daughter; the two teenagers employed at the hotel, together at the furthest corner of the room; and in a low chair nearly obscured by shadows, a black-haired woman who raised a haunted face to Lynley, hollow-cheeked, dark-eyed, with an undercurrent of passion held in savagely tight rein. Irene Sinclair, Lynley guessed, the victim's sister.

But none of these was the one person Lynley was looking for, and he passed his eyes over the group once again until he found the director of the play, recognising him from the olive skin, black hair, and sombre eyes of the Welsh. Rhys Davies-Jones was standing by the chair that Lady Helen had just vacated. He had moved when she did, as if to prevent her from confronting the police alone. He stopped, however, when it became apparent to everyone that this particular policeman was no stranger to Lady Helen Clyde.

Across the width of the room and through the gulf created by the conflict of their cultures, Lynley looked at Davies-Jones, feeling an aversion take hold of him, one so strong that it seemed a physical illness. *Helen's lover*, he thought, and then more fiercely to convince himself of the fact's grim immutability: *This is Helen's lover.*

No man could have looked less likely for the role. The Welshman was at least ten years Helen's senior, quite possibly more. With curly hair going to grey at the temples and a thin weathered face, he was wiry and fit like his Celtic ancestors. Also like them, he was neither tall nor handsome. His features were sharp and stony. But Lynley could not deny that the look of the man spoke of both intelligence and inner strength, qualities that Helen would recognise—and value—beyond any others.

"Sergeant Havers," Lynley's voice cut through the continued protestations, eliminating them abruptly, "take Lady Helen to her room and allow her to get dressed. Where are the keys?"

Wide-eyed and white-faced, a young girl came forward. Mary Agnes Campbell, finder of the body. She held out a silver tray on which someone had deposited all of the hotel keys, but her hands were shaking, so the tray and its contents jangled discordantly. Lynley's eyes took it in, then moved to the assembled company.

"I locked all the rooms and collected the keys immediately after she . . . the body was discovered this morning." Lord Stinhurst resumed his seat by the fire, a couch which he was sharing with one of the two older women. Her hand groped for his, and their fingers intertwined. "I'm not certain what the procedure is in a case like this," Stinhurst concluded, in explanation, "but that seemed the best."

When Lynley looked less than willing to receive this bit of news with appreciation, Macaskin interjected, "Everyone was in the drawing room when we arrived this morning. His lordship had done us the service of locking them in."

"How helpful of Lord Stinhurst." It was Sergeant Havers, speaking in a voice so polite that it sounded like steel.

"Find your key, Helen," Lynley said. Her eyes had never left his face since he'd first spoken to her. He could feel them on him now, her gaze warm, like a touch. "The rest of you may be expected to be inconvenienced awhile longer."

Into the storm of fresh protests that greeted this remark, Lady Helen started to respond, but Joanna Ellacourt expertly wrested the stage from her by crossing the room to Lynley. The lighting became her, and Joanna walked like a woman who knew how to use the moment. Her long, unpinned hair moved like sun-shot silk upon her shoulders.

"Inspector," she murmured, motioning gracefully towards the door, "I feel I *may* ask you . . . if it's not too much. I should be only too grateful to be given just a few moments to myself. Somewhere. Out of here. In my own room, perhaps, but if that's not possible, just in any room. Anywhere. With a single chair on which I could sit and ponder and gather my wits once again. Five minutes only. If you would be so good as to see to it for me, I should feel in your debt. After this dreadful day."

Her performance was lovely, Blanche Dubois in Scotland. But Lynley had no intention of acting the part of her gentleman from Dallas.

"I'm sorry," he replied, "I'm afraid you shall have to rely on the kindness of strangers other than myself." And then he repeated, "Find your key, Helen."

Lady Helen made a gesture Lynley recognised, a prelude to speaking. He turned away. "We'll be in the Sinclair room," he said to Havers. "Let me know when she's dressed. Constable Lonan, see that the rest of them stay here for now."

Angry voices swelled again. Lynley ignored them and left the room. St. James and Macaskin followed.

LEFT WITH THIS group of la-de-da suspects, so atypical of what one usually came across in a murder investigation, Barbara Havers was only too delighted to make her own assessments of their potential guilt. She had the time to do so as Lady Helen returned to Rhys Davies-Jones and exchanged a few quiet words with him beneath the general din of expostulations and imprecations that followed Lynley's departure.

They were quite the lot, Barbara decided. Chic and well tailored and divinely turned out. With the exception of Lady Helen, they were a veritable advertisement for how to dress for a murder. And how to act once the police arrive: righteous indignation, calls for solicitors, nasty remarks. So far, they were living up to her every expectation. At any moment, no doubt one of them would mention a close connection with his MP, an intimacy with Mrs. Thatcher, or a notable figure on his family tree. They were all the same, such swells, such toffs.

All but that one pinch-faced woman who had managed to shrink her considerable frame into an ill-shaped heap on the settee, as far away as possible from the man with whom she shared it. *Elizabeth Rintoul*, Barbara thought. *Lady* Elizabeth Rintoul, to be exact. Lord Stinhurst's only daughter.

She was acting as if the man seated next to her carried a particularly virulent strain of disease. Cringed into a corner of the couch, she held a navy cardigan closed at her throat and pressed both arms tightly, painfully to her sides. Her feet were planted on the floor in front of her, shod in the kind of flat-soled, plain black shoes that are generally labelled *sensible*. They stuck out like angular blobs of oil from beneath an unappealing black flannel skirt. Lint dotted it liberally. She added nothing whatsoever to the conversation going on about her. But something in her posture suggested bones that were brittle and about to break.

"Elizabeth, dear," murmured the woman opposite her. She wore the kind of meaningful, ingratiating smile one directs to a recalcitrant child misbehaving before company. Obviously, this was Mum, Barbara decided, Lady Stinhurst herself, dressed in a fawn-coloured twinset and amber beads, ankles neatly crossed and hands folded in her lap. "Perhaps Mr. Vinney's drink could be replenished."

Elizabeth Rintoul's dull eyes moved to her mother. "Perhaps," she responded. She made the word sound foul.

Casting a pleading glance at her husband as if for support, Lady Stinhurst persisted. She had a gentle, uncertain voice, the sort one expects from maiden ladies not accustomed to speaking to children. She lifted a hand nervously to hair that was expertly coloured and styled to fight off the reality of fast-encroaching old age. "You see, darling, we've been sitting so long now and I really don't believe Mr. Vinney's had anything at all since half past two."

It was far more than a hint. It was a blatant suggestion. The bar was just across the room and Elizabeth was to wait upon Mr. Vinney like a debutante with her very first beau. The directions were clear enough. But Elizabeth wasn't about to follow them. Instead, contempt flashed across her features, and she dropped her eyes to a magazine in her lap. She mouthed a singularly unladylike response, one word only. Her mother could not possibly misread or misunderstand it.

Barbara watched the exchange between them with some fascination. The Lady Elizabeth looked well over thirty years old— probably skating closer to forty. She was hardly of an age to need a prod from Mum in the man department. But prod was certainly what Mum had in mind. In fact, in spite of Elizabeth's unveiled hostility, Lady Stinhurst made a movement that looked very much as if she intended to shove Elizabeth in the direction of Mr. Vinney's arms.

Not that Jeremy Vinney himself appeared willing. Next to Elizabeth, *The Times* journalist was doing his best to ignore the conversation entirely. He probed at his pipe with a stainless steel tool and eavesdropped unashamedly on what Joanna Ellacourt was saying at her end of the room. She was angry and making no secret about the fact.

"She's made wonderful fools of us all, hasn't she? What a lark for her! What a bloody good laugh!" the actress cast a scathing look at Irene Sinclair, who still sat in her low chair far away from the rest of them, as if her sister's death somehow had served to make her own presence unwelcome. "And who do *you* imagine benefits from last night's little change in the script? Me? Not on your life! Well, I won't stand for it, David. I damn well won't stand for it."

David Sydeham sounded conciliatory as he answered his wife. "Nothing's settled yet, Jo. Far from it now. Once she changed the script, your contract may well have become void."

"You *think* the contract is void. But you don't have it here, do you? We can't look at it, can we? You don't know if it's void at all. Yet you expect me to believe—to take your word after all that's happened—that merely a change in characterisation makes a contract void? Pardon my disbelief, will you? Pardon my incredulous shriek of laughter. And give me another gin. *Now.*"

Sydeham wordlessly jerked his head at Robert Gabriel, who pushed a bottle of Beefeaters in his direction. It was two-thirds empty. Sydeham poured his wife a drink and returned the bottle to Gabriel, who grasped it and murmured with laughter catching at his voice:

" 'I have thee not and yet I see thee still . . . Come, let me clutch thee.' " Gabriel leered at Joanna and poured himself another drink. "Sweet shades of the regionals, Jo, m'love. Wasn't that our first?

Hmm, no, perhaps not." He managed to make it sound more like a sexual encounter than a production of *Macbeth*.

Scores of her school chums had swooned over Gabriel's Peter Pan good looks fifteen years ago, but Barbara had never been able to see his appeal. Nor, apparently, did Joanna Ellacourt. She favoured him with a smile that hurled daggers of an entirely different sort.

"Darling," she responded, "how could I *ever* forget? You dropped ten lines in the middle of act two, and I carried you all the way to the end. Frankly, I've been waiting for those multitudinous seas to become incarnadine for the last seventeen years."

Gabriel gave a snort of laughter. "West End Bitch," he announced. "Ever true to form."

"You're drunk."

Which was certainly more than halfway true. As if in response to this, Francesca Gerrard stood up uneasily, pushing herself away from the couch she was sharing with her brother, Lord Stinhurst. She seemed to want to take control of the situation, perhaps to act out the role of hotel proprietress in even so inconsequential a manner as she chose when she turned to Barbara.

"If we could have some coffee . . ." Her hand fluttered up to a collection of coloured beads which she wore across her chest like mail. Contact with them seemed to give her courage. She spoke again, with more authority. "We'd like some coffee. Will you arrange it?" When Barbara didn't reply, she turned to Lord Stinhurst. "Stuart . . ."

He spoke. "I'd appreciate your arranging for a pot of coffee," he said to Barbara. "Some of the party want sobering up."

Barbara gave fleeting and delighted thought to how many opportunities she would ever have again to put an earl in his place.

"Sorry," she replied tartly. And then she said to Lady Helen, "If you'll come with me now, I should guess the inspector will want to see you first."

LADY HELEN CLYDE felt more than a little numb as she fumbled her way across the library. She told herself that it was the lack of food, the endless and appalling day, the ghastly discomfort of sitting hour after hour in her nightclothes in a room that had continually alternated between subfreezing and claustrophobic. Reaching the doorway, she gathered the greatcoat about her with as much dignity as she could muster and stepped out into the hall. Sergeant Havers was an unacknowledged companion behind her.

"Are you quite all right, Helen?"

Gratefully, Lady Helen turned to see that St. James had waited for her. He stood in the shadows just outside the door. Lynley and Macaskin had already disappeared up the stairs.

She smoothed her hand against her hair in an attempt to arrange it but gave up the effort with a small, chagrined smile. "Can you possibly imagine what it's been like to spend an entire day with a roomful of individuals who communicate directly with Thespis?" she asked St. James. "We've run the gamut since half past seven this morning. From rage to hysteria to grief to paranoia. Frankly, by noon, I would have sold my soul for just one of Hedda Gabler's pistols." She drew the greatcoat up to her throat and held it closed at her neck, stifling a shiver. "But I'm fine. At least, I think so." Her eyes took in the stairs and then moved back to St. James. "Whatever's wrong with Tommy?"

Behind her, Sergeant Havers moved with inexplicable sharpness, but it was a gesture Lady Helen couldn't clearly see. St. James, she noted, took his time about replying, using a moment to brush at the leg of his trousers. There was nothing on them for his attention, however, and when he chose to speak, it was to ask a question of his own.

"What on earth are you doing here, Helen?"

She glanced back at the closed library door. "Rhys invited me. He was to direct Lord Stinhurst's new production for the opening of the Agincourt Theatre, and this weekend was to be a run-through— a sort of preliminary reading of the new script."

"Rhys?" St. James repeated.

"Rhys Davies-Jones. You don't remember him? My sister used to see him. Years ago. Before he . . ." Lady Helen twisted a button at the throat of the greatcoat, hesitating, wondering how much to say. She settled on, "He's been working in regional theatre over the past two years. This was to be his first London production since . . . *The Tempest*. Four years ago. We were there. Surely you remember." She saw that he did.

"Lord," St. James said with some reverence. "Was that Davies-Jones? I'd completely forgotten."

Lady Helen wondered how that was even possible, for it was something she knew she could never forget: that awful night at the theatre when Rhys Davies-Jones, the director, had taken the stage himself and everyone had seen he was inches short of delirious. Shoving actors and actresses alike to one side, chasing demons only he could see, he had publicly ended his career with a vengeance. She could see it all still—the stage, the pandemonium, the devastation he had wrought upon himself and others. For it had been during the act 4 speech when his drunken frenzy broke into the lovely words, blotting out both his past and future in an instant, leaving, indeed, not a single rack behind.

"He spent four months in hospital after that. He's quite . . . recovered now. I ran into him early last month in the Brompton Road. We had dinner and . . . well, ever since we've seen a good deal of each other."

"His recovery must be complete indeed if he's working with Stinhurst, Ellacourt, and Gabriel. Lofty company for—"

"A man of his reputation?" Lady Helen frowned down at the floor, touching her slippered foot delicately to one of the pegs that held the wood in place. "Yes, I suppose. But Joy Sinclair was his cousin. They were very close, and I think she saw the opportunity to give him a second chance in London theatre. She was instrumental in talking Lord Stinhurst into giving Rhys the contract."

"She had influence with Stinhurst?"

"I've got the impression Joy had influence with everyone."

"Meaning?"

Lady Helen hesitated. She was not a woman given to saying anything that might denigrate others, even in a murder investigation. Doing so now went against the grain, even with St. James, always a man she could trust implicitly, waiting for her answer. She gave it reluctantly, prefacing it with a quick look at Sergeant Havers to read her face for its degree of discretion.

"Apparently she had an affair with Robert Gabriel last year, Simon. They had a tremendous row about it only yesterday afternoon. Gabriel wanted Joy to tell his former wife that he slept with her just once. Joy refused. It . . . well, the row was heading towards violence when Rhys burst into Joy's room and broke it up."

St. James looked perplexed. "I don't understand. Did Joy Sinclair know Robert Gabriel's wife? Did she even know he was married?"

"Oh yes," Lady Helen answered. "Robert Gabriel was married for nineteen years to Irene Sinclair. Joy's sister."

INSPECTOR MACASKIN unlocked the door and admitted Lynley and St. James into Joy Sinclair's room. He felt for the wall switch, and two serpentine bronze ceiling fixtures spilled light down on the wealth of contradictions below. It was, Lynley saw, a beautiful room, the sort one expects the play's star performer to be given, not its author. Expensively papered in green and yellow, it was furnished with a four-poster Victorian bed and nineteenth-century chest of drawers, wardrobe, and chairs. A comfortably faded Axminster carpet covered the oak floor, and the boards creaked with age when they walked across it.

Yet the room was still very much the scene of a brutal crime, and the frigid air was a rich effluvium of blood and destruction. The bed acted as centrepiece with its writhing confusion of blood-soaked linens and its single, deadly gash that spoke eloquently of the manner in which the woman had died. Donning latex gloves, the three men approached it with a fair degree of respect: Lynley taking in the room with a sweeping glance, Macaskin pocketing Francesca Gerrard's master keys, and St. James scrutinising those scant feet and inches of horrifying catafalque as if they could reveal to him the identity of their maker.

As the other two watched, St. James removed a small folding ruler from his pocket and, leaning over the bed, delicately probed the ugly puncture at the centre top. The mattress was unusual, wool-filled in the manner of a tick. Packing of this sort would make it soothingly comfortable, moulded to shoulders, hips, and the small of one's back. And it had the additional benefit of having shaped itself cooperatively round the intrusive murder weapon, faultlessly reproducing the direction of entry.

"One thrust," St. James said to the others over his shoulder. "Right-handed, delivered from the left side of the bed."

Inspector Macaskin spoke curtly. "Possible for a woman?"

"If the dirk was sharp enough," St. James responded, "it would take no great force to drive it through a woman's neck. Another woman could have done it." He looked pensive. "But why is it that one can't really imagine a woman committing a crime such as this?"

Macaskin's eyes were on the immense stain that was not yet dry upon the mattress. "Sharp, yes. Damned sharp," he said moodily. "A killer covered with blood?"

"Not necessarily. I should guess that he would have blood on his right hand and arm, but if he managed it quickly and shielded himself with the bed linen, he might well have got away with just a spot or two. And that, if he didn't panic, could easily be wiped off on one of the sheets and that spot on the sheet then mingled in with the blood that the wound produced."

"What about his clothing?"

St. James examined the two pillows, set them on a chair, and peeled back the bottom sheet from the mattress a careful inch at a time. "The killer might well have worn no clothes at all," he noted. "It would be far easier to see to it in the nude. Then he could return to his room, or to her room," this with a nod at Macaskin, "and wash the blood off with soap and water. If there was any on him in the first place."

"That would be a risk, wouldn't it?" Macaskin asked. "Not to mention cold as the dickens."

St. James paused to compare the hole in the sheet with that in the mattress. "The entire crime was a risk. Joy Sinclair might well have awakened and screamed like a banshee."

"If she was asleep in the first place," Lynley noted. He had gone to the dressing table near the window. A jumble of articles took up its surface: make-up, hair brushes, hair dryer, tissues, a mass of jewellery among which were three rings, five silver bangles, and two strings of coloured beads. A gold hoop earring lay on the floor. "St. James," Lynley said, his eyes on the table, "when you and Deborah go to an hotel, do you lock the door?"

"As soon as possible," he replied with a smile. "But I suppose that comes from living in the same house with one's father-in-law. A few days out of his presence and we become hopeless reprobates, I'm ashamed to say. Why?"

"Where do you leave the key?"

St. James looked from Lynley to the door. "In the keyhole, generally."

"Yes." From the dressing table, Lynley picked up the door key by the metal ring that attached the key to its plastic identification tab. "Most people do. So why do you suppose Joy Sinclair locked the door and put the key on the dressing table?"

"There was an argument last night, wasn't there? She was part of it. She may well have been distracted or upset when she came in. She may have locked the door and tossed the key there in a fit of temper."

"Possibly. Or perhaps she wasn't the one who locked the door at all. Perhaps she didn't come in by herself but with someone else who did the locking up while she waited in the bed." Lynley noticed that Inspector Macaskin was pulling at his lip. He said to him, "You don't agree?"

Macaskin chewed on the side of his thumb for a moment before he dropped his hand with a look of distaste, as if it had climbed to his mouth of its own volition. "As to someone being with her," he said, "no, I don't think so."

Lynley dropped the key back on to the dressing table and went to the wardrobe, opening the doors. Inside, clothes hung in a haphazard arrangement; shoes were tossed to the back; a pair of blue jeans was in a heap on the floor; a suitcase yawned, displaying stockings and brassieres.

Lynley looked through these items and turned back to Macaskin. "Why not?" he asked him as St. James crossed the room to the chest of drawers and began going through it.

"Because of what she was wearing," Macaskin explained. "You couldn't have recognised much from the CID photographs, but she had on a man's pyjama top."

"Doesn't that make it even more likely that someone was with her?"

"You're thinking that she had on the pyjama top of whoever came to see her. I can't agree."

"Why not?" Lynley closed the wardrobe door and leaned against it, his eyes on Macaskin.

"Realistically then," Macaskin began with the assurance of an exponent who has given his subject a great deal of prior thought, "does a man bent on seduction go to a woman's room in his oldest pyjamas? Top she had on was thin, washed many times and worn through at the elbows in two separate spots. At least six or seven years old, I should guess. Possibly older. Not exactly what one would expect a man to have on or, for that matter, to leave as a memento for a woman to wear after a night of lovemaking."

"Now you describe it," Lynley said thoughtfully, "it sounds more like a talisman, doesn't it?"

"Indeed." Lynley's agreement seemed to encourage Macaskin to warm to his topic. He paced the distance from bed to dressing table and from there to the wardrobe, using his hands for emphasis. "And supposing it had always belonged to her and came from no man at all. Would she wait for a lover in her oldest bedclothes? I hardly think so."

"I agree," St. James said from the chest of drawers. "And considering that we've not one reasonable sign of a struggle, we have to conclude that even if she wasn't asleep when the murderer entered—if it was someone she let in the room for a friendly chat—she certainly was asleep when he plunged the dirk through her throat."

"Or perhaps not asleep," Lynley said slowly. "But taken completely by surprise, by someone she had reason to trust. But in that case, wouldn't she have locked the door herself?"

"Not necessarily," Macaskin said. "The murderer could have locked it, killed her, and—"

"Returned to Helen's room," Lynley finished coldly. His head snapped towards St. James. "By God—"

"Not yet," St. James replied.

THEY GATHERED at a small magazine-covered table by the window and sat surveying the room companionably. Lynley flipped through the assortment of periodicals, St. James lifted the lid of the teapot on the abandoned morning tray and gave consideration to the transparent film that had formed on the liquid, and Macaskin tapped a pen in staccato against the bottom of his shoe.

"We've two lapses of time," St. James said. "Twenty minutes or more between the discovery of the body and the call to the police. Then nearly two hours between the call to the police and their arrival here." He gave his attention to Macaskin. "And your crime-scene men weren't able to go over the room thoroughly before you had the call from your CC, ordering you back to the station?"

"That's right."

"Then you may as well have them go over the room now if you want to phone for them. I don't expect we'll gain much from the effort, though. Any amount of apocryphal evidence could have been planted in here during that time."

"Or removed," Macaskin noted blackly. "With only Lord Stinhurst's word that he locked all the doors and waited for us and did nothing else."

That remark struck a chord in Lynley. He got to his feet and went without speaking from the chest of drawers to the wardrobe to the dressing table. The other two watched as he opened doors and drawers and looked behind furniture.

"The script," he said. "They were here to work on a script, weren't they? Joy Sinclair was the author. So where is it? Why are there no notes? Where *are* all the scripts?"

Macaskin jumped to his feet. "I'll see to that," he said and vanished in an instant.

As the one door closed behind him, the second door opened. "We're ready in here," Sergeant Havers said from Lady Helen's room.

Lynley looked at St. James. He peeled off his gloves. "I'm not the least looking forward to this," he admitted.

*   *   *

LADY HELEN had never really thought about how much her self-confidence was tied up in a daily bath. Having been forbidden that simple luxury, she had become ridiculously consumed by a need to bathe that was thwarted by Sergeant Havers' simple, "Sorry. I have to stay with you and I should guess you'd rather not have me scrubbing your back." As a result, she felt at odds with herself, like a woman forced to wear skin that was not her own.

At least they had compromised on make-up, although seeing to her face under the watchful eye of the detective sergeant made Lady Helen distinctly uncomfortable, as if she were a mannequin on display. This feeling increased while she dressed, pulling on clothing that first came to hand without the least regard for what it was or how it looked upon her. She knew only the cool movement of silk, the scratchy pull of wool. As to what the garments were, as to whether they matched one another or were a battle of colours taking her appearance down to perdition, she could not have said.

And all the time she could hear St. James, Lynley, and Inspector Macaskin in the next room. They were not talking at any particular volume, yet she heard them with ease. So she wondered what on earth she would tell them when they asked her—as they no doubt would—why she had never managed to hear a single sound in the night from Joy Sinclair. She was still pondering this question when Sergeant Havers opened the second door to let St. James and Lynley into the room.

She turned to face them. "What a mess I am, Tommy," she said with a cheerful smile. "You must swear by every sartorial god there is that you'll never tell anyone I was wearing a dressing gown and slippers at four in the afternoon."

Without answering, Lynley stopped by an armchair. It was high-backed, upholstered in a pattern that matched the room's wallpaper—roses on cream—and set on an angle three feet from the door. He appeared to be examining it for no particular reason and at some considerable length. Then he bent, and from behind it he picked up a man's black tie which he laid across the back of the chair with steady deliberation. With a final look round the room, he nodded at Sergeant Havers, who opened her notebook. At all this, Lady Helen's additional score of light-hearted preliminary remarks, designed to break through the professional reticence that she had encountered from Lynley in the library, died a sudden death. He had the upper hand. Lady Helen saw in an instant how he meant to use it.

"Sit down, Helen." When she would have chosen another place, he said, "At the table, please."

Like the arrangement of furniture in Joy Sinclair's room, the table was placed beneath a bay window, the curtains undrawn. Darkness had fallen quickly outside, and the pane reflected both ghostly reflections and gold streaks of lamplight from the bedside table against the far wall. A cobwebbing of frost patterned itself against the window outside, and Lady Helen knew that if she put her hand to the glass, it would feel burning cold, like a clear sheet of ice.

She walked to one of the chairs. They were eighteenth-century pieces upholstered in yet unfaded tapestry bearing a mythological scene. Lady Helen knew she should recognise the young man and nymph-like woman who reached out to each other in the pastoral setting—indeed, she knew that Lynley himself probably did. But whether it was Paris eager for the promised reward after rendering judgement, or Echo pining for Narcissus, she could not have said. And more, at the moment, she didn't particularly care.

Lynley joined her at the table. His eyes rested on the telling items that covered it: a bottle of cognac, an overfull ashtray, and a Delft plate of oranges, one partially peeled but then discarded, yet still exuding a faint citrus scent. He took these in as Sergeant Havers pulled the dressing table's stool over to join them and St. James made a slow circuit of the room.

Lady Helen had seen St. James work a hundred times before. She knew how unlikely it was that any detail would escape him. Yet, watching his familiar routine directed at her this time, she felt a tightening of muscles as she witnessed him engage in a cursory examination of the tops of chest of drawers and dressing table, of wardrobe and floor. It was like a violation, and when he threw back the covers of her unmade bed and ran his eyes speculatively over the sheets, her self-control snapped.

"My God, Simon, is that absolutely necessary?"

None of them answered. But their silence was enough. And the combination of having been locked up for nearly nine hours like a common criminal and sitting here now while they proposed to question her dispassionately—as if they were not all three tied together by years of pain and friendship—caused anger to swell like a tumour within her. She fought against it with limited success. Her eyes moved back to Lynley, and she made herself ignore the sounds of St. James' movement in the room behind her.

"Tell us about the row that occurred last night."

From their behaviour, Lady Helen had expected Lynley's first question to concern itself with the bedroom. This unexpected start took her by surprise, disarming her momentarily as he no doubt intended.

"I wish I could. All I know for certain is that it involved the play Joy Sinclair was writing. Lord Stinhurst and she had a terrible quarrel about it. Joanna Ellacourt was furious as well."

"Why?"

"From what I could gather, the play Joy brought with her for this weekend run-through was considerably different from the play that everyone signed on to do in London. She did announce at dinner that she'd made a few changes here and there, but evidently the changes were far more extensive than anyone was prepared for. It was still a murder mystery, but little else was the same. So the argument grew from there."

"When did all this occur?"

"We'd gone into the sitting room to do a read-through of the script. The quarrel broke out not five minutes into it. It was so odd, Tommy. They'd hardly begun when Francesca—Lord Stinhurst's sister—absolutely leaped to her feet, as if she'd had the most dreadful shock of her life. She began shouting at Lord Stinhurst, saying something like, 'No! Stuart, stop her!' and then she tried to get out of the room. Only she became confused, or lost her way, because she backed directly into a large curio cabinet and smashed it to pieces. I can't think how she managed not to cut herself to shreds in the process, but she didn't."

"What was everyone else doing?"

Lady Helen sketched out each person's behaviour as best she remembered it: Robert Gabriel staring at Stuart Rintoul, Lord Stinhurst, obviously waiting for him either to deal with Joy or to go to his sister's aid; Irene Sinclair growing pale to the very lips as the situation escalated; Joanna Ellacourt flinging her script down and stalking out of the room in a rage, followed a moment later by her husband David Sydeham; Joy Sinclair smiling across the walnut reading table at Lord Stinhurst, and that smile apparently firing him into action so that he jumped to his feet, grabbed her arm, and dragged her into the morning room next door, slamming the door behind them. Lady Helen concluded with:

"And then Elizabeth Rintoul went after her aunt Francesca. She appeared . . . it was hard to tell, but she may have been crying, which seems a bit out of character for her."

"Why?"

"I don't know. Elizabeth seems to have given up crying some time ago," Lady Helen replied. "She's given up on lots of things, I think. Joy Sinclair, among them. They used to be close friends, from what Rhys told me."

"You haven't mentioned what he did after the read-through," Lynley pointed out. But he gave her no time to answer, saying instead, "Stinhurst and Joy Sinclair had the quarrel by themselves, then? The others weren't involved?"

"Only Stinhurst and Joy. I could hear their voices from the morning room."

"Shouting?"

"A bit from Joy. But actually I didn't hear much from Stinhurst. He doesn't seem to be the kind of man who has to raise his voice to get one's attention, does he? So the only thing I really heard clearly was Joy shouting hysterically about someone called Alec. She said Alec knew and Lord Stinhurst killed him because of it."

Next to her, Lady Helen heard Sergeant Havers' indrawn breath, which was followed by a speculative look in Lynley's direction. Immediately comprehending, Lady Helen hurried on to say:

"But surely that was a metaphorical statement, Tommy. A bit like, 'If you do that, you'll kill your mother.' You know what I mean. And at any rate, Lord Stinhurst didn't even respond to it. He just left, saying something like as far as he was concerned, she was through. Or words to that effect."

"And after that?"

"Joy and Stinhurst went upstairs. Separately. But they both looked dreadful. As if neither had won the argument and both wished it had never come about. Jeremy Vinney tried to say something to Joy when she came out into the hall, but she wouldn't talk. She may have been crying as well. I couldn't tell."

"Where did you go from there, Helen?" Lynley was studying the ashtray, the cigarette butts that littered it and the ashes that dusted the tabletop in mourning, grey mixed with black.

"I heard someone in the drawing room and went in to see who it was."

"Why?"

Lady Helen considered lying, manufacturing an amusing description of herself governed by curiosity, prowling about the house like a youthful Miss Marple. She chose the truth instead.

"Actually, Tommy, I'd been looking for Rhys."

"Ah. Disappeared, had he?"

She bristled at Lynley's tone. "Everyone had disappeared." She saw that St. James had finished his perusal of the room. He took a seat in the armchair near the door and leaned back against it, listening. Lady Helen knew he would take no notes. But he would remember every word.

"Was Davies-Jones in the drawing room?"

"No. Lady Stinhurst—Marguerite Rintoul—was there. And Jeremy Vinney. Perhaps he'd caught the scent of a story that he wanted to write for his newspaper because he seemed to be trying to question her about what had happened. With no success. I spoke to her as well because . . . frankly, she seemed to be in some sort of stupor. She did talk to me briefly. And strangely enough, she said something very similar to what Francesca had said earlier to Lord Stinhurst in the sitting room. 'Stop her.' Or something like that."

"Her? Joy?"

"Or perhaps Elizabeth, her daughter. I'd just mentioned Elizabeth. I think I'd said, 'Shall I fetch Elizabeth for you?' "

As she spoke, feeling very much a potential suspect being interrogated by the police, Lady Helen became aware of other sounds in the house: the steady scratching of Sergeant Havers' pencil upon her notebook paper; doors being unlocked at the other end of the corridor; the voice of Macaskin directing a search; and below in the library, upon the opening and closing of the door, angry shouting. Two men. She couldn't identify them.

"What time did you come to your room last night, Helen?"

"It must have been half past twelve. I didn't notice."

"What did you do when you got here?"

"I got undressed, got ready for bed, read for a time."

"And then?"

Lady Helen made no immediate reply. She was watching Lynley's face, completely free to do so since he would not meet her eyes. His features in repose had always combined every classical beauty possible in a man, but as he continued to ask his questions, Lady Helen saw those features begin to take on a grim impenetrability that she had never seen before and could not have guessed that he even possessed. Confronted with it, she felt entirely cut off from him for the very first time in their long and close friendship, and in a desire to put an end to this division, she reached a hand forward, not with the intention of touching him but in a miming of contact where contact apparently would not be allowed. When he did not respond with anything that could have been taken for acknowledgement, she felt compelled to speak honestly.

"You seem terribly angry, Tommy. Please. Tell me. What is it?"

Lynley's right fist clenched and unclenched in a movement so quick that it looked like a reflex. "When did you start smoking?"

At that, Lady Helen heard the abrupt cessation of Sergeant Havers' writing. She saw, past Lynley, St. James' movement in his chair. And she knew that, for some reason, her question had allowed Lynley to reach a decision, one that advanced him from police work into a new arena altogether, an arena not at all governed by the manuals, codes, and procedures that formed the rigid boundaries of his job.

"You know I don't smoke." She withdrew her hand.

"What did you hear last night?" Lynley asked. "Joy Sinclair was murdered between two and six in the morning."

"Nothing, I'm afraid. It was terribly windy, enough to rattle the windows. That must have drowned out any noise from her room. If there was any noise."

"And, of course, even if it hadn't been windy, you weren't alone, were you? You were . . . distracted, I should guess."

"You're right. I wasn't alone." She saw the muscles tighten at Lynley's mouth. Otherwise, he was motionless.

"What time did Davies-Jones come to your room?"

"At one."

"And he left?"

"Shortly after five."

"You saw a watch."

"He woke me. He was dressed. I asked the time. He told me."

"And between one and five, Helen?"

Lady Helen felt a quick surge of disbelief. "What is it exactly that you want to know?"

"I want to know what happened in this room between one and five. To use your own word: exactly." His voice was ice.

Past the wretchedness she felt at the question itself, at the brutal intrusion into her life and the implied assumption that she would be only too willing to answer it, Lady Helen saw Sergeant Havers' mouth drop open. She closed it quickly enough, however, when Lynley's frosty glance swept over her.

"Why are you asking me this?" Lady Helen asked Lynley.

"Would you like a solicitor to explain exactly what I can and cannot ask in a murder investigation? We can telephone for one if you think it's necessary."

This wasn't her friend, Lady Helen thought bleakly. This wasn't her laughing companion of more than a decade. This was a Tommy she didn't know, a man to whom she could give no rational response. In his presence, a tumult of emotions argued for precedence within her: anger, anguish, desolation. Lady Helen felt them attack like an onslaught, not one after another but all at once. They gripped her with punishing, unforgiving force, and when she was able to speak, her words struggled desperately for indifference.

"Rhys brought me cognac." She indicated the bottle on the table. "We talked."

"Did you drink?"

"No. I'd had some earlier. I wanted none."

"Did he have any?"

"No. He . . . isn't able to drink."

Lynley looked towards Havers. "Tell Macaskin's men to check the bottle."

Lady Helen read the thought behind the order. "It's sealed!"

"No. I'm afraid it isn't." Lynley took Havers' pencil and applied it to the foil at the top of the cognac. It came off effortlessly, as if it had once been removed and then reapplied to wear the guise of a closure.

Lady Helen felt ill. "What are you saying? That Rhys brought something with him this weekend to drug me? So that he could safely get away with murdering Joy Sinclair—my God, his own *cousin*—and have me as an alibi for his innocence? Is that what you think?"

"You said you talked, Helen. Am I to understand that, having refused his offer of a drink of whatever is in this bottle, you spent the remainder of the night in scintillating conversation together?"

His refusal to answer her question, his rigid adherence to the formality of police interrogation when it served his needs, his casual decision to fix blame upon a man and then bend the facts to fit it, outraged her. Carefully, deliberately, giving each separate syllable its own private position in the balance on which she measured the gravity of what he was doing to their friendship, she replied.

"No. Of course there's more, Tommy. He made love to me. We slept. And then, much later, I made love to him."

Whatever she had hoped for, Lynley showed absolutely no reaction to her words. Suddenly the smell of burnt tobacco from the ashtray was overwhelming. She wanted to fling it from sight. She wanted to fling it at him.

"That's all?" he asked. "He didn't leave you during the night? He didn't get out of bed?"

He was too damnably quick for her. When she couldn't keep the answer off her face, he said, "Ah. Yes. He did get out of bed. What time please, Helen?"

She looked down at her hands. "I don't know."

"Had you been asleep?"

"Yes."

"What awakened you?"

"A noise. I think it was a match. He was smoking, standing by the table."

"Dressed?"

"No."

"Just smoking?"

She hesitated momentarily. "Yes. Smoking. Yes."

"But you noticed something more, didn't you?"

"No. It's just that . . ." He was dragging words from her. He was compelling her to say things that belonged unspoken.

"That what? You noticed something about him, something not quite right?"

"No. *No.*" And then Lynley's eyes—shrewd, brown, insistent—held her own. "I went to him and his skin was damp."

"Damp? He'd bathed?"

"No. Salty. He was . . . his shoulders . . . perspiring. And it was so cold in here."

Lynley looked automatically to Joy Sinclair's room. Lady Helen continued.

"Don't you see, Tommy? It was the cognac. He wanted it. He was desperate. It's like an illness. It had nothing at all to do with Joy."

She might not have spoken, for Lynley was clearly following his own line of thought. "How many cigarettes did he have, Helen?"

"Five. Six. What you see here."

He was designing a pattern. Lady Helen could see it. If Rhys Davies-Jones had taken the time to smoke the six cigarettes that lay crushed in the ashtray, if she had not awakened until he was smoking the very last one, what else might he have done? Never mind the fact that she knew perfectly well how he had spent the time while she slept: fighting off legions of demons and ghouls that had drawn him to the bottle of cognac like a man with an unquenchable thirst. In Lynley's mind, he had used the time to unlock the door, murder his cousin, and return, his body broken out with the sweat of apprehension. Lady Helen read all of that in the stillness—like a void—that followed her sentence.

"He wanted a drink," she said simply. "But he can't drink. So he smoked. That's all."

"I see. May I assume he's an alcoholic?"

Her throat felt numb. *It's only a word,* Rhys would have said with his gentle smile. *A word alone has no power, Helen.* "Yes."

"So he got out of bed, and you never awakened. He smoked five or six cigarettes, and you never awakened."

"And you want to add that he unlocked the door to murder Joy Sinclair and I never awakened, don't you?"

."His prints are on the key, Helen."

"Yes, they are! I've no doubt of it! He locked the door before he took me to bed. Or are you going to say that was part of his plan? To make certain I saw him lock the door so I could explain away his fingerprints later? Is that how you have it worked out?"

"It's what you're doing, isn't it?"

SHe drew in a broken breath. "What a rotten thing to say!"

"You slept through his getting out of bed, you slept through his smoking one cigarette after another. Are you going to try to argue now that, in reality, you're a light sleeper, that you would have known had Davies-Jones left your room?"

"I would have known!"

Lynley looked over his shoulder. "St! James?" he asked evenly. And those two words took the entire affair out of the realm of control.

Lady Helen sprang to her feet. Her chair toppled over. Her hand came down brutally against Lynley's face. It was a blow of lightning swiftness, driven by the power of her rage.

"You filthy bastard!" she cried and headed for the door.

"Stay where you are," Lynley ordered.

She whirled and faced him. "Arrest me, Inspector." She left the room, slamming the door behind her.

St. James followed her at once.

4

BARBARA HAVERS closed her notebook. It was a studied movement, one that bought her time while she thought. Across from her, Lynley felt in the breast pocket of his jacket. Although colour still splodged his face where Lady Helen had struck him, his hands were quite steady. He brought out his cigarette case and lighter, used them both and handed them over. Barbara did likewise although after inhaling once, she grimaced and crushed out the cigarette.

Not a woman who ever spent a great deal of time analysing her emotions, Barbara did so now, realising with some confusion that she had wanted to intervene in what had just occurred. All Lynley's questions had, of course, been fairly standard police procedure, but the manner in which he had asked them and the nasty insinuations carried in his tone had made Barbara want to throw herself into the fray as Lady Helen's champion. She couldn't understand why. So she thought about it in the aftermath of Lady Helen's departure, and she found her answer in the myriad ways that the young woman had shown kindness to her in the months since Barbara had been assigned to work with Lynley.

"I think, Inspector," Barbara ran her thumb back and forth on a crease in the cover of her notebook, "that you were more than a bit out of line just now."

"This isn't the time for a row about procedure," Lynley replied. His voice was dispassionate enough, but Barbara could hear its taut control.

"It has nothing to do with procedure, does it? It has to do with decency. You treated Helen like a scrubber, Inspector, and if you're about to answer that she acted like a scrubber, I might suggest you take a good look at one or two items in your own chequered past and ask yourself how well they'd appear in a scrutiny the likes of which you just forced her to endure."

Lynley drew on his cigarette, but, as if he found the taste unpleasant, he stubbed it out in the ashtray. As he did so, a jerk of his hand spilled ashes across the cuff of his shirt. Both of them stared at the resulting contrast of black grime against white.

"Helen had the misfortune of being in the wrong place at the wrong time," Lynley replied. "There was no way to get round it, Havers. I can't give her special treatment because she's my friend."

"Is that right?" Barbara asked. "Well, I'll be fascinated to see how that line plays out when we have the two old boys together for a confidential little chat."

"What are you talking about?"

"Lords Asherton and Stinhurst sitting down for a chew. I can hardly wait for the chance to see you treat Stuart Rintoul with the same iron glove that you used on Helen Clyde. Peer to peer, chap to chap, Etonian to Etonian. Isn't that how it plays? But as you've said, none of that will get in the way of Lord Stinhurst's unfortunate placement of himself at the wrong place at the wrong time." She knew him well enough to see his quick rise to anger.

"And what is it exactly that you would have me do, Sergeant? Ignore the facts?" Coolly, Lynley began to tick them off. "Joy Sinclair's hall door is locked. The master keys are, for all intents and purposes, unavailable. Davies-Jones' prints are on the key to the only other door that gives access to the room. We have a period of time that is unaccounted for because Helen was asleep. All that, and we haven't even begun to consider where Davies-Jones was until one in the morning when he showed up at Helen's door, or why Helen, of all people, was put into this room in the first place. Convenient, isn't it, when you consider that we have a man coincidentally coming here in the middle of the night to seduce Helen while his cousin is being murdered in the very next room?"

"And that's the rub, isn't it?" Barbara pointed out. "*Seduction*, not murder."

Lynley picked up the cigarette case and lighter, slipped them back in his pocket, and got to his feet. He didn't respond. But Barbara did not require him to do so. A response was pointless when she knew very well that his stiff-upper-lip breeding had a propensity towards deserting him in moments of personal crisis. And the truth of the matter was that the instant she had seen Lady Helen in the library, had seen Lynley's face when Lady Helen crossed the room to him with that ridiculous greatcoat hanging forlornly to her heels, Barbara had known that, for Lynley, the situation had the potential of developing into a personal crisis of some considerable proportions.

Inspector Macaskin appeared at the bedroom door. Fury played on his features. His face was flushed, his eyes snapped, his skin looked tight. "Not one script in the house, Inspector," he announced. "It appears our good Lord Stinhurst has burnt every last one."

"Well, la-de-da-da," Barbara murmured to the ceiling.

IN THE LOWER NORTH corridor, which was one-fourth of a quadrangle surrounding a courtyard where untouched snow reached nearly to the height of the leaded windows, a door gave out onto the estate grounds. To one side of this door, Francesca Gerrard had established a storage area—a jumble of discarded Wellingtons, fishing gear, rusty gardening tools, mackintoshes, hats, coats, and scarves. Lady Helen knelt on the floor in front of this clutter, throwing aside one boot after another, furiously seeking a mate to the one she had already pulled on. She heard the distinctive sound of St. James' awkward footsteps coming down the stairs, and she rooted frantically among gumboots and fishing baskets, determined to get out of the house before St. James found her.

But the perverse acuity that had always allowed him to know most of her thoughts before she was even aware of thinking them led him directly to her now. She heard his strained breathing from his rapid descent of the stairs and did not need to look up to know that his face would be pinched with irritation at his body's weakness. She felt his tentative touch on her shoulder. She jerked away.

"I'm going out," she said.

"You can't. It's far too cold. Beyond that, I'd have too hard a time following you in the dark, and I want to talk to you, Helen."

"I don't think we have anything to say to each other, do we? You had your place at the peep show. Or did you want to tip the tart?"

She looked up at that, saw his reaction to her words in the sudden darkening of his smoky blue eyes. But rather than rejoice in her ability to wound him, she was defeated at once. She ceased her search, and stood, with one boot on and another uselessly in her hand. St. James reached out, and Lady Helen felt his cool, dry fingers close over her own.

"I felt just like a whore," she whispered. Her eyes were dry and hot. She was far beyond tears. "I'll never forgive him."

"I'll not ask that of you. I've not come to excuse Tommy, merely to say that he was hit squarely in the face today with several monumental truths. Unfortunately, he wasn't prepared to deal with any of them. But he'll have to be the one to explain that to you. When he can."

Lady Helen plucked miserably at the top of the boot she held. It was black and smudged along its upper ridge with a stickiness that made it look even blacker.

"Would you have answered his question?" she asked abruptly.

St. James smiled, a warm transformation of his otherwise unattractive, angular face. "You know, I always envied your ability to sleep through anything, Helen. Fire, flood, or thunder. I would lie next to you for hours, wide awake, and steadily curse you for having a conscience so unclouded that nothing ever got in the way of your sleep. I used to think that I could have marched the Queen's Household Cavalry right through the bedroom and you wouldn't even have noticed. But I wouldn't have answered him. There are some things, in spite of everything that's happened, that are just between the two of us. Frankly, that's one of them."

Lady Helen felt the tears then, a hot flurry behind her eyelids which she blinked back, looking away, trying to find her voice. St. James didn't wait for her to do so. Rather, he drew her gently towards a narrow bench that rested on splintered legs along one of the walls. Several coats hung on pegs above it, and he removed two of them, draping one round her shoulders and using the other himself to ward off the chill that invaded the storage area.

"Aside from the changes Joy had made to the script, did anything else strike you that might have led up to the row last night?" he asked.

Lady Helen considered the hours she had spent with the group from London prior to the turmoil in the sitting room. "I couldn't say for certain. But I do think everyone's nerves were strung."

"Whose in particular?"

"Joanna Ellacourt's, for one. From what I could gather at cocktails last night, she was already a bit overwrought by the thought that Joy might be writing a play that was going to be a vehicle to resurrect her sister's career."

"That would certainly have bothered her, wouldn't it?"

Lady Helen nodded. "Besides the opening of the new Agincourt Theatre, the production was to celebrate Joanna's twentieth year on the stage, Simon, so its focus was supposed to be on her, not on Irene Sinclair. But I got the impression that she didn't think it would be." Lady Helen explained the brief scene she had witnessed in the drawing room last night, when the company had gathered before dinner. Lord Stinhurst had been standing near the piano with Rhys Davies-Jones, flipping through a set of designs for costumes, when Joanna Ellacourt joined them, slinking across the room in a semi-bodiceless coruscating gown that gave new definition to dressing for dinner. She had taken up the drawings for her own perusal, but her face revealed in an instant how she felt about what she saw.

"Joanna didn't like Irene Sinclair's costumes," St. James guessed.

"She claimed that every one of them showed Irene off . . . like a vamp, I think she said. She crumpled the drawings up, told Lord Stinhurst that his costume people would have to redesign if he wanted *her* in the play, and threw them all on the fire. She was absolutely livid, and I think that once she began reading the play in the sitting room, she saw in Joy's changes that her worst fears were confirmed, and that's why she threw down the script and left. And Joy . . . well, I couldn't help feeling that she enjoyed the sensation and the disruption she was causing."

"What was she like, Helen?"

It wasn't an easy question to answer. Physically, Joy Sinclair had been striking. Not beautiful, Lady Helen explained, she looked like a gypsy, with olive skin and black eyes, possessing the sort of features that belong on a Roman coin, finely boned, chiselled, and stamped with both intelligence and strength. She was a woman who radiated sensuality and life. Even a quick impatient gesture to her earlobe to remove an earring somehow could become a movement fraught with promise.

"Promise for whom?" St. James asked.

"That's hard to say. But I should guess that Jeremy Vinney was the most interested man here. He jumped up to join her the moment she came into the drawing room last evening—she was the last to arrive—and he stuck right to her side at dinner as well."

"Were they lovers?"

"She didn't act as if there was anything between them other than friendship. He mentioned having tried to reach her on the telephone and leaving a dozen or so messages on her answering machine over the past week. And she just laughed and said that she was terribly sorry he'd gone ignored but she wasn't even listening to her answering machine because she was six months overdue on a book she had contracted with her publisher, so she didn't want to feel guilty by listening to the messages asking her where it was."

"A book?" St. James asked. "She was writing both a book *and* a play?"

Lady Helen laughed regretfully. "Incredible, wasn't she? And to think that I feel industrious if I manage to answer a letter within five months of receiving it."

"She sounds like a woman who might well inspire jealousy."

"Perhaps. But I think it was more that she alienated people unconsciously." Lady Helen told him of Joy's light-hearted comments during cocktails about a Reingale painting that hung over the fireplace in the drawing room. It was a depiction of a white-gowned Regency woman, surrounded by her two children and a frisky terrier who nosed at a ball. "She said she'd never forgotten that painting, that as a child visiting Westerbrae, she'd liked to imagine herself as that Reingale woman, safe and secure and admired, with two perfect children to adore her. She said something like, what more could one ask for than that and isn't it strange how life turns out. Her sister was sitting right below the painting as she spoke, and I remember noticing how Irene began to flush horribly, like a rash was spreading up her neck and across her face."

"Why?"

"Well, of course, Irene had once been all those things, hadn't she? Safe and secure, with a husband and two children. And then Joy had come along and destroyed it all."

St. James looked sceptical. "How can you be sure that Irene Sinclair was reacting to what her sister had said?"

"I can't, of course. I know that. Except at dinner, when Joy and Jeremy Vinney were talking together and Joy was making all sorts of amusing comments about her new book, entertaining the whole table with stories about some man she'd been trying to interview in the Fens, Irene . . ." Lady Helen hesitated. It was difficult to put into words the chilling effect Irene Sinclair's behaviour had had upon her. "Irene was sitting quite still, staring at the candles on the table and she . . . it was rather dreadful, Simon. She drove the tines of her fork right into her thumb. But I don't think she felt a thing."

ST. JAMES reflected upon the tops of his shoes. They were smudged with dried mud from the drive, and he bent to wipe them off. "Then Joanna Ellacourt must have been wrong about Irene's role in this changed version of the play. Why would Joy Sinclair be writing for her sister if she continued to alienate her at every juncture?"

"As I said, I think the alienation was unconscious. And as for the play, perhaps Joy felt guilty. After all, she had destroyed her sister's marriage. She couldn't give that back to her. But she could give her back her career."

"But in a play with Robert Gabriel? After a messy divorce that Joy herself had likely helped cause? Doesn't that smack of sadism to you?"

"Not if no one else in London was willing to give Irene a chance, Simon. Evidently, she's been out of circulation for a good many years. This may well have been her only opportunity for a second go on stage."

"Tell me about the play."

As Lady Helen recalled, Joy Sinclair's description of the new version of the play—prior to the actors' actually seeing it—had been deliberately provocative. When asked about it by Francesca Gerrard, she had smiled up and down the length of the dining table and said, "It takes place in a house much like this. In the dead of winter, with ice sheeting the road and not a soul in miles and no way to escape. It's about a family. And a man who dies, and the people who had to kill him. And why. Especially why." Lady Helen had expected to hear wolves howling next.

"It sounds as if she intended that as a message for someone."

"It does, doesn't it? And then when we were all gathered in the sitting room and she began going over the changes in the plot, she said much the same thing."

The plot concerned itself with a family and their thwarted New Year's Eve celebration. According to Joy, the oldest brother was a man possessed of a terrible secret, a secret that was about to rip apart the fabric of everyone's life.

"And then they began to read," Lady Helen said. "I wish I had paid more attention to *what* they were reading, but it was so stuffy in the sitting room—no, it was more like a pan of water about to come to a boil—that I didn't really follow much of what they had to say. All I remember for a certainty is that just before Francesca Gerrard went a bit mad, the older brother in the story—Lord Stinhurst was reading the part since it hadn't been cast yet—had just received a telephone call. He decided that he had to leave at once, saying that after twenty-seven years, he wasn't about to become another vassal. I'm fairly certain those were the words. And that's when Francesca leaped to her feet and the evening collapsed."

"Vassal?" St. James repeated blankly.

She nodded. "Odd, isn't it? Of course, since the play had nothing to do with feudalism, I thought it was something wildly avant-garde, with me just too dim to understand what it meant."

"But they understood?"

"Lord Stinhurst, his wife, Francesca Gerrard, and Elizabeth. Decidedly. But I do think, aside from their irritation at the late changes in the script, everyone else was as confused as I was." Lady Helen ran her fingers unconsciously round the top of the boot she still held. "Altogether, I had the impression that the play was supposed to serve a noble purpose that didn't quite come off. A noble purpose for everyone. It was to honour Stinhurst's achievement vis-à-vis the renovated Agincourt, it was to celebrate Joanna Ellacourt's career on the stage, it was to bring Irene Sinclair back into the theatre, it was to get Rhys back into directing a major production in London. Perhaps Joy even intended a part for Jeremy Vinney as well. Someone mentioned that he'd started out as an actor before turning to dramatic criticism, and frankly, other than to continue following the Agincourt story, there doesn't seem to be any other real reason for him to have come to the read-through. So you see," she concluded with an urgency in her voice that she could not hide from him, "it doesn't seem reasonable that any of *those* people would have murdered Joy, does it?"

St. James smiled at her fondly. "Especially Rhys." His words were exceptionally gentle.

Lady Helen met his eyes, saw the kindness and compassion behind them, felt she couldn't bear it, and looked away. Yet she knew that, above all people, he was the single person who would understand. So she spoke. "Last night with Rhys. It was . . . the first time in years that I felt so loved, Simon. For what I am, for my faults and my virtues, for my past and my future. I haven't had that with a man since . . ." She hesitated, then finished what needed to be said. "Since I had it with you. And I never expected to have it again. That was to be my punishment, you see. For what happened between us all those years ago. I deserved it."

St. James shook his head sharply, without reply. After a moment he said, "If you concentrate, Helen, are you certain you heard nothing last night?"

Lady Helen answered his question with one of her own. "The first time you made love to Deborah, what else did you notice besides her?"

"You're right, of course. The house could have burned to the ground for all I would have known. Or cared, for that matter." He got to his feet, hung his coat back on the peg, and held out his hand for hers. When she gave it to him, his brow furrowed. "My God, what have you done to yourself?" he asked.

"Done?"

"Your hand, Helen."

Her eyes dropped, and she saw that her fingers had somehow become laced with blood, black with it underneath her fingernails. She started at the sight.

"Where . . . I don't . . ."

More blood, she saw, smeared along the side of her skirt, drying to brown on the wool. She looked for the source, spied the boot she had been holding, and picked it up, examining the sticky substance round its top, black upon black in the dull light of the storage area. Wordlessly, she handed it to St. James.

He upended the boot on the bench, thumped it soundly against the wood, and dislodged a large glove, at one time leather and fur but now nothing more than a pulpy mass of Joy Sinclair's blood. Not yet dried, not yet done for.

HALF THE SIZE of the library, the Westerbrae sitting room to the left of the wide baronial stairway seemed to Lynley an odd choice of locations for any large group to meet in. Yet it was still set up for the reading of Joy Sinclair's play, with a concentric arrangement of tables and chairs at the room's centre for the actors, and peripheral observation points along its walls for everyone else. Even the scent in the room bore witness to last night's ill-fated gathering: tobacco, burnt matches, coffee dregs, and brandy.

When Lord Stinhurst entered under the watchful eye of Sergeant Havers, Lynley directed him to sit in an unwelcoming ladder-back chair near the fireplace. A coal fire burned in the small grate there, cutting the chill in the room. Outside the closed door, the scene-of-crime men from Strathclyde CID were making an unusually noisy arrival.

Stinhurst took his designated seat cooperatively, crossing one well-tailored leg over the other, refusing a cigarette. He was impeccably dressed, the personification of weekend-in-the-country. Yet, in spite of his movements, which carried the assurance of a man used to the stage, used to being under the eyes of hundreds of people at once, he looked physically drained, whether from exhaustion or from the effort of holding together the women in his family during this time of crisis, Lynley could not have said. But he took the opportunity of observing the man while Sergeant Havers leafed through the pages of her notebook.

Cary Grant, Lynley thought in summation of Stinhurst's general appearance and liked the comparison. Although Stinhurst was in his seventies, his face had lost none of the extraordinarily hand-some, strong-jawed force of its youth, and his hair, shafted obliquely by the amiable low light of the room, was variations on silver, roughly textured and full as it had always been. With a body on which there was no spare flesh, Stinhurst belied the term *old age*, living proof that relentless industry was the key to youth.

Yet, underneath this pleasant, surface perfection, Lynley sensed strong undercurrents being mastered, and he decided that control was the key to understanding the man. He appeared to excel at maintaining it: over his body, over his emotions, over his mind. This last was acutely alive and, as far as Lynley could tell, perfectly capable of deciding how best to tamper with a mountain of evidence. At the moment, Lord Stinhurst manifested only one sign of agita-tion in the face of this interview, pressing together the thumb and forefinger of his right hand in repeated, forceful spasms. The flesh under the nails alternately whitened and blushed as circulation was interrupted and then restored. Lynley found the gesture interesting and wondered if Stinhurst's body would continue to reveal his increasing tension.

"You look a great deal like your father," Stinhurst said. "But I suppose you hear that frequently."

Lynley saw Havers' head come up with a snap. "Generally not, in my line of work," he replied. "I'd like you to explain why you've burnt Joy Sinclair's scripts."

If Stinhurst was disconcerted by Lynley's unwillingness to recog-nise any bond between them, he did not show it. Rather, he said, "Without the sergeant, please."

Gripping her pencil more firmly, Havers regarded the older man with eyes narrowed in contempt at his lord-of-the-manor dismissal of her. She waited for Lynley's response and flashed a brief, satisfied smile when he said firmly, "That's not possible." Hearing that, she settled back into her chair.

Stinhurst didn't move. He had not, in fact, even glanced at Sergeant Havers before he requested her removal. He merely said, "I have to insist, Thomas."

The use of his given name was a stimulus that brought back to Lynley not only Havers' angry challenge to treat Lord Stinhurst with an iron glove, but also the trepidation he had earlier felt about his assignment to this case. It set off every alarm.

"That's not one of your rights, I'm afraid."

"My . . . rights?" Stinhurst offered the smile of a cardplayer with a winning hand. "This entire fantasy that says I have to speak with you is just that, Thomas. A fantasy. We don't have that kind of legal system. You and I both know it. The sergeant goes or we wait for my solicitor. From London."

Stinhurst might have been mildly disciplining a fractious child. But there was absolute reality behind his words, and in the space of time that it had taken to hear them, Lynley saw the alternatives, a legal minuet with the man's attorney or a momentary compromise that could well be used to purchase some truth. It had to be done.

"Step outside, Sergeant," he told Havers, his eyes unwavering from the other man.

"Inspector . . ." Her voice was unbearably restrained.

"See to Gowan Kilbride and Mary Agnes Campbell," Lynley went on. "It will save us some time."

Havers drew a tense breath. "May I speak to you outside, please?"

Lynley allowed her that much, following her into the great hall and closing the door behind them. Havers gave rapid scrutiny to the left and right, wary of listeners. When she spoke, her voice was a whisper, fierce and angry.

"What the hell are you doing, Inspector? You can't question him alone. Let's chat about the procedure you've been so bloody fond of throwing in my face these last fifteen months."

Lynley felt unmoved by her quick flare of passion. "As far as I'm concerned, Sergeant, Webberly threw procedure out the window the moment he got us involved in this case without a formal request from Strathclyde CID. I'm not about to spend time agonising over it now."

"But you've got to have a witness! You've got to have the notes! What's the point of questioning him if you've nothing written down to use against . . ." Sudden comprehension dawned on her face. "Unless, of course, you know right now that you intend to believe every blessed word his sweet lordship has to say!"

Lynley had worked with the sergeant long enough to know when a conversational skirmish was about to escalate into verbal warfare. He cut her off.

"At some point, Barbara, you're going to have to decide whether an uncontrollable factor such as a person's birth is reason enough to distrust him."

"What's that supposed to mean? I'm supposed to *trust* Stinhurst? He's destroyed a stack of evidence, he's sitting smack in the middle of a murder, he's refusing to cooperate. And I'm supposed to *trust* him?"

"I wasn't talking about Stinhurst. I was talking about myself."

She gaped at him, speechless. He turned back to the door, pausing with his hand on the knob.

"I want you to see to Gowan and Mary Agnes. I want notes. I want them precise. Use Constable Lonan to assist. Is that clear?"

Havers shot him a look that would have withered flowers. "Perfectly . . . sir." Slamming her notebook shut, she stalked off.

When Lynley returned to the sitting room, he saw that Stinhurst had adjusted to the new conditions, his shoulders and spine releasing their wire-tight grip on his posture. He seemed suddenly less unyielding and far more vulnerable. His eyes, the colour of fog, focussed on Lynley. They were unreadable.

"Thank you, Thomas."

This easy shift in persona—a chameleon passage from hauteur to gratitude—was a glaring reminder to Lynley that Stinhurst's lifeblood flowed not through his veins but through the aisles of the theatre.

"As to the scripts," Lynley said.

"This murder has nothing to do with Joy Sinclair's play." Lord Stinhurst gave his attention not to Lynley but to the shattered front of the curio cabinet next to the door. He left his chair and went to it, retrieving the disembodied head of a Dresden shepherdess from the remaining crumble of broken porcelain that still lay inside, heaped upon the bottom shelf. He carried it back to his seat.

"I don't imagine Francie yet realises that she broke this piece last night," he remarked. "It'll be a blow. Our older brother gave it to her. They were very close."

Lynley wasn't about to play hunt the thimble through the man's family history. "If Mary Agnes Campbell found the body at six-fifty this morning, why did the police not log your call until seven-ten? Why did it take twenty minutes for you to phone for help?"

"I wasn't even aware until this moment that twenty minutes had elapsed," Stinhurst replied.

Lynley wondered how long he had rehearsed that response. It was clever enough, the type of nonanswer to which no further comment or accusation could be attached.

"Then why don't you tell me exactly what happened this morning," he said with deliberate courtesy. "Perhaps we can account for the twenty minutes that way."

"Mary Agnes found the . . . Joy. She went immediately for my sister, Francesca. Francesca came for me." Lord Stinhurst seemed to be ready for Lynley's next thought, for he went on to say, "My sister was panicked. She was terrified. I don't imagine she thought to phone the police herself. She'd always depended upon her husband Phillip to be the master of any unpleasant situation. As a widow, she merely turned that dependence on me. That's not abnormal, Thomas."

"And that's all?"

Stinhurst's eyes were on the porcelain head he held gingerly in his palm. "I told Mary Agnes to gather everyone into the drawing room."

"They cooperated?"

He looked up. "They were in shock. One doesn't really expect a member of one's party to be stabbed through the neck during the night." Lynley raised an eyebrow. Stinhurst explained, "I had a look at the body when I locked her room this morning."

"You were fairly clear-headed for a man who's just encountered his first corpse."

"I think one ought to be clear-headed when there's a murderer in one's midst."

"You're sure of that?" Lynley asked. "You never considered that the murderer might have come from outside the house?"

"The nearest village is five miles away. It took the police nearly two hours to get here this morning. Do you really see someone coming in on snowshoes or skis to do away with Joy during the night?"

"Where did you place the call to the police?"

"From my sister's office."

"How long were you in there?"

"Five minutes. Perhaps less."

"Is that the only call you made?"

The question clearly took Stinhurst off guard. His face looked shuttered. "No. I telephoned my secretary in London. At her flat."

"Why?"

"I wanted her to know about the . . . situation. I wanted her to cancel my engagements on Sunday evening and Monday."

"How farsighted of you. But all things considered, wouldn't you agree that it's a bit odd to be thinking about your personal engagements directly after discovering that a member of your party has been murdered?"

"I can't help what it looks like. I just did it."

"And what were the engagements that you had to cancel?"

"I've no idea. My secretary keeps my engagement book with her. I merely work off the daily schedule she gives me." He concluded impatiently, as if in the need of a defence, "I'm out of the office frequently. It's easier this way."

Yet, Lynley thought, Stinhurst did not have the look of a man who required that his life be arranged round elements that made it easier and more liveable. So the last two statements wore the guise of both fencing and prevaricating. Lynley wondered why Stinhurst had even made them.

"How does Jeremy Vinney fit into your weekend plans?"

It was a second question for which Stinhurst seemed unprepared. But this time his hesitation bore the quality of thoughtful consideration rather than evasion. "Joy wanted him here," he answered after a moment. "She told him about the read-through we were going to have. He'd been covering the renovation of the Agincourt with a series of articles in *The Times*. I suppose this weekend seemed like a natural extension of those stories. He phoned me and asked if he could come along. It seemed harmless enough, the possibility of good press prior to the opening. And at any rate, he and Joy appeared to know each other quite well. She was insistent that he come."

"But why would she want him here? He's the arts critic, isn't he? Why would she want him to have access to her play so soon in the process of production? Or was he her lover?"

"He could have been. Men always found Joy immensely attractive. Jeremy Vinney wouldn't have been the first."

"Or perhaps his interest was solely in the script. Why did you burn it?"

Lynley made sure that the question had the ring of inevitability. Stinhurst's face reflected a patient recognition of this fact.

"Burning the scripts had nothing to do with Joy's death, Thomas. The play as it stood wasn't going to be produced. Once I withdrew my support—and I did that last night—it would have died on its own."

"Died. Interesting choice of words. Then why burn the scripts?"

Stinhurst did not reply. His eyes were on the fire. That he was struggling with a decision was more than obvious. The fact played across his features like a battle. But who the opposing forces were and what was at stake in the victory were fine points of the conflict that were not yet clarified.

"The scripts," Lynley said again, implacably.

Stinhurst's body gave a convulsive movement akin to a shudder. "I burned them because of the subject matter Joy had chosen to explore," he said. "The play was about my wife Marguerite. And her love affair with my older brother. And the child they had thirty-six years ago. Elizabeth."

5

GOWAN KILBRIDE was in a new kind of agony. It began the moment Constable Lonan opened the library door and called out that the London police wanted to speak with Mary Agnes. It increased in intensity when Mary Agnes jumped to her feet, displaying an undisguised eagerness for the encounter. And it reached its zenith with the knowledge that for the past fifteen minutes she had been gone from his sight and his determined—if hardly adequate—protection. Worse still, she was now under the sure, the entirely adequate, the decidedly masculine protection of New Scotland Yard.

Which was the source of the problem.

Once the police group from London—but most particularly the tall, blond detective who appeared to be in charge—had left the library after their brief encounter with Lady Helen Clyde, Mary Agnes had turned to Gowan, her eyes ablaze. "He's *haiven*," she had breathed.

That remark boded ill, but, like a fool for love, Gowan had been willing to take the conversation further.

"Haiven?" he'd asked irritably.

"Tha' policeman!" And then Mary Agnes had gone on rhapsodically to catalogue Inspector Lynley's virtues. Gowan felt them tattooed into his brain. Hair like Anthony Andrews, a nose like Charles Dance, eyes like Ben Cross, and a smile like Sting. No matter that the man had not bothered to smile once. Mary Agnes was perfectly capable of filling in details when necessary.

It had been bad enough to be in fruitless competition with Jeremy Irons. But now Gowan saw that he had the entire front line of Britain's theatrical performers to contend with, all embodied in a single man. He ground his teeth bitterly and writhed in discomfort.

He was sitting in a cretonne-covered chair whose material felt like a stiff second skin after so many hours. Next to him—moved carefully out of everyone's way only a quarter hour into their group incarceration—Mrs. Gerrard's treasured Cary Globe rested on an impossibly ornate, gilded stand. Gowan stared at it morosely. He felt like kicking it over. Better yet, he felt like heaving it through the window. He was desperate for escape.

He tried to quell the need by forcing himself to consider the library's charms, but he found there were none. The white plaster octagons on the ceiling needed paint, as did the garlands that ornamented their centres. Years of coal fires and cigarette smoke had taken their toll, and what looked like deep shadows in the nooks and crannies of the raised decoration was really soot, the kind of grime that promised a miserable two weeks or more of work in the coming months. The bookshelves, too, spoke of added misery. They held hundreds of volumes—perhaps even thousands—bound in leather and, behind the glass, all smelling equally of dust and disuse. Another job of cleaning and drying and repairing and . . . *Where* was Mary Agnes? He had to find her. He had to get out.

Near him, a woman's voice rose in a tear-filled plea. "My God, please! I can't stand this another moment!"

Within the last weeks, Gowan had developed a mild dislike of actors in general. But in the past nine hours, he had found he'd developed a hardy loathing of one group in the very particular.

"David, I've reached my breaking point. Can't you *do* something to get us out of here?" Joanna Ellacourt was wringing her hands as she spoke to her husband, pacing the floor and smoking. Which, Gowan thought, she'd been doing all day. The room smelled like a smouldering rubbish heap largely because of her. And it was interesting to note that she had only reached this newest level of nervous agitation when Lady Helen Clyde reentered the room and promised the possibility of attention being directed somewhere other than upon the great star herself.

From his wing chair, David Sydeham's hooded eyes followed his wife's slim figure. "What would you have me do, Jo? Batter down the door and club that constable over the head? We're at their mercy, *ma belle.*"

"Sit, Jo darling." Robert Gabriel extended a well-tended hand to her, beckoning her to join him on the couch by the fire. The coals there had burned down to small grey lumps speckled with glowing rose. "You're doing nothing more than unstringing your nerves. Which is exactly what the police would like you to do, would like all of us to do, in fact. It makes their job easier."

"And you're hell-bent on not doing that, I dare say," Jeremy Vinney put in just a pitch above *sotto voce*.

Gabriel's temper flared. "What the hell is that supposed to mean?"

Vinney ignored him, struck a match, and applied it to his pipe.

"I asked you a question!"

"And I'm choosing not to answer it."

"Why, you miserable—"

"We all know Gabriel had a row with Joy yesterday," Rhys Davies-Jones said reasonably. He was sitting furthest from the bar, in a chair next to the window whose curtains he had recently pulled back. Black night yawned through the glass. "I don't think any of us need make veiled references to it in the hope that the police will get the point."

"Get the *point*?" Robert Gabriel's voice held the cutting edge of his ire. "Nice of you to have *me* fingered for the murder, Rhys, but I'm afraid it won't wash. Not a bit of it."

"Why? Have you an alibi?" David Sydeham asked. "The way it looks to me, you're one of the very few people at significant risk, Gabriel. Unless, of course, you can produce a second party with whom you spent the night." He smiled sardonically. "What about the little girl? Is that what Mary Agnes is up to right now, trotting out stories about your technique? That must be keeping the coppers on the edge of their seats, all right. An intimate description of what it's like for a woman to have you between her legs. Or was Joy's play heading us towards that kind of revelation last night?"

Gabriel surged to his feet, knocking against a brass floor lamp. Its arc of light flashed wildly round the room. "I bloody well ought to—"

"Stop it!" Joanna Ellacourt put her hands over her ears. "I can't stand it! Stop!"

But it was too late. The quick exchange of words had struck Gowan like fists. He leaped out of his chair. In four steps he made it across the room to Gabriel and furiously whipped the actor around to face him.

"Damn ye tae hell!" he shouted. "Did ye titch Mary Agnes?"

But the answer didn't interest him. Seeing Gabriel's face, Gowan needed no response. They were a match for size, but the boy's fury made him stronger. It crested within him, firing him to fight. His single punch put Gabriel flat on the floor, and he fell upon him, one hand at the man's throat, the other solidly delivering nasty and well-placed blows to his face.

"Wha' did ye dae tae Mary Agnes?" Gowan roared as he struck.

"Jesus God!"

"Stop him!"

Fragile composure—that thin shell of civility—disintegrated into uproar. Limbs flailed viciously. Hoarse cries charged the air. Glassware smashed onto the hearth. Feet kicked and jolted abandoned furniture to one side. Gowan's arm encircled Gabriel's neck, and he dragged the man, panting and sobbing, to the fire.

"Tell me!" Gowan forced Gabriel's handsome face, now twisted with pain, over the fender, within an inch of the coals. "Tell me, ye bystart!"

"Rhys!" Irene Sinclair backed stiffly into her chair, her face ashen. "Stop him! Stop him!"

Davies-Jones and Sydeham climbed past the overturned furniture and the frozen figures of Lady Stinhurst and Francesca Gerrard, who cowered together like two versions of Lot's wife. They reached Gowan and Gabriel, struggled uselessly to haul them apart. But Gowan held the actor in a grip made unbreakable by the force of his passion.

"Don't believe him, Gowan," Davies-Jones said urgently into the boy's ear. He gripped his shoulder hard, jerking him to sensibility. "Don't lose yourself like this. Let him be, lad. *Enough.*"

Somehow the words—and the implication of complete understanding behind them—reached past Gowan's red tide of anger. Releasing Robert Gabriel, he tore himself away from Davies-Jones and fell to his side on the floor, gasping convulsively.

He realised, of course, the gravity of what he had done, the fact that he would lose his job—and Mary Agnes—because of it. But beyond the enormity of his behaviour, it was the torment of loving and being unloved in return that drove the threat from him, entirely blind to the impact it might have on others in the room, seeking only to wound as he had been wounded.

"I know bluidy all! An' I'll tell the police! An' ye'll pay!"

"Gowan!" Francesca Gerrard cried out in horror.

"Better speak now, lad," Davies-Jones said. "Don't be a fool to talk like that when there's a killer in the room."

Elizabeth Rintoul had not moved once during the altercation.

Now she stirred, as if from a deep sleep. "No. Not here. Father's gone to the sitting room, hasn't he?"

"I SHOULD GUESS you see Marguerite as she is now, a sixty-nine-year-old woman very much near the end of her resources. But at thirty-four, when all this occurred, she was lovely. Lively. And eager—so eager to live."

Restlessly, Lord Stinhurst had gone to a different chair, not one of those in the centre of the room, but one on its perimeter, well out of the light. He sat forward in it, leaning his arms on his knees, and he studied the floral carpet as he talked, as if its muted arabesque pattern held answers for him. His voice was toneless. It was the voice of a man giving a recitation that had to be got through with no expenditure of emotion.

"She and my brother Geoffrey fell in love shortly after the war."

Lynley said nothing. But he wondered how, even at a distance of thirty-six years, any man could speak of such a monumental act of disloyalty with so little affect. Stinhurst's lack of emotion spoke of a man who was dead inside, who could no longer afford to let himself be touched, who single-mindedly pursued excellence in his career so that he never had to face the agony rife in his personal life.

"Geoff had been decorated numerous times. He came back from the war a hero. I suppose it was natural that Marguerite was attracted to him. Everyone was. He had a way about him . . . an air." Stinhurst paused reflectively. His hands sought each other and pressed hard together.

"You served in the war as well?" Lynley asked.

"Yes. But not like Geoffrey. Not with his flair, not with his devotion. My brother was like a fire. He blazed through life. And like a fire, he attracted lesser creatures to him, weaker creatures. Moths. Marguerite was one of them. Elizabeth was conceived on a trip that Marguerite made alone to my family's home in Somerset. It was during the summer and I'd been gone two months, travelling from spot to spot in order to direct regional theatre. Marguerite had wanted to come with me, but frankly, I felt I would be burdened with her, with having to . . . keep her entertained. I thought," he didn't bother to disguise his self-contempt, "that she would be in the way. My wife was no fool, Thomas. She still isn't, for that matter. She could read my reluctance to have her about, so she stopped badgering me to take her. I ought to have realised what that meant, but I was too much caught up in the theatre to understand that Marguerite was making arrangements of her own. I didn't know at the time that she went to Geoffrey. I only knew at the end of the summer that she was pregnant. She would never tell me whose child it was."

That Lady Stinhurst had refused her husband this knowledge made perfect sense to Lynley. But that Stinhurst, in the face of it, had carried on with the marriage made no sense at all. "Why did you not divorce her? Messy as it would have been, surely you would have gleaned some peace of mind."

"Because of Alec," Stinhurst replied. "Our son. As you said yourself, a divorce like that would have been messy. More than messy. At that time it would have produced an attendant scandal that, God knows, would have spread across the front page of every newspaper for months. I couldn't let Alec be tormented like that. I wouldn't. He meant too much to me. More, I suppose, than my marriage itself."

"Last night Joy accused you of killing Alec."

A weary smile touched Stinhurst's lips, comprising equal parts sorrow and resignation. "Alec . . . my son was in the RAF. His plane went down in a test flight over the Orkney Islands in 1978. Into . . ." Stinhurst blinked quickly and made a change in his position. "Into the North Sea."

"Joy knew that?"

"Of course. But she was in love with Alec. They wanted to marry. She was devastated by his death."

"You opposed the marriage?"

"I wasn't delighted by it. But I didn't actively oppose it. I merely suggested that they wait until Alec had done his time in the military."

It was a decidedly odd choice of words. "Done his time?"

"Every man in my family has gone into the military. When that pattern has been in motion for three hundred years, one doesn't want one's son to be the first Rintoul to break it." For the first time Stinhurst's voice was clouded by a wisp of emotion. "But Alec didn't want to do it, Thomas. He wanted to study history, to marry Joy, to write, and perhaps teach at university. And I—blind fool of a patriot with more love for my family tree than for my own son—I gave him no peace until I'd persuaded him to do his duty. He chose the Royal Air Force. I think he believed it would take him farthest from conflict." Stinhurst looked up quickly and commented as if in defence of his son, "It wasn't danger he was afraid of. He merely couldn't stomach war. Not an unnatural reaction from a decent historian."

"Did Alec know about the affair his mother and uncle had?"

Stinhurst lowered his head again. The conversation appeared to be ageing him, diminishing the very last of his resources. It was a remarkable change in such an otherwise youthful man. "I thought not. I hoped not. But now I know, according to what Joy said last night, he did."

So the wasted years, the entire charade—performed to protect Alec—had been for nothing. Stinhurst's next words echoed Lynley's thought.

"I've always been so blasted civilised. I wasn't about to become Chillingsworth to Marguerite's Hester Prynne. So we lived the charade of Elizabeth's being my daughter until New Year's Eve of 1962."

"What happened?"

"I discovered the truth. It was a chance remark, a slip of the tongue that effectively put my brother Geoffrey in Somerset instead of London where he was supposed to be that particular summer. Then I knew. But I suppose I had always suspected as much."

Stinhurst stood abruptly. He walked to the fireplace, threw several lumps of coal onto the blaze, and watched the flames take them. Lynley waited, wondering if the activity was part of the man's need to quell emotion or to conceal his past.

"There was . . . I'm afraid we had a terrible fight. Not an argument. A physical fight. It was here at Westerbrae. Phillip Gerrard, my sister's husband, put an end to it. But Geoffrey got the worst of it. He left shortly after midnight."

"Was he fit to leave?"

"I suppose he thought he was. God knows, I didn't try to stop him. Marguerite tried, but he wouldn't have her near him. He tore out of here in a passionate frenzy, and less than five minutes later he was killed on the switchback just below Hillview Farm. He hit ice, missed the turn. The car flipped over. He broke his neck. He was . . . burned."

They were silent. A piece of coal tumbled to the hearth and singed the edge of the carpet. The air became scented with the acrid odour of burnt wool. Stinhurst swept the ember back to the grate and finished his story.

"Joy Sinclair was here at Westerbrae that night. She'd come up for the holidays. She was one of Elizabeth's school friends. She must have heard bits and pieces of the argument and put them all together. God knows, she always had a passion for setting the record straight. And what better way to get her vengeance upon me for inadvertently causing Alec's death?"

"But that was ten years ago. Why would she wait so long for her revenge?"

"Who was Joy Sinclair ten years ago? How could she have taken revenge then—a twenty-five-year-old woman merely at the start of her career? Who would have listened to her? She was no one. But now—an award-winning author with a reputation for accuracy— now she could command an audience that would listen. And how cleverly she did it after all, writing one play in London but bringing a different play here to Westerbrae. With no one the wiser until we actually began the reading last night. With a journalist present to pick out the most lubricious of the facts. Of course, it didn't get quite as far as Joy had hoped it would. Francesca's reaction put an end to the reading long before the worst of the details in our sordid little family saga came to light. And now an end has been put to the play as well."

Lynley marvelled at the man's words, at the bald indication of culpability they contained. Surely Stinhurst understood to what degree they blackened him?

"You must see how bad it looks that you burned those scripts," Lynley said.

Stinhurst's gaze dropped to the fire momentarily. A shadow moved against his brow, etched darkness on his cheek. "It can't be helped, Thomas. I had to protect Marguerite and Elizabeth. God knows, I owe them that much. Especially Elizabeth. They're my family." His eyes met Lynley's, flat and opaque with a full genera-tion of pain. "I should think that you, of all people, would under-stand how much a man's family means to him."

And the hell of it was that he did understand. Completely.

For the first time Lynley noticed the Briar Rose paper on the walls of the sitting room. It was, he realised, the very same paper that hung in his mother's day room at Howenstow, the very same paper that no doubt hung on the walls of day rooms and morning rooms and sitting rooms of countless great houses throughout the country. Late Victorian, it had a distracting pattern of dull yellow roses battling with leaves that, with age and smoke, had become more grey than green.

Without preliminary observation, Lynley could have closed his eyes and described the rest of the room, so similar was it to his mother's in Cornwall: a fireplace of iron and marble and oak, two pieces of porcelain on each end of the mantel, a walnut longcase clock in one corner, one small case of favourite books. And always the photographs, on a satinwood table within the window's embrasure.

Even here, he could see the similarities. How generic their pictorial family histories really were.

So he understood. Good God, how he understood. The concerns of family, the duty and devotion to having been born with a particular blend of blood in his veins, had been effectively haunting Lynley for most of his thirty-four years. The ties of blood constrained him; they thwarted his desires; they bound him to tradition and demanded his adherence to a life that was claustrophobic. Yet there was no escape. For even if one gave up titles and land, one did not give up roots. One did not give up blood.

THE WESTERBRAE dining room offered the kind of lighting guaranteed to take ten years off anyone's age. Brass sconces on the panelled walls managed this, aided by candelabra spaced evenly along the gleaming surface of the lengthy mahogany table. Barbara Havers stood at one end of this, Inspector Macaskin's floor plan of the house spread out in front of her. She was comparing it to her notes, her eyes screwed up against the smoke from a cigarette which she held between her lips, its ash amazingly long, as if she were attempting a world-record length. Nearby, whistling "Memories" with the sort of passionate conviction that would have done Betty Buckley proud, one of Macaskin's crime-scene men was dusting for prints on an ornamental circle of Scottish dirks that hung on the wall above the sideboard. They were part of a larger display of halberds and muskets and Lochaber axes, all equally eager to be lethal.

Squinting down at the floor plan, Barbara tried to reconcile what Gowan Kilbride had told her with what she wanted to believe about the facts in the case. It wasn't easy going. It strained credibility. She was relieved when the sound of footsteps in the hall gave her an excuse to devote her attention to something else. She looked up, dislodging the tobacco soot down the front of her crewneck sweater. Irritably, she brushed at it, leaving a smudge of grey like a thumb print on the wool.

Lynley came in. Avoiding the print man, he nodded towards a far door. Barbara picked up her notebook and followed him through the warming room, the china room, and into the kitchen. It was fragrant with the odours of meat seasoned with rosemary, with tomatoes simmering in some kind of sauce on the stove. At a centralised worktable, a harried woman bent over a cutting board, chopping potatoes into mince-like pieces with a particularly deadly looking knife. She was costumed entirely in white from head to toe, an effect that gave her more the look of a scientist than of a cook.

"Folks do hae t' eat their dinner," she explained tersely when she saw Barbara and Lynley, although the way she wielded the implement looked more like self-defence than preparing a meal.

Barbara heard Lynley murmur an appropriate culinary response before he walked on, leading her through another door at the far corner of the kitchen and down three steps into the scullery. This room was cramped and poorly lit, but it had the combined virtues of privacy and heat, the latter emanating from an enormous old boiler that wheezed noisily in one corner of the room and dripped rusty water onto the cracked tile floor. The atmosphere was not unlike a steam bath, overhung with an almost imperceptible miasma of mildew and wet wood. Just behind the boiler, the back stairs led to the upper floor of the house.

"What did Gowan and Mary Agnes have to say?" Lynley asked when he had shut the door behind them.

Barbara went to the sink, extinguished her cigarette under the tap, and tossed it into the rubbish. She shoved her short brown hair behind her ears and stopped to pick a piece of tobacco off her tongue before giving her attention to her notebook. She was displeased with Lynley and troubled by the fact that she couldn't quite decide why. Whether it was for dismissing her from the sitting room earlier, or for the way she anticipated he would react to her notes, she didn't know. But whatever the source of her aggravation, she felt it like a splinter. Until it worked its way out into the open, the skin that housed it would fester.

"Gowan," she said briefly, leaning against the warped wooden counter. It was wet from a recent washing, and she felt a ridge of damp seep through her clothes. She moved away. "It seems he had a rather nasty clash with Robert Gabriel in the library just before he and I met. That may well have gone far in lubricating his tongue."

"What sort of clash?"

"A quick brawl in which our silken Mr. Gabriel apparently got himself hammered. Gowan made sure I knew about that, as well as about the row he overheard between Gabriel and Joy Sinclair yesterday afternoon. They'd had an affair, it seems, and Gabriel was hot to have Joy tell his former wife—Irene Sinclair, as a matter of fact, Joy's sister—that he only bedded Joy once."

"Why?"

"I've the impression Robert Gabriel very much wants Irene Sinclair back and that he thought Joy could help him in his reconciliation if she'd only tell Irene that their fling was strictly a one-time encounter. But Joy refused to do so. She said she wouldn't deal in lies."

"Lies?"

"Yes. Evidently theirs wasn't a one-time encounter at all because, according to Gowan, when Joy refused to cooperate, Gabriel said something to her like," Barbara consulted her notes, " 'You little hypocrite. For one entire year you screw me in every bug-infested rat hole in London and now you stand there and tell me you don't deal in lies!' And they continued to argue until Gabriel finally went after her. He had her down on the floor, in fact, when Rhys Davies-Jones managed to get in and separate them. Gowan was bringing someone's luggage up the stairs when all this was going on. He got quite an eyeful of everything because Davies-Jones left the door open when he burst into Joy's room."

"What set Gowan and Gabriel off in the library?"

"A remark someone made—Sydeham, I think—about Mary Agnes Campbell, alluding to her being Gabriel's alibi for last night."

"How much truth is there to that?"

Barbara considered the question for a moment before answering. "It's hard to tell. Mary Agnes seems rather smitten with the theatre. She's attractive, has a nice body. . . ." Barbara shook her head. "Inspector, that man must be a good twenty-five years her senior. I can see why he might want to dandle her, but I can't see for a moment why she'd go along with the idea. Unless, of course . . ." She thought about the possibilities, intrigued to find that there was one that actually worked.

"Havers?"

"Hmm? Well, Robert Gabriel might have looked like her ticket to a new life. You know the sort of thing. The star-struck girl meets the established actor, sees the kind of life he can offer her, and gives herself to him in the hope he'll take her with him when he leaves."

"Did you ask her about it?"

"I wasn't able to. I didn't hear about the row between Gowan and Gabriel until after I'd spoken to Mary Agnes. I've not got back to her yet." And that was because of what Gowan had said, because of what she knew Lynley would make of the boy's information.

He seemed to read her mind. "What was Gowan able to tell you about last night?"

"He saw a lot after the read-through broke up because he had to clean up a mess of liqueurs that he'd dropped in the great hall when Francesca Gerrard banged into him as she left the sitting room. It took him nearly an hour. Even with Helen's help, by the way."

Lynley ignored the final reference, saying only, "And?"

Barbara knew what Lynley wanted, but she delayed a bit by focussing on the minor players in the drama, whose comings and goings Gowan had remembered in astonishing detail. Lady Stinhurst, clad in black, wandering aimlessly between drawing room, dining room, sitting room, and great hall until after midnight when her husband came from above stairs to fetch her; Jeremy Vinney finding excuses to follow Lady Stinhurst, murmuring questions which she steadfastly ignored; Joanna Ellacourt, storming down an upstairs corridor in a violent fit of temper after a loud argument with her husband; Irene Sinclair and Robert Gabriel closeting themselves in the library. The house had eventually fallen into relative calm at about half past twelve.

Barbara heard Lynley say with his usual perspicacity, "But that's not all Gowan saw, I imagine."

Her teeth pulled at the inside of her lower lip. "No, that's not all. Later, after he'd gone to bed, he heard footsteps in the corridor outside his door. He's right on the corner, where the lower northwest wing meets the great hall. He's not certain of the time except that it was well after half past twelve. Close to one, he thinks. He was curious because of all the excitement in the evening. So he got out of bed, cracked his door, and listened."

"And?"

"More footsteps. And then a door opened and closed." Barbara wasn't particularly eager to relate the rest of Gowan's tale, and she knew her face reflected that reluctance. Nonetheless, she plodded forward and completed the story, relating how Gowan had left his room, gone to the end of the corridor, and peered out into the great hall. It was dark—he'd shut off the lights himself just minutes before—but the exterior estate lights managed to provide a faint illumination.

Barbara saw from the swift change of Lynley's expression that he read what was coming. "He saw Davies-Jones," he said.

"Yes. But he was coming out of the library, not the dining room where the dirks are, Inspector. He had a bottle. It must have been the cognac he took up to Helen." She waited for Lynley to offer the inevitable, the conclusion she had already worked out for herself. A trip to pick up a dirk in the dining room was every bit as convenient as one to pick up cognac thirty feet away in the library. And always there remained the fact that Joy Sinclair's hall door had been locked.

However, Lynley merely said, "What else?"

"Nothing. Davies-Jones went upstairs."

Lynley nodded grimly. "Let's do so ourselves."

He led Barbara towards the back stairway. Narrow, uncarpeted, lit only by two unshaded bulbs, and entirely devoid of decoration, it would take them to the west wing of the house.

"What about Mary Agnes?" Lynley asked as they climbed.

"She didn't hear a sound during the night according to the statement I had from her prior to this new Gabriel-twist. Just the wind, she said. But of course, she may well have heard *that* from Gabriel's room, not her own. However, there was one curious item, and I think you need to hear it." She waited until Lynley paused and turned on the stair above her. Near his left hand, a largish stain marred the wall, much the shape of Australia. It looked like a patch of damp. "Immediately after she found the body this morning, Mary Agnes went for Francesca Gerrard. They fetched Lord Stinhurst together. He went into Joy's room, came out a moment later, and ordered Mary Agnes to go back to her own room and wait for Mrs. Gerrard to come for her."

"I'm not certain I see your point, Sergeant."

"My point is that Francesca Gerrard didn't come back to fetch Mary Agnes from her room for the next twenty minutes. And only *then* did Lord Stinhurst tell Mary Agnes to begin waking the household and telling them to come to the drawing room. In the meantime, he placed some phone calls from Francesca's office—it's next to Mary Agnes' bedroom, so she could hear his voice. And, Inspector, he *received* two calls as well."

When Lynley didn't react to this piece of information, Barbara felt her earlier irritation begin to bite. "Sir, you've not forgotten Lord Stinhurst, have you? You know who he is: the man who ought to be on his way to the police station right now for destruction of evidence, interfering with the police, and murder."

"That's a bit premature," Lynley remarked.

His calm rubbed the sore of Barbara's irritation.

"Is it?" she demanded. "And at what point did you make *that* fine decision?"

"I've heard nothing so far to convince me that Lord Stinhurst murdered Joy Sinclair." Lynley's voice was a model of patience. "But even if I thought that he might have done so, I'm not about to arrest a man on the strength of his having burned a stack of scripts."

"*What?*" Barbara's own voice rasped. "You've made your decision about Stinhurst already, haven't you? Based on one conversation with a man who spent the first ten years of his career on the bloody stage and no doubt turned in his finest performance right here tonight, explaining himself away to you! That's rich, Inspector. Police work you can be proud of!"

"Havers," Lynley said quietly, "step back in line."

He was pulling rank. Barbara heard the warning. She knew she ought to back down, but she wasn't about to at a moment when she was so completely in the right. "What did he tell you that has you so convinced of his innocence, Inspector? That he and Daddy were school chums at Eton? That he'd like to see more of you round the London club? Or better yet, that his destroying evidence had nothing at all to do with the murder and you can trust him to tell you the truth about it since he's a real gent, just like you!"

"There's more involved than that," Lynley said, "and I'm not about to discuss it—"

"With the likes of me! Oh, rot!" she finished.

"Get that blasted chip off your shoulder and you might find yourself a person that other people want to confide in," Lynley snapped. But he spun from Barbara quickly and didn't move on.

She could tell that he regretted his loss of control at once. She had pushed him to it, wanting his anger to bubble and boil over just as her own had done earlier when he had locked her out of the sitting room. But she saw quite clearly how little ground she would gain in his estimation with this sort of manipulative behaviour. She berated herself for her temperamental stupidity. After a moment, she spoke.

"Sorry," she said wretchedly. "I was off, Inspector. Out of line. Again."

Lynley didn't immediately respond. They stood on the stairs, caught by a tension that seemed painfully immutable, each involved in a separate misery. Lynley appeared to rouse himself only with an effort.

"We make an arrest on the strength of evidence, Barbara."

She nodded calmly, her brief passion spent. "I know that, sir. But I think . . ." He wouldn't want to hear it. He would hate her. She plunged on. "I think you're ignoring the obvious so that you can head directly towards Davies-Jones, not on the strength of evidence at all, but on the strength of something else that . . . perhaps you're afraid to admit."

"That isn't the case," Lynley replied. He continued up the stairs.

At the top, Barbara identified each room for him as they passed it: Gabriel's the closest to the rear stairway, then Vinney's, Elizabeth Rintoul's, and Irene Sinclair's. Across the hall from this last was Rhys Davies-Jones' room, where the west corridor turned right, widened, and led into the main body of the house. All the doors here were locked, and as they walked along the hallway where portraits displayed several generations of sombre-faced Gerrard ancestors and delicately worked sconces intermittently cast half-circles of light on the pale walls, St. James met them, handing Lynley a plastic bag.

"Helen and I found this stuffed into one of the boots downstairs," he said. "According to David Sydeham, it's his."

6

DAVID SYDEHAM did not look like the kind of man to whom a woman of Joanna Ellacourt's fame and reputation would have stayed married for nearly two decades. Lynley knew the fairy-tale version of their relationship, the sort of romantic drivel that tabloids feed up for their customers to read on the underground during rush-hour commutes. It was fairly standard stuff, how a twenty-nine-year-old midland booking agent—the son of a country cleric—with little more than good looks and unshakeable self-confidence to recommend him, had discovered a nineteen-year-old Nottingham girl doing a tousle-haired Celia in a back-alley theatre; how he persuaded her to throw her lot in with his, rescuing her from the grim working-class environment into which she had been born; how he provided her with drama coaches and voice lessons; how he nurtured her career every step of the way until she emerged, as he had long known she would, the most sought-after actress in the country.

Twenty years later, Sydeham was still handsome enough in a sensual way, but it was a handsomeness gone to seed, a sensuality given sway too often with unfortunate consequences. His skin showed the inchoate signs of dissipation. There was rather too much flesh under his chin and a decided puffiness to his hands and face. Like the other men at Westerbrae, Sydeham had not been given the opportunity to shave that morning, and he looked even the worse for wear because of this. A substantial growth of beard shadowed his face, accenting the deep circles under his heavily lidded eyes. Still, he dressed with a remarkable instinct for making the best of what he had. Although his was the body of a bull, he encased it in jacket, shirt, and trousers that were obviously cut specifically to fit him. They had the look of money, as did his wristwatch and signet ring which flashed gold in the firelight as he took a seat in the sitting room. Not a hard-backed chair, Lynley noted, but a comfortable armchair in the semi-darkness of the room's periphery.

"I'm not entirely certain that I understand your function here this weekend," Lynley said as Sergeant Havers closed the door and took her seat at the table.

"Or my function at all?" Sydeham's face was bland.

It was an interesting point. "If you wish."

"I manage my wife's career. I see to her contracts, book her engagements, run interference for her when the pressure mounts. I read her scripts, coach her with her lines, manage her money." Sydeham appeared to perceive a change in Lynley's expression. "Yes," he repeated, "I manage her money. All of it. And there's quite a bit. She makes it, I invest it. So I'm a kept man, Inspector." Upon this last remark, he smiled without the slightest trace of humour. His skin seemed thin enough when it came to the superficial inequities in his relationship with his wife.

"How well did you know Joy Sinclair?" Lynley asked.

"Do you mean did I kill her? I'd only met the woman at half past seven. And while Joanna wasn't altogether happy with the manner in which Joy had taken to revising her play, I generally negotiate improvements with playwrights. I don't kill them if I don't like what they've written."

"Why wasn't your wife happy with the script?"

"All along, Joanna had been suspicious that Joy was attempting to create a vehicle to bring her sister back to the stage. At Joanna's expense. Joanna's would be the name that would bring in the audience and the critics, but Irene Sinclair's performance would be spotlighted for them to see. At least, that was Jo's fear. And when she saw the revised script, she jumped to conclusions and felt the worst had actually come true." Sydeham slowly lifted both arms and shoulders. It was a curious, Gallic shrug. "I . . . we had quite a row about it after the read-through, in fact."

"What sort of row?"

"The sort of row married couples always have. A look-at-what-you-got-me-into row. Joanna was determined not to go on with the play."

"And that's been taken care of rather nicely for her, hasn't it?" Lynley remarked.

Sydeham's nostrils flared. "My wife didn't kill Joy Sinclair, Inspector. Nor, for that matter, did I. Killing Joy would hardly have put an end to our real problem." He moved his head abruptly from Lynley and Havers, focussing on the table that stood under the sitting-room window and on the silver-framed photographs arrayed on it.

Lynley saw the other man's remark for the fishing line it was and decided to take the bait. "Your real problem?"

Sydeham's head swivelled back to them. "Robert Gabriel," he said broodingly. "Robert bleeding Gabriel."

Lynley had learned years before that silence was as useful a tool of interrogation as any question he might ask. The attendant tension it nearly always caused was a form of appanage, one of the few benefits to carrying a warrant card from the police. So he said nothing, letting Sydeham simmer himself into further disclosure. Which he did, almost immediately.

"Gabriel's been after Joanna for years. He fancies himself some kind of cross between Casanova and Lothario, only it never worked with Jo, in spite of all his efforts. She can't stand the bloke. Never has."

Lynley was amazed to hear this revelation, considering the reputation Ellacourt and Gabriel had for sizzling across the stage. Evidently, Sydeham recognised this reaction, for he smiled as if in acknowledgement and went on.

"My wife is one hell of an actress, Inspector. She always was. But the truth of the matter is that Gabriel put his hands up her skirt one time too many during *Othello* last season, and she was through with him. Unfortunately, she didn't tell me how determined she was never to perform with him again until it was too late. I'd already negotiated the deal with Stinhurst for this new production. And I saw to it personally that Gabriel had a part in it as well."

"Why?"

"Simple business. Gabriel and Ellacourt have chemistry. People pay to see chemistry. And I thought Joanna could take care of herself well enough if she had to appear with Gabriel again. She did it in *Othello*, bit him like a shark when he went for tongue during a stage kiss, and laughed like hell about it afterwards. So I didn't think that one more play with Gabriel would set her off the way it did. Then like a fool, when I found out how absolutely dead set against him she was, I lied to her, told her that Stinhurst had insisted that Gabriel be in the new production. But unfortunately, last night, Gabriel let it out of the bag that I was the one who had wanted him in the play. And that was part of what set Joanna off."

"And now that it's certain there's to be no play?"

Sydeham spoke with ill-concealed impatience. "Joy's death does nothing to change the fact that Joanna's still under contract to do a play for Stinhurst. So is Gabriel. And Irene Sinclair, for that matter. So Jo's working with both of them whether she likes it or not. My guess is that Stinhurst will take them back to London and start putting together another production as soon as he can. So if I wanted to help Joanna—or at least put an end to the anger between us—I'd be orchestrating a quick end to either Stinhurst or Gabriel. Joy's death put a stop to Joy's play. Believe me, it didn't really do a thing to benefit Joanna."

"To benefit yourself, perhaps?"

Sydeham gave Lynley a long look of evaluation. "I don't see how anything that hurts Jo might benefit me, Inspector."

There was certainly truth to that, Lynley admitted to himself. "When did you last have your gloves with you?"

Sydeham appeared to want to continue their previous discussion. Nonetheless, he answered cooperatively enough. "Yesterday afternoon when we arrived, I think. Francesca asked me to sign the register, and I would have taken my gloves off to do so. Frankly, I don't know what I did with them after that. I don't remember putting them back on, but I might have shoved them in the pocket of my coat."

"That was the last time you saw them? You didn't miss them?"

"I didn't need them. Joanna and I didn't go out again, and I'd no need to put them on in the house. I didn't even know they were missing until your man brought the one into the library a few minutes ago. The other may be in my coat pocket or even on the reception desk if I left them there. I simply don't remember."

"Sergeant?" Lynley nodded towards Havers who got up, left the room, and returned in a moment with the second glove.

"It was on the floor between the wall and the reception desk," she said and laid it on the table.

All of them gave a moment over to examining the glove. The leather was rich, comfortably worn, and initialled on the inner wrist with the letters *DS* in intricate scrollwork. The faint scent of saddle soap spoke of a recent cleaning, but no remnants of that preservative clung to seams or to lining.

"Who was in the reception area when you arrived?" Lynley asked.

Sydeham's face wore the meditative expression of looking back upon an activity that one thinks at the time is unimportant in order, in retrospect, to place persons and events in their correct positions. "Francesca Gerrard," he said slowly. "Jeremy Vinney came briefly to the door of the drawing room and said hello." He paused. He was using his hands as he talked, illustrating each person's position in the air in front of him in a process of visualisation. "The boy. Gowan was there. Perhaps not immediately, but he'd have had to be eventually since he came for our luggage and showed us up to our room. And . . . I'm not entirely certain, but I think I may have seen Elizabeth Rintoul, Stinhurst's daughter, darting into one of the rooms along that corridor off the entrance hall. Someone was down there, at any rate."

Lynley and Havers exchanged speculative glances. Lynley directed Sydeham's attention towards the plan of the house which Havers had brought with her into the sitting room. It was spread out on the central table, next to Sydeham's glove. "Which room?"

Sydeham pushed out of his chair, came to the table, and ran his eyes over the plan. He scrutinised it conscientiously before he replied. "It's hard to say. I only caught a glimpse, as if she were trying to avoid us. I just assumed it was Elizabeth because she's peculiar that way. But I should guess this last room." He pointed to the office.

Lynley considered the implications. The master keys were kept in the office. They were locked in the desk, Macaskin had said. But then he had gone on to say that Gowan Kilbride may have had access to them. If that were the case, the locking of the desk may well have been a casual matter at best, sometimes done and sometimes ignored. And on the day of the arrival of so large a party, surely the desk would have been unlocked, the keys easily accessible to anyone involved in preparing the rooms. Or to anyone at all who knew about the existence of the office: Elizabeth Rintoul, her mother, her father, even Joy Sinclair herself.

"When was the last time you saw Joy?" Lynley asked.

Sydeham shifted restlessly on his feet. He looked as if he wanted to go back to his chair. Lynley decided he wanted him standing.

"A while after the read-through. Perhaps half past eleven. Perhaps later. I wasn't paying much attention to the time."

"Where?"

"In the upstairs corridor. She was heading towards her room." Sydeham looked momentarily uncomfortable but continued. "As I said before, I'd had a row with Joanna over the play. She'd stormed out of the read-through, and I found her in the gallery. We had some fairly nasty words. I don't much care for rowing with my wife. I was feeling low afterwards, so I was going to the library to fetch myself a bottle of whisky. That's when I saw Joy."

"Did you speak to her at all?"

"She didn't look very much like she wanted to speak to anyone. I just brought the whisky back to my room, had a few drinks, well . . . maybe four or five. Then I simply slept it off."

"Where was your wife all this time?"

Sydeham's eyes drifted to the fireplace. His hands automatically sought the pockets of his grey tweed jacket, perhaps in a fruitless search for cigarettes to still his nerves. Obviously, this was the question he had hoped to avoid answering.

"I don't know. She'd left the gallery. I don't know where she went."

"You don't know," Lynley repeated carefully.

"That's right. Look, I learned a good number of years ago to leave Joanna to herself when she's in a temper, and she was in a fair one last night. So that's what I did. I had the drinks. I fell asleep, passed out, call it whatever you want to. I don't know where she was. All I can say is that when I woke up this morning—when the girl knocked on the door and babbled at us to get dressed and meet in the drawing room—Joanna was in bed beside me." Sydeham noticed that Havers was writing steadily. "Joanna was upset," he asserted. "But it was at me. No one else. Things have been . . . a bit off between us for a while. She wanted to be away from me. She was angry."

"But she did return to your room last night?"

"Of course she did."

"What time? In an hour? In two? In three?"

"I don't know."

"But surely her movement in the room would have awakened you."

Sydeham's voice grew impatient. "Have you ever slept off a binge, Inspector? Pardon the expression, but it would have been like waking the dead."

Lynley persisted. "You heard nothing? No wind? No voices? Nothing at all?"

"I told you that."

"Nothing from Joy Sinclair's room? She was on the other side of yours. It's hard to believe that a woman could meet her death without making a sound. Or that your own wife could be in and out of the room without your awareness. What other things might have gone on without your knowledge?"

Sydeham looked sharply from Lynley to Havers. "If you're pinning this on Jo, why not on me as well? I was alone for part of the night, wasn't I? But that's a problem for you, isn't it? Because, saving Stinhurst, so was everyone else."

Lynley ignored the anger that rode just beneath Sydeham's words. "Tell me about the library."

There was no alteration in expression at this sudden, new direction in the questioning. "What about it?"

"Was anyone there when you went for the whisky?"

"Just Gabriel."

"What was he doing?"

"The same as I was about to. Drinking. Gin by the smell of it. And no doubt hoping for something in a skirt to wander by. Anything in a skirt."

Lynley picked up on Sydeham's black tone. "You don't much like Robert Gabriel. Is it merely because of the advances he's made towards your wife, or are there other reasons?"

"No one here much likes Gabriel, Inspector. No one anywhere much likes him. He gets by on sufferance because he's such a bloody good actor. But frankly, it's a mystery to me why he wasn't murdered instead of Joy Sinclair. He was certainly asking for it from any number of quarters."

It was an interesting observation, Lynley thought. But more interesting was the fact that Sydeham had not answered the question.

APPARENTLY, Inspector Macaskin and the Westerbrae cook had decided to carry a burgeoning conflict to the sitting room, and they arrived at the door simultaneously, bearing two disparate messages. Macaskin insisted upon being the first heard, with the white-garbed cook lurking in the background, wringing her hands together as if every wasted moment brought a soufflé closer to perdition in her oven.

Macaskin gave David Sydeham a head-to-toe scrutiny as the man moved past him into the hall. "We've done all that's to be done," he said to Lynley. "Fingerprinted the whole lot. Clyde and Sinclair rooms are sealed off, crime-scene men are done. Drains appear clean, by the way. No blood anywhere."

"A clean kill save for the glove."

"My man will test that." Macaskin jerked his head towards the library and went on curtly. "Shall I let them out? Cook says she's got dinner and they've asked for a bit of a wash."

The request, Lynley saw, was out of character for Macaskin. Giving the reins of an investigation over to another officer was not an accustomed routine for the Scot, and even as he spoke, the tips of his ears grew red against his fine, grey hair.

As if she recognised a concealed message within Macaskin's words, the cook belligerently continued, "Ye canna keep them from fude. 'Tisna richt." Clearly, it was her expectation that the police *modus operandi* was to put the entire group on bread and water until the killer was found. "I do hae a bit prepared. They've ha nowt but one wee san'wich a' day, Inspector. Unlike the police," she nodded meaningfully, "who hae been feeding themsel' since this mornin' from what I can tell by lookin' a' my kitchen."

Lynley flipped open his pocket watch, surprised to see that it was half past eight. He couldn't have been less hungry himself, but since the crime-scene men were finished, there was no further purpose to keeping the group from adequate food and from the relatively restricted, supervised freedom of the house. He nodded his approval.

"Then we'll be off," Macaskin said. "I'll leave Constable Lonan with you and get back myself in the morning. I've a man ready to take Stinhurst to the station."

"Leave him here."

Macaskin opened his mouth, closed it, opened it again, throwing protocol to the wind long enough to say, "As to those scripts, Inspector."

"I'll see to it," Lynley said firmly. "Burning evidence isn't murder. He can be dealt with when the time arrives." He saw Sergeant Havers move in a recoiling motion, as if she wished to distance herself from what she saw as a poor decision.

For his part, Macaskin seemed to consider arguing the point and decided to let it go. His official good-night comprised the brusque words: "We've put your things in the northwest wing. You're in with St. James. Next to Helen Clyde's new room."

Neither the political manoeuvring nor the sleeping arrangements of the police were of interest to the cook, who had remained in the doorway, eager to resolve the culinary dispute that had brought her to the sitting room in the first place. "Twenty minutes, Inspector." She turned on her heel. "Bey on time."

It was a fine point of conclusion. And that is how Macaskin used it.

RELEASED at last from their day's confinement in the library, most of the group were still in the entrance hall when Lynley asked Joanna Ellacourt to step into the sitting room. His request, made so soon after his interview with her husband, reduced the small cluster of people to breath-holding suspense, as if they were waiting to see how the actress would respond. It was, after all, couched as a request. But none of them were foolish enough to believe that it was an invitation that might be politely rebuffed should Joanna choose to do so.

It looked as if she was considering that as a possibility, however, walking a quick line between outright refusal and hostile coopera-tion. The latter seemed ascendant, and as she approached the sitting-room door, Joanna gave vent to the umbrage she felt after a day of incarceration by favouring neither Lynley nor Havers with so much as a word before she passed in front of them and took a seat of her own choosing, the ladder-back chair by the fire that Sydeham had avoided and Stinhurst had only reluctantly occupied. Her choice of it was intriguing, revealing either a determination to see the interview through in the most forthright manner possible or a desire to choose a location where the benefits of firelight playing upon her skin and hair might distract an idle watcher at a crucial moment. Joanna Ellacourt knew how to play to an audience.

Looking at her, Lynley found it hard to believe that she was nearly forty years old. She looked ten years younger, possibly more, and in the forgiving light of the fire that warmed her skin to a translucent gold, Lynley found himself recalling his first sight of François Boucher's *Diana Resting*, for the splendid glow of Joanna's skin was the same, as were the delicate shades of colour across her cheeks and the fragile curve of her ear when she shook her hair back. She was absolutely beautiful, and had her eyes been brown instead of cornflower blue, she might herself have posed for Bou-cher's painting.

No wonder Gabriel's been after her, Lynley thought. He offered her a cigarette which she accepted. Her hand closed over his to steady the lighter's flame with fingers that were long, very cool, flashing several diamond rings. It was a stagey sort of movement, intentionally seductive.

"Why did you argue with your husband last night?" he asked.

Joanna raised a well-shaped eyebrow and spent a moment taking in Sergeant Havers from head to toe, as if in an evaluation of the policewoman's grubby skirt and soot-stained sweater. "Because I'd grown tired of being on the receiving end of Robert Gabriel's lust for the last six months," she replied frankly, and paused as if in the expectation of a response—a nod of sympathy, perhaps, or a cluck of disapproval. When it became evident that none was forthcoming, she was forced to continue her story. Which she did, her voice a bit tight. "He had a nice hard-on every night in my last scene in *Othello*, Inspector. Just about the time he was supposed to smother me, he'd begin squirming about on the bed like a pubescent twelve-year-old who's just discovered how much fun he can have with that sweet little sausage between his legs. I'd had it with him. I thought David understood as much. But apparently he didn't. So he arranged a new contract, forcing me to work with Gabriel again."

"You argued about the new play."

"We argued about everything. The new play was just part of it."

"And you objected to Irene Sinclair's role as well."

Joanna flicked cigarette ash onto the hearth. "As far as I was concerned, my husband couldn't have manipulated this affair with more resounding idiocy. He put me in the position of having to fight off Robert Gabriel for the next twelve months at the same time as trying to keep Gabriel's ex-wife from climbing up my back on the way to her new, superlunary career. I won't lie to you, Inspector. I'm not at all sorry that this play of Joy's is finished. You may say that's an open admission of guilt if you like, but I'm not about to sit here and play the mourner over the death of a woman I scarcely knew. I suppose that gives me a motive to kill her, as well. But I can't help that."

"Your husband says that you were out of your room for part of last night."

"So I had the opportunity to do Joy in? Yes, I suppose it looks that way."

"Where did you go after your row in the gallery?"

"To our room, at first."

"What time was this?"

"Shortly after eleven, I imagine. But I didn't stay there. I knew David would be coming back, sorry about it all and eager to make it up in his usual fashion. And I wanted none of it. Or of him. So I went to the music room next to the gallery. There's an ancient gramophone there and some even more ancient records. I played show tunes. Francesca Gerrard appears to be quite an Ethel Merman fan, by the way."

"Would someone have heard you?"

"As corroboration, you mean?" She shook her head, apparently unconcerned by the fact that her alibi thus had absolutely no grounds for credibility. "The music room's off by itself in the northeast corridor. I doubt anyone would have heard. Unless Elizabeth was doing her usual routine, snooping at doors. She seems to excel at it."

Lynley let that one go by. "Who was in the reception area when you arrived yesterday?"

Joanna fingered a few strands of her firelit hair. "Aside from Francesca, I don't recall anyone in particular." Her brow furrowed thoughtfully. "Except Jeremy Vinney. He came to the drawing room door and said a few words. I do remember that."

"Curious that Vinney's presence sticks in your mind."

"Not at all. Years ago he had a small part in a production I did in Norwich. And I remember thinking when I saw him yesterday that he has about as much stage presence now as he did then. Which is to say he has none. He's always looked like someone who's just dropped fifteen lines and can't think how to ad-lib his way out of the mess. He couldn't even manage to rhubarb successfully. Poor man. The stage was not his gift, I'm afraid. But then he's awfully dumpy to play any significant role."

"What time did you return to your room last night?"

"I'm really not certain, as I didn't check the time. It's not the sort of thing one does as a matter of course. I just played records until I was sufficiently cooled off." She gazed at the fire. Her unruffled composure altered a degree as she ran a hand along the fine crease in her trousers. "No, that's not quite true, is it? I wanted to make certain David had time to fall asleep. Face-saving, I suppose, although when I think about it now, why I wanted to give him a chance to save face is beyond me."

"To save face?" Lynley queried.

Joanna smiled quickly, without apparent cause. It appeared to be a distraction, a way of automatically concentrating an audience's attention on her beauty rather than the quality of her performance. "David is in the wrong about this entire contract situation with Robert Gabriel, Inspector. And had I come back sooner, he would have wanted to put the anger between us at rest. But . . ." She looked away again, touching the tip of her tongue to her lips as if in the need to buy time. "I'm sorry. I just don't think I can tell you after all. Silly of me, isn't it? I suppose you might even want to arrest me. But there are some things . . . I know David wouldn't have told you himself. But I couldn't go back to our room until he was asleep. I just couldn't. Please understand."

Lynley knew she was asking for permission to cease talking, but he said nothing, merely waiting for her to continue. When she did so, she kept her face averted, and she drew on her cigarette several times before crushing it out altogether.

"David would have wanted to make it up. But he hasn't been able to . . . for nearly two months now. Oh, he would have tried anyway. He'd have felt he owed me that. And if he failed, everything would have been that much worse between us. So I stayed out of the room until I thought he'd be asleep. Which he was. And I was glad of it."

This was a fascinating piece of information, to be sure. It made the longevity of the Ellacourt-Sydeham marriage even more difficult to understand. As if in recognition of this fact, Joanna Ellacourt spoke again. Her voice became sharp, unclouded by either sentiment or regret.

"David's my history, Inspector. I'm not ashamed to admit that he made me what I am. For twenty years he's been my biggest supporter, my biggest critic, my best friend. One doesn't throw that over simply because life gets a little inconvenient now and again."

Her final statement declared marital loyalty more eloquently than anything Lynley had ever heard. Nonetheless, it was difficult for him to put aside David Sydeham's evaluation of his wife. She was, indeed, one hell of an actress.

FRANCESCA GERRARD'S bedroom was tucked far away into the corner of the upper northeast corridor, where the hallway narrowed and an old disused harp, covered haphazardly, cast a Quasimodo shadow against the wall. No portraits hung here. No tapestries served as buffers against the cold. Here were no overt illustrations of comfort and security. Only monochromatic plaster, showing the tracery of age like fine webbing, and a paper-thin carpet running along the floor.

Casting a hasty look behind her, Elizabeth Rintoul slipped down this hallway and paused at her aunt's door, listening intently. From the upper west corridor, she could hear the rumble of voices. But from inside the room there was nothing. She tapped her fingernails against the wood, a nervous movement that resembled the pecking of small birds. No one called entrance. She knocked again.

"Aunt Francie?" A whisper was all she was willing to risk. Again there was no response.

She knew her aunt was inside, for she'd seen her walk down this corridor not five minutes past when the police had finally unlocked all their rooms. So she tried the doorknob. It turned, feeling slippery under her sweaty hand.

Inside, the air held a smell of musty pomanders, sweetly suffocating face powder, pungent analgesic, and inexpensive cologne. The room's furnishings acted as companion pieces to the bleak paucity of decoration in the corridor outside: a narrow bed, a single wardrobe and chest of drawers, a cheval glass that cast strangely green reflections, distorted so that foreheads were bulbous and chins were too small.

Her aunt had not always used this as her bedroom. It was only after her husband's death that she had moved to this part of the house, as if its inconvenience and inelegance were part of the process of mourning him. She appeared to be engaged in that process now, for she was sitting upright on the very edge of the bed, her attention given to a studio photograph of her husband that was hanging on the wall, the room's sole decoration. It was a solemn picture, not at all the Uncle Phillip that Elizabeth remembered from her childhood, but undeniably the melancholy man he had become. After New Year's Eve. After Uncle Geoffrey.

Elizabeth shut the door quietly behind her, but as the wood scraped against the strike plate, her aunt gave a choked, mewling gasp. She rose swiftly from the bed and spun, both hands raised in front of her like claws, as if in defence.

Elizabeth stiffened. How a gesture, so simple, could bring everything back, a memory suppressed and believed forgotten. A six-year-old girl, wandering happily out to the stable in Somerset; seeing the kitchen maids squatting to look through a fissure in the building's stone wall where the mortar had worn away; hearing them whisper to her *Come and see some nancy boys, luv*; not knowing what it meant but eager—always so pathetically eager—to be friends; bending to the peephole and seeing two stableboys, their clothes strewn carelessly round a stall, one of them on all fours and the other rearing and plunging and snorting behind him and both of their bodies sheened with a sweat that glistened like oil; frightened and recoiling from the sight only to hear the girls' stifled laughter. Laughter at *her*. At her innocence and her blind naïveté. And wanting to strike out at them, to hurt them, to claw at their eyes. With hands just like Aunt Francie's were now.

"Elizabeth!" Francesca dropped her arms. Her body sagged. "You startled me, my dear." ·

Elizabeth watched her aunt warily, afraid to contend with any other memories that might be stirred by another inadvertent gesture. Francesca, she saw, had begun to make herself ready for dinner when her husband's picture had drawn her into the reverie that Elizabeth had interrupted. Now she was peering at her reflection in the mirror as she ran a brush through her thinning grey hair. She smiled at Elizabeth, but her lips quivered to belie whatever air of tranquillity she was straining to project.

"As a girl, you know, I got used to looking in the mirror without seeing my own face. People say it can't be done, but I mastered it. I can do my hair, my make-up, my earrings, anything. And I never have to see how homely I am."

Elizabeth didn't bother to offer a soothing denial. Denial was insult, for her aunt spoke the truth. She *was* homely and had always been so, burdened by a long, horsey face, a preponderance of teeth, and very little chin. Possessing a gangling body, she was all arms, legs, and elbows, the recipient of every genetic curse of the Rintoul family. Elizabeth had often thought that homeliness was the reason her aunt wore so much costume jewellery, as if it might somehow distract one's attention from the gross misfortunes of her face and body.

"You mustn't mind, Elizabeth," Francesca was saying gently. "She means well. She *does* mean well. You mustn't mind so awfully much."

Elizabeth felt her throat close. How well her aunt knew her. How completely she had always understood. " 'Get Mr. Vinney a drink, darling. . . . His glass is almost empty.' " Bitterly, she mimicked her mother's retiring voice. "I wanted to die. Even with the police. Even with Joy. She can't stop. She won't stop. It won't ever end."

"She wants your happiness, my dear. She sees it in marriage."

"Like her own, you mean?" The words tasted like acid.

Her aunt frowned. She put her brush on the chest of drawers, placing her comb neatly across its bristles. "Have I shown you the photographs Gowan gave to me?" she asked brightly, pulling open the top drawer. It squeaked and stuck. "Silly dear boy. He saw a magazine with those before-and-after pictures and decided we'd do a set of the house. Of each room as we renovate it. And then perhaps we'll display them all in the drawing room when everything's done.

Or perhaps an historian might find them of interest. Or we could always use them to . . ." She struggled with the drawer, but the wood was swollen with the winter damp.

Elizabeth watched her wordlessly. It was always the way within the circle of the family: unanswered questions, secrets, and withdrawal. They were all conspirators whose collusion insisted upon ignoring the past so that it would go away. Her father, her mother, Uncle Geoffrey, and Granda. And now Aunt Francie. Her loyalties, too, were to the ties of blood.

There was no point in staying in the room any longer. Only one thing needed to be said between them. Elizabeth steadied herself to say it.

"Aunt Francie. Please."

Francesca looked up. She still held on to the drawer, still pulled at it fruitlessly, without realising that she was only making its inutility even more pronounced.

"I wanted you to know," Elizabeth said. "You need to know. I . . . I'm afraid I didn't manage things properly at all last night."

Francesca at last dropped her grip on the drawer. "In what way, my dear?"

"It's just that . . . she wasn't alone. She wasn't even in her room. So I didn't have a chance to talk to her at all, to give her your message."

"It doesn't matter, darling. You did your best, didn't you? And at any rate, I—"

"No! Please!"

Her aunt's voice—as always—was warm with compassion, with understanding how it felt to be barren of ability or talent or hope. In the face of this unconditional acceptance, Elizabeth felt the dry choking of fruitless tears. She couldn't bear to weep—in either sorrow or pain—so she turned and left the room.

"BLUIDY THING!"

Gowan Kilbride had just about reached his point of no return in his ability to survive nonstop aggravation. The situation in the library had been bad enough, but afterwards it had grown worse with the knowledge, neither admitted to nor denied by the girl herself, that Mary Agnes had allowed Robert Gabriel the very liberties that were forbidden to Gowan's own pleasure. And now, after all that, to be sent to the scullery by Mrs. Gerrard with directions to do something about the *bloody* boiler that hadn't worked properly in fifty years . . . It was beyond a person's ability to endure.

With a curse, he threw his spanner down onto the floor where it promptly chipped an old tile, bounced once, and slid under the fiery coils of the infernal water heater.

"Damn! Damn! Damn!" Gowan fumed with rising anger.

He squatted on the floor, poked about with his arm, and immediately burned himself on the metal underside of the boiler.

"Jesus flippin' Christ!" he howled, throwing himself to one side and staring at the old mechanism as if it were a malevolent, living being. He kicked it viciously, kicked it again. He thought about Robert Gabriel with Mary Agnes and kicked it a third time, which dislodged one of the rusting pipes. Steaming water began to spray out in a hissing arc.

"Oh hell!" Gowan snapped. "Burn an' rot an' worms eat yer insides!"

He grabbed a piece of towelling from the scullery sink and wrapped it round the pipe to grasp it without further damage to himself. Wrestling the piece into inadequate submission, sputtering against the fine hot spray that shot against his face and his hair, he lay on his chest. With one hand he forced the pipe back into place, and with the other he sought the spanner that he had dropped, finally locating it back against the far wall. He scrabbled against the floor to inch his way closer to the tool. His fingers were mere centimetres from it when suddenly the entire scullery went black, and Gowan realised that on top of everything else, the single light bulb in the room had just burnt out. The only light left came from the boiler itself, a thin useless glow of red that was shining directly into his eyes. It was the final blow.

"Ye shittin' piece of crile!" he cried. "Ye damn pie-eyed sheemach! Ye veecious piece o' sussy! Ye—"

And then, with no warning, he knew that he wasn't alone.

"Who's there? Cum here an' help me!"

There was no answer.

"Here! Richt on the fluir!"

And still no response.

He turned his head, tried and failed to pierce the gloom. He was about to call out again—and louder this time, for the hair on the back of his neck had begun to rise with consternation—when there was a rush of movement in his direction. It sounded as if half a dozen people were storming him at once.

"Hey—"

A blow cut off his voice. A hand gripped his neck and smashed his head to the floor. Pain roared through his temples. His fingers loosened their hold on the pipe and water shot out directly into his face, blinding him, searing him, scalding his flesh. He struggled wildly to free himself but was shoved savagely onto the burning pipe so that the gush of water entered his clothes, blistering his chest, his stomach, and his legs. His clothing was wool, and it clung to him like a sealant, holding the liquid like acid upon his skin.

"Gaaaa—"

He tried to cry out as agony, terror, and confusion ripped through him. But a knee dropped onto the small of his back, and the hand twined in his hair forced his head to turn and ground his forehead, nose, and chin into the pool of steaming water forming on the tile.

He felt the bridge of his nose crack, felt the skin scrape from his face. And just as he began to understand that his unseen assailant meant to drown him in less than one inch of water, he heard the unmistakable *snick* of metal on tile.

The knife entered his back a second later.

THE LIGHT switched on again.

Quick footsteps climbed the stairs.

7

"I SUPPOSE the more important question is whether you believe Stinhurst's story," St. James pointed out to Lynley.

They were in their corner bedroom, where the northwest wing of the house met the main body. It was a small room, adequately furnished in beechwood and pine, inoffensively papered with stripes of creeping jenny on a field of pale blue. The air held that vaguely medicinal smell of cleanser and disinfectant, disagreeable but not overwhelming. From the window, Lynley could see across a recess to the west wing where Irene Sinclair was moving listlessly in her room, a dress draped over her arm as if she couldn't decide whether to put it on or to forget the business entirely. Her face looked etiolated, an elongated white oval framed by black hair, like an artist's study of the power of contrast. Lynley dropped the curtain and turned to find that his friend had begun changing his clothes for dinner.

It was an awkward ritual, made worse because St. James' father-in-law was not there to assist him, made worse because the entire need for assistance in what for anyone else would have been a simple procedure had its genesis on a single night of Lynley's own drunken carelessness. He watched St. James, caught between wanting to offer him help and knowing that the offer would be politely rebuffed. The leg brace was uncovered, the crutches were used, the shoes were untied, and always St. James' face remained entirely indifferent, as if he had not been lithe and athletic a mere decade before.

"Stinhurst's story had the ring of truth, St. James. It's not exactly the kind of tale one spins to get out of a murder charge, is it? What could he possibly hope to gain from disparaging his own wife? If anything, the case against him looks blacker now. He's given himself a solid motive for murder."

"One that can't be verified," St. James argued mildly, "unless you check with Lady Stinhurst herself. And something tells me that Stinhurst is betting you're too much the gentleman to do so."

"I'll do it, of course. If it becomes necessary."

St. James dropped one of his shoes onto the floor and began attaching his leg brace to another. "But let's go beyond what he's assuming your reaction will be, Tommy. Let's consider for a moment that his story *is* true. It would be clever of him, wouldn't it, to outline his motive for murder so obviously. That way you needn't dig for it, needn't be additionally suspicious when you uncover it. Taken to the extreme, you needn't even suspect him of the murder in the first place since he's been perfectly honest with you about everything from the start. It's clever, isn't it? Too clever by half. And what better way to develop a crucial need to destroy the evidence than by acquiescing to Jeremy Vinney's presence here as well, a man likely to pursue any embarrassing story once Joy was killed."

"You're arguing that Stinhurst knew in advance that Joy's revisions of the play would turn it into an exposé of his wife and brother's affair. But that really doesn't hold with Helen being given the room adjoining Joy's, does it? Or with the locked hall door. Or with Davies-Jones' fingerprints all over that key."

St. James didn't disagree. He merely remarked, "If it comes to that, Tommy, I suppose one could say that it also doesn't hold with the fact that Sydeham was alone for a part of the night. As was his wife, as it turns out. So either one of them had the opportunity to kill her."

"Opportunity, perhaps. Everyone appears to have had the opportunity. But motive is a problem. Not to mention the fact that Joy's door was locked, so whoever did it either had access to those master keys or got in through Helen's room. We'll always go back to that, you see."

"Stinhurst could have had access to the keys, couldn't he? He told you himself that he's been here before."

"As have his wife, his daughter, and Joy. All of them with access to the keys, St. James. Even David Sydeham may have had access to them if he went down the corridor later on in the afternoon to see which room Elizabeth Rintoul had disappeared into when she saw him and Joanna Ellacourt arrive. But that's stretching things, isn't it? Why would he be curious about Elizabeth Rintoul's hiding place? More, why would Sydeham kill Joy Sinclair? To spare his wife a production with Robert Gabriel? It doesn't wash. Apparently, she's tightly under contract to appear with Gabriel anyway. Killing Joy accomplished nothing."

"We go back to that point, don't we? Joy's death seems to benefit one person only: Stuart Rintoul, Lord Stinhurst. Now that she's dead, the play that promised to be so embarrassing for him is never to be produced. By anyone. It looks bad, Tommy. I don't see how you can ignore such a motive."

"As to that—"

A knock sounded on the door. Lynley answered it to find Constable Lonan standing in the corridor, carrying a lady's shoulder bag that was encased in plastic. He held it stiffly before him in both hands, like a butler presenting a tray of questionable hors d'oeuvres.

"It's Sinclair's," the constable explained. "The inspector thought you might want to have a look at the contents before the lab goes over the bag for prints."

Lynley took it from him, laid it on the bed, and pulled on the latex gloves that St. James wordlessly passed him from the open valise at his feet. "Where was it found?"

"In the drawing room," Lonan replied. "On the window seat behind the curtains."

Lynley looked at him sharply. "Hidden?"

"Looks like she just tossed it there the same way she tossed about everything in her room."

Lynley unzipped the plastic, slipping the shoulder bag out onto the bed. The other two men watched curiously as he opened it and spilled out its contents. They comprised an interesting array of articles which Lynley sorted through slowly, dividing them into two piles. Into one pile he placed those objects common to a hundred thousand handbags hanging from the arms of a hundred thousand women: a set of keys attached to a large, brass ring, two inexpensive ballpoint pens, an opened pack of Wrigley's, a single matchbook, and a pair of dark glasses in a new leather case.

The rest of the contents went into the second pile where they attested to the fact that, like many women, Joy Sinclair had imbued even so mundane an object as a black shoulder bag with the singular stamp of her personality. Lynley thumbed through her chequebook first, scanning the entries for anything unusual and finding nothing. Apparently the woman had not been overly concerned with the state of her finances, since she had not balanced the book in at least six weeks. This financial nonchalance had its explanation in her wallet, which held nearly one hundred pounds in notes of varying denominations. But neither chequebook nor wallet retained Lynley's interest once his eyes fell upon the final two objects Joy Sinclair had carried with her—an engagement calendar and a small, hand-sized tape recorder.

The calendar was new, its pages scarcely having seen use at all. The weekend at Westerbrae was blocked out, as was a luncheon with Jeremy Vinney two weeks past. There were references to a theatre party, a dental appointment, some sort of anniversary, and three engagements marked *Upper Grosvenor Street*—each one crossed out as if none had been kept. Lynley turned the page to the successive month, found nothing, turned again. Here the single word *P. Green* was written across one entire week, *chapters 1–3* across the week after that. There was nothing else save a reference to *S birthday* jotted down on the twenty-fifth.

"Constable," Lynley said thoughtfully, "I'd like to keep this for now. The contents, not the bag itself. Will you check that with Macaskin before he pushes off?"

The constable nodded and left the room. Lynley waited until the door closed behind him before he turned back to the bed, picked up the tape recorder, and with a glance at St. James switched it on.

She had a perfectly lovely voice, throaty and musical. It was husky, a come-hither sort of voice with the kind of inadvertent sensuality that some women consider a blessing and others a curse. The sound switched on and off, in varying tempos with differing backgrounds—traffic, the underground, a quick blare of music—as if she grabbed the recorder out of her shoulder bag to save a sudden thought wherever it happened to strike her.

"Try to put Edna off at least two more days. There's nothing to report. Perhaps she'll believe I've had flu. . . . That penguin! She used to love penguins. It'll be perfect. . . . For God's sake, don't let Mum forget Sally again this year. . . . John Darrow believed the best about Hannah until circumstances forced him to believe the worst. . . . See about tickets and a decent place to stay. Take a heavier coat this time. . . . Jeremy. Jeremy. Oh Lord, why be in such a lather about him? It's hardly a lifetime proposition. . . . It was dark, and although the winter storm . . . wonderful, Joy. Why not simply go with a dark and stormy night and have done with creativity once and for all. . . . Remember that peculiar smell: decaying vegetables and flotsam washed down the river by the last storm. . . . The sound of frogs and pumps and the unremittingly flat land. . . . Why not ask Rhys how best to approach him? He's good with people. He'll be able to help. . . . Rhys wants to—"

Lynley switched off the recorder at this. He looked up to find St. James watching him. In a play for time before the inevitable came into the open between them, Lynley gathered up the articles and placed them all into a plastic bag which St. James had produced from his valise. He folded it closed, took it to the chest of drawers.

"Why haven't you questioned Davies-Jones?" St. James asked.

Lynley returned to the foot of the bed, to his suitcase which lay on a luggage stand there. Flipping this open, he pulled out his dinner clothes, giving himself time to consider his friend's question.

It would be easy enough to say that the initial circumstances had not allowed him to question the Welshman, that there was a logic to the manner in which the case had developed so far and he had intuitively followed the logic to see where it would lead. There was truth in that explanation as well. But beyond that truth, Lynley recognised an additional, unpleasant reality. He was struggling with a need to avoid confrontation, a need with which he had not yet come to terms, so foreign was it to him.

In the next room, he could hear Helen, her movements light and brisk and efficient. He had heard her thus a thousand and one times over the years, heard her without noticing. The sounds were amplified now, as if with the intention of imprinting themselves permanently onto his consciousness.

"I don't want to hurt her," he said at last.

St. James was attaching his leg brace to a black shoe, and he paused in the effort, shoe in one hand, brace in the other. His face, usually so noncommittal, reflected surprise. "You've certainly an odd way of showing it, Tommy."

"You sound just like Havers. But what would you have me do? Helen's determined to be absolutely blind to the obvious. Shall I point out the facts to her now, or hold my tongue and let her become even more involved with the man so that she's thoroughly devastated when she discovers how he's used her?"

"If he's used her," St. James said.

Lynley pulled on a clean shirt, buttoned it in a poorly hidden agitated fashion, and knotted his tie. "If! Just what do you conjecture his visit to her room last night was all about, St. James?"

His question was met with no reply. Lynley could feel his friend's eyes on his face. His fingers fumbled with the mess he had made of his tie. "Oh, damn and blast!" he muttered savagely.

* * *

AT THE KNOCK, Lady Helen opened her door, expecting to find Sergeant Havers or Lynley or St. James in the corridor, ready to escort her to dinner as if she were either the prime suspect or a key witness in need of police protection. Instead, it was Rhys. He said nothing, his expression hesitant, as if he was wondering what his reception might be. But when Lady Helen smiled, he entered the room and pushed the door shut behind him.

They looked at each other like guilty lovers, hungry for a surreptitious meeting. The need for quiet, for stealth, for a declaration of unity heightened sensitivity, heightened desire, heightened and strengthened the newly forged bond between them. When he held out his arms, Lady Helen more than willingly sought their refuge.

With a wordless longing, he kissed her forehead, her eyelids, her cheeks, and at last her mouth. Her lips parted in response and her arms tightened round him, holding him closer to her as if his presence might obliterate the worst of the day. She felt the length of his body create its sweet agony of pressure against her own, and she began to tremble, shot through with a dizzying, unexpected bolt of desire. It came upon her from nowhere, running through her blood like a liquid fire. She buried her face against his shoulder, and his hands moved upon her with possessive knowledge.

"Love, love," Rhys whispered. He said nothing more, for at his words, she turned her head and sought his mouth again. After some moments, he murmured, "Aw bey browden on ye, lassie," and then added with a torn chuckle, "But I suppose you've noticed that."

Lady Helen lifted her hand to smooth his hair back from his temples where it was peppered with grey. She smiled, feeling somehow comforted and not entirely certain why this should be so. "Where on earth did a black-hearted Welshman ever learn to speak Scots?"

At that, his mouth twisted, his arms stiffened momentarily, and Lady Helen knew before he answered that she had innocently asked the wrong question. "In hospital," he said.

"Oh Lord. I'm so sorry. I didn't think—"

Rhys shook his head, pulled her closer to him, resting his cheek against her hair. "I've not told you about any of it, have I, Helen? I think it's something I didn't want you to know."

"Then don't—"

"No. The hospital was just outside of Portree. On Skye. In the dead of winter. Grey sea, grey sky, grey land. Boats leaving for the mainland with me wishing to be on any one of them. I used to think that Skye would drive me to drink on a permanent basis. That kind of place tests one's mettle as nothing else ever does. To survive, it all came down to clandestine pulls at a whisky bottle or proficiency in Scots. I chose Scots. That, at least, was guaranteed by my roommate, who refused to speak anything else." His fingers touched her hair, a mere ghost of a caress. It seemed tentative, unsure. "Helen. For God's sake. Please. I don't want your pity."

It was his way, she thought. It was always his way. He would cut through like that, moving past the potential of any meaningless expression of compassion that stood between him and the rest of the world. For pity kept him at a disadvantage, prisoner of an illness that could not be cured. She took his pain as her own.

"How could you ever believe I feel pity? Is that what you think was between us last night?"

She heard his ragged sigh. "I'm forty-two years old. Do you know that, Helen? Is that fifteen years your senior? Good God, is it more?"

"Twelve years."

"I was married once, when I was twenty-two. Toria was nineteen. Both of us fresh from the regionals and thinking we'd become the next West End wonders."

"I didn't know that."

"She left me. I'd been doing a winter's season round Norfolk and Suffolk—two months here, a month there. Living in grimy bed-sits and foul-smelling hotels. Thinking none of it was really half bad since it put food on the table and kept the children in clothes. But when I got back to London, she was gone, home to Australia. Mum and Dad and security. More than mere bread on the table. Shoes on her feet." His eyes were bleak.

"How long had you been married?"

"Only five years. But quite long enough, I'm afraid, for Toria to come to terms with the worst about me."

"Don't say—"

"*Yes.* I've only seen my children once in the past fifteen years. They're teenagers now, a boy and a girl who don't even know me. And the worst of it is that it's my own fault. Toria didn't leave because I was a failure in the theatre, although God knows my chances of success were fairly dim. She left because I was a drunkard. I still am. A drunkard, Helen. You must never forget that. I mustn't let you forget it."

She repeated what he had said himself one night as they walked together against the wind along the edge of Hyde Park: "Well, it's only a word, isn't it? It only has the power we're willing to give it."

He shook his head. She could feel the heavy beating of his heart. "Have they questioned you yet?" she asked.

"No." His cool fingers rested on the nape of her neck, and he spoke over her head carefully, as if each word was chosen with deliberation. "They do think I killed her, don't they, Helen?"

Her arms tightened of their own volition, speaking the answer for her. He went on. "I've been considering how they might think I did it. I came to your room, brought you cognac to make you drunk, made love to you as a distraction, then stabbed my cousin. Why, of course, remains to be seen. But no doubt they'll think of something soon enough."

"The cognac was unsealed," Lady Helen whispered.

"Do they think I put something in it? Good God. And what about you? Do you think that as well? Do you think I came to you, intent upon drugging you and then murdering my cousin?"

"Of course not." Looking up, Lady Helen saw a mixture of fatigue and sadness melt together on his face, tempered by relief.

"When I got out of your bed, I unsealed it," he said. "God knows I wanted the stuff. I felt desperate to have it. But then you woke up. You came to me. And frankly, I discovered that I wanted you more."

"You don't need to tell me."

"I was inches from a drink. Centimetres. I haven't felt like that in months. If you hadn't been there . . ."

"It doesn't matter. I was there. I'm here now."

Voices came to them from the room next door: Lynley's raised hotly for a moment, followed by St. James' placid murmur. They listened. Rhys spoke.

"Your loyalties are going to be tested brutally through this, Helen. You know that, don't you? And even if you're presented with irrefutable truths, you're going to have to decide for yourself why I came to your room last night, why I wanted to be with you, why I made love to you. And, most of all, what I was doing all that time while you slept."

"I don't need to decide," Lady Helen declared. "There aren't two sides to this story as far as I'm concerned."

Rhys' eyes darkened to black. "There are. His and mine. And you know it."

*   *   *

WHEN ST. JAMES and Lynley entered the drawing room, they saw it was destined to be a most unpleasant dinner. The assembled group could not have placed themselves across the oriental carpet with any more effective staging to depict their displeasure with the fact that they would be sitting down to dine with New Scotland Yard.

Joanna Ellacourt had selected a centre-stage location. Having established herself somewhere between sitting and draping on a rosewood chaise near the fireplace, she favoured the two newcomers with a glacial look before she turned away, sipped on what looked like white-capped pink syrup, and cast her eyes upon the George II chimneypiece as if its pale green pilasters needed memorising. The others were gathered round her on couches and chairs; their desultory conversation ceased entirely at the entrance of the two men.

Lynley's eyes swept over the group, making a quick note of the fact that some of them were missing, making especial note of the fact that among the missing were Lady Helen and Rhys Davies-Jones. At a drinks trolley at the far end of the room, Constable Lonan sat like a guardian angel, keeping sharp eyes on the company as if in the expectation that one or more of them might commit some new act of violence. Lynley and St. James went to join him.

"Where are the others?" Lynley asked.

"Not down yet," Lonan replied. "The one lady just got in here herself."

Lynley saw that the lady in question was Lord Stinhurst's daughter, Elizabeth Rintoul, and she was approaching the drinks trolley like a woman going to her execution. Unlike Joanna Ellacourt, who had dressed for the dinner in clinging satin as if it were a social occasion of the highest order, Elizabeth wore a tan tweed skirt and bulky green sweater, both decidedly old and ill-fitting, the latter decorated with three moth holes that made an isosceles triangle high on her left shoulder.

She was, Lynley knew, thirty-five years old, but she looked far older, like a woman approaching spinsterly middle age in the worst possible way. Her hair, perhaps in an unsuccessful attempt to achieve strawberry blonde, had been coloured an artificial shade of brown that had since gone brassy. It was heavily permed so that it formed a screen from behind which she could observe the world. Both the colour and the style suggested a choice made from a magazine photograph and not one that took into consideration the demands of her complexion or the shape of her face. She was very gaunt, with features that were pinched and pointed. Her upper lip was beginning to develop the creasing lines of age.

Uneasiness limned itself on her bloodless face as she crossed the room. One hand caught at her skirt and squeezed the material. She didn't bother to introduce herself, didn't bother with any introductory formality at all. It was clear that she had waited more than twelve hours to ask her question and was not about to be put off another moment. Nonetheless, she didn't actually look at Lynley as she spoke. Her eyes—shadowed inexpertly with a peculiar shade of aquamarine—merely touched his face to establish contact and from that moment forward remained riveted on the wall just beyond him, as if she were addressing the painting that hung there.

"Do you have the necklace?" she asked stiffly.

"I beg your pardon?"

Elizabeth's hands splayed out against her skirt. "My aunt's pearl necklace. I gave it to Joy last night. Is it in her room?"

There was a murmur from the group at the fireplace, and Francesca Gerrard got to her feet. Coming to Elizabeth's side, she put her hand on her elbow, attempting to draw her back to the others. She kept her eyes off the police.

"It's all right, Elizabeth," she murmured. "Really. Quite all right."

Elizabeth jerked away. "It's not all right, Aunt Francie. I didn't want to give it to Joy in the first place. I knew it wouldn't work. Now that she's dead, I want you to have it back." Still, she looked at no one. Her eyes were bloodshot, a condition that her eyeshadow only heightened.

Lynley looked at St. James. "Were there pearls in the room?" The other man shook his head.

"But I took the necklace to her. She wasn't in her room yet. She'd gone to . . . So I asked him to . . ." Elizabeth stopped, her face working. Her eyes sought and then fastened on Jeremy Vinney. "You didn't give it to her, did you? You said you would, but you didn't. What have you done with that necklace?"

Vinney's gin and tonic stopped midway to his lips. His fingers, too plump and overly hairy, tightened on the glass. Clearly, the accusation came as a surprise. "I? Of course I gave it to her. Don't be absurd."

"You're lying!" Elizabeth shrilled. "You said she didn't want to talk to anyone! And you put it in your pocket! I heard the two of you in your room, you know! *I* know what you were after! But when she wouldn't let you do it, you followed her back to her room, didn't you? You were angry! You killed her! And then you took the pearls as well!"

Vinney was on his feet at that, a quick man in spite of the weight he carried. He tried to push aside David Sydeham, who grabbed his arm.

"You dried-up little shrew," he flared. "You were so goddamned jealous of her, you probably killed her yourself! Snooping about, listening at doors. That's about as close as you've come to having any, isn't it?"

"Jesus God, Vinney—"

"And what were you doing with her?" Angry colour shot across Elizabeth's cheeks in patches. Her lips contorted into a sneer. "Hoping to get your own creative juices up by bleeding off hers? Or smelling her up like every other man here?"

"Elizabeth!" Francesca Gerrard pleaded weakly.

"Because I know why you came! I know what you were after!"

"She's mad," Joanna Ellacourt muttered in disgust.

Lady Stinhurst broke at that. She spat a response at the actress. "Don't you say that! Don't you dare! You sit there like an ageing Cleopatra who needs men to—"

"*Marguerite!*" Her husband's voice boomed. It shattered everyone to silence, nerve-strung and brittle.

The tension was broken by footsteps on the stairs and in the hall. A moment later the remaining members of the party entered the room: Sergeant Havers, Lady Helen, Rhys Davies-Jones. Robert Gabriel appeared less than a minute behind them.

His eyes darted from the tense group by the fireplace to the others near the drinks trolley, to Elizabeth and Vinney, squaring off in anger. It was an actor's moment and he knew how to use it.

"Ah." He smiled gaily. "We are indeed all in the gutter, aren't we? But I wonder which of us are looking at the stars?"

"Certainly not Elizabeth," Joanna Ellacourt replied curtly and turned back to her drink.

From the corner of his eye, Lynley saw Davies-Jones draw Lady Helen towards the drinks trolley and pour her a dry sherry. *He even knows her habits,* Lynley thought dismally and decided that he had had his fill of the entire group.

"Tell me about the pearls," he said.

Francesca Gerrard felt for the single string of cheap beads she wore. They were puce-coloured; they argued dramatically with the green of her blouse. Ducking her head, raising a nervous hand to her mouth as if to hide her prominent teeth from scrutiny, she spoke with a well-bred hesitation, as if better manners told her it was unwise to intrude.

"I . . . It's my fault, Inspector. I'm afraid that last night I did ask Elizabeth to offer the pearls to Joy. They aren't priceless, of course, but I thought if she needed money. . . ."

"Ah. I see. A bribe."

Francesca's eyes went to Lord Stinhurst. "Stuart, won't you . . . ?" The words wavered uneasily. Her brother didn't reply. "Yes. I thought she might be willing to withdraw the play."

"Tell him how much the pearls are worth," Elizabeth insisted hotly. "Tell him!"

Francesca made a delicate moue of distaste, clearly unused to discussing such matters in public. "They were a wedding present from Phillip. My husband. They were . . . perfectly matched so—"

"They were worth more than eight thousand pounds," Elizabeth snapped.

"I had of course always intended to pass them on to my own daughter. But since I have no children—"

"They were going to go to our little Elizabeth," Vinney finished triumphantly. "So who better to have nicked them from Joy's room? You nasty little bitch! Clever to point the finger at me!"

Elizabeth made a precipitate move towards him. Her father rose and intercepted her. The entire scene was about to be lived through once again. But Mary Agnes Campbell arrived in their midst, coming to stand hesitantly in the doorway, her eyes large and round, her fingers playing at the tips of her hair. Francesca spoke to her in an effort to divert the tide of passion.

"Dinner, Mary Agnes?" she asked inanely.

Mary Agnes scanned the room. "Gowan?" she responded. "He isna wi' ye? Nae wi' the police? Cuik wants him . . ." Her voice fell off. "Ye havena seen . . ."

Lynley looked from St. James to Havers. All of them shared a moment of the unthinkable. All of them moved. "See that no one leaves the room," Lynley directed Constable Lonan.

THEY WENT in separate directions, Havers up the stairs, St. James down the lower northeast corridor, and Lynley into the dining room, through the china and warming rooms. He burst into the kitchen. The cook started in surprise, a steaming kettle in her hand. Broth spilled over the side in an aromatic stream. Above them, Lynley heard Havers pounding down the west corridor. Doors crashed open. She called the boy's name.

Seven steps and Lynley was at the scullery door. The knob turned in his hand, but the door wouldn't open. Something blocked the passage.

"Havers!" he shouted, and in rising anxiety at the absence of reply, "Havers! Damn and blast!"

Then he heard her flying down the back staircase, heard her pause, heard her cry of incredulity, heard the unbelievable sound of water, the sound of sloshing like a child in a wading pond. Precious seconds passed. And then her voice like a bitter draught of medicine one expects but hopes not to swallow:

"Gowan! Christ!"

"Havers, for God's sake—"

There was movement, something dragging. The door eased open a precious twelve inches, giving Lynley access to the heat and the steam and the heart of malevolence.

His back muddied and gummed by crimson, Gowan had been lying on his stomach across the top step of the scullery, apparently in an effort to escape the room and the scalding water that poured from the boiler and mixed with the cooling water on the floor. It was inches deep, and Havers waded back across it, seeking the emergency valve that would shut it off. When she found it, the room was plunged into an eerie stillness that was broken by the cook's voice on the other side of the door.

"Is it Gowan? Is it the lad?" And she began a keening that reverberated like a musical instrument against the kitchen walls.

But when she paused, a second sound racked the hot air. Gowan was breathing. He was alive.

Lynley turned the boy to him. His face and neck were a puckered, red mass of boiled flesh. His shirt and trousers were cooked onto his body. "Gowan!" Lynley cried. And then, "Havers, phone for an ambulance! Get St. James!" She did not move. "Blast it, Havers! Do as I say!"

But her vision was transfixed on the boy's face. Lynley spun back, saw the initial glazing of Gowan's eyes, knew what it meant.

"Gowan! No!"

For an instant, Gowan seemed to try desperately to respond to the shout, to accept the call back from the darkness. He took a stertorous breath, wracked with bloody phlegm.

"Didn't . . . *see* . . ."

"What?" Lynley urged. "Didn't see what?"

Havers leaned forward. "Who? Gowan, *who?*"

With an enormous effort, the boy's eyes sought her. But he said nothing more. His body shuddered once and was still.

*   *   *

LYNLEY FOUND that he had grasped hold of Gowan's shirt in a frantic attempt to infuse his tortured body with life. Now he released him, letting the corpse rest back upon the step, and a monumental sense of outrage filled him. It began as a howling, curling deep within muscles, tissues, and organs, screaming to get out. He thought of the wasted life—the generations of life callously destroyed—in the single young boy who had done . . . *what?* Who had paid for what crime? What chance remark? What piece of knowledge?

His eyes burned, his heart pounded, and for a moment he chose to ignore the fact that Sergeant Havers was speaking to him. Her voice broke wretchedly.

"He pulled the ruddy thing out! Oh my God, Inspector, he must have pulled it out!"

Lynley saw that she had gone back to the boiler in the corner of the room. She was kneeling on the floor, mindless of the water, a torn piece of towel in her hand. Using it, she lifted something from the pool and Lynley saw it was a kitchen knife, the very same knife he had seen in the hands of the Westerbrae cook a few short hours before.

8

THERE WASN'T ENOUGH space in the scullery, so Inspector Macaskin did his pacing in the kitchen. His left hand ran along the worktable in the centre of the room; he gnawed at the fingers of his right with vicious concentration. His eyes flicked from the windows that presented him blankly with his own reflection to the closed door leading towards the dining room. From there he could hear the raised wail of a woman's voice, and the voice of a man, raw with anger. Gowan Kilbride's parents from Hillview Farm, meeting with Lynley, flailing him mercilessly with the first fury of their grief. On the floor above them, behind closed and guarded doors, the suspects waited for their summons from the police. *Again*, Macaskin thought. He cursed himself soundly, his conscience shredded by the belief that had he not suggested letting everyone out of the library for dinner, Gowan Kilbride might well be alive.

Macaskin swung around as the scullery door opened and St. James stepped out with Strathclyde's medical examiner. He hurried to join them. Over their shoulders, he could see two other crime-scene men still at work in the small room, doing what they could to collect what evidence had not been obliterated by water and steam.

"Right branch of the pulmonary artery is my guess without a full postmortem," the examiner murmured to Macaskin. He was stripping off a pair of gloves, which he stuffed into his jacket pocket.

Macaskin directed a querying look at St. James.

115

"It could be the same killer." St. James nodded. "Right-handed. One blow."

"Man or woman?"

St. James blew out a reflective breath. "My guess is a man. But I wouldn't rule out the possibility of a woman."

"But surely we're talking about considerable strength!"

"Or a rush of adrenaline. A woman could do it if she were driven."

"Driven?"

"Blind rage, panic, fear."

Macaskin bit down too hard on his finger. He tasted blood. "But who? *Who?*" he demanded of no one.

WHEN LYNLEY unlocked the door to Robert Gabriel's room, he found the man sitting much like a solitary prisoner in a cell. He had chosen the least comfortable chair in the room and he leaned forward in it, his arms on his legs, his manicured hands dangling uselessly in front of him.

Lynley had seen Gabriel on the stage, most memorably as Hamlet four seasons past, but the man close-up was very different from the actor who swept the audience along with him through the tortured psyche of a Danish prince. In spite of the fact that he was not much past forty, Gabriel was starting to look worn out. There were pouches under his eyes, and a fatty layer had begun to take up permanent residence round his waist. His hair was well cut and perfectly combed, but in spite of a gel that attempted to encourage it into a modern style, it was thin upon his skull, artificial-looking as if he had enhanced its colour in some way. At the crown of his head, its thickness barely sufficed to cover a bald spot that made a small but growing tonsure. Youthfully dressed, Gabriel appeared to favour trousers and shirt of a colour and weight that seemed more appropriate to a summer in Miami Beach than a winter in Scotland. They were contradictions, notes of instability in a man one would expect to be self-assured and at ease.

Lynley nodded Havers towards a second chair and remained standing himself. He chose a spot near a handsome hardwood chest of drawers where he had an unobstructed view of Gabriel's face. "Tell me about Gowan," he said. The sergeant crackled through the pages of her notebook.

"I always thought my mother sounded just like the police," was Gabriel's weary response. "I see I was right." He rubbed at the back of his neck as if to rid it of stiffness, then sat up in his chair and reached for the travel alarm clock on the bedside table. "My son gave this to me. Look at the silly thing. It doesn't even keep proper time any longer, but I've not been able to bring myself to toss it in the rubbish. I'd call that paternal devotion. Mum would call it guilt."

"You had a row in the library late this afternoon."

Gabriel gave a derisive snort. "We did. It seems Gowan believed that I'd been savouring one or two of Mary Agnes' finer qualities. He didn't much like it."

"And had you?"

"Christ. Now you sound like my ex-wife."

"Indeed. That doesn't go far to answering my question, however."

"I'd spoken to the girl," Gabriel snapped. "That's all."

"When was this?"

"I don't know. Sometime yesterday. Shortly after I arrived. I was unpacking and she knocked on the door, ostensibly to deliver fresh towels, which I didn't need. She stayed to chat, long enough to find out if I had any acquaintance with a list of actors who appear to be running neck and neck at the top of her marital-prospect list." Gabriel waited belligerently and when no additional question came forth he said, "All right, all *right!* I may have touched her here and there. I probably kissed her. I don't know."

"You *may* have touched her? You don't know if you kissed her?"

"I wasn't paying attention, Inspector. I didn't know I would have to account for every second of my time with the London police."

"You talk as if touching and kissing are knee-jerk reactions," Lynley pointed out with impassive courtesy. "What does it take for you to remember your behaviour? Complete seduction? Attempted rape?"

"All right! She was willing enough! And I didn't kill that boy over it."

"Over what?"

Gabriel had at least enough conscience to look uncomfortable. "Good God, just a bit of nuzzle. Perhaps a feel beneath her skirt. I didn't take the girl to bed."

"Not then, at least."

"Not at all! Ask her! She'll tell you the same." He pressed his fingers to his temples as if to quell pain. His face, bruised from his run-in with Gowan, looked riven by exhaustion. "Look, I didn't know Gowan had his eye on the girl. I hadn't even seen him then. I didn't know he existed. As far as I was concerned, she was free for the taking. And, by God, she didn't protest. She could hardly do that, could she, when she was doing her best to manage a feel of her own."

The actor's last statement rang with a certain pride, the kind evidenced by men who feel compelled to talk about their sexual conquests. No matter how puerile the reported seduction appears to others, in the speaker it always meets some undefined need. Lynley wondered what it was in Gabriel's case.

"Tell me about last night," he said.

"There's nothing to tell. I had a drink in the library. Spoke to Irene. After that, I went to bed."

"Alone?"

"Yes, as hard as that may be for you to believe, alone. Not with Mary Agnes. Not with anyone else."

"That takes away an alibi, though, doesn't it?"

"Why in God's name would I need an alibi, Inspector? Why would I want to kill Joy? All right, I had an affair with her. I admit my marriage fell apart because of it. But if I wanted to kill her, I would have done so last year when Irene found out and divorced me. Why wait until now?"

"Joy wouldn't cooperate in the plan you had, would she, the plan to win your wife back? Perhaps you knew that Irene would come back to you if Joy would tell her that she'd been to bed with you only once. Not again and again over a year, but once. Except that Joy had no intention of lying to benefit you."

"So I killed her because of that? When? How? There's not a person in the house who doesn't know her door was locked. So what did I do? Hide in the wardrobe and wait for her to fall asleep? Or better yet, tiptoe back and forth through Helen Clyde's room and hope she wouldn't notice?"

Lynley refused to let himself become involved in a shouting match with the man. "When you left the library this evening, where did you go?"

"I came here."

"Immediately?"

"Of course. I wanted a wash. I felt like hell."

"Which stairs did you use?"

Gabriel blinked. "What do you mean? What other stairs are there? I used the stairs in the hall."

"Not those right next door to this very room? The back stairs? The stairs in the scullery?"

"I had no idea they were even there. It's not my habit to prowl about houses looking for secondary access routes to my room, Inspector."

His answer was clever enough, impossible to verify if no one had seen him in the scullery or the kitchen within the last twenty-four hours. Yet certainly Mary Agnes had used the stairs when she worked on this floor. And the man wasn't deaf. Nor were the walls so thick that he would hear no footsteps.

It appeared to Lynley that Robert Gabriel had just made his first mistake. He wondered about it. He wondered what else the man was lying about.

Inspector Macaskin poked his head in the door. His expression was calm, but the four words he said held a note of triumph.

"We've found the pearls."

"THE GERRARD woman had them all along," Macaskin said. "She handed them over readily enough when my man got to her room for the search. I've put her in the sitting room."

Sometime since their earlier meeting that night, Francesca Gerrard had decided to deck herself out in a grating array of costume jewellery. Seven strands of beads in varying colours from ivory to onyx had joined those of puce, and she was sporting a line of metallic bracelets that made her movements sound as if she were in shackles. Discoidal plastic earrings striped violently in purple and black were clipped to her ears. Yet the tawdry display seemed the product of neither eccentricity nor self-absorption. Rather, it appeared however questionably to be a substitute for the ashes which women of other cultures pour upon their heads at the time of a death.

Nothing was quite so clear as the fact that Francesca Gerrard was grieving. She sat at the table in the centre of the room, one arm pressed tightly into her waist, one fist clenched between her eyebrows. Swaying slowly from side to side, she wept. The tears were not spurious. Lynley had seen enough mourning to know when he was faced with the real thing.

"Get something for her," he said to Havers. "Whisky or brandy. Sherry. Anything. From the library."

Havers went to do so, returning a moment later with a bottle and several glasses. She poured a few tablespoons of whisky into one of the tumblers. Its smoky scent struck at the air like a sound.

With a gentleness unusual in her, Havers pressed the glass into Francesca's hand. "Drink a bit," she said. "Please. Just to steady yourself."

"I can't! I can't!" Nonetheless, Francesca allowed Sergeant Havers to lift the glass to her lips. She took a grimacing swallow, coughed, took another. Then she said brokenly, "He was . . . I liked to pretend he was my son. I've no children. Gowan . . . It's my *fault* that he's dead. I asked him to work for me. He didn't really want to. He wanted to go to London. He wanted to be like James Bond. He had dreams. And he's dead. And I'm to blame."

Like people afraid of making any sudden movements, the others in the room took seats surreptitiously, Havers at the table with Lynley, St. James and Macaskin out of Francesca's line of vision.

"Blame is part of death," Lynley said quietly. "I bear equal responsibility for what's happened to Gowan. I'm not likely to forget it."

Francesca looked up, surprised. Clearly, she had not expected such an admission from the police.

"Part of myself feels lost. It's as if . . . No, I can't explain." Her voice quavered, then held.

Any man's death diminishes me, because I am involved in mankind. Exposed for years to death in a thousand and one horrible varieties, Lynley understood far better than Francesca Gerrard could ever have realised. But he said only, "You'll find that, in a case like this, a burial of grief comes hand-in-hand with justice. Not at once, of course. But eventually."

"And you need me for that. Yes. I do understand." She drew herself up, blew her nose shakily on a wadded tissue from her pocket, took another hesitant sip of whisky. Her eyes brimmed with tears again. Several escaped in a wet trail from cheeks to lips.

"How did you come to have the necklace in your room?" Lynley asked. Sergeant Havers took out her pencil.

Francesca hesitated. Her lips parted twice to speak before she was able to go on. "I took it back last night. I would have told you earlier in the drawing room. I wanted to. But when Elizabeth and Mr. Vinney began . . . I didn't know what to do. Everything happened so quickly. And then Gowan . . ." She faltered on the name, like a runner stumbling and not righting himself properly.

"Yes. I see. Did you go to Joy's room for the necklace or did she bring it to you?"

"I went to her room. It was on the chest of drawers by the door. I suppose I had changed my mind about her having it."

"You took it back as easily as that? There was no discussion?"

Francesca shook her head. "There couldn't have been. She was asleep."

"You saw her? You got into her room? Was the door unlocked?"

"No. I'd gone without my keys because I thought at first it might be unlocked. Everyone knew each other, after all. There was no reason to lock doors. But hers *was* locked, so I went to the office for the master keys."

"The key wasn't in her lock from the inside?"

Francesca frowned. "No . . . It couldn't have been, could it, or I wouldn't have been able to unlock it with my own."

"Take us through exactly what you did, Mrs. Gerrard."

Willingly, Francesca retraced her route from her bedroom to Joy's where she turned the door handle only to find the room locked; from Joy's room to her own where she picked up her desk key from her chest of drawers; from her room to her office where she took the master keys from the bottom drawer of her desk; from her office to Joy's room where she unlocked the door quietly, saw the necklace in the light from the corridor, took it, and relocked the door; from Joy's room to her office where she returned the keys; from her office back to her own room where she replaced the necklace in her jewellery box.

"What time was this?" Lynley asked.

"Three-fifteen."

"Exactly?"

She nodded and went on to explain. "I don't know whether you've ever done anything impulsive that you regret, Inspector. But I regretted parting with the pearls directly after Elizabeth took them to Joy. I lay in bed trying to decide what to do. I didn't want a confrontation with Joy, I didn't want to burden my brother Stuart with anything else. So I . . . well, I suppose I stole them, didn't I? And I know it was three-fifteen because I had been lying awake watching the clock and that's what time it was when I finally decided to do something about getting my necklace back."

"You said Joy was asleep. Did you see her? Hear her breathing?"

"The room was so dark. I . . . I suppose I assumed she was asleep. She didn't stir, didn't speak. She . . ." Her eyes widened. "Do you mean she might have been dead?"

"Did you actually see her in the room at all?"

"You mean in the bed? No, I couldn't see the bed. The door was in the way and I hadn't opened it more than a few inches. I just thought, of course . . ."

"What about your desk in your office? Was it locked?"

"Oh yes," she replied. "It's always locked."

"Who has keys to it?"

"I have one key. Mary Agnes has the other."

"And could anyone have seen you going from your room to Joy's? Or going to the office? On either of the two trips?"

"I didn't notice anyone. But I suppose . . ." She shook her head. "I just don't know."

"But you would have passed any number of rooms to make the trips, wouldn't you?"

"Of course, anyone on the main corridor could have seen me if they were up and about. But surely I would have noticed that. Or heard a door opening."

Lynley went to join Macaskin who was already on his feet, examining the floor plan that was still spread out upon the table from their earlier interview with David Sydeham. Four rooms had immediate access to the main corridor besides the rooms belonging to Lady Helen and Joy Sinclair: Joanna Ellacourt and David Sydeham's room, Lord Stinhurst and his wife's, the unused room of Rhys Davies-Jones, and Irene Sinclair's at the junction of the main corridor and the west wing of the house.

"Surely there's truth to what the woman is saying," Macaskin muttered to Lynley as they looked the floor plan over. "Surely she would have heard something, seen something, been alerted to the fact that she was being watched."

"Mrs. Gerrard," Lynley said to her over his shoulder, "are you absolutely certain that Joy's door was locked last night?"

"Of course," she replied. "I thought of sending a note with her tea this morning, to tell her I'd taken the necklace back. Perhaps I really should have. But then—"

"And you did take the keys back to your desk?"

"Yes. Why do you keep asking me about the door?"

"And you locked the desk again?"

"Yes. I know I did that. It's something I always do."

Lynley turned from the table but remained next to it, his eyes on Francesca. "Can you tell me," he asked her, "how Helen Clyde came to be given a room adjoining Joy Sinclair's? Was that coincidental?"

Francesca's hand rose to her beads, an automatic movement, companion to thought. "Helen Clyde?" she repeated. "Was it Stuart who suggested . . . No. That's not right, is it? Mary Agnes took the call from London. I remember because Mary's spelling is a bit phonetic, and the name she'd written was unfamiliar. I had to get her to say it for me."

"The name?"

"Yes. She'd written down *Joyce Encare*, which of course made no sense until she said it. *Joy Sinclair*."

"Joy had telephoned you?"

"Yes. So I returned the call. This was . . . it must have been last Monday evening. She asked if Helen Clyde might have the room next to hers."

"Joy asked for Helen?" Lynley queried sharply. "Asked for her by name?"

Francesca hesitated. Her eyes dropped to the plan of the house, then rose back to meet Lynley's. "No. Not exactly by name. She merely said that her cousin was bringing a guest and could that guest be given the room next to hers. I suppose I assumed she must have known. . . ." Her voice faltered as Lynley pushed himself away from the table.

He looked from Macaskin to Havers to St. James. There was no point in further procrastination. "I'll see Davies-Jones now," he said.

RHYS DAVIES-JONES did not appear to be cowed in the presence of the police, in spite of the escort of Constable Lonan who had followed him like an unfortunate reputation from his room, down the stairs, and right to the door of the sitting room. The Welshman evaluated St. James, Macaskin, Lynley, and Havers with a look entirely straightforward, the deliberate look of a man intent upon showing that he had nothing to hide. *A dark horse which had never been thought of . . .* Lynley nodded him to a seat at the table.

"Tell me about last night," he said.

Davies-Jones gave no perceptible reaction to the question other than to move the liquor bottle out of his line of vision. He played the tips of his fingers round the edge of a packet of Players that he took from his jacket pocket, but he did not light one. "What about last night?"

"About your fingerprints on the key to the door that adjoined Helen's and Joy's rooms, about the cognac you brought to Helen, about where you were until one in the morning when you showed up at her door."

Again, Davies-Jones did not react, either to the words themselves or to the current of hostility that ran beneath them. He answered frankly enough. "I took cognac up to her because I wanted to see her, Inspector. It was stupid of me, a rather adolescent way of getting into her room for a few minutes."

"It seems to have worked well enough."

Davies-Jones didn't respond. Lynley saw that he was determined to say as little as possible. He found himself instantly equally determined to wring every last fact from the man. "And your fingerprints on the key?"

"I locked the door, both doors in fact. We wanted privacy."

"You entered her room with a bottle of cognac and locked both the doors? Rather a blatant admission of your intentions, wouldn't you say?"

Davies-Jones' body tensed fractionally. "That's not how it happened."

"Then do tell me how it happened."

"We talked for a bit about the read-through. Joy's play was supposed to have brought me back into London theatre after my . . . trouble, so I was rather upset about the way everything turned out. It was more than a little bit obvious to me that whatever my cousin had in mind in getting us all up here to look at the revisions in her script, putting on a play had little enough to do with it. I was angry at having been used as a pawn in what was clearly some sort of vengeance game Joy was playing against Stinhurst. So Helen and I talked. About the read-through. About what in God's name I would do from here. Then, when I was going to leave, Helen asked me to stay the night with her. So I locked the doors." Davies-Jones met Lynley's eyes squarely. A faint smile touched his lips. "You weren't expecting it to have happened quite that way, were you, Inspector?"

Lynley didn't reply. Rather, he pulled the whisky bottle towards him, twisted off its cap, poured himself a drink. The liquor flashed through his body satisfactorily. Deliberately, he set the glass down on the table between them, a full inch still in it. At that, Davies-Jones looked away, but Lynley didn't miss the tight movements of the man's head, the tension in his neck, traitors to his need. He lit a cigarette with unsteady hands.

"I understand you disappeared right after the read-through, that you didn't show up again until one in the morning. How do you account for the time? What was it, ninety minutes, nearly two hours?"

"I went for a walk," Davies-Jones replied.

Had he claimed that he had gone swimming in the loch, Lynley could not have been more surprised. "In a snowstorm? With a wind-chill factor of God only knows how far below freezing, you went for a walk?"

Davies-Jones merely said, "I find walking a good substitute for the bottle, Inspector. I would have preferred the bottle last night, frankly. But a walk seemed like the smarter alternative."

"Where did you go?"

"Along the road to Hillview Farm."

"Did you see anyone? Speak to anyone?"

"No," he replied. "So no one can verify what I'm telling you. I understand that perfectly. Nonetheless, it's what I did."

"Then you also understand that as far as I'm concerned you could have spent that time in any number of ways."

Davies-Jones took the bait. "Such as?"

"Such as collecting what you'd need to murder your cousin."

The Welshman's answering smile was contemptuous. "Yes. I suppose I could have. Down the back stairs, through the scullery and kitchen, into the dining room, and I'd have the dirk without anyone seeing me. Sydeham's glove is a problem, but no doubt you can tell me how I managed to get it without him being the wiser."

"You seem to know a great deal about the layout of the house," Lynley pointed out.

"I do. I spent the early part of the afternoon looking it over. I've an interest in architecture. Hardly a criminal one, however."

Lynley fingered the tumbler of whisky, swirling it meditatively. "How long were you in hospital?" he asked.

"Isn't that a bit out of your purview, Inspector Lynley?"

"Nothing that touches this case is out of my purview. How long were you in hospital for your drinking problem?"

Davies-Jones answered stonily. "Four months."

"A private hospital?"

"Yes."

"Costly venture."

"What's that supposed to mean? That I stabbed my cousin for her money to pay my bills?"

"Did Joy have money?"

"Of course she had money. She had plenty of money. And you can rest assured she didn't leave any of it to me."

"You know the terms of her will, then?"

Davies-Jones reacted to the pressure, to being in the close presence of alcohol, to having been led so expertly into a trap. He stubbed out his cigarette angrily in the ashtray. "Yes, blast you! And she's left every last pound to Irene and her children. But that's not what you wanted to hear, is it, Inspector?"

Lynley seized the opportunity he had gained through the other man's anger. "Last Monday Joy asked Francesca Gerrard that Helen

Clyde be given a room next to hers. Do you know anything about that?"

"That *Helen* . . ." Davies-Jones reached for his cigarettes, then pushed them away. "No. I can't explain it."

"Can you explain how she knew Helen would be with you this weekend?"

"I must have told her. I probably did."

"And suggested that she might want to get to know Helen? And what better way than by asking to be given adjoining rooms."

"Like schoolgirls?" Davies-Jones demanded. "Rather transparent for a ruse leading to murder, wouldn't you say?"

"I'm certainly open to your explanation."

"I don't bloody have one, Inspector. But my guess is that Joy wanted Helen next to her to act as a buffer, someone without a vested interest in the production, someone who wouldn't be likely to come tapping at her door, hoping for a chat about line and scene changes. Actors are like that, you know. They generally don't give a playwright much peace."

"So you mentioned Helen to her. You planted the idea."

"I did nothing of the kind. You asked for an explanation. That's the best I can do."

"Yes. Of course. Except that it doesn't hold with the fact that Joanna Ellacourt had the room on the other side of Joy's, does it? No buffer there. How do you explain it?"

"I don't. I have absolutely no idea what Joy was thinking. Perhaps she had no idea herself. Perhaps it means nothing and you're looking for meaning wherever you can find it."

Lynley nodded, unaffected by the anger in the implication. "Where did you go once everyone was let out of the library this evening?"

"To my room."

"What did you do there?"

"I showered and changed."

"And then?"

Davies-Jones' eyes made their way to the whisky. There was no noise at all save for a rustle from one of the others in the room, Macaskin fishing a roll of mints from his pocket. "I went to Helen."

"Again?" Lynley asked blandly.

His head snapped up. "What the hell are you suggesting?"

"I should guess that would be obvious enough. She's provided several rather good alibis for you, hasn't she? First last night and now this evening."

Davies-Jones stared at him incredulously before he laughed. "My God, that's absolutely unbelievable. Do you think Helen's stupid? Do you think she's so naïve that she'd allow a man to do that to her? And not once, but twice? In twenty-four hours? What kind of a woman do you think she is?"

"I know exactly the kind of woman Helen is," Lynley responded. "One absolutely vulnerable to a man who claims to be in possession of a weakness that only *she* can cure. And that's how you played it, isn't it? Right into her bed. If I bring her down here now, no doubt I'll discover that this evening in her room was just another variation on last night's tender theme."

"And by God, you can't bear the thought of that, can you? You're so sick with jealousy that you stopped seeing straight the moment you knew I'd slept with her. Face the facts, Inspector. Don't twist them about to pin something on me because you're too goddamned afraid to take me on in any other way."

Lynley moved sharply in his chair, but Macaskin and Havers were on their feet at once. That brought him to his senses. "Get him out of here," he said.

BARBARA HAVERS waited until Macaskin himself had ushered Davies-Jones from the room. She watched to ensure they were left in complete privacy before she cast a long, supplicating look in St. James' direction. He joined her at the table with Lynley, who had put on his reading spectacles and was looking through Barbara's notes. The room was taking on a more than lived-in look, with glasses, plates of half-eaten food, overfull ashtrays, and notebooks scattered about. The air smelled as if a contagion were alive in it.

"Sir."

Lynley raised his head and Barbara saw with a wrench that he looked awful, fagged out, drawn through a wringer of his own devising.

"Let's look at what we have," she suggested.

Over the top of his spectacles, Lynley's eyes went from Barbara to St. James. "We have a locked door," he replied reasonably. "We have Francesca Gerrard locking it with the only key available besides the one across the room on the dressing table. We have a man in the next room with a clear means of access. Now we're looking for a motive."

No, Barbara thought weakly. She kept her voice even and impartial. "You must admit that it's purely coincidental that Helen's room and Joy's room adjoined each other. He *couldn't* have known in advance about that."

"Couldn't he? A man with a self-professed interest in architecture? There are homes with adjoining rooms all over the country. It hardly takes a university degree to guess there would be two here. Or that Joy, after specifically requesting a room by Helen's, would be given one of them. I imagine no one else was phoning Francesca Gerrard with special requests of that nature."

Barbara refused to submit. "Francesca herself could have killed Joy as matters stand now, sir. She was in the room. She admits it. Or she could have given the key to her brother and let him do the job."

"It always comes back to Lord Stinhurst for you, doesn't it?"

"No, that's not it."

"And if you want to go with Stinhurst, what about Gowan's death? Why did Stinhurst kill him?"

"I'm not arguing that it's Stinhurst, sir," Barbara said, trying to hold on to her patience, her temper, and her need to shout out Stinhurst's motive until Lynley was forced to accept it. "For that matter, Irene Sinclair could have done it. Or Sydeham or Ellacourt, since they were both on their own. Or Jeremy Vinney. Joy was in his room earlier. Elizabeth told us as much. For all we know, he wanted Joy, got himself squarely rejected, went to her room and killed her in a fit of anger."

"And how did he lock the door when he left?"

"I don't know. Perhaps he went out the window."

"In a storm, Havers? You're stretching it more than I am." Lynley dropped her notes onto the table, removed his spectacles, rubbed his eyes.

"I see that Davies-Jones had access, Inspector. I see that he had opportunity, as well. But Joy Sinclair's play was to resurrect his career, wasn't it? And he had no way of knowing for certain whether the play was finished just because Stinhurst withdrew his support. Someone else well might have financed it. So it seems to me that he's the only person in the house with a solid motive for keeping the woman alive."

St. James spoke. "No. There's another, isn't there, if it comes to regenerating dying careers? Her sister, Irene."

"I DID WONDER when you would get to me."

Irene Sinclair stepped back from the door. She walked to her bed and sat down, her shoulders slumped. In deference to the lateness of the hour, she had changed into her nightclothes, and like the woman itself, her garments were restrained. Flat-heeled slippers, a navy flannel dressing gown under which the high neck of a white nightdress rose and fell with her steady breathing. There was something, however, oddly impersonal about her clothing. It was serviceable, indeed, yet adhering strictly to a norm of perceived propriety, it was exceedingly chilling, as if designed and worn to hold life itself at bay. Lynley wondered if the woman ever slopped round the house in old blue jeans and a tattered jersey. Somehow, he doubted it.

Her resemblance to her sister was remarkable. In spite of the fact that he had observed Joy only through the photographs of her death, Lynley could easily recognise in Irene those features she had shared with her sister, features unaffected by the five or six years that separated them in age: prominent cheekbones, broad brow, the slight squaring of jawline. She was, he guessed, somewhere in her early forties, a statuesque woman with the sort of body other women long for and most men dream of taking into their beds. She had a face that might have belonged to Medea and black hair in which the grey was beginning to streak back dramatically from the left peak of her forehead. Any other woman, remotely insecure, would have coloured it long ago. Lynley wondered if the thought had even crossed Irene's mind. He studied her wordlessly. Why on earth had Robert Gabriel ever found the need to stray?

"Someone has probably told you already that my sister and my husband had an affair last year, Inspector," she began, keeping her voice low. "It's no particular secret. So I don't mourn her death as I ought to, as I probably shall eventually. It's just that when your life's been torn apart by two people you love, it's difficult to forgive and forget. Joy didn't need Robert, you see. I did. But she took him anyway. And that still hurts when I think of it, even now."

"Was their affair over?" Lynley asked.

Irene's attention drifted from Havers' pencil to the floor. "Yes." The single word had the distinct flavour of a lie, and she continued at once, as if to hide this fact. "I even knew when it started between them. One of those dinner parties where people have too much to drink and say things they wouldn't otherwise say. That night Joy announced that she'd never had a man who'd been able to satisfy her in only one go. That, of course, was the sort of thing Robert would take as a personal challenge that had to be attended to without delay. Sometimes what hurts me the most is the fact that

Joy didn't love Robert. She never loved anyone at all after Alec Rintoul died."

"Rintoul's been a recurring theme this evening. Were they ever engaged?"

"Informally. Alec's death changed Joy."

"In what way?"

"How can I explain it?" she replied. "It was like a fire, a rampage. It was as if Joy decided that she would start living with a vengeance once Alec was gone. But not to enjoy herself. Rather, to destroy herself. And to take as many of us down with her as she could. It was a sickness with her. She went through men, one after another, Inspector. She devoured them. Rapaciously. Hatefully. As if no one could ever begin to make her forget Alec and she was daring each and every one of them to try."

Lynley walked to the bed, placed the contents from Joy's shoulder bag onto the counterpane. Irene considered the objects listlessly.

"Are these hers?" she asked.

He handed her Joy's engagement calendar first. Irene seemed reluctant to take it, as if she would come across knowledge within it that she would rather not possess. However, she identified what notations she could: appointments with a publisher in Upper Grosvenor Street, the birthday of Irene's daughter Sally, Joy's self-imposed deadline for having three chapters of a book done.

Lynley pointed out the name scrawled across one entire week. *P. Green.* "Someone new in her life?"

"Peter, Paul, Philip? I don't know, Inspector. She might have been going off on holiday with someone, but I couldn't say. We didn't speak to one another very often. And then, when we did, it was mostly business. She probably wouldn't have told me about a new man in her life. But it wouldn't surprise me at all to know that she had one. That would have been more than typical of her. Really." Disconsolately, Irene fingered one or two other items, the wallet, the matchbook, the chewing gum, the keys. She said nothing else.

Watching her, Lynley pressed the button on the small tape recorder. Irene shrank infinitesimally at the sound of her sister's voice. He let the machine play. Through the cheerful comments, through the vibrant excitement, through the future plans. He couldn't help thinking, as he listened to Joy Sinclair once again, that she didn't sound at all like a woman bent upon destroying anyone. Halfway through it, Irene raised a hand to her eyes. She bent her head.

"Does any of that mean anything to you?" Lynley asked.

Irene shook her head blindly, a passionate movement, a second patent lie.

Lynley waited. She seemed to be attempting to withdraw from him, moving further into herself both physically and emotionally. Shrivelling up through a concerted act of will. "You can't bury her this way, Irene," he said quietly. "I know that you want to. I understand why. But you know if you try it, she'll haunt you forever." He saw her fingers tighten against her skull. The nails caught at her flesh. "You don't have to forgive her for what she's done to you. But don't put yourself into a position of doing something for which you cannot forgive yourself."

"I *can't* help you." Irene's voice sounded distraught. "I'm not sorry my sister's dead. So how can I help you? I can't help myself."

"You can help by telling me anything about this tape." And ruthlessly, mercilessly, Lynley played it again, hating himself for doing so at the same time as he acknowledged it was part of the job, it had to be done. Still, at the end, there was no response from her. He rewound the tape, played it again. And then again.

Joy's voice was like a fourth person in the room. She coaxed. She laughed. She tormented. She pleaded. And she broke her sister the fifth time through the tape, on the words, "For God's sake, don't let Mum forget Sally again this year."

Irene snatched the recorder, shut it off with hands which fumbled on the buttons, and flung it back onto the bed as if touching it contaminated her.

"The *only* reason my mother ever remembered my daughter's birthday is because Joy reminded her," she cried. Her face bore the signs of anguish, but her eyes were dry. "And still I hated her! I hated my sister every minute and I wanted her to die! But not like this! Oh *God*, not like this! Have you any idea what it's like to want a person dead more than anything in the world and then to have it happen? As if a mocking deity listened to your wishes and only granted the foulest ones you possess?"

Good God, the power of simple words. He knew. Of course, he knew. In the timely death of his own mother's lover in Cornwall, in ways that Irene Sinclair could never hope to understand. "It sounds as if some of what she said was to be part of a new work. Do you recognise the place she's describing? The decaying vegetables, the sound of frogs and pumps, the flat land?"

"No."

"The circumstance of a winter storm?"

"No!"

"The man she mentions, John Darrow?"

Irene's hair swung out in an arc as she turned her head away. At the sudden movement, Lynley said, "John Darrow. You recognise the name."

"Last night at dinner. Joy talked about him. She said something about wining and dining a dreary man called John Darrow."

"A new man she's involved with?"

"No. No, I don't think so. Someone—I think it was Lady Stinhurst—had asked her about her new book. And John Darrow came up. Joy was laughing the way she always did, making light of the difficulties she's been having with the writing, saying something about information she needed and was trying to get. It involved this John Darrow. So I think he's connected with the book somehow."

"Book? Another play, you mean?"

Irene's face clouded. "Play? No, you've misunderstood, Inspector. Aside from an early play six years ago and the new piece for Lord Stinhurst, my sister didn't write for the theatre. She wrote books. She used to be a journalist, but then she took up documentary nonfiction. Her books are all about crimes. Real crimes. Murders, mostly. Didn't you know that?"

Murders mostly. Real crimes. Of course. Lynley stared at the little tape recorder, hardly daring to believe that the missing piece to the triangular puzzle of motive-means-opportunity would be given to him so easily. But there it was, what he had been seeking, what he had known instinctively he would find. A motive for murder. Still obscure, but merely waiting for the details to flesh it out into a coherent explanation. And the connection was there on the tape as well, in Joy Sinclair's very last words: ". . . ask Rhys how best to approach him. He's good with people."

Lynley began replacing Joy's belongings in the bag, feeling uplifted yet at the same time filled with a hard edge of anger at what had happened here last night, and at the price he was going to have to pay personally to see that justice was done.

At the door, with Havers already out in the corridor, he was stopped by Irene Sinclair's last words. She stood near the bed, backed by inoffensive wallpaper and surrounded by a suitable bedroom suite. A comfortable room, a room that took no risks, threw out no challenges, made no demands. She looked trapped within it.

"Those matches, Inspector," she said. "Joy didn't smoke."

*   *   *

MARGUERITE RINTOUL, Countess of Stinhurst, switched out the bedroom light. The gesture was not born of a desire to sleep, since she knew very well that sleep would be an impossibility for her. Rather, it was a last vestige of feminine vanity. Darkness hid the tracery of lines that had begun to network and crumple her skin. In it, she felt protected, no longer the plump matron whose once beautiful breasts now hung pendulous inches short of her waist; whose shiny brown hair was the product of weavings and dyes expertly orchestrated by the finest hairdresser in Knightsbridge; whose manicured hands with their softly buffed nails bore the spotting of age and caressed absolutely nothing any longer.

On the bedside table she placed her novel, laying it down so that its lurid cover lined up precisely with the delicate brass inlay etched against the rosewood. Even in the darkness, the book's title leered up at her. *Savage Summer Passion.* So pathetically obvious, she told herself. So useless as well.

She looked across the room to where her husband sat in an armchair by the window, given over to the night, to the weak starlight that filtered through the clouds, to the amorphous shapes and shadows upon the snow. Lord Stinhurst was fully clothed, as was she, sitting upon the bed, her back against the headboard, a wool blanket thrown across her legs. She was less than ten feet away from him, yet they were separated by a chasm of twenty-five years of secrecy and suppression. It was time to bring it to an end.

The thought of doing so was paralysing Lady Stinhurst. Every time she felt that the breath she was taking was the breath that would allow her to speak at last, her entire upbringing, her past, her social milieu rose in concert to strangle her. Nothing in her life had ever prepared her for a simple act of confrontation.

She knew that to speak to her husband now was to risk everything, to step into the unknown, to hazard coming up against the insurmountable wall of his decades of silence. Having tested these waters of communication periodically before, she knew how little might be gained from her efforts and how horribly her failure would sit upon her shoulders. Still, it was time.

She swung her legs over the side of the bed. A momentary dizziness took her by surprise when she stood, but it passed quickly enough. She padded across to the window, acutely aware of the deep cold in the room and the nasty tightness in her stomach. Her mouth tasted sour.

"Stuart." Lord Stinhurst did not move. His wife chose her words carefully. "You must talk to Elizabeth. You must tell her everything. You *must*."

"According to Joy, she already knows. As did Alec."

As always, those last three words fell heavily between them, like blows against Lady Stinhurst's heart. She could still see him so clearly—alive and sensitive and achingly young, meeting the terrifying end that was destined for Icarus. But burning, not melting, out of the sky. *We are not meant to outlive our children*, she thought. *Not Alec, not now.* She had loved her son, loved him instinctively and devotedly, but invoking his memory—like a raw wound in both of them that time had only caused to fester—had always been one of her husband's ways of putting an end to unpleasant conversations. And it had always worked. But not tonight.

"She knows about Geoffrey, yes. But she doesn't know it all. You see, she heard the argument that night. Stuart, Elizabeth heard the fighting." Lady Stinhurst stopped, seeking a response from him, seeking some kind of sign that would tell her it was safe to continue. He gave her nothing. She plunged on. "You spoke to Francesca this morning, didn't you? Did she tell you about her talk with Elizabeth last night? After the read-through?"

"No."

"Then I shall. Elizabeth saw you leave that night, Stuart. Alec and Joy saw you as well. They were all watching from a window upstairs." Lady Stinhurst felt her voice wavering. But she forced herself to continue. "You know how children are. They see part, hear part, and assume the rest. Darling. Francesca said that Elizabeth believes you killed Geoffrey. Apparently, she's thought that . . . since the night it happened."

Stinhurst made no reply. Nothing changed about him, not the even flow of his breathing, not his upright posture, not his steady gaze on the frozen grounds of Westerbrae. His wife tentatively put her fingers on his shoulder. He flinched. She dropped her hand.

"Please. Stuart." Lady Stinhurst hated herself for the tremor behind her words, but she couldn't stop them now. "You must tell her the truth. She's had twenty-five years of believing you're a murderer! You can't let it continue. My God, you can't do that!"

Stinhurst didn't look at her. His voice was low. "No."

She couldn't believe him. "You didn't kill your brother! You weren't even responsible! You did everything in your power—"

"How can I destroy the only warm memories Elizabeth has? She has so little, after all. For God's sake, at least let her keep that."

"At the expense of her love for you? No! I won't have it."

"You will." His voice was implacable, bearing the sort of unquestionable authority that Lady Stinhurst had never once disobeyed. For to disobey was to step out of the role she had been playing her entire life: daughter, wife, mother. And nothing else. As far as she knew, there was only a void beyond the narrow boundaries set up by those who governed her life. Her husband spoke again. "Go to bed. You're tired. You need to sleep."

As always, Lady Stinhurst did as she was told.

IT WAS PAST TWO in the morning when Inspector Macaskin finally left, with a promise to telephone with the postmortems and the forensic reports as soon as he could. Barbara Havers saw him out and returned to Lynley and St. James in the sitting room. They were at the table, with the items from Joy Sinclair's shoulder bag spread out before them. The tape recorder was playing yet another time, Joy's voice rising and falling with the broken messages that Barbara had long ago memorised. Hearing it now, she realised that the recording had begun to take on the quality of a recurring nightmare, and Lynley the quality of a man obsessed. His were not quantum leaps of intuition in which the misty image of crime-motive-perpetrator took recognisable shape. Rather, they bore the appearance of contrivance, of an attempt to find and assess guilt where only by the wildest stretching of the imagination could it possibly exist. For the first time in that endless harrowing day, Barbara began to feel uneasy. In the long months of their partnership, she had come to realise that, for all his exterior gloss and sophistication, for all his trappings of upper-class splendour that she so mightily despised, Lynley was still the finest DI she had ever worked with. Yet Barbara knew intuitively that the case he was building now was wrong, founded on sand. She sat down and reached restlessly for the book of matches from Joy Sinclair's bag, brooding upon it.

It bore a curious imprint, merely three words, *Wine's the Plough*, with the apostrophe an inverted pint glass spilling lager. Clever, Barbara thought, the sort of amusing memento one picks up, stuffs into a handbag, and forgets about. But she knew that it was only a matter of time before Lynley would grasp at the matchbook as another piece of evidence affirming Davies-Jones' guilt. For Irene Sinclair had said that her sister did not smoke. And all of them had seen that Davies-Jones did.

"We need physical evidence, Tommy," St. James was saying. "You know as well as I that all this is purest conjecture. Even Davies-

Jones' prints on the key can be explained away by the statement Helen gave us."

"I'm aware of that," Lynley replied. "But we'll have the forensic report from Strathclyde CID."

"Not for several days, at least."

Lynley went on as if the other man had not spoken. "I've no doubt that some piece of evidence will turn up. A hair, a fibre. You know as well as I how impossible it is to carry off a perfect crime."

"But even then, if Davies-Jones was in Joy's room earlier in the day—and from Gowan's report, he was—what have you gained by the presence of one of his hairs or a fibre from his coat? Besides, you know as well as I that the crime scene was contaminated by the removal of the body, and there's not a barrister in the country who won't know it as well. As far as I'm concerned, it comes back to motive again and again. The evidence is going to be too weak. Only a motive can give it strength."

"That's why I'm going to Hampstead tomorrow. I've a feeling that the pieces are lying there, ready to be put together in Joy Sinclair's flat."

Barbara heard this statement with disbelief. It was beyond consideration that they should leave so soon. "What about Gowan, sir? You've forgotten what he tried to tell us. He said he didn't see someone. And the only person he told me he saw last night was Rhys Davies-Jones. Don't you think that means he was trying to change his statement?"

"He didn't finish the sentence, Havers," Lynley replied. "He said two words, *didn't see*. Didn't see whom? Didn't see what? Davies-Jones? The cognac he was supposed to be carrying? He expected to see him with something in his hand because he came out of the library. He expected liquor. A book. But what if he only thought that's what he saw? What if he realised later that what he saw was something quite different, a murder weapon?"

"Or what if he didn't see Davies-Jones at all and that's what he was trying to tell us? What if he only saw someone else attempting to look like Davies-Jones, perhaps wearing his overcoat? It could have been anyone."

Lynley stood abruptly. "Why are you so determined to prove the man is innocent?"

From his sharp tone, Barbara knew what direction his thoughts were taking. But he wasn't the only one with a gauntlet to throw down. "Why are *you* so determined to prove that he's guilty?"

Lynley gathered Joy's belongings. "I'm looking for guilt, Havers.

It's my job. And I believe the guilt lies in Hampstead. Be ready by half past eight."

He started for the door. Barbara's eyes begged St. James to intercede in an area where she knew she could not go, where friendship had stronger ties than the logic and rules that govern a police investigation.

"Are you certain it's wise to go back to London tomorrow?" St. James asked slowly. "When you think of the inquest—"

Lynley turned in the doorway, his face caught by the cavern of shadows in the hall. "Havers and I can't give professional evidence here in Scotland. Macaskin will handle it. As for the rest of them, we'll collect their addresses. They're not about to leave the country when their livelihood's tied up on the London stage."

With that, he was gone. Barbara struggled to find her voice. "I think Webberly's going to have his head over this. Can't you stop him?"

"I can only try to reason with him, Barbara. But Tommy's no fool. His instincts are sound. If he feels he's onto something, we can only wait to see what he finds."

In spite of St. James' assurance, Barbara's mouth was dry. "Can Webberly sack him for this?"

"I suppose it depends on how it all turns out."

Something in his guarded statement told her everything she wanted to know. "You think he's wrong, don't you? You think it's Lord Stinhurst, too. God in heaven, what's wrong with him? What's happened to him, Simon?"

St. James picked up the bottle of whisky. "Helen," he said simply.

THE KEY in his hand, Lynley hesitated at Lady Helen's door. It was half past two. No doubt she would be asleep by now, his intrusion both disruptive and unwelcome. But he needed to see her. And he didn't lie to himself about the purpose of this visit. It had nothing to do with police work. He knocked once, unlocked the door and went in.

Lady Helen was on her feet, coming across the room, but she halted when she saw him. He closed the door. He said nothing at first, merely noting the details and striving to understand what they might imply.

Her bed was undisturbed, its yellow and white counterpane pulled up round the pillows. Her shoes, slim black pumps, were on the floor next to it. They were the only article of clothing that she had removed other than her jewellery: gold earrings, a thin chain, a delicate bracelet on the nightstand. This last object caught his eyes, and for a painful moment he considered how small her wrists were that such a piece could encircle them so easily. There was nothing else to see in the room, save a wardrobe, two chairs, and a dressing table in whose mirror they both were reflected, warily confronting one another like two mortal enemies come upon each other unexpectedly and without sufficient energy or will to do battle again.

Lynley walked past her to the window. The west wing of the house stretched into the darkness, scattered lights making bright slits against black where curtains were not fully drawn, where others waited, like Helen, for the morning. He closed the curtains.

"What are you doing?" Her voice was chary.

"It's far too cold in here, Helen." He touched the radiator, felt its ineffective tingle of warmth, and went to the door to speak to the young constable stationed at the top of the stairs. "Would you see if there's an electric fire somewhere?" Lynley asked him. When the man nodded, he shut the door again and faced her. The distance between them seemed enormous. Hostility thickened the air.

"Why have you locked me in here, Tommy? Do you expect me to hurt someone?"

"Of course not. Everyone's locked in. It'll be over in the morning."

There was a book on the floor next to one of the chairs. Lynley picked it up. It was a murder mystery, he saw, well thumbed through with typical, whimsical Helen-notations in the margins: arrows and exclamation points, underlinings and comments. She was always determined that no author would ever pull the wool over her eyes, convinced that she could solve any literary conundrum far sooner in its pages than could he. Because of this, he'd been the recipient of her discarded, dog-eared books for the better part of a decade. *Read this, Tommy darling. You shall never sort it out.*

At the memory's sudden force, he felt stricken with sorrow, desolate, utterly alone. And what he had come to say would only serve to make the situation worse between them. But he knew he had to speak to her, whatever the cost.

"Helen, I can't bear to see you do this to yourself. You're trying to replay St. James to a different ending. I don't want you to do it."

"I don't know what you're talking about. None of this has anything to do with Simon." Lady Helen remained where she was, across the room from him, as if to step in his direction were to surrender in some way. And she would never do that.

Lynley thought he saw a small bruise low on her neck where the collar of her teal blouse dipped towards the swell of her breasts. But when she moved her head, the bruise disappeared, a trick of light, a product of unhappy imagination.

"It does," he said. "Or haven't you noticed yet how very much like St. James he is? Even his alcoholism is St. James all over again with a simple difference in disability. Except that this time, you won't walk out on him, will you? You won't go gratefully when he tries to send you away."

Lady Helen's head turned from him. Her lips parted, then closed. He saw that she would allow him these moments of castigation, but she would offer no defence. His punishment would be never to know, never to understand completely what had drawn her to the Welshman, to be forced into guesswork that she would never affirm. He accepted this knowledge with rising anguish. Still, he wanted to touch her, feeling desperate for contact, for a moment of her warmth.

"I know you, Helen. And I understand how guilt feeds on itself. Who on earth could possibly understand that better than I? I crippled St. James. But you've always believed that your sin was worse, haven't you? Because inside, where you would never have to admit it, you were relieved all those years ago when he broke your engagement. Because then you would never have to face life with a man who could no longer do all those things that, at the time, seemed so absurdly important. Skiing, bathing at resorts, dancing, hiking, having a wonderful time."

"Damn you." Her voice was no more than a whisper. When she met his eyes, her face was white. It was a warning. He ignored it, compelled to go on.

"For ten years you've had yourself on the rack over leaving St. James. And now you see an opportunity to put it all right, to make up for everything: for letting him go off to Switzerland to convalesce alone, for letting yourself be driven off when he needed you; for shirking a marriage that appeared to have responsibilities far outweighing its pleasures. Davies-Jones is going to be your redemption, isn't he? You plan to make him whole again, just as you could have done—and didn't do—for St. James. And then you'll be able to forgive yourself at last. That's it, isn't it? That's how it's to be played."

"I think you've said enough," she said stiffly.

"I haven't." Lynley sought the words to break through to her; it was imperative that she understand. "Because he isn't like St. James at all beneath the surface. Please. Listen to me, Helen. Davies-Jones isn't a man you've known intimately, inside and out, since your eighteenth birthday. He's a relative stranger to you, someone you can't really know."

"A murderer, in other words?"

"Yes. If you will."

She flinched from the easiness of his admission, but her slender body drew strength from the passion of her reply. Muscles became tense across her face and neck, even—to his imagination—beneath the soft sleeves of her blouse.

"With me too blinded by love or remorse or guilt or whatever it is that prevents me from seeing what's so patently obvious to you?" She flung her hand sharply towards the doorway, to the house beyond it, to the room she had occupied and what had happened within it. "Exactly when did he set this murder in motion? He left the house after the read-through. He didn't get back till one."

"On his own report, yes."

"You're saying he lied to me, Tommy. But I *know* he didn't. I know he walks when he needs to drink. He told me that in London. I even walked with him out by the loch after he broke up the row between Joy Sinclair and Gabriel yesterday afternoon."

"And don't you see how clever that was, how all of that was to set you up to believe him when he said he'd been out walking again last night? He needed your compassion, Helen, if you were to allow him to stay in your room. And what better way to get it than to say he'd been out walking off his need to drink. He could hardly have gained your sympathy so effectively by hanging about after the read-through, could he?"

"Do you actually want me to believe that Rhys murdered his cousin while I was asleep, that he then came back into my room, and made love to me for a second time? It's completely absurd."

"Why?"

"Because I *know* him."

"You've been to bed with him, Helen. I think you'll agree that knowing a man is more complicated than falling into bed with him for a few steamy hours, no matter how pleasant they may have been."

Her dark eyes alone bore the wound made by his words. When she spoke again, it was with heavy irony. "You choose your words well. Congratulations. They do hurt."

Lynley felt his heart twist. "I don't want you to be hurt! God in heaven, can't you see that? Can't you see that I'm trying to keep you from harm? I'm sorry about what's happened. I'm sorry for the foul way I treated you earlier. But none of that goes any distance to change the facts of last night. Davies-Jones used you to gain access to her, Helen. He used you again after he saw to Gowan this evening. He plans to go on using you unless I can stop him. And I intend to stop him. Whether you help me or not."

She lifted her hand to her throat, clutched at the collar of her blouse. "Help you? My God, I think I'd rather die."

Her words and the bitterness of her tone struck Lynley like a blow. He might have answered but was spared the necessity by the police constable who had managed to find a single-bar electric fire to keep her warm through what remained of the night.

9

BARBARA HAVERS paused on the wide drive before going back into the house. Snow had fallen again during the night, but it was a light fall, insufficient to close roads but enough to make walking on the estate grounds wet, cold, and unpleasant. Nonetheless, after a foully sleepless night, she had risen shortly after dawn and had set out through the snow, determined to rid herself of the turmoil of mixed loyalties that were plaguing her.

Logic told Barbara that her primary responsibility was to New Scotland Yard. Adherence right now to procedures, to judges' rules, to Force regulations would add to the likelihood of her receiving a promotion the next time an inspector's position came open. After all, she had taken the examination only last month—she could swear for certain that she'd passed it this time—and the last four courses at the training centre had earned her the highest possible marks. So the time was right for advancement, or as nearly right as it was ever going to be, if she only played this entire affair wisely.

Thomas Lynley was what made everything so difficult. Barbara had spent practically every working hour over the last fifteen months in Lynley's presence, so she was not at all oblivious of the qualities that had made him a superb member of the Force, a man who had risen from constable to sergeant to detective inspector in his first five years. He was quick-witted and intuitive, gifted with both compassion and humour, a man liked by his colleagues and well trusted by Superintendent Webberly. Barbara knew how lucky she was to be working with Lynley, knew how deserving he was of her absolute faith. He put up with her moods, stoically listened to her ravings even when her most virulent attacks were directed against him, still encouraged her to think freely, to offer her own opinions, to disagree openly. He was unlike any other officer she had ever known, and she owed him personal debts that went far beyond her having been returned to CID from her demotion to uniformed patrol fifteen months back.

So now she had to decide where her true loyalties lay, to Lynley or to advancement in her career. For in her forced hike through the woods this morning, she had inadvertently come upon a piece of information that bore the unmistakable stamp of being part of the puzzle. And she had to decide what to do with it. More, no matter what she decided, she had to understand exactly what it meant.

The air was stinging in its icy purity. Barbara felt its sharp stab in her nose and throat, in her ears and against her eyes. Yet she breathed it in deeply five or six times, squinting against the brilliant purity of sunlit snow, before she trudged across the drive, stamped her feet roughly against the stone steps, and walked into the great hall of Westerbrae.

It was nearly eight. There was movement in the house, footsteps in the upper corridor and the sound of keys turning in locks upstairs. A smell of bacon and the rich perfume of coffee gave normality to the morning—as if the events of the past thirty-two hours had only been part of an extended nightmare—and the low murmur of pleasant voices came from the drawing room. Barbara walked in to find Lady Helen and St. James sitting in a soft pool of sunlight at the east end of the room, sharing coffee and conversation. They were alone. As Barbara watched them together, St. James shook his head, reached out and rested his hand for a moment upon Lady Helen's shoulder. It was a gesture of infinite gentleness, of understanding, the wordless binding of a friendship that made the two of them together stronger and more viable than either one could ever be alone.

Seeing them, Barbara was struck by the thought of how easy it was to make a decision when she considered it in the light of friendship. Indeed, between Lynley and her career there was no choice at all. She had no real career without him. She crossed the room to join them.

Both looked as if they, too, had experienced a restless night. The lines on St. James' face were more sharply defined than usual, and Lady Helen's fine skin had a fragile look about it, like a gardenia that would bruise at the slightest touch. When St. James automatically began to rise in greeting, Barbara waved the social nicety to one side.

"Can you come outside with me?" she asked them. "I've found something in the woods that I think you ought to see." St. James' face registered the impossibility of his being able to navigate the snow drifts, and Barbara hastily sought to reassure him. "There's a brick walk for part of the way. And I've flattened enough of a path in the forest itself, I think. It's only about sixty yards into the trees."

"What it is?" Lady Helen asked.

"A grave," Barbara replied.

THE FOREST had been planted to the south of a pathway that circled the great house. It was not the sort of woodland that would have sprung up naturally in this moor-filled area of Scotland. There were English and sessile oaks, beeches, walnuts, and sycamores mixed in with pines. A narrow path led through them, marked out by small circles of yellow paint that had been dotted onto the trunks of the trees.

The forest was a place of that unearthly kind of silence that comes from the heavy insulation of snow upon tree branches and ground. No wind moved, and although the raw burst of an automobile engine pierced the stillness momentarily, it died off quickly, leaving in its wake only the restless lapping of water in the loch some twenty yards down the slope to their left. The going was not easy, for even though Sergeant Havers had indeed flattened a primitive path through the woods, the snow was deep and the ground irregular, no place for a man who had difficulty enough on a surface that was flat and dry.

It took fifteen minutes to make a four-minute walk, and, in spite of Lady Helen's supportive arm, St. James was damp-faced from exertion when Havers finally led them off the main path onto a smaller branch that rose gently through a copse towards a knoll. During the summer, heavy foliage would probably have hidden both the knoll and the little track from the view of anyone on the main path from the house. But in the winter, hydrangeas that otherwise would have been vibrant with clusters of pink and blue flowers, and walnuts that would have created a verdant screen of protection, were bare, giving anyone free access to the plot of ground at the knoll's top. It was an area about twenty-five feet square, bounded by an iron fence. White powder dusted this, hiding the fact that long ago the fence had surrendered to rust.

Lady Helen was the first to speak. "What on earth is a graveyard doing here? Is there a church nearby?"

Havers indicated the direction the main path took towards the south. "There's a locked chapel and a family vault not too much further along. And an old pier on the loch just below it. It looks like they've boated their way to burials."

"Like the Vikings," St. James said absently. "What have we here, Barbara?" He pushed open the gate, wincing at the shriek of its unoiled metal. There was one set of footsteps in the snow already.

"I had a look," Havers explained. "I'd already gone along to the family chapel and had a look there. So when I saw this on my way back, I was curious. See for yourself. Tell me what you think."

While Havers waited at the gate, St. James and Lady Helen crunched through the snow to the single gravestone that rose from it like a solitary grey augury, scratched by a bare elm branch that drooped heavily onto its top. It was not a terribly old stone, certainly not as old as those found in tumbling graveyards throughout the country. Yet it was very much abandoned, for the black residue of lichen ate at the meagre carving and St. James guessed that in midsummer, the yard itself would be wildly overgrown with cow parsley and weeds. Nonetheless, the words upon the stone were legible, only partially effaced by weather and neglect.

Geoffrey Rintoul, Viscount Corleagh
1914–1963

Quietly, they studied the lonely grave. A dense chunk of snow fell from a branch above it and disintegrated on the stone.

"Is that Lord Stinhurst's older brother?" Lady Helen asked.

"It looks that way," Havers replied. "Curious, wouldn't you say?"

"Why?" St. James' eyes swept across the plot, looking for other graves. There were none.

"Because the family home's in Somerset, isn't it?" Havers replied.

"It is." St. James knew that Havers was watching him, knew that she was attempting to gauge how much Lynley had told him of his private conversation with Lord Stinhurst. He tried to sound completely detached.

"So what's Geoffrey doing buried here? Why isn't he in Somerset?"

"I believe he died here," St. James replied.

"You know as well as I that nobs like these bury their own in family plots, Simon. Why wasn't this particular body taken home?

Or," she queried before he could answer, "if you're going to say that it wasn't possible for them to take the body home, then why wasn't he buried in the Gerrard family plot just a few hundred yards further down the path?"

St. James chose his words with care. "Perhaps this was a favourite spot of his, Barbara. It's peaceful, no doubt quite beautiful in the summer with the loch just below it. I can't think that it means all that much."

"Not even when you consider that this man, Geoffrey Rintoul, was Stinhurst's older brother, and the *rightful* Lord Stinhurst in the first place?"

St. James' eyebrows raised quizzically. "You're not suggesting that Lord Stinhurst murdered his brother in order to gain the title? Because if that's the case, wouldn't it make a lot more sense, if he wished to cover up a murder, to take his brother home and bury him with attendant pomp and circumstance in Somerset?"

Lady Helen had been listening to their exchange quietly, but she spoke at the mention of burials. "There's something not quite right here, Simon. Francesca Gerrard's husband—Phillip Gerrard—isn't buried in the family plot either. He's on a small island in the loch, just a bit off shore. I saw the island from my window right after my arrival, and when I commented upon it to Mary Agnes—it has a curious tomb on it that looks like a folly—she told me all about it. According to Mary Agnes, that's where Francesca's husband, Phillip, insisted upon being buried. *Insisted*, Simon. It was in the terms of his will. I should guess it's a bit of local colour because Gowan told me the exact same thing when he brought up my luggage not fifteen minutes later."

"There you have it," Havers put in. "Something awfully strange is going on with these two families. And you certainly can't argue that *this* is a Rintoul family graveyard here. Not without any other graves. Besides, the Rintouls aren't even Scots! Why would they bury one of their family here unless—"

"They had to," Lady Helen murmured.

"Or wanted to," Havers finished triumphantly. She crossed the little yard and stood in front of St. James. "Inspector Lynley's told you about his interrogation of Lord Stinhurst, hasn't he? He's told you everything Stinhurst said. What's going on?"

For a moment, St. James considered lying to Havers. He also considered telling her the brutal truth: that what Lynley had told him had been said in confidence and was none of her business. But he had a sense that she had not brought them out on this trek as an exercise in attempting to affix blame for the last two days' deaths upon Stuart Rintoul, Lord Stinhurst. She could have done that easily enough by insisting that Lynley himself be the one to look at this solitary grave, by arguing its peculiarity with him. The fact that Havers had not done so suggested one of two things to St. James. Either she was collecting her own evidence in an attempt to aggrandise herself and denigrate Lynley in front of their superiors at Scotland Yard, or she was seeking his own help to prevent Lynley from making a colossal mistake.

Havers turned her back on him, walking away. "It's all right. I ought not to have asked that. You're his friend, Simon. Of course he'd talk to you." She pulled her woollen cap down roughly so that it covered her forehead and ears, looking cheerlessly down at the loch.

Watching her, St. James decided that she deserved the truth. She deserved the tribute of someone's trust and the opportunity to prove herself worthy of it. He told her Lord Stinhurst's story as Lynley had related it to him.

Havers listened, doing nothing more than tugging at one or two dead weeds along the fence while St. James spun out the twisted tale of love and betrayal that had ended with Geoffrey Rintoul's death. Her eyes, narrowed against the gleam of sunlight on the snow, rested on the tombstone nearby. When St. James was done, she asked only one question.

"Do you believe it?"

"I can't think why a man in Lord Stinhurst's position would defame his own wife to anyone. Even," this as Havers was about to speak, "to save his own skin."

"Too noble for that?" Her tone was cutting.

"Not at all. Too proud."

"Then if, as you say, it's a matter of pride, a matter of appearances, wouldn't he have kept up appearances one hundred percent?"

"What do you mean?"

Lady Helen spoke. "If Lord Stinhurst wanted to pretend that *everything* was status quo, Simon, wouldn't he have taken Geoffrey home for burial in Somerset in addition to keeping his marriage alive all these years? As a matter of fact, it seems that taking his brother home would have been—in the long run—far less painful than staying married for the next thirty-six years to a woman who had made a fool of him with his own brother."

There was clear-eyed sense in that, typical of Helen. St. James had to admit it to himself even if he didn't say it aloud. But evidently he would not have to. For Sergeant Havers appeared to read it in his face.

"Please. Help me get to the bottom of the Rintoul family," she said desperately. "Simon, I swear that Stinhurst has something to bury. And I think Inspector Lynley's been given the shovel to see to it himself. Perhaps by the Yard. I don't know."

St. James hesitated, thinking about the difficulties he would be creating for himself—poised precariously between Lynley's trust and Havers' unwavering belief in Stinhurst's guilt—if he agreed to help her. "It won't be easy. If Tommy finds out you've gone your own way on this, Barbara, there'll be hell to pay. Insubordination."

"You'll be finished in CID," Lady Helen added quietly. "You'll be back on the street."

"Don't you think I know that?" Havers' face, though pale, was resolute and unflinching. "And who's going to be finished if there *is* a cover-up being generated? And if it comes to light through the efforts of some reporter—someone like Jeremy Vinney, by God—sniffing it out on his own? At least this way, if I'm involved in looking into Stinhurst, the inspector's protected. For all anyone will know, he's ordered me to do it."

"You care for Tommy, don't you?"

Havers looked away at once from Lady Helen's sudden query. "Most of the time I hate the miserable fop," she replied. "But if he's given the sack, it's not going to be over some berk like Stinhurst."

St. James smiled at the ferocity of her reply. "I'll help you," he said. "For what it's worth."

ALTHOUGH the broad walnut sideboard bore a heavy burden of chafing dishes, all exuding a variety of breakfast odours from kippers to eggs, the dining room held only one occupant when Lynley entered. Elizabeth Rintoul's back was to the door and, apparently indifferent to the sound of his footsteps, she did not turn her head to see who was joining her for the meal. Rather, she toyed a fork against the single sausage on her plate, rolling it back and forth, her eyes making a study of the shiny trail of grease it left, snail-like, in its wake. Lynley joined her, carrying a cup of black coffee and a single slice of cold toast.

She was, he presumed, dressed for the journey back to London with her parents. But like her garments of last evening, her black skirt and grey jumper were overlarge, and although she wore black tights to match them, a small ladder in the ankle promised to lengthen as the day drew on. Over the back of her chair was draped a curious full-length cape, midnight blue in colour, a sort of Sarah Woodruff garment that one might wear for striking dramatic poses on the Cobb. It certainly didn't seem to fit in with the general scheme of Elizabeth's personality.

That she wasn't eager to spend any time with Lynley became evident the moment he sat down across from her. Stoney-faced, she pushed back her chair and began to rise.

"I've been given to understand that Joy Sinclair was engaged to your brother Alec at one time," Lynley observed as if she'd made no movement.

Her eyes didn't shift from her plate. She settled back down and began cutting the sausage into wafer-thin slices, eating none of them. Her hands were extraordinarily large, even for a woman of her height, and their knuckles were knobby and unattractive. Deep scratches covered them, Lynley noted. Several days old.

"Cats." Elizabeth's voice was a shade less than surly. Lynley chose not to reply to the evasive monosyllable, so she went on by saying, "You're looking at my hands. The scratches are from my cats. They don't much like it when one breaks up their copulating. But there are some activities that I frankly prefer not go on on my bed."

It was a double-edged remark, telling in its inadvertent admission. Lynley wondered what an analyst would make of it.

"Did you want Joy to marry your brother?"

"It hardly matters now, does it? Alec's been dead for years."

"How did she come to meet him?"

"Joy and I were at school together. She came home with me for half-terms occasionally. Alec was there."

"And they got on?"

At this, Elizabeth raised her head. Lynley marvelled that a woman's face could be so completely devoid of expression. It looked like an inexpertly painted mask. "Joy got on with all men, Inspector. It was her special gift. My brother was just one of a long line of her suitors."

"Yet I've the impression she took him far more seriously than the others."

"Of course. Why not? Alec professed his love often enough to sound like a perfect sap at the same time as he massaged her ego. And how many of the others could offer her the promise of being Countess of Stinhurst once Daddy popped off?" Elizabeth began arranging the pieces of her sausage into a pattern on her plate.

"Did her relationship with your brother put a strain on your friendship?"

A breath of laughter shot through her nose like a gust of angry wind. "Our friendship was defined by Alec, Inspector. Once he died, I served no further purpose in Joy Sinclair's life. I saw her only once after Alec's memorial service, in fact. Then she disappeared without a second thought."

"Until this weekend."

"Yes. Until this weekend. That's the kind of friends we were."

"Is it your habit to travel with your parents on a theatrical outing such as this?"

"Not at all. But I'm fond of my aunt. It was a chance to see her. So I came." An unpleasant smile played round Elizabeth's mouth, quivered at her nostrils, and disappeared. "Of course, there was also Mummy's plan for my lusty liaison with Jeremy Vinney. And I couldn't disappoint her when she was depending so much upon this being the weekend that my rose was finally plucked, if that's not too much of a metaphor for you."

Lynley ignored the implication. "Vinney's known your family long," he concluded.

"Long? He's known Daddy forever, on both sides of the footlights. Years ago in the regionals, he fancied himself the next Olivier, but Daddy set him straight. So Vinney moved on to drama criticism, where he's been ever since, happily getting his jollies by trashing as many productions in a year as he can. But this new play . . . well, it was something close to my father's heart. The Agincourt re-opening and all. So I suppose my parents wanted me to be here to ensure good reviews. You know what I mean, just in case Vinney decided to respond to a . . . shall we say, less than delectable bribe?" She swept a hand rudely down the length of her body. "Myself in exchange for a favourable commentary in *The Times*. It would meet the needs of both my parents, don't you see? My mother's desire to have me properly serviced at last. My father's desire to take London in triumph."

She had deliberately returned to her prior theme in spite of Lynley's offer to turn the tide of conversation. Cooperatively, he took up her thought.

"Is that why you went to Jeremy Vinney's room the night Joy died?"

Elizabeth's head shot up at that. "Of course not! Smarmy little man with fingers like hairy sausages." She stabbed her fork at her plate. "As far as I was concerned, Joy could have the little beast. I think he's pathetic, rubbing up to theatre people in the hope that hanging about might give him the talent he lacked to make it on the stage years ago. *Pathetic!*" The sudden burst of passion seemed to disconcert her. As if to negate it, she shifted her eyes and said, "Well, perhaps that's why Mummy considered him such a suitable candidate for me. Two little blobs of pathos, drifting into the sunset together. God, what a romantic thought."

"But you went to his room—"

"I was looking for Joy. Because of Aunt Francie and her bloody pearls. Although now I think about it, Mummy and Aunt Francie probably had the entire scene planned out in advance. Joy would rush off to her room, salivating over her new acquisition, leaving me alone with Vinney. No doubt Mummy had already been in his room with flower petals and holy water, and all that was left was the act itself. What a pity. All that effort she went to, only to have it wasted on Joy."

"You seem fairly certain about what was going on between them in Vinney's room. I do wonder about that. Did you see Joy? Are you certain she was with him? Are you sure it wasn't somebody else?"

"I . . ." Elizabeth stopped. She toyed jerkily with knife and fork. "Of *course* it was Joy. I heard them, didn't I?"

"But you didn't see her?"

"I heard her voice!"

"Whispering? Murmuring? It was late. She'd have kept it low, wouldn't she?"

"It was Joy! Who else could it have been? And what else would be going on between them after midnight, Inspector? Poetry readings? Believe me, if Joy went to a man's room, it was with only one thing on her mind. I *know* it."

"She did that with Alec when she visited at your home?"

Elizabeth's mouth shut, tightened. She went back to her plate.

"Tell me what you did when you left the read-through the other night," Lynley said.

She moved the sliced sausage into a neat little triangle. Then with the knife, she began cutting the circular pieces in half. Each slice was sparely made and carried out with acute concentration. It was a moment before she replied. "I went to my aunt. She was upset. I wanted to help."

"You're fond of her."

"You seem surprised, Inspector. As if it's a miracle of sorts that I could be fond of anything. Is that right?" In the face of his refusal to rise to her taunting, she put down knife and fork, pushed her chair fully back, and regarded him straightforwardly. "I took Aunt Francie to her room. I put a compress on her head. We talked."

"About?"

Elizabeth smiled one last time, but it was, inexplicably, a reaction that seemed to mix both amusement and the knowledge of having bested an opponent. "*The Wind in the Willows*, if you really must know," she said. "You're familiar with the story, aren't you? The toad. The badger. The rat. And the mole." She stood, reached for her cape, and swung it round her shoulders. "Now if there's nothing more, Inspector, I've things to see to this morning."

That said, she left him. Lynley heard her bark of laughter echo in the hall.

IRENE SINCLAIR had herself just heard the news when Robert Gabriel found her in what Francesca Gerrard optimistically labelled her games room. Behind the last door in the lower northeast corridor, almost obscured behind a pile of disused outdoor garments, the room was completely isolated, and once inside, Irene welcomed its smell of mildew and wood rot and the pervasive congestion of dust and grime. Obviously, the renovation of the house had not reached this far corner yet. Irene found herself glad of it.

An old billiard table sat in the centre of the room, its baize covering loosely rippled, the netting under most of the pockets either torn or missing altogether. There were cue sticks on a rack on the wall, and Irene fingered these absently as she made her way to the window. No curtains covered it, a condition that contributed to the numbing want of heat. Since she wore no coat, she held her body tightly and rubbed her hands along her arms, pressing hard against the wool sleeves of her dress, feeling the answering friction like a kind of pain.

From the window there was little to see, just a grove of winterbare alders beyond which the slate top of a boathouse seemed to be sprouting from a hillock like a triangular excrescence. It was an optical illusion, fabricated from the angle of the window and the height of the hill. Irene considered this idea, brooding over the continuing place that illusions seemed to be making in her life.

"God in heaven, Renie. I've been looking for you everywhere. What are you doing in here?" Robert Gabriel crossed the room to her. He had come in noiselessly, managing to shut the warped door without a sound. He was carrying his overcoat and said in explanation of it, "I was just about to go outside and start a search." He dropped the coat on her shoulders.

It was a meaningless enough gesture, yet Irene still felt a distinct aversion to his touch. He was so near that she could smell the cologne he wore and the last vestige of coffee fighting with toothpaste upon his breath. It made her feel ill.

If Gabriel noticed, he gave no sign. "They're letting us leave. Have they made an arrest? Do you know?"

She couldn't bring herself to look at him. "No. No arrest. Not yet."

"Of course, we're to be available for the inquest. God, what a dashed inconvenience it is to have to run back and forth from London. But at least it's better than having to stay in this ice pit. The hot water's entirely gone, you know. And little hope of having repairs done on that old boiler for at least three days. That's taking roughing it to the limit, isn't it?"

"I heard you," she said. Her voice was a whisper, small and despairing. She felt him looking at her.

"Heard?"

"I *heard* you, Robert. I heard you with her the other night."

"Irene, what are you—"

"Oh, you needn't worry that I've told the police. I wouldn't do that, would I? But that's why you've come looking for me, I dare say. To make sure my pride ensures my silence."

"No! I don't even know what you're talking about. I'm here because I want to take you back to London. I don't want you to be going off on your own. There's no telling—"

"Here's the most amusing part," Irene interrupted acidly. "I'd actually come looking for you. God help me, Robert, I think I was ready to have you back. I'd even—" To her shame, her voice broke and she moved away from him as if by that she would regain her self-control. "I'd even brought you a picture of our James. Did you know he was Mercutio at school this year? I had two photographs made, one of James and one of you in a double frame. Remember that photo of you as Mercutio all those years ago? Of course, you don't look very much alike because James has my colouring, but all the same I thought you'd want to have the pictures. Mostly because of James. No, I'm lying to myself. And I swore last night that I'd stop it. I wanted to bring you the pictures because I hated you and I loved you and just for a moment the other night when you and I were together in the library, I *thought* there was a chance. . . ."

"Renie, for the love of God—"

"No! I heard you! It was Hampstead all over again! Exactly! And they say that life doesn't repeat itself, don't they? What a filthy laugh! All I needed to do was open the door to find you a second time having my sister. Just as I did last year, with the only difference being that I was alone this time. At least our children would have been spared a second go at the sight of their father sweating and panting and moaning over their lovely aunt Joy."

"It isn't—"

"What I think?" Irene felt her face quiver with encroaching tears. Their presence angered her—that he should *still* be able to reduce her to this. "I don't want to hear it, Robert. No more clever lies. No more, 'It only happened once.' No more anything."

He grabbed her arm. "Do you think I killed your sister?" His face looked ill, perhaps from lack of sleep, perhaps from guilt.

She laughed hoarsely, shaking him off. "Killed her? No, that's not at all your style. Dead, Joy was absolutely no good to you, was she? After all, you aren't the least bit interested in screwing a corpse."

"That didn't happen!"

"Then what did I hear?"

"I don't know what you heard! I don't know *who* you heard! Anyone could have been with her."

"In *your* room?" she demanded.

His eyes widened in panic. "In *my* . . . Renie, good God, it's not what you think!"

She flung his coat off her shoulders. Dust leaped from the floor when it dropped. "It's worse than knowing you've always been a filthy liar, Robert. Because now I realise that *I've* become one. God help me. I used to think that if Joy died I'd be free of the pain. Now I believe I'll only be free of it when you're dead as well."

"How can you say that? Is that what you really want?"

She smiled bitterly. "With all my heart. God, *God!* With all my heart!"

He stepped away from her, away from the coat on the floor between them. His face was ashen. "So be it, love," he whispered.

LYNLEY FOUND Jeremy Vinney outside on the drive, stowing his suitcase into the boot of a hired Morris. Vinney was muffled against the cold in coat, gloves, and scarf; his breath steamed the air. His high domed forehead gleamed pinkly where the sun struck it and he looked, surprisingly, as if he were perspiring. He was also, Lynley noted, the first to leave. A decidedly strange reaction in a newspaperman. Lynley crossed the drive to him, his footsteps grating against the gravel and ice. Vinney looked up.

"Making an early start of it," Lynley remarked.

The journalist nodded towards the house where dark early morning shadows were painted like ink along the stone walls. "Not really a spot for lingering, is it?" He slammed the boot lid home and checked to see that it was securely locked. Fumbling a bit with his keys, he dropped them and cleared his throat raspily as he bent to retrieve them in their worn leather case. When he finally looked at Lynley, it was to reveal a face upon which grief played subtly, the way it often does when an initial shock has been lived through and the immensity of a loss begins to be measured against the endlessness of time.

"Somehow," Lynley said, "I should think a journalist would be the last to leave."

At this, Vinney gave an abrupt, little laugh. It seemed self-directed, punitive, and unkind. "Hot after a story at the scene of the crime? Looking for a good ten inches of space on page one? Not to mention a byline and a knighthood for having solved the crime single-handedly? Is that how you see it, Inspector?"

Lynley answered the question by asking one. "Why were you actually here this weekend, Mr. Vinney? Every other presence can be accounted for in one way or another. But you remain a bit of a mystery. Can you shed some light on it for me?"

"Didn't you get a good enough picture from our attractive Elizabeth last evening? I was wild to get Joy in bed. Or better yet, I was picking her brains for material to bolster my career. Choose either one."

"Frankly, I'd prefer the reality."

Vinney swallowed. He seemed discomfited, as if he expected something other than equanimity from the police. Bellicose insistence upon the truth, perhaps, or a finger stabbed provocatively into his chest. "She was my friend, Inspector. Probably my best friend. Sometimes I think my only friend. And now she's gone." His eyes looked burnt out as he turned them towards the untroubled surface of the loch in the distance. "But people don't understand that kind of friendship between a man and a woman, do they? They want to make something of it. They want to cheapen it up."

Lynley was not untouched by the man's distress. He noticed, however, that Vinney had sidestepped his question. "Was Joy the one who actually arranged for you to be here? I know you did the

phoning to Stinhurst, but did she smooth the way? Was it her idea?"
When Vinney nodded, he asked, "Why?"

"She said she was worried about how Stinhurst and the actors
would receive the revisions she'd made to the play. She wanted a
friend along, she said, for moral support should things not go her
way. I'd been following the Agincourt renovation for months. It
seemed reasonable that I might ask to be included in the setting-up
of the play for its opening. So I came. To support her, as she asked.
But I didn't support her at all in the end, did I? She may as well have
been here alone."

"I saw your name in her engagement book."

"I shouldn't be surprised. We met for lunch regularly. We've done
so for years."

"At these meetings, did she tell you anything about this weekend? What it would be like? What to expect?"

"Just that it was a read-through and that I might find it an
interesting story."

"The play itself?"

Vinney didn't answer at first. His vision appeared fixed on
nothing. When he replied, however, his voice sounded thoughtful,
as if he'd been struck by an idea unconsidered before. "Joy said she
wanted me to think about writing an early article on the play. It
would be a piece about the stars, the plot, perhaps the format she
was using. Coming here would give me an idea about how the play
would be staged. But I . . . I could easily have got that information
in London, couldn't I? We see . . . saw . . . each other often enough.
So could she . . . could she have been worried that something like
this might happen to her, Inspector? Good God, could she have
hoped I'd see to it that the truth were told?"

Lynley commented upon neither the man's apparent belief in
the inability of the police to ferret out the truth nor the egotistical
likelihood of a single journalist's being able to do it for them.
Nonetheless, he catalogued the fact that Vinney's remark was aston-
ishingly close to Lord Stinhurst's own assessment of the columnist's
presence.

"Are you saying she was concerned about her safety?"

"She didn't say that," Vinney admitted honestly. "And she didn't
act concerned."

"Why was she in your room the other night?"

"She said she was too keyed up to sleep. She'd had it out with
Stinhurst and went to her room. But she felt restless, so she came
to mine. To talk."

"What time was this?"

"A bit after midnight. Perhaps a quarter past."

"What did she talk about?"

"The play at first. How she was bound and determined to see to it that it was produced, with or without Stinhurst. And then about Alec Rintoul. And Robert Gabriel. And Irene. She felt rotten about everything that had happened to Irene, you know. She . . . she was desperate for her sister to get back with Gabriel. That's why she wanted Irene in the play. She thought if the two of them were thrown together enough, nature would take its course. She said she wanted Irene's forgiveness and knew she couldn't have it. But more than that, I think she wanted to forgive herself. And she couldn't do that as long as Gabriel and her sister were apart."

It was a glib enough recital, seemingly straightforward. Yet Lynley's instincts told him there was more to be said about Joy's nocturnal visit to Vinney's room.

"You make her sound rather saintly."

Vinney shook his head in denial. "She wasn't a saint. But she was a decent friend."

"What time did Elizabeth Rintoul come to your room with the necklace?"

Vinney brushed the snow from the Morris' roof before answering. "Not long after Joy came in. I . . . Joy didn't want to talk to her. She expected it would be another row about the play. So I kept Elizabeth out. I only opened the door a crack; she couldn't see inside. So when I wouldn't invite her in, of course she assumed Joy was in my bed. That's fairly typical of her. Elizabeth can't conceive that members of the opposite sex might just be friends. With her, a conversation with a man is an access route to some sort of sexual encounter. It's rather sad, I think."

"When did Joy leave your room?"

"Shortly before one."

"Did anyone see her leave?"

"There was no one about. I don't think anyone saw her, unless Elizabeth was peering out her door somehow. Or maybe Gabriel. My room was between both of theirs."

"Did you see Joy to her room?"

"No. Why?"

"Then she might not have gone there at once. If, as you said, she thought she wouldn't be able to sleep."

"Where else would she go?" Understanding swept across his face.

"To meet someone? No. She wasn't interested in any of these people."

"If, as you say, Joy Sinclair was merely your friend, how can you be certain that she didn't share something more than friendship with someone else? With one of the other men here this weekend. Or one of the women, perhaps."

At the second suggestion, Vinney's face clouded. He blinked and looked away. "There were no lies between us, Inspector. She knew everything. I knew everything. Surely she would have told me if . . ." He stopped, sighing, rubbing the back of his gloved hand wearily across his forehead. "May I be off? What else is there to say? Joy was my friend. And now she's dead." Vinney spoke as if there were a connection between the last two ideas.

Lynley couldn't help wondering if there was. Curious about the man and his relationship with Joy Sinclair, he chose another subject.

"What can you tell me about a man called John Darrow?"

Vinney dropped his hand. "Darrow?" he repeated blankly. "Nothing. Should I know who he is?"

"Joy did. Evidently. Irene said she even mentioned him at dinner, perhaps in reference to her new book. What can you tell me about it?" Lynley watched Vinney's face, waiting to see a flicker of recognition from the man with whom Joy had ostensibly shared everything.

"Nothing." He appeared embarrassed about this apparent contradiction in what he had previously said. "She didn't talk about her work. There was nothing."

"I see." Lynley nodded thoughtfully. The other man shifted his weight back and forth on his feet. He played his keys from one hand to the other. "Joy carried a tape recorder in her shoulder bag. Did you know?"

"She used it whenever a thought struck her. I knew that."

"She made reference to you on it, asking herself why she was in such a lather over you. Why might she have said that?"

"In a lather over *me!*" His voice rose incredulously.

" 'Jeremy. Jeremy. Oh Lord, why be in such a lather over him? It's hardly a lifetime proposition.' Those were her words. Can you shed light on them?"

Vinney's face was tranquil enough, but the unrest in his eyes betrayed him. "No. I can't. I can't think what she meant. We didn't have that sort of friendship. At least not on my side. Not at all."

Six denials. Lynley knew his man well enough to discern the fact that his last remarks had deliberately misdirected the conversation.

Vinney wasn't a good liar. But he was skilled in seizing the moment and using it cleverly. He'd just done so. But why?

"I won't keep you any longer, Mr. Vinney," Lynley concluded. "No doubt you're anxious to get back to London."

Vinney looked as if he wanted to say more, but instead he got into the Morris and switched on its ignition. At first the car made that rolling sound that comes from an engine unwilling to start. But then it coughed and fired into life, releasing exhaust fumes dyspeptically. Vinney cranked down the window while the front wipers worked to free the windscreen of snow.

"She was my friend, Inspector. Just that. Nothing more." He reversed the car. The tyres spun fiercely on a patch of ice before gaining hold on the gravel. He shot down the drive towards the road.

Lynley watched Vinney's departure, intrigued by the man's compulsion to repeat that last remark, as if it contained an underlying meaning that a detective's close scrutiny would instantly reveal. For some reason—perhaps because of the distant presence of Inverness—it took him back to Eton and a fifth form's passionate debate over the obsessions and compulsions evidenced by Macbeth, that pricking of conscience spurring his tormented references to sleep once the deed was done. *What need is going unfulfilled in the man despite his successful completion of the act that he thought would bring him joy?* His pacing literature master would ask the question insistently, pointing at this boy or that for assessments, evaluations, speculations, defence. *Needs drive compulsions. What need? What need?* It was a very good question, Lynley decided.

He felt for his cigarette case and started back across the drive just as Sergeant Havers and St. James came round the corner of the house. Snow clung to their trouser legs as if they'd been thrashing in it. Lady Helen was right behind them.

For an awkward moment, the four of them stared at one another wordlessly. Then Lynley said, "Havers, put a call in to the Yard, will you? Let Webberly know we're on our way back to London this morning."

Havers nodded, disappearing through the front door. With a quick glance from Lady Helen to Lynley, St. James did likewise.

"Will you come back with us, Helen?" Lynley asked when they were alone. He put his cigarette case back into his pocket, unopened. "It'll be a quicker trip for you. We've a helicopter waiting near Oban."

"I can't, Tommy. You know that."

Her words were not unkind. But they were unmercifully final.

There seemed to be nothing more for them to say to each other. Still, Lynley found himself struggling to break her reserve in some manner, no matter how shadowy or inconsequential. It was inconceivable that he should part from her this way. And that's what he told her, before common sense or pride or stiff propriety could prevent him from doing so.

"I can't bear your going away from me like this, Helen."

She was caught before him in a streak of sunlight. It slanted through her hair, turning it the colour of a fine, old brandy. Just for a moment her lovely dark eyes held an unreadable emotion. Then it vanished.

"I must go," she said quietly, passed by him and entered the house.

It's like a death, Lynley thought. *But without a proper burial, without a period of mourning, without an end to lamentation.*

IN HIS CLUTTERED London office, Superintendent Malcolm Webberly placed the telephone receiver back into its cradle.

"That was Havers," he said. In a characteristic gesture, he raked his right hand through his thinning, sandy hair and pulled on it roughly, as if to encourage his incipient baldness.

Sir David Hillier, Chief Superintendent, did not move from the window where he had been standing for the last quarter hour, his eyes placidly evaluating the serried collection of buildings that composed the city skyline. As always, he was impeccably dressed, and his posture suggested a man at ease with success, comfortable with navigating the treacherous straits of political power. "And?" he asked.

"They're on their way back."

"That's all?"

"No. According to Havers, they're tracking a lead to Hampstead. Apparently, Sinclair was working on a book there. At her home."

Hillier's head turned slowly but with the sun behind him, his face was in shadow. "A book? In addition to the play?"

"Havers wasn't all too clear about it. However, I got the impression it was something that struck Lynley, something that he feels he must follow through."

Hillier smiled coolly at this. "Thank God for Inspector Lynley's remarkably creative intuition."

"He's my best man, David," Webberly said bitterly.

"And he'll follow orders, of course. As will you." Hillier turned back to his contemplation of the city.

10

IT WAS HALF past two when Lynley and Havers finally reached Joy Sinclair's small corner house. Located in the fashionable Hampstead area of London, the white brick building was a testament to the author's success. Its front window, hung with diaphanous ivory curtains, bowed out over a patch of garden where pruned rose bushes, dormant star jasmine, and tight-budded camellias grew. Two window boxes spilled ivy down the front and up the walls of the house, particularly near the doorway whose narrow shingled pediment was nearly lost beneath lush, bronze-veined leaves. Although the house faced Flask Walk, its garden entry was on Back Lane, a narrow cobbled avenue that climbed towards Heath Street a block away, where traffic moved smoothly, almost without sound.

Followed by Havers, Lynley unhooked the wrought iron gate and crossed the flagstone pathway. The day was windless but the air was raw, and a watery winter sunshine caught upon the brass lighting fixture to the left of the door and upon the polished post slot at its centre.

"Not bad digs," Havers commented with grudging admiration. "Your basic bricked-in garden, your basic nineteenth-century lamp post, your basic tree-shaded street lined with your very basic BMWs." She jerked a thumb at the house. "Must have set her back a few quid."

"From what Davies-Jones said about the terms of her will, I've the impression she could afford it," Lynley replied. He unlocked the door and motioned Havers inside.

They found themselves in a small anteroom, marble-tiled and unfurnished. A collection of several days' letters lay scattered on the floor, pushed through the slot in the door by the postman. They were the kind of collection one might expect in the post of a successful author: five circulars, an electricity account, eleven letters addressed to Joy in care of her publisher and forwarded on, a telephone account, a number of small envelopes that looked like invitations, several business-size envelopes with a variety of return addresses. Lynley handed them to Havers.

"Have a look through these, Sergeant."

She took them and they went on into the house, through an opaque glass door that led into a long hall. Here, two doors opened along the left wall and a staircase rose along the right. At the far end of the corridor, afternoon shadows filled what appeared to be the kitchen.

Lynley and Havers entered the sitting room first. The room shone in a filtered gold light that fell in three oblique shafts through a large bay window across a carpet the colour of mushrooms which had the look and smell of having been newly laid. But there was very little else to reveal the personality of the house's owner, other than low-slung chairs grouped round calf-high tables that spoke of a penchant for modern design. This was affirmed by Joy Sinclair's choice of art. Three oils after the fashion of Jackson Pollock leaned against one wall, waiting to be hung, and on one of the tables an angular marble sculpture stood, its subject indeterminate.

Double doors on the eastern wall opened into the dining room. It too was furnished sparingly, with that same taste for the sleek paucity of modern design. Lynley walked to the set of four French doors behind the dining table, frowning at the simplicity of their locks and the ease of entry they would afford the least skilled burglar. Not, he admitted to himself, that Joy Sinclair had much here worth stealing, unless the market for Scandinavian furniture was booming or the paintings in the sitting room were the real thing.

Sergeant Havers pulled out one of the dining chairs and sat down at the table, spreading the mail in front of her, pursing her lips thoughtfully. She began slitting it open. "Popular lady. Must be a dozen different invitations in here."

"Hmm." Lynley looked out at the brick-walled back garden, a square not much larger than the area required to hold one thin ash tree, a circlet of ground beneath it for planting flowers, and a patch of lawn covered by a thin layer of snow. He went on into the kitchen.

The pervasive feeling of anonymous ownership here was much the same as in the other two rooms. Black-fronted appliances broke into a long row of white cabinets, a scrubbed pine breakfast table with two chairs stood against one wall, and bright splashes of primary colour had strategic places throughout the room: a red cushion here, a blue tea kettle there, a yellow apron on a hook behind the door. Lynley leaned against the counter and studied it all. Houses always had a way of revealing their owners to him, but this house had a look of deliberate artificiality, something created by an interior designer who had been given free rein by a woman absolutely uninterested in her personal environment. The result was a tasteful showpiece of restrained success. But it told him nothing.

"Horrendous telephone bill," Havers called from the dining room. "Looks like she spent most of her time chatting it up with half a dozen chums round the world. She seems to have asked for a print out of her calls."

"Such as?"

"Seven calls to New York, four to Somerset, six to Wales and . . . let me see . . . ten to Suffolk. All very brief save for two longer ones."

"Made at the same time of day? Made one after another?"

"No, over five days. Last month. Interspersed with the calls to Wales."

"Check on all the numbers." Lynley started down the hall towards the stairs as Havers slit open another envelope.

"Here's something, sir." She read out to him, " 'Joy, You've answered none of my calls nor any of my letters. I shall expect to hear from you by Friday or the matter will have to be turned over to our legal department. Edna.' "

Lynley paused, his foot on the first step. "Her publisher?"

"Her editor. And it's on publishing house stationery. Sounds like trouble, doesn't it?"

Lynley reflected on earlier information: the reference on the tape recording to putting Edna off, the crossed-out appointments on Upper Grosvenor Street in Joy's engagement calendar.

"Telephone the publishing house, Sergeant. Find out what you can. Then do the same for the rest of the long-distance calls on the print out. I'm going up above."

While Joy Sinclair's personality had seemed absent on the lower floor of the house, her presence asserted itself with chaotic abandon once Lynley reached the top of the stairs. Here was the life centre of the building, an eclectic jumble of personal possessions collected and treasured. Here, Joy Sinclair was everywhere, in the photographs covering the walls of the narrow hall, in an overfull storage cabinet stuffed with everything from linens to crusty paintbrushes, in the curtain of lingerie in the bathroom, even in the air, which held the faint fragrance of bath powder and perfume.

Lynley went into the bedroom. It was a riot of multicoloured pillows, battered rattan furniture, and clothes. On the table next to her unmade bed stood a photograph that he examined briefly. An arrow-thin, sensitive-looking young man stood by the fountain in the Great Court of Trinity College, Cambridge. Lynley noted the way his hair grew back from his forehead, recognised something familiar in the set of his shoulders and head. Alec Rintoul, he guessed, and replaced it. He went on to the front of the house. Here, Joy's study was no different from the other rooms, and upon his first look at it, Lynley wondered how anyone could manage to produce a book in an atmosphere so totally devoid of order.

He stepped over a pile of manuscripts near the door and walked to the wall where two maps were hung above a word processor. The first map was large, a regulation district map of the sort bookstores sell to tourists who want to make a thorough scrutiny of a particular area of the country. This one was for Suffolk, although parts of Cambridgeshire and Norfolk were included on it. Evidently, Joy had been using it for some sort of research, Lynley saw, for the name of a village was circled heavily in red ink, and some two inches from it a large X had been drawn not far from Mildenhall Fen. Lynley put on his spectacles to get a better look. *Porthill Green*, he read beneath the red circle.

And then, a moment later, he made the connection. *P. Green* in Joy's engagement diary. Not a person at all, but a place.

Further circles appeared here and there on the map: Cambridge, Norwich, Ipswich, Bury St. Edmunds. Routes were traced out from each of these to Porthill Green and from Porthill Green out to the X near Mildenhall Fen. Lynley considered the implications attached to the presence of the map as below him he heard Sergeant Havers making one telephone call after another, muttering to herself occasionally when a response displeased her or when she was kept waiting or a line was engaged.

Lynley dropped his eyes to the second map on the wall. This was hand-drawn and rough, a pencilled depiction of a village with buildings common to any spot in England. They were only identified in the most generic of terms as *church, greengrocers, pub, cottage, petrol station.* The map told him nothing. Unless, of course, it was a rough delineation of Porthill Green. And even then it only indicated Joy's interest in the spot. Not why she was interested, or what she would have done had she gone there.

Lynley gave his attention to her desk. Like everything else in the room, it had the appearance of disordered confusion, of the sort in which the originator of the mess knows exactly where everything is but of which no other human being could ever make sense. Books, maps, notebooks, and papers covered its surface, as well as an unwashed teacup, several pens, a stapler, and a tube of heat-producing analgesic to be rubbed on tired muscles. He considered it for several minutes as Havers' voice continued its rise and fall of conversation below him.

There had to be some strange system involved, Lynley thought, looking through it. And it wasn't too long before he understood what it was. Although the piles of material made no superficial sense as a whole, taken individually, they were perfectly rational. One stack of books seemed to be reference materials. There were three psychology texts dealing with depression and suicide, two textbooks on the workings of the British police. Another stack was a collection of newspaper articles, all detailing one sort of death or another. A third stack contained a collection of booklets and pamphlets describing various sections of the country. A last stack was correspondence, thick and probably gone unanswered.

He looked through this, ignoring the fan letters, working on instinct, hoping it would guide him to something significant. He found it thirteen letters into the stack.

It was a brief note from Joy Sinclair's editor, fewer than ten sentences long. When, the editor asked, might we expect to see the first draft of *Hanging's Too Good?* You're six months overdue on it and as your contract stipulates . . .

Suddenly everything on Joy's desk began to take on a marked coherence. The texts on suicide, the workings of the police, the articles about death, the title of a new book. Lynley felt the tightening of excitement that always came with knowing he was on the right track.

He turned back to the word processor. It had two disks in it, he saw, both a program disk and one that would contain Joy's work.

"Havers," he shouted, "what do you know about computers?"

"A minute," she returned. "I've got . . ." Her voice lowered as she spoke into the phone.

Impatiently, Lynley switched the machine on. In a moment, directions appeared on the screen. It was far simpler than he would have ever imagined. Within a minute he was looking at Joy's working copy of *Hanging's Too Good*.

Unfortunately, the sum total of her manuscript—six months overdue to her publishers and no doubt the cause of her dispute with them—was one simple sentence: "Hannah decided to kill herself on the night of March 26, 1973." That was it.

Fruitlessly, Lynley searched for something else, using every direction that the computer program had to offer him. But nothing was there. Either her work had been erased, or that single sentence was as far as Joy Sinclair had gone. *No wonder her editor is frothing at the mouth and talking about legal action*, Lynley thought.

He switched the machine off and gave his attention back to her desk. He spent the next ten minutes trying to find something more in the material there. Failing that, he went to her filing cabinet and began searching through its four drawers. He was on his second one when Havers came into the room.

"Anything?" she asked him.

"A book called *Hanging's Too Good*, someone named Hannah who decided to commit suicide, and a place called Porthill Green, *P. Green*, I should guess. What about you?"

"I've begun to get the feeling that no one goes to work in New York much before noon, but I was able to find out that the New York number was for a literary agent."

"And the others?"

"The Somerset call was to Stinhurst's home."

"What about the letter from Edna? Did you telephone the publishing house about it?"

Havers nodded. "Joy sold a proposal to them early last year. She wanted to do something different, not a study of a criminal and victim which was her usual bent, but a study of a suicide, what led up to it and its aftereffects. The publisher bought the proposal—they've not had to worry about her meeting deadlines before this. But that was the end of it. She never gave them a thing. They've been after her for months. In fact, the reaction to her death sounded as if one of them may have been praying for it on a nightly basis."

"What about the other numbers?"

"The number in Suffolk was an interesting one," Havers replied. "A boy answered—sounded like a teenager. But he didn't have the slightest idea who Joy Sinclair was or why she might have been phoning his number."

"So what's so interesting about that?"

"His name, Inspector. Teddy Darrow. His father's name is John. And he was speaking to me from a pub called Wine's the Plough. And that pub is sitting right in the middle of Porthill Green."

Lynley grinned, felt that swift surge of power that comes from validation. "By God, Havers. Sometimes I think we're one hell of a team. We're onto it now. Can't you feel it?"

Havers didn't respond. She was browsing through the material on the desk.

"So we've found the John Darrow that Joy talked about both at dinner and on her tape," Lynley mused. "We've the explanation for the reference on her calendar to *P. Green*. We've the reason for the matchbook in her shoulder bag—she must have been in the pub. And now we're looking for a connection between Joy's book and John Darrow, between John Darrow and Westerbrae." He looked at Havers sharply. "But there was another set of phone calls, wasn't there? To Wales."

Lynley watched her leaf through the newspaper clippings on the desk in an apparent need to scrutinise each one of them. She didn't appear to be reading, however. "They were to Llanbister. To a woman called Anghared Mynach."

"Why did Joy phone her?"

Again, there was hesitation. "She was looking for someone, sir."

Lynley's eyes narrowed. He closed the filing drawer whose contents he had been examining. "Who?"

Havers frowned. "Rhys Davies-Jones. Anghared Mynach is his sister. He was staying with her."

BARBARA SAW in Lynley's face the swift assimilation of a series of ideas. She knew quite well the set of facts he was combining in his mind: the name John Darrow that was mentioned at dinner the night Joy Sinclair was murdered; the reference to Rhys Davies-Jones on Joy's tape recorder; the ten telephone calls to Porthill Green, and mixed in with those calls, six to Wales. Six calls made to Rhys Davies-Jones.

To avoid a discussion of all of this, Barbara went to the pile of manuscripts lying near the study door. She began riffling through them curiously, noting the range of Joy Sinclair's interest in murder and death: an outline for a study of the Yorkshire Ripper, an unfinished article on Crippen, at least sixty pages of material on Lord Mountbatten's death, a bound galley from a book called *The*

Knife Plunges Once, three heavily edited versions of another book called *Death in Darkness.* But there was something missing.

As Lynley involved himself again with the filing cabinet, Barbara went to the desk. She opened the top drawer. In it, Joy had kept her computer disks, two long rows of floppy black squares, all labelled by subject on the upper right-hand corner. Barbara flipped through them, reading the titles. And as she did so, the knowledge began to flourish within her, like a growth that was swelling, not with malignancy but with tension. The second and third drawers were much the same, containing stationery, envelopes, ribbons for the printers, staples, ancient carbon paper, tape, scissors. But not what she was looking for. Nothing like that at all.

When Lynley moved to the bookshelves and began looking through the materials there, Barbara went to the filing cabinet.

"I've been through that, Sergeant," Lynley said.

She sought an excuse. "Just a hunch, sir. It'll only take a moment."

The fact was that it took nearly an hour, but by that time Lynley had removed the jacket from a copy of Joy Sinclair's most recent book, putting this into his pocket before going on into the bedroom and from there to the storage cabinet at the top of the stairs where Barbara could hear him rooting systematically through the assortment of belongings. It was after four o'clock when she concluded her search of the files and rested back on her heels, satisfied with the validity of her hypothesis. Her only decision now was whether to tell Lynley or to hold her tongue until she had more facts, facts that he would be incapable of brushing aside.

Why, she wondered, had he not noticed it himself? How could he possibly have missed it? With the glaring absence of material right before his eyes, he was seeing only what he wanted to see, what he needed to see, a trail of guilt leading directly to Rhys Davies-Jones.

This guilt was so seductive a presence that it had become for Lynley an effective smokescreen hiding the one crucial detail that he had failed to note. Joy Sinclair had been in the midst of writing a play for Stuart Rintoul, Lord Stinhurst. And nowhere in the study was there a single reference to it. Not a draft, not an outline, not a list of characters, not a scrap of paper.

Someone had been through the house before them.

*   *   *

"I'LL DROP YOU in Acton, Sergeant," Lynley said when they were back outside. He headed down the street towards his car, a silver Bentley that had collected a small group of admiring schoolboys who were peering into its windows and running pious hands along its gleaming wings. "Let's plan on an early start out to Porthill Green tomorrow. Half past seven?"

"Fine, sir. But don't bother about Acton. I'll catch the Tube. It's just up on the corner of Heath Street and the high."

Lynley paused, turned back to her. "Don't be ridiculous, Barbara. That'll take an age. A change of stations and God only knows how many stops. Get in the car."

Barbara heard it as the order it was and looked for a way to deflect it without raising his ire. She couldn't possibly waste the time of having him drive her all the way home. Her day was far from over, in spite of what he thought.

Without considering how unlikely it would sound to him, she took a stab with the first excuse that came into her mind. "Actually, I've a date, sir," she said. And then knowing how ridiculous the idea was, she smoothed over the absurdity with, "Well, it's not a date exactly. It's someone I've met. And we thought . . . well, perhaps we'd have dinner and see that new film at the Odeon." She winced inwardly at that last piece of creativity and took a moment to pray that there *was* a new film at the Odeon. Or at least if there wasn't, that he wouldn't be the wiser.

"Oh. I see. Well. Anyone I know?"

Hell, she thought. "No, just a bloke I met last week. At the supermarket, actually. We banged trolleys somewhere between tinned fruit and tea."

Lynley smiled at that. "Sounds exactly the way a meaningful relationship starts. Shall I drop you at the Tube?"

"No. I could do with the walk. I'll see you tomorrow, sir."

He nodded, and she watched him stride towards his car. In an instant he was surrounded by the eager children who had been admiring it.

"This your car, mister?"

"How much it cost?"

"Those seats leather?"

"C'n I drive it?"

Barbara heard Lynley laugh, saw him lean against the car, fold his arms, and take a moment to engage the group in friendly conversation. *How like him*, she thought. *He's had all of three hours sleep in the last thirty-three, he's facing the fact that half of his*

*world may be as good as in ruins, and still he takes the time to
listen to children's chatter.* Watching him with them—fancying
from this distance that she could see the lines of laughter round his
eyes and the quirky muscle that crooked his smile—she found
herself wondering what she might actually be capable of doing to
protect the career and integrity of a man like that.

Anything, she decided, and began her walk to the Tube.

SNOW WAS FALLING when Barbara arrived at the St. James home on
Cheyne Row in Chelsea that evening at eight. In the tawny glow of
the street lamps, snowflakes looked like slivers of amber, floating
down to blanket pavement, cars, and the intricate wrought iron of
balconies and fences. The flurry was mild by way of winter storms,
but even so, enough to snarl the traffic on the Embankment a block
away. The usual roar of passing cars was considerably muted, and
the occasional horn, honking in a burst of temper, explained why.

Joseph Cotter, who played the unusual dual role of manservant
and father-in-law in St. James' life, answered the door to Barbara's
knock. He was, she guessed, no older than fifty, a balding man of
short, solid physique, so physically unlike his willowy daughter
that for some time after she had first met Deborah St. James, Barbara
had had no idea that she was even related to this man. He was
carrying a coffee service on a silver tray and doing his best to avoid
trampling a small, long-haired dachshund and a plump grey cat who
were vying for attention at his feet. All of them threw grotesquely
shaped shadows against the dark panelling on the wall.

"Off wi' you, Peach! Alaska!" he said, before he turned his ruddy
face to greet Barbara. The animals retreated a respectable six inches.
"Come in, Miss . . . Sergeant. Mr. St. James is in the study." He
looked Barbara over critically. " 'Ave you eaten yet, young lady?
Those two 'ave only finished just now. Let me get you a bite in a
tick, shall I?"

"Thank you, Mr. Cotter. I could do with something. I haven't
had a thing since this morning, I'm afraid."

Cotter shook his head. "Police," he said, in brief and eloquent
disapproval. "You just wait in 'ere, miss. I'll fix you up something
nice."

He knocked once on the door at the foot of the stairs and without
waiting for a response, swung it open. Barbara followed him into St.
James' study, a room of tall, crowded bookshelves, scores of photo-

graphs, and intellectual jumble, one of the most pleasant locations in the Cheyne Row house.

A fire had been lit, and the room's mixed odours of leather and brandy formed a comfortable redolence, not unlike that one might find in a gentleman's club. St. James occupied a chair by the hearth, his bad leg resting upon a worn ottoman, while across from him, Lady Helen Clyde was curled into a corner of the couch. They were sitting quietly, in the manner of an old married couple or of friends too close to need the bridge of conversation.

" 'Ere's the sergeant now, Mr. St. James," Cotter said, bustling forward with the coffee, which he set down on a low table in front of the fire. Flames there cast a glow against the porcelain, flickered like moving gold in a reflection on the tray. "An' she's not 'ad a bite to eat, so I'll see to that at once if you'll do the coffee on your own."

"I think we can manage that without disgracing you more than two or three times, Cotter. And if there's any chocolate cake left, would you cut another piece for Lady Helen? She's longing to have one, but you know how she is. Far too well bred to ask for more."

"He's lying as usual," Lady Helen interjected. "It's for himself but he knows how you'll disapprove."

Cotter looked from one to the other, undeceived by their exchange. "*Two* pieces of chocolate cake," he said meaningfully. "An' a meal for the sergeant as well." Flicking at the arm of his black jacket, he left the room.

"You look about done in," St. James said to Barbara when Cotter was gone.

"We *all* look done in," Lady Helen added. "Coffee, Barbara?"

"At least ten cups," she replied. She tugged off her coat and knit cap, tossed them down on the couch, and walked to the fire to thaw out her numb fingers. "It's snowing."

Lady Helen shuddered. "After this past weekend, those are the last two words I look forward to hearing." She handed St. James a cup of coffee and poured out two more. "I do hope your day was more productive than mine, Barbara. After spending five hours exploring Geoffrey Rintoul's past, I've begun to feel as though I'm working for one of those committees in the Vatican who recommend candidates for canonisation." She smiled at St. James. "Can you bear to hear it all again?"

"I long to," he replied. "It allows me to examine my own disreputable past and feel suitable guilt over it."

"As well you should." Lady Helen returned to the couch, shaking back a few feathery strands of hair that fell against her cheek. She slipped off her shoes, curled her legs underneath her, and sipped her coffee.

Even in exhaustion, she was graceful, Barbara noticed. Utterly confident. Completely at ease. Being in her presence was always an exercise in feeling ungainly and decidedly unattractive, and observing the woman's understated elegance, Barbara wondered how St. James' wife placidly endured the fact that her husband and Lady Helen worked side by side three days each week in his forensic laboratory on the top floor of the house.

Lady Helen reached for her handbag and pulled from it a small, black notebook. "After several hours with Debrett's and Burke's and *Landed Gentry*—not to mention a forty-minute stretch on the telephone with my father, who knows everything about everyone who's ever had a title—I've managed to come up with a rather remarkable portrait of our Geoffrey Rintoul. Let me see." She opened the notebook, and her eyes skimmed down the first page. "Born November 23, 1914. His father was Francis Rintoul, fourteenth Earl of Stinhurst, and his mother was Astrid Selvers, an American debutante in the fashion of the Vanderbilts who apparently had the audacity to die in 1925, leaving Francis with three small children to raise. He did so, with outstanding success, considering Geoffrey's accomplishments."

"He never remarried?"

"Never. It doesn't even appear that he engaged in discreet affairs, either. But sexual disinclination seems to run in the family, as you shall note momentarily."

"How does that fit?" Barbara asked. "Considering the affair between Geoffrey and his sister-in-law."

"A possible inconsistency," St. James acknowledged.

Lady Helen continued. "Geoffrey was educated at Harrow and Cambridge. Graduated from Cambridge in 1936 with a first in economics and assorted honours in speech and debate which went on and on forever. But he didn't come to anyone's particular attention until October of 1942, and really, he appeared to be the most astonishing man. He was fighting with Montgomery at the twelve-day battle at El Alamein in North Africa."

"His rank?"

"Captain. He was part of a tank crew. Apparently in one of the worst days of the fighting, his tank was hit, incapacitated, and ignited by a German shell. Geoffrey managed to get two wounded men out, dragging them more than a mile to safety. All in spite of the fact that he was wounded himself. He was awarded the Victoria Cross."

"Hardly the sort of man one expects to find buried in an isolated grave," Barbara commented.

"And there's more," Lady Helen said. "At his own request, and in spite of the severity of his wounds that could well have put him out of action for the remainder of the war, he finished it up in the Allied front in the Balkans. Churchill was trying to preserve some British influence there in the face of potential Russian predominance, and evidently Geoffrey was a Churchill man through and through. When he came home, he moved into a job in Whitehall working for the Ministry of Defence."

"I'm surprised a man like that didn't stand for Parliament."

"He was asked. Repeatedly. But he wouldn't do it."

"And he never married?"

"No."

St. James made a movement in his chair, and Lady Helen held out a hand to stop him. She rose herself and poured him a second cup of coffee, without a word. She merely frowned when he used the sugar too heavily and took the sugar bowl from him entirely when he dipped a spoon into it for the fifth time.

"Was he homosexual?" Barbara asked.

"If he was, then he was discretion itself. Which applies to any affairs he may have had. Not a whisper of scandal about him. Anywhere."

"Not even anything that attaches him to Lord Stinhurst's wife, Marguerite Rintoul?"

"Absolutely not."

"He's too good to be true," St. James remarked. "What do you have, Barbara?"

As she was about to pull her own notebook from the pocket of her coat, Cotter entered with the promised food, cake for St. James and Lady Helen and a platter of cold meats, cheeses, and bread for Barbara. With, she saw, a third piece of cake to end her improvised meal. She smiled her thanks and Cotter gave her a friendly wink, checked the coffeepot, and disappeared through the door. His footsteps sounded on the stairs in the hall.

"Eat first," Lady Helen advised. "With this chocolate cake in front of me, I'm afraid I shall be markedly distracted from anything you say. We can go on when you've finished your dinner."

With a grateful nod for the nicely veiled understanding so typical of Lady Helen, Barbara fell upon the food eagerly, devouring three pieces of meat and two large wedges of cheese like a prisoner of war. Finally, with the cake before her and another cup of coffee, she pulled out her notebook.

"A few hours browsing through the public library and all I could find is that Geoffrey's death appeared to be an entirely straightforward affair. Most of this is from the newspaper accounts of the inquest. There was a tremendous storm on the night he died at Westerbrae, or actually in the early morning hours of January 1, 1963."

"That much is believable, considering what the weather was like this last weekend," Lady Helen noted.

"According to the officer in charge of the investigation—an Inspector Glencalvie—the section of the road where the accident occurred was sheeted with ice. Rintoul lost control on the switchback, went right over the side, and rolled the car several times."

"He wasn't thrown out?"

"Apparently not. But his neck was broken and his body was burned."

Lady Helen turned to St. James at this. "But couldn't that mean—"

"No body-swapping in this day and age, Helen," he interrupted. "No doubt they had dental charts and X rays to identify him. Was anyone a witness to the accident, Barbara?"

"The closest they could get to a witness was the owner of Hillview Farm. He heard the crash and was first on the scene."

"And he is?"

"Hugh Kilbride, Gowan's father." They ruminated upon this information for a moment. The fire crackled and popped as the flames reached a hard bubble of sap. "So I kept thinking," Barbara went on slowly, "what did Gowan really mean when he said those two words *didn't see* to us? Of course, at first I thought it had something to do with Joy's death. But perhaps it didn't at all. Perhaps it referred to something his father had told him, a secret he was keeping."

"It's a possibility, to be sure."

"And there's something else." She told them about her search through Joy Sinclair's study, about the absence of any materials that referred to the play she had been writing for Lord Stinhurst.

St. James' interest was piqued. "Was there any sign of forcible entry to the house?"

"None that I noticed."

"Could someone else have had a key?" Lady Helen asked, then

went on to say, "But that's not quite right, is it? Everyone with an interest in the play was at Westerbrae, so how could her house . . . Unless someone rushed back to London and managed to get everything out of the study before you arrived. Yet that doesn't seem at all likely, does it? Or even possible. Besides, who would have a key?"

"Irene, I imagine. Robert Gabriel. Perhaps even . . ." Barbara hesitated.

"Rhys?" Lady Helen asked.

Barbara felt a stirring of discomfort. She could read worlds into the manner in which Lady Helen had said the man's name. "Possibly. There were a number of phone calls to him on her telephone bill. They were interspersed with calls to a place called Porthill Green." Her loyalty to Lynley prevented her from saying anything else. The ice she was walking on in this private investigation was insubstantial enough without giving Lady Helen any information which she might inadvertently or deliberately pass on to someone else.

But Lady Helen required no further information. "And Tommy thinks that Porthill Green somehow gives Rhys a motive for murder. Of course. He's looking for a motive. He told me as much."

"And yet, none of this takes us any closer to understanding Joy's play, does it?" St. James looked at Barbara. "*Vassal,*" he said. "Does that mean anything to you?"

She frowned. "Feudalism and fiefs. Should it mean something more?"

"It's somehow connected to all of this," Lady Helen answered. "It's the only part of the play that stuck in my mind."

"Why?"

"Because it made no sense to anyone but the members of Geoffrey Rintoul's family. And it made perfect sense to them. They reacted when they heard the character say that he wasn't about to become another vassal. It seemed to be some sort of familial code word that only they understood."

Barbara sighed. "So where do we go from here?"

Neither St. James nor Lady Helen had an answer for her. They fell into several minutes of meditation that were broken by the sound of the front door opening and a young woman's pleasant voice calling, "Dad? I'm home. Absolutely freezing and in desperate need of food. I'll eat anything. Even steak and kidney pie, so you can see how immediately in danger of starvation I am." Her light laughter followed.

Cotter's voice replied sternly from one of the upper floors. "Your 'usband's eaten every crumb in the 'ouse, luv. And that'll teach you to leave the poor man to 'is own devices all these hours. What's the world comin' to?"

"Simon? He's home so soon?" Footsteps sounded hurriedly in the hall, the study door burst open, and Deborah St. James said eagerly, "My love, you didn't—" She stopped abruptly when she saw the other women. Her eyes went to her husband and she pulled off a beret the colour of cream, loosing an undisciplined mass of coppery red hair. She was dressed in business clothes—a fine coat of ivory wool over a grey suit—and she carried a large metal camera case which she set down near the door. "I've been doing a wedding," she explained. "And together with the reception, I thought I'd never escape. You're all of you back from Scotland so soon? What's happened?"

A smile broke over St. James' face. He held out his hand and his wife crossed the room to him. "I know *exactly* why I married you, Deborah," he said, kissing her warmly, tangling his hand in her hair. "Photographs!"

"And I always thought it was because you were absolutely mad for my perfume," she replied crossly.

"Not a bit of it." St. James pushed himself out of his chair and went to his desk. There, he rooted through a large drawer and pulled out a telephone directory which he opened quickly.

"Whatever are you doing?" Lady Helen asked him.

"Deborah's just given us the answer to Barbara's question," St. James replied. "Where do we go from here? To photographs." He reached for the telephone. "And if they exist, Jeremy Vinney is the one man who can get them."

11

PORTHILL GREEN was a village that looked as if it had grown, like an unnatural protuberance, out of the peat-rich earth of the East Anglian Fens. Close to the centre of a rough triangle created by the Suffolk and Cambridgeshire towns of Brandon, Mildenhall, and Ely, the village was not a great deal more than the intersection of three narrow lanes that wound through fields of sugar beets, traversing chalky brown canals by means of bridges barely the width of a single car. It sat in a landscape largely given over to the colours grey, brown, and green—from the cheerless winter sky, to the loamy fields dotted irregularly by patchy snow, to the vegetation that bordered the lanes in thick abundance.

The village possessed little to recommend itself. Nine buildings of knapped flint and four of plaster, carelessly half-timbered in a drunken pattern, lined the high street. Those that were places of business announced that fact with signs of chipped and sooty paint. A lone petrol station, with pumps that appeared to be fabricated largely from rust and glass, stood sentry on the outskirts of the village. And at the end of the high street, marked by a weather-smoothed Celtic cross, lay a circle of dirty snow under which no doubt grew the grass for which the village was named.

Lynley parked here, for the green lay directly across from Wine's the Plough, a building no different from any of the other sagging structures on the street. He examined it while next to him Sergeant Havers buttoned her coat beneath her chin and gathered her notebook and shoulder bag.

Lynley could see that, originally, the pub had simply been called The Plough, and that on either side of its name had been fixed the words *Wines* and *Liquors*. The latter had fallen off sometime in the past, however, leaving merely a dark patch on the wall where the word had once been, the shape of its letters still legible. Rather than replace *Liquors*, or even repaint the building for that matter, to the first word had been added an apostrophe by means of a tin mug nailed into the plaster. Thus the building was renamed, no doubt to someone's amusement.

"It's the same village, Sergeant," Lynley said after a cursory examination through the windscreen. Aside from a liver-coloured mongrel sniffing along an ill-formed hedge, the place might have been abandoned.

"Same as what, sir?"

"As that drawing posted in Joy Sinclair's study. The petrol station, the greengrocers. There's the cottage set back behind the church as well. She'd been here long enough to become familiar with the place. I've no doubt someone will remember her. You take care of the high while I have a word with John Darrow."

Havers reached for the door handle with a sigh of resignation. "Always the footwork," she groused.

"Good exercise to clear your head after last night."

She looked at him blankly. "Last night?"

"Dinner, film? The chap from the supermarket?"

"Oh, *that*," Havers said, fidgeting in her seat. "Believe me, it was very forgettable, sir." She got out of the car, letting in a gust of air that commingled the faint odours of the sea, dead fish, and rotting debris, and strode over to the first building, disappearing behind its weathered black door.

By pub hours it was early yet, the drive from London having taken them less than two hours, so Lynley was not surprised to find the door locked when he tried to enter Wine's the Plough across the street. He stepped back from the building and looked above to what seemed to be a flat, but his observation gained him nothing. Limp curtains served as a barrier against prying eyes. No one was about at all, and there was no automobile or motorbike to indicate that the building was currently under anyone's ownership. Nonetheless, when Lynley peered through the grimy windows of the pub itself, a missing slat in one of the shutters revealed a light shining in a far doorway that appeared to lead to the building's cellar stairs.

He returned to the door and knocked upon it soundly. Within moments, he heard heavy footsteps. They trudged to the door.

"Not opened," a man's gravelly voice said behind it.

"Mr. Darrow?"

"Aye."

"Would you open the door please?"

"Y'r business is?"

"Scotland Yard CID."

That got a reaction, although not much of one. The door was unbolted and held open a mere six or seven inches. "All's in order in here." Eyes the shape and size of hazelnuts, the colour of a brown gone bad with yellow, dropped to the identification that Lynley held.

"May I come in?"

Darrow didn't look up as he considered the request and the limited responses available to him. "Not about Teddy, is it?"

"Your son? No, it's nothing to do with him."

Apparently satisfied, the man held the door open wider, stepped back, and admitted Lynley into the pub. It was a humble establishment, in keeping with the village it served. Its sole decoration appeared to be a variety of unlit signs behind and above the Formica-topped bar, identifying the liquors sold on the premises. There was very little furniture: half a dozen small tables surrounded by stools and a bench running beneath the front windows. This was padded, but the cushion was sun-bleached from its original red to rusty pink, and dark stains patterned it. A stinging burnt smell tinctured the air, a combination of cigarette smoke, a dead fire in a blackened fireplace, and windows too long closed against the winter weather.

Darrow positioned himself behind the bar, perhaps with the intention of treating Lynley like a customer in spite of the hour and his police identification. For his part, Lynley followed suit in front of it although it meant standing and he would much rather have conducted this interview at one of the tables.

Darrow, he guessed, was in his mid-forties, a rough-looking man who projected a decided air of suppressed violence. He was built like a boxer, squat, with long, powerful limbs, a barrel chest, and incongruously small, well-shaped ears which lay flat against his skull. His clothes suited him. They suggested a man able to make the transition from publican to brawler in the time it would take to ball up a fist. He wore a wool shirt, with cuffs turned up to reveal hirsute arms, and a pair of loose-fitting trousers for ease of movement. Evaluating all this, Lynley doubted that any fist fights broke out in Wine's the Plough unless Darrow himself provoked them.

He had in his pocket the jacket of *Death in Darkness*, which he had taken from Joy Sinclair's study. Removing it, he folded it so that the author's smiling photograph was facing up. "Do you know this woman?" he asked.

Recognition flickered unmistakably in Darrow's eyes. "I know her. What of it?"

"She was murdered three nights ago."

"I was here three nights ago," Darrow replied. His tone was surly. "Saturday's my busiest. Anyone in the village'll tell you as much."

It wasn't at all the reaction Lynley had been expecting. Perhaps surprise, perhaps confusion, perhaps reserve. But a reflex denial of culpability? That was unusual, to say the least.

"She's been here to see you," Lynley stated. "She telephoned this pub ten times in the last month."

"What of it?"

"I expect you to tell me that."

The publican seemed to be evaluating the even quality of Lynley's voice. He appeared disconcerted that his show of belligerent uncooperation produced virtually no reaction in the London detective. "I was having none of her," he said. "She wanted to write a flipping book."

"About Hannah?" Lynley asked.

The tightening of Darrow's jaw tensed every muscle in his face. "Aye. Hannah." He went to an upturned bottle of Bushmill's Black Label and pushed a glass against its spigot. He drained the whisky, not in a single gulp but in two or three slow swallows, all taken with his back to Lynley. "Have one?" he asked, drawing himself another.

"No."

The man nodded, drank again. "She came out of nowhere," he said. "Bringing a clutch of newspaper clippings about this and that book that she'd written, and going on about awards she'd received and . . . I don't know what else. And she plain expected me to give her Hannah and be thankful for the attention. Well, I wouldn't. I wasn't having it. And I wasn't having my Teddy exposed to that kind of muck. It's bad enough with his mum doing herself in and providing the local ladies with gossip till he was ten years old. I wasn't about to have it start again. Raking it all up. Upsetting the lad."

"Hannah was your wife?"

"Aye. My wife."

"How did Joy Sinclair happen to know about her?"

"Claimed she'd been studying up on suicides for nine or ten

months to find one she thought interesting, and she'd read of Hannah's. Caught her eye, she said." His voice was sour. "Can you credit that, man? *Caught her eye.* Han wasn't a person to her. She was a piece of meat. So I told her to fuck herself. In just those words."

"Ten telephone calls suggests that she was rather persistent."

Darrow snorted. "Made no difference. She was getting nowhere. Teddy was too young to know what had happened. So she couldn't talk to him. And she was getting nothing from me."

"May I take it that without your cooperation, there could be no book?"

"Aye. No book. Nothing. And that's the way it was going to stay."

"When she came to see you, was she alone?"

"Aye."

"Never anyone with her? Perhaps someone waiting out in the car?"

Darrow's eyes narrowed suspiciously. They darted to the windows and back. "What d'you mean?"

It had seemed a straightforward question to Lynley. He wondered if Darrow was temporising. "Did she come with a companion?"

"She was always alone."

"Your wife killed herself in 1973, didn't she? Did Joy Sinclair ever give you any indication why a suicide that long ago was of interest to her?"

Darrow's face darkened. His lips curled with loathing. "She liked the chair, Inspector. She was good enough to tell me that. She liked the bleeding chair."

"The chair?"

"Right. Han lost a shoe when she kicked over the chair. And the woman fancied that. She called it . . . *poignant.*" He turned back to the Bushmill's. "Begging your pardon if I don't particularly care that someone murdered the bitch."

ST. JAMES and his wife were both working at their respective interests on the top floor of their house, St. James in his forensic laboratory and Deborah in her developing room that adjoined it. The door between the two was open and looking up from the report that he was compiling for the defence team in an upcoming trial, St. James engaged in a moment of simple pleasure, watching his wife. She was frowning over a collection of her photographs, a pencil stuck behind one ear and a mass of curly hair drawn back from her face with a set of combs. The light above glittered against her head like a halo. Much of the rest of her was in shadow.

"Hopeless. Pathetic," she murmured, scribbling on the back of one picture and tossing another into a rubbish box at her feet. "Blasted light . . . God in heaven, Deborah, where did you learn the basic elements of composition! . . . Oh Lord, this is even *worse!*"

St. James laughed at that. Deborah looked up. "Sorry," she said. "Am I distracting you?"

"You always distract me, my love. Far too much, I'm afraid. And especially when I've been away from you for twenty-four hours or more."

A faint colour rose in her cheeks. "Well, after a year, I'm glad to hear there's a bit of romance left between us. I . . . silly though, isn't it? Were you really only gone one night to Scotland? I missed you, Simon. I find that I don't care for going to bed without you any longer." Her blush deepened when St. James got down from his tall stool and crossed the lab to join her in the semi-darkness of the developing room. "No, my love . . . I really didn't mean . . . Simon, we'll get no work done like this," she said in insincere protest when he took her into his arms.

St. James laughed quietly, said, "Well, we'll get other things done, won't we?" and kissed her. A long moment later, he murmured appreciatively against her mouth, "Lord. Yes. Far more important things, I think."

They parted guiltily at the sound of Cotter's voice. He was pounding up the stairway, talking several volumes louder than he usually did.

"Just up 'ere, they both are," he boomed. "Workin' in the lab, I should guess. Deb's got 'er snaps out and Mr. St. James is doin' a report o' some sort. 'Tis just up above. Not a bit of a climb. We'll be there in a tick."

This last pronouncement was made louder than all the others. Deborah laughed when she heard it. "I never know whether to be appalled or amused by my father," she whispered. "How *can* he possibly be wise to what we're up to all the time?"

"He sees the way I look at you, and that's evidence enough. Believe me, your father knows exactly what I have on my mind." St. James dutifully returned to his lab and was writing away upon his report when Cotter appeared at the door with Jeremy Vinney behind him.

" 'Ere you are," Cotter said expansively. "Bit of a climb that, isn't it?" He cast a look here and there as if to make certain he hadn't caught his daughter and her husband *in flagrante delicto*.

Vinney betrayed no surprise at the stentorian manner in which Cotter had heralded his arrival. Rather he came forward, a manila folder in one hand. His portly face bore the signs and shadows of fatigue, and on his jawline ran a thin line of whiskers that he'd missed in shaving. He had not as yet bothered to take off his overcoat.

"I think I have what you need," he said to St. James as Cotter directed an affectionate scowl at his daughter's impish smile before departing. "Perhaps a bit more. The fellow who covered Geoffrey Rintoul's inquest in sixty-three is one of our senior editors now, so we rooted through his files this morning and came up with three photographs and a set of old notes. They're hardly legible since they were done in pencil, but we might be able to make something out of them." He gave St. James a look that endeavoured to read beneath the surface. "Did Stinhurst kill Joy? Is that where you're heading?"

The question was a logical conclusion to everything that had gone before, and not an unreasonable one for the journalist to ask. But St. James was not unaware of what it implied. Vinney played a triple role in the drama that had occurred at Westerbrae, as newsman, friend of deceased, and suspect. It was to his advantage to have that last entitlement removed entirely in the eyes of the police, to see that suspicion passed on to someone else. And after a show of fine, journalistic cooperation, what better person to see that it was done than St. James himself, known to be Lynley's friend? He answered Vinney cautiously.

"There's merely a small oddity about Geoffrey Rintoul's death that has us intrigued."

If the journalist was disappointed with the obliquity of the reply, he was careful not to show it. "Yes. I see." He shrugged out of his overcoat and accepted the introduction to St. James' wife. Placing the manila folder onto the lab table, he drew out its contents, a sheaf of papers and three tattered pictures. When he spoke again, it was with professional formality. "The inquest notes are quite complete. Our man was hoping for a feature on it, considering Geoffrey Rintoul's distinguished past, so he was careful about the details. I think you can rely on his accuracy."

The notes were written on yellow paper which did not make the faded pencil any easier to read. "It says something about an argument," St. James remarked, looking them over.

Vinney drew a lab stool over to the table. "The testimony of the

family was fairly straightforward at the inquest. Old Lord Stinhurst—Francis Rintoul, the present earl's father—said there had
been quite a row before Geoffrey took off that New Year's Eve."

"A row? About what?" St. James scanned for the details as
Vinney supplied them.

"Apparently a semi-drunken spat that started delving into the
family history."

That was very close to what Lynley had reported of his conversation with the current earl. But it was hard for St. James to believe
that old Lord Stinhurst would have discussed his two sons' love
triangle before a coroner's jury. Family loyalty would have precluded
that. "Did he give any specifics?"

"Yes." Vinney pointed to a section midway down the page.
"Apparently Geoffrey was hot to get back to London and decided to
take off that night in spite of the storm. His father testified that he
didn't want him to go. Because of the weather. Because he hadn't
seen much of Geoffrey for the past six months and wanted to keep
him there while he could. Evidently, their recent relationship hadn't
been smooth, and the old earl saw this New Year's gathering as a
way to heal the breach between them."

"What sort of breach?"

"I gathered that the earl had taken Geoffrey under considerable
fire for not marrying. I suppose he wanted Geoffrey to feel duty
bound to shore up the ancestral house. At any rate, that was what
was at the heart of the trouble in their relationship." Vinney studied
the notes before he went on delicately, as if he had come to
understand how important a show of impartiality might be when
discussing the Rintoul family. "I do get the impression that the old
man was used to having things his way. So when Geoffrey decided
to return to London, his father lost his temper and the argument
grew from there."

"Is there any indication why Geoffrey wanted to return to
London? A woman friend that his father wouldn't have approved of?
Or perhaps a relationship with a man that he wanted to keep under
wraps?"

There was an odd, unaccountable hesitation, as if Vinney were
trying to read St. James' words for an additional meaning. He cleared
his throat. "There's nothing to indicate that. No one ever came
forward to claim an illicit relationship with him. And consider the
tabloids. If someone had been involved with Geoffrey Rintoul on
the side, he or she would probably have come forward and sold the
story for a good deal of money once he was dead. God knows that's

the way things were happening in the early sixties, with call girls servicing what seemed like half the top ministers in the government. You remember Christine Keeler's tales about John Profumo. That set the Tories reeling. So it does seem that if someone Geoffrey Rintoul was involved with needed the money, he or she would merely have followed in Keeler's footsteps."

St. James responded pensively. "There *is* something in what you're saying, isn't there? Perhaps more than we realise. John Profumo was state secretary for war. Geoffrey Rintoul worked for the Ministry of Defence. Rintoul's death and inquest were in January, the very same month that John Profumo's sexual relationship with Keeler was brewing in the press. Is there some sort of connection between these people and Geoffrey Rintoul that we're failing to see?"

Vinney seemed to warm to the plural pronoun. "I wanted to think so. But if any call girl had been involved with Rintoul, why would she have held her tongue when the tabloids were willing to pay a fortune for a juicy story about someone in government?"

"Perhaps it wasn't a call girl at all. Perhaps Rintoul was involved with someone who didn't need the money and certainly wouldn't have benefitted from the disclosure."

"A married woman?"

Once again they were back to Lord Stinhurst's original story about his brother and his wife. St. James pushed past it. "And the testimony of the others?"

"They all supported the old earl's story of the argument, Geoffrey going off in a rage, and the accident on the switchback. There was something rather odd, however. The body was badly burned, so they had to send to London for X rays and dental charts to use in the formal identification. Geoffrey's physician, a man called Sir Andrew Higgins, brought them personally. He did the examination along with Strathclyde's pathologist."

"Unusual but not out of the range of belief."

"That's not it." Vinney shook his head. "Sir Andrew was a longtime school friend of Geoffrey's father. They'd been at Harrow and Cambridge together. They were in the same London club. He died in 1970."

St. James supplied his own conclusion to this new revelation. Sir Andrew may have hidden what needed to be hidden. He may have brought forth only what needed to be brought forth. Yet, all the disjointed pieces of information considered, the time period—January 1963—struck St. James as the most relevant item. He couldn't have said why. He reached for the photographs.

The first was of a group of black-garbed people about to climb into a row of parked limousines. St. James recognised most of them. Francesca Gerrard clinging to the arm of a middle-aged man, presumably her husband Phillip; Stuart and Marguerite Rintoul bending over to speak to two bewildered children, obviously Elizabeth and her older brother Alec; several people forming a conversational circle on the steps of the building in the background, their faces blurry. The second picture was of the accident site with its scar of burnt land. Standing next to it was a roughly dressed farmer, a border collie at his side. Hugh Kilbride, Gowan's father, St. James speculated, the first on the scene. The last picture was of a group leaving a building, most likely the site of the inquest itself. Once again, St. James recognised the people he had met at Westerbrae. But this photograph contained several unfamiliar faces.

"Who are these people? Do you know?"

Vinney pointed as he spoke. "Sir Andrew Higgins is directly behind the old Earl of Stinhurst. Next to him is the family solicitor. You know the others, I presume."

"Save this man," St. James said. "Who is he?" The man in question was behind and to the right of the old Earl of Stinhurst, his head turned in conversation to Stuart Rintoul, who listened, frowning, one hand pulling at his chin.

"Not a clue," Vinney said. "The chap who took the notes for the story might know, but I didn't think to ask him. Shall I take them back and have a go?"

St. James thought about it. "Perhaps," he said slowly, and then turned to the darkroom. "Deborah, will you have a look at these please?" His wife joined them at the table, gazing over St. James' shoulder at the photographs. After giving her a moment to evaluate them, St. James said, "Can you do a set of enlargements from this last one? Individual pictures of each person, mostly each face?"

She nodded. "They'd be quite grainy, of course, certainly not the best quality, but recognisable. Shall I set up to do it?"

"Please, yes." St. James looked at Vinney. "We shall have to see what our current Lord Stinhurst has to say about these."

THE POLICE in Mildenhall had conducted the investigation into Hannah Darrow's suicide. Raymond Plater, the investigating officer, was, in fact, now the town's chief constable. He was a man who wore authority like a suit of clothes into which he had grown more and more comfortable with the passage of time. So he was not the least concerned to have Scotland Yard CID popping up on his doorstep to talk about a case fifteen years closed.

"I remember it, all right," he said, leading Lynley and Havers into his well-appointed office. He adjusted beige venetian blinds in a manner of proud ownership, then picked up a telephone, dialled three numbers, and said, "Plater here. Will you bring me the file on Darrow, Hannah. D-a-r-r-o-w. It'll be in 1973. . . . A closed case . . . Right." He swivelled his chair to a table behind his desk and tossed back over his shoulder, "Coffee?"

When the other two accepted his offer, Plater did the honours with an efficient-looking coffee maker, passing steaming mugs over to them along with milk and sugar. He himself drank appreciatively, yet with remarkable delicacy for a man so energetic and so fierce of feature. With its implacable jaw and clear Nordic eyes, his face reflected the savage Viking warriors from whom he no doubt had taken his blood.

"You're not the first to come asking about the Darrow woman," he said, leaning back in his chair.

"The writer Joy Sinclair was here," Lynley responded, and to Plater's quickly cocked head, added, "She was murdered this past weekend in Scotland."

The chief constable's adjustment in position indicated his interest. "Is there a connection?"

"Merely a gut feeling at the moment. Did Sinclair come to you alone?"

"Yes. Persistent she was, too. Arrived without an appointment, and as she wasn't a member of the Force, there was a bit of a wait." Plater smiled. "Just over two hours, as I recall. But she put in the time, so I went ahead and saw her. This was . . . sometime early last month."

"What did she want?"

"Conversation mostly. A look at what we had on the Darrow woman. Ordinarily I wouldn't have made it available to anyone, but she had two letters of introduction, one from a Welsh chief constable she'd worked with on a book and another from a detective superintendent somewhere in the south. Devon, perhaps. Beyond that, she'd an impressive list of credentials—at least two Silver Daggers, I recall—that she wasn't above showing off to convince me she wasn't hanging about the entrance hall in the hope of an hour's natter."

A deferential knock upon the door heralded a young constable who handed his chief a thick folder and made himself scarce. Plater opened the folder and drew out a stack of police photographs.

They were, Lynley saw, standard crime-scene work. Starkly black and white, they still depicted death with grim attention to detail, going so far as to include an elongated shadow cast by the hanging body of Hannah Darrow. There was little else to see. The room was virtually unfurnished, with an open-beam ceiling, a floor of wide but badly pitted planks, and rough-hewn wooden walls. These appeared to be curved, small four-paned windows their only decoration. A plain cane-seated chair lay on its side beneath the body, and one of her shoes had fallen off and rested against a rung. She had not used rope, but rather what appeared to be a dark scarf, attached to a hook in a ceiling beam, and her head hung forward with long blonde hair curtaining the worst distortion of her face.

Lynley scrutinised the photographs, one after another, feeling a twinge of uncertainty. He handed them to Havers and watched as she sorted through them, but she returned them to Plater without remark.

"Where were the photographs taken?" he asked the chief constable.

"She was found in a mill out on Mildenhall Fen, about a mile from the village."

"Is the mill still there?"

Plater shook his head. "Torn down three or four years past, I'm afraid. Not that it would do you too much good to see it. Although," his voice was momentarily reflective, "the Sinclair woman asked to see it as well."

"Did she?" Lynley asked thoughtfully. He wondered about that request and considered what John Darrow had told him: Joy had taken ten months to find the death she wanted to write about. "Are you absolutely certain this was a suicide?" he asked the chief constable.

In answer, Plater riffled through the file. He brought out a single piece of notebook paper. Torn in several places, it bore the trace of creases from having been crumpled and then pressed in among other papers to smooth it out. Lynley scanned the few words, written in a large, childish script with rounded letters and tiny circles used in place of periods and dots.

> I must go, it's time . . . There's a tree that's dead, but it
> goes on swaying in the wind with the others. So it seems to

me that if I die, I'll still have a part in life, one way or another. Good-bye, my darling.

"Pretty straightforward, that," Plater commented.

"Where was this found?"

"On the kitchen table at her home. With the pen right beside it, Inspector."

"Who found it?"

"Her husband. Evidently, she was supposed to help him in the pub that night. When she didn't show up, he went upstairs to their flat. He saw the note, panicked, ran out looking for her. When he couldn't find her, he came back, closed the pub, and got up a group of men for a proper search. She was found in the mill," Plater referred to the file, "shortly after midnight."

"Who found her?"

"Her husband. Accompanied," he noted hastily when he saw Lynley start to speak, "by two blokes from the village who were no particular friends of his." Plater smiled affably. "I expect you're thinking what we all thought at first, Inspector. That Darrow lured his wife out to the mill, strung her up, and fashioned the note himself. But we checked on that angle. The note's genuine enough. Our writing people verify that. And although both their prints were on the paper—Hannah's and her husband's—his are explained away easily enough. He'd picked up the paper from the kitchen table where she'd left it for him. Hardly questionable behaviour under the circumstances. Besides, Hannah Darrow was wearing plenty of ballast that night to make certain she did the job right and proper. She had on two wool coats and two heavy sweaters. And you can't tell me her husband talked her into going for an evening stroll all done up like that."

THE AGINCOURT THEATRE was tucked between two far more impressive structures on a narrow street off Shaftesbury Avenue. To its left was the Royal Standard Hotel, complete with a uniformed doorman who scowled at pedestrians and traffic alike. To its right was the Museum of Theatrical History, its front windows filled with a dazzling display of Elizabethan costumes, weaponry, and props. Sandwiched between these two, the Agincourt had the appearance of neglect and disrepair, qualities disproved the moment one walked through its doors.

When Lady Helen Clyde entered shortly before noon, she paused in surprise. The last time she had seen a production here the building had been under different ownership, and although its former gloomy Victorian interior had possessed a certain Dickensian charm, Lord Stinhurst's renovation was breathtaking. She had read about it in the paper, of course, but nothing had prepared her for such a metamorphosis. Stinhurst had given both architects and designers free rein in orchestrating the theatre's improvements. Following a no-holds-barred philosophy of interior design, they had gutted the building completely, achieving light and space through their creation of an entrance that soared with three full floors of open balconies, and through their use of colours that contrasted sharply with the soot-covered exterior which the building presented to the street. Admiring the wealth of creativity that had altered the theatre, Lady Helen allowed herself to forget some of the trepidation with which she had been anticipating her coming interview.

With Sergeant Havers and St. James, she had gone over the details until nearly midnight. Together, the three of them had explored every avenue of approach for this visit to the Agincourt. Since Havers was unable to get to the theatre without Lynley's knowledge and do the job properly under the aegis of the police, it was left to the devices of either Lady Helen or St. James to encourage Lord Stinhurst's secretary to talk about the telephone calls which her employer claimed she had placed for him on the morning that Joy Sinclair's body was found.

Their late night discussion ended with a consensus that Lady Helen was the likeliest one among them to encourage an offering of confidences from anyone. All that had sounded reasonable enough at midnight—even a bit complimentary if one wanted to take it that way—but it was far from reassuring right now with the Agincourt's offices a mere ten steps away and Stinhurst's secretary waiting unwittingly in one of them.

"Helen? Have you come to join the newest fray?"

Rhys Davies-Jones was standing at the auditorium door, a mug in his hand. Lady Helen smiled and joined him at the bar where coffee was brewing noisily, emitting a pungent smell that was in large part chicory.

"Worst coffee in the world," Davies-Jones acknowledged. "But one develops a taste for it over time. Will you have some?" When she declined, he poured himself a mug. The liquid was black, resembling overused motor oil.

"What newest fray?" she asked him.

"Perhaps *fray* isn't the best choice of words," he admitted. "It's more like political manoeuvring among our tender players for the best part in Stinhurst's new production. With the only difficulty being that the play hasn't been decided upon yet. So you can well imagine the jockeying for position that's been going on for the last two hours."

"*New* production?" Lady Helen asked. "You don't mean that Lord Stinhurst intends to go on with a play after what's happened to Joy and Gowan?"

"He has no choice, Helen. We're all of us under contract to him. The theatre's due to open in less than eight weeks. It's a new production or he loses his shirt. I can't say he's at all happy about it, however. And he's going to be a good sight unhappier the moment the press start storming him about what happened to Joy. I can't think why the media haven't picked up on the story." He touched Lady Helen's hand lightly where it lay on the bar. "That's why you're here, isn't it?"

She hadn't thought she would see him, hadn't considered what she might say if she did. Unprepared for his question, she answered with the first thing that came into her mind, not even thinking for the moment about why she was lying.

"Actually, no. I found myself in the neighbourhood. I thought you might be here, so I took the chance of dropping in."

His eyes remained perfectly steady on her own, but they managed to convey how ridiculous her story sounded. He was not the kind of man who wanted his ego massaged by an attractive woman seeking him out. Nor was she the kind of woman who would ever do so. He knew that quite well.

"Right. Yes, I see." He studied his coffee, moved the mug from one hand to the other. When he spoke again, it was with an altered tone, one deliberately light and unaffected. "Come into the auditorium then. There's not much to see since we've got virtually nothing at all done. But there have been sparks aplenty. Joanna's been harassing David Sydeham all morning with an endless list of complaints that she wants him to handle, and Gabriel's been attempting to pour oil on their troubled waters. He's managed to alienate nearly everyone present, but most particularly Irene. The meeting may well turn into a brawl, yet it does have some amusement value. Will you join us?"

After the manufactured excuse for her presence at the theatre, Lady Helen knew she could hardly refuse. So she followed him into the dark auditorium and took a seat in the very last row. He smiled at her politely and began to walk towards the brightly lit stage where the players, Lord Stinhurst, and several other people were gathered round a table, their voices raised in discussion.

"Rhys," she called. When he turned back to her, she said, "May I see you tonight?"

It was part contrition and part desire. But which was the greater and more pressing, she could not have said. She knew only that she couldn't leave him today on a lie.

"I'm sorry, but I can't, Helen. I've a meeting with Stuart . . . Lord Stinhurst about the new production."

"Oh. Yes, of course. I wasn't thinking. Then perhaps sometime . . ."

"Tomorrow night? For dinner, if you're free. If that's what you want."

"I . . . yes. Yes, it's what I want. *Truly.*"

He stood in shadow, so she could not see his face. She could only hear his words and the fragile core of tenderness behind them. The timbre of his voice told her the cost of his speaking at all. "Helen. I woke up this morning knowing with perfect certainty that I love you. So much. God help me, but I don't understand why no other moment in my life has ever been quite as frightening."

"Rhys—"

"No. Please. Tell me tomorrow." He turned decisively and walked down the aisle, up the steps to join the others.

Left alone, Lady Helen forced her eyes to remain on the stage, but her thoughts would not. Instead, they attached themselves stubbornly to a reflection on loyalty. If this encounter with Rhys were a test of her devotion to him, she saw that, without even thinking, she had failed it miserably. And she wondered if that momentary failure meant the very worst, if in her heart she questioned what Rhys had really done two nights ago while she was asleep at Westerbrae. The very thought was devastating. She despised herself.

Getting to her feet, she returned to the entrance hall and approached the office doors. She decided against an elaborate fabrication. She would face Stinhurst's secretary with the truth.

That commitment to honesty would, in this case, be a wise decision.

"IT'S THE CHAIR, Havers," Lynley was saying once again, possibly for the fourth or fifth time.

The afternoon was growing unbearably cold. A frigid wind had swept in from The Wash and was tearing across the Fens, unbroken by woodland or hills. Lynley made the turn back towards Porthill

Green just as Barbara concluded her third examination of the suicide photographs and replaced them in the Darrow file that Chief Constable Plater had loaned them.

She shook her head inwardly. As far as she could tell, the case he was building was more than tenuous; it was virtually nonexistent. "I don't see how you can possibly reach any viable conclusion from looking at a picture of a chair," she said.

"Then *you* look at it again. If she hanged herself, how would she tip the chair onto its *side?* It couldn't have been done. She could have kicked at the back of it, or even turned it sideways and *still* kicked at the back of it. But in either case, the chair would have fallen onto its back, not onto its side. The only way for the chair to end up in that position at Hannah Darrow's own doing would be if she had twisted her foot into the space between the seat and the back and actually tried to toss the thing."

"It could have happened. She was missing a shoe," Barbara reminded him.

"Indeed. But she was missing her right shoe, Havers. And if you look again, you'll see that the chair was tipped over to her left."

Barbara saw that he was determined to win her to his way of thinking. There seemed little point to a further protest. Nonetheless, she felt compelled to argue. "So what you're saying is that Joy Sinclair, in innocently researching a book about a suicide, fell upon a murder instead. How? Out of all the suicides in the country, how could she possibly have stumbled onto one that was a murder? Good God, what do you think the odds are for doing that?"

"But consider *why* she was attracted to Hannah Darrow's death in the first place, Havers. Look at all the oddities involved that would have made it stand out glaringly in comparison to any others she looked at. The location: the Fens. A system of canals, periodic floods, land reclaimed from the sea. All the natural characteristics that have made it the inspiration of everyone from Dickens to Dorothy Sayers. How did Joy describe it on her tape? "The sound of frogs and pumps, the unremittingly flat land.' Then there's the site of the suicide: an old abandoned mill. The bizarre clothing she was wearing: two wool coats over two wool sweaters. And then the inconsistency that surely must have struck Joy the moment she saw those police photos: the position of that chair."

"If it *is* an inconsistency, how do you explain the fact that Plater himself overlooked it during the investigation? He doesn't exactly seem to be your bumbling Lestrade type."

"By the time Plater got there, all the men from the pub had been searching for Hannah, *all* of them convinced that they were looking for a suicide. And when they found her and telephoned for the police, they reported a suicide. Plater was predisposed to believe that's exactly what he was looking at when he got to the mill. So he'd lost objectivity before he ever saw the body. And he was given fairly convincing evidence that Hannah Darrow had indeed intended to kill herself when she left her flat. The note."

"But you heard Plater say it was genuine enough."

"Of course it's genuine," Lynley said. "I'm certain it's her handwriting."

"Then how do you explain—"

"Good God, Havers, look at the thing. Is there a single misspelled word in it? Is there a point of punctuation that she even missed?"

Barbara took it out, glanced at it, turned to Lynley. "Are you trying to say that this is something Hannah Darrow *copied*? Why? Was she practising her handwriting? Acting out of sheer boredom? Life in Porthill Green looks like it might be less than ducky, but I don't exactly see a village girl whiling away her time by improving her script. And even if she did, are you going to argue that Darrow found this note somewhere and realised how he could use it? That he had the foresight to stow it away until the time was right? That he put it out on the kitchen table? That he . . . what? Killed his wife? How? When? And how did he get her to wear all those clothes? And even if he managed it all without raising anyone's suspicion, how on earth is he connected to Westerbrae and Joy Sinclair's death?"

"Through the telephone calls," Lynley said. "Wales and Suffolk over and over. Joy Sinclair innocently telling her cousin Rhys Davies-Jones about her frustrations in dealing with John Darrow, not to mention her budding suspicions about Hannah's death. And Davies-Jones biding his time, suggesting that Joy arrange to have a room next to Helen, then finishing her off the moment he saw his chance."

Barbara heard him, incredulous. Once again she saw how he was turning and interpreting all the facts skilfully, using only what he needed to take him closer to an arrest of Davies-Jones. "*Why!*" she demanded in exasperation.

"Because there's a connection between Darrow and Davies-Jones. I don't know what it is yet. Perhaps an old relationship. Perhaps a debt to be paid. Perhaps mutual knowledge. But whatever it is, we're getting closer to finding it."

12

WINE'S THE PLOUGH was just minutes short of its midafternoon closing when Lynley and Havers entered. John Darrow made no secret of his displeasure at seeing them.

"Closing," he barked.

Lynley ignored the man's implied refusal to speak with them. Instead, he approached the bar, opened the file, and took out Hannah Darrow's suicide note. Next to him, Havers flipped open her notebook. Darrow watched all this with his mouth pressed into a hostile line.

"Tell me about this," Lynley suggested, passing the note across to him.

The man gave it a moment's sullen, cursory attention, but he said nothing. Instead, he began gathering the pint glasses that lined the bar, dousing them furiously into a pan of murky water beneath it.

"How much education did your wife have, Mr. Darrow? Did she finish school? Did she go to university? Or was she self-educated? A great reader, perhaps?"

Darrow's scowling face revealed a stumbling search through Lynley's words for a trap. Apparently not finding one, he said shortly, "Hannah didn't hold with books. She'd had enough of school at fifteen."

"I see. But interested in the Fens, was she? The plant life and such?"

The man's lips moved in a quick snarl of contempt. "What d'you want with me, pommy boy? Have your say and get out."

"She writes here about trees. And a tree that died but still sways in the wind. Rather poetic, wouldn't you say? Even for a suicide message. What is this note really, Darrow? When did your wife write it? Why did she? Where did you find it?" There was no reply. Wordlessly, Darrow continued washing glasses. They clanked and scraped angrily against the metal pan. "On the night she died, you left the pub. Why?"

"I went looking for her. I'd been up to the flat, found that"— Darrow's sharp nod indicated the note—"in the kitchen, went out to find her."

"Where?"

"The village."

"Knocking on doors? Looking in sheds? Searching through houses?"

"No. She wasn't likely to kill herself in someone's house now, was she?"

"And you knew for a certainty that she *was* going to kill herself?"

"It bloody well says that!"

"Indeed. Where did you look for her?"

"Here and there. I don't remember. It's fifteen years past. I didn't heed it at the time. And it's buried now. Am I clear on that, man? It's *buried*."

"It *was* buried," Lynley acknowledged. "Quite successfully so, I should guess. But then Joy Sinclair came here and began an exhumation. And it looks very much as if someone was afraid of that. Why did she telephone you so many times, Darrow? What did she want?"

Darrow swung both arms up from the dishwater. Irately, he slammed them onto the bar. "I've told you! The bitch wanted to talk about Hannah, but I was having none of it. I didn't want her raking up the past and mucking about with our lives. We're *over* it. God damn you, we're going to stay that way. Now, get out of here or make a fucking arrest."

Regarding the other man calmly, Lynley made no reply, so the implication behind Darrow's last statement grew with every moment. His face began to mottle. The veins in his arms seemed to swell.

"An arrest," Lynley repeated. "Odd that you should suggest that, Mr. Darrow. Why on earth should I want to make an arrest for a suicide? Except we both know, don't we, that this wasn't a suicide. And I believe that Joy Sinclair's mistake was telling you that it didn't much look like a suicide to her."

"Get out!" Darrow roared.

Lynley took his time about gathering the materials back into the folder. "We'll be back," he said pleasantly.

BY FOUR O'CLOCK that afternoon, the company assembled at the Agincourt Theatre had, after seven hours of politics and debate, settled on a playwright for the theatre's opening production: Tennessee Williams, a revival piece. The play itself was still open to discussion.

From the back of the auditorium, St. James observed the group on the stage. They had narrowed the field down to the relative merits of three possibilities, and from what St. James could tell, things were swinging in Joanna Ellacourt's direction. She was arguing strongly against *A Streetcar Named Desire*, her aversion to it rising, it seemed, out of a quick calculation of how much stage time Irene Sinclair would have if, however incongruously, she played Stella. There appeared to be no doubt at all as to the casting of Blanche Dubois.

Lord Stinhurst had been displaying a remarkable degree of patience for the quarter hour that St. James had been watching. In an unusual display of magnanimity, he had allowed all the players, the designers, the director, and the assistants to have their say about the crisis facing the company and the pressing need to get into production as soon as possible. Now, he got to his feet, kneading his fingers into the small of his back.

"You'll have my decision tomorrow," he told them. "We've been together long enough for now. Let's meet again in the morning. At half past nine. Be ready to read."

"No hints for us, Stuart?" Joanna Ellacourt asked, stretching languorously and leaning back in her chair so that her hair fell like a shimmering gold veil in the light. Next to her, Robert Gabriel affectionately ran three fingers down its length.

"None at all, I'm afraid," Lord Stinhurst replied. "I've not quite made up my mind."

Joanna smiled up at him, moving her shoulder to disengage Gabriel's hand from her hair. "Tell me what I can do to persuade you to decide in my favour, darling."

Gabriel gave a low, guttural laugh. "Take her up on it, Stuart. God knows our darling Jo excels at persuading."

No one spoke for a moment in answer to that remark, fully laced though it was with innuendo. No one even moved at first, save for David Sydeham, who raised his head slowly from the script he was examining and levelled his eyes on the other man. His face was deadly, rife with hostility, but Gabriel did not seem the least affected.

Rhys Davies-Jones threw down his own script. "Christ, you're an ass," he said to Gabriel wearily.

"And I once thought Rhys and I would never agree upon anything," Joanna added.

Irene Sinclair moved her chair back from the table. Harshly, it abraded the stage floor. "Right. Well. I'll be off." She spoke agreeably enough before making her exit down the main aisle of the theatre. But when she passed St. James, he saw how she was working to control her face, and he wondered how and why she had ever endured a marriage to Robert Gabriel.

While the other players, the assistants, and the designers began to drift off towards the wings, St. James got to his feet and went to the front of the auditorium. It was not overlarge, perhaps seating only five hundred people, and a grey haze of stale cigarette smoke hung over its open thrust stage. He mounted the steps.

"Have you a moment, Lord Stinhurst?"

Stinhurst was having a low-voiced conversation with a spindly young man who carried a clipboard and wrote with knotted concentration. "See to it that we've enough copies for tomorrow's read-through," he said in conclusion. Only then did he look up.

"So you lied to them about not having your mind made up," St. James observed.

Stinhurst didn't reply to this at once. Rather, he called out, "We've no need for all this light now, Donald," and in answer the stage leaped with cavernous shadows. Only the table itself was illuminated. Stinhurst sat down at it, took out pipe and tobacco, and laid them both down.

"Sometimes it's easier to lie," he admitted. "I'm afraid it's one of the behaviours a producer grows adept at over time. If you've ever been in the midst of a tug-of-war of creative egos, you'd know what I mean."

"This seems to be a particularly inflammable group."

"It's understandable. They've been through a bit of hell these past three days." Stinhurst packed his pipe. His shoulders were stiff, a marked contrast to the weariness of his voice and face. "I don't imagine this is a social call, Mr. St. James."

St. James handed him the stack of enlargements which Deborah had made from the photograph taken at Geoffrey Rintoul's inquest. On each new photograph appeared a single face and occasionally part of a torso, but nothing else. There was nothing to indicate that the people had once all been part of one group. Deborah had been particularly careful about that.

"Will you identify these people for me?" St. James asked.

Stinhurst fingered through the lot, turning each one slowly, his pipe ignored. St. James could see the marked hesitation in his movements, and he wondered if the man would actually cooperate. Stinhurst was no doubt well aware of the fact that he was not obliged to reveal a thing. Nonetheless, he also appeared to know exactly how a refusal to respond would be interpreted by Lynley if he learned of it. So St. James only hoped that Stinhurst believed he was here in some official capacity at Lynley's behest. After a thorough perusal, the man laid all the photographs out in a line and indicated each as he spoke.

"My father. My sister's husband, Phillip Gerrard. My sister, Francesca. My wife, Marguerite. My father's solicitor—he died some years ago and I can't remember his name at the moment. Our physician. Myself."

Stinhurst had omitted the very man whose identity they needed. St. James pointed to the photograph he had laid next to that of his sister. "And this man in profile?"

Stinhurst's brow creased. "I don't know. I can't say I've ever seen him before."

"Odd," St. James said.

"Why?"

"Because in the original photo from which all of these were taken, he's talking to you. And for some reason you look in that picture as if you know him quite well."

"Indeed. I may have at the time. But my brother's inquest was twenty-five years ago. And at this distance, I don't think I can be expected to remember everyone who was there."

"That's true," St. James replied and considered the fascinating fact that he had not mentioned that the photographs were from Geoffrey Rintoul's inquest at all.

Stinhurst was getting to his feet. "If there's nothing else, Mr. St. James, I've things to see to before my day ends here."

He did not look at the photographs again as he spoke, gathering

pipe and tobacco, readying himself to leave. And that was so unlikely a human reaction. It was as if the man had to keep his eyes
from them lest his face reveal more than he had been willing to say.
One thing was a certainty, St. James concluded. Lord Stinhurst
knew exactly who the man in the photograph was.

CERTAIN KINDS of lighting refuse to lie about the relentless, ineluc-
table process of ageing. They are entirely unforgiving, capable of
exposing flaws and baring the truth. Direct sunlight, the harsh
overhead fluorescent lights of a business establishment, the flood
lights used to film without soft-focus filters—these are proficient at
doing their worst. In her dressing room, Joanna Ellacourt's make-up
table appeared to have this sort of lighting as well. At least it did
today.

The air was quite cool, the way she always liked it in order to
keep the flowers fresh when they arrived from a score of admirers
before her performances. There were no flowers now. Instead, the
air held that combination of odours peculiar to every dressing room
she had ever inhabited, the mingling scents of cold cream, astrin-
gent, and lotion that littered the tabletop. Joanna was only dimly
aware of this scent as she stared unflinchingly at her reflection and
forced her eyes to rest upon each telling harbinger of approaching
middle age: the incipient wrinkles from nose to chin; the delicate
webbing round her eyes; the first ringed indentations on her neck,
prelude to the old-age cording that could never be disguised.

She smiled in self-mockery at the thought that she had escaped
nearly everything that had constituted the psychological quicksand
of her life. Her family's grubby five-room council house in Nottingham; the sight of her father sitting daily in unshaven gloom at his
window, a machinist on the dole whose dreams had died; the sound
of her mother whining about the cold that persistently seeped
through the poorly sealed windows, or the black and white telly
whose knobs were broken off so that the sound remained at a
constant nerve-shattering pitch; the future that each of her sisters
had chosen, one that repeated the history of their parents' marriage,
an endless, bone-grinding repetition of producing babies at intervals
of eighteen months and living without either hope or joy. She had
escaped all that. But she could not escape that process of slow
decomposition that awaits every man.

Like so many egocentric creatures whose beauty dominates the
stage and the screen and the covers of countless magazines, she had

thought for a time that she might elude it. She had, in fact, grown to believe that she *would*. For David had always allowed her to do so.

Her husband had been more than her liberation from the miseries of Nottingham. David had been the one true constant in a fickle world in which fame is ephemeral, in which the critics' apotheosis of a new talent could mean the ruin of an established actress who has given her life to the stage. David knew all about that, knew how it frightened her, and through his continual support and love—in spite of her tantrums, her demands, her flirtations—he had assuaged her fears. Until Joy Sinclair's play had come along, changing everything irrevocably between them.

Fixing her eyes on her reflection without really seeing it, Joanna felt the anger all over again. No longer the fire that had consumed her with such irrational, revenge-seeking intensity on Saturday night at Westerbrae, it had burned itself down to a glowing pilot, capable of igniting her central passion at the least provocation.

David had betrayed her. She forced herself to think of it again and again, lest the decades of their shared intimacy insinuate themselves into her consciousness and demand that she forgive him. She would never do so.

He had known how much she had depended upon *Othello* being the last time she performed with Robert Gabriel. He had known how much she despised Gabriel's pursuit of her, flavoured with accidental encounters, casually inadvertent movements that grazed his hand across the very tips of her breasts, longing stage kisses in front of enormous audiences who grew to believe it was part of the show, private double-edged compliments attached to references to his sexual prowess.

"Like it or not, you and Gabriel have magic when you're on the stage together," David had said.

Not the least bit jealous, not the least bit concerned. She had always wondered why. Until now.

He had lied to her about Joy Sinclair's play, telling her that Robert Gabriel's participation was Stinhurst's idea, telling her that Gabriel couldn't possibly be dropped from the cast. But she knew the real truth although she couldn't bear to face what it implied. To insist upon Gabriel's being sacked would mean a decrease in revenues for the show itself, which would cut into her percentage—into David's percentage. And David liked his money. His Lobb shoes, his Rolls, his home on Regent's Park, his cottage in the country, his Savile Row wardrobe. If all this could be maintained, what did it matter that his wife would have to fight off Robert Gabriel's sweaty advances for another year or so? She'd been doing it for more than a decade, after all.

When her dressing-room door opened, Joanna didn't bother to turn from the make-up table, for the mirror provided a more than adequate view of the door. Even if this had not been the case, she knew who was entering. After all, she'd had twenty years of hearing them to recognise any one of her husband's movements—his steady footsteps, the rasp of a match when he lit a cigarette, the rustle of cloth against his skin when he dressed, the slow relaxation of his muscles when he lay down to sleep. She could identify any and all of them; in the end they were so uniquely David.

But she was beyond considering any of that now. So she reached for hairbrush and hairpins, pushed her make-up case to one side, and began to see to her hair, counting the strokes from one to one hundred as if each took her further away from the long stretch of history she shared with David Sydeham.

He didn't speak when he entered the room. He merely walked to the chaise as he always did. But this time he did not sit. Nor did he speak until she finally finished with her hair, dropped her brush to the table, and turned to look at him expressionlessly.

"I suppose I can rest a bit more easily if I simply know why you did it," he said.

LADY HELEN arrived at the St. James home shortly before six that evening. She felt both discouraged and disheartened. Even a tray in St. James' study, burdened with fresh scones, cream, tea, and sandwiches, did little to brighten her.

"You look as if you could do with a sherry," St. James observed once she had removed her coat and gloves.

Lady Helen dug through her handbag for her notebook. "That sounds exactly what I need," she agreed heavily.

"No luck?" Deborah asked. She was sitting on the ottoman to the right of the hearth, sneaking an occasional bit of scone down to Peach, the scruffy little dachshund who waited patiently at her feet, occasionally testing the flavour of her ankle with a delicate and loving pink tongue. Nearby, the grey cat Alaska was curled happily onto a pile of papers in the centre of St. James' desk. Although his eyes slitted open, he did not otherwise stir at Lady Helen's entrance.

"It's not exactly that," she replied, gratefully accepting the glass of sherry which St. James brought her. "I've the information we want. It's only that . . ."

"It doesn't go far to helping Rhys," St. James guessed.

She shot him a smile that she knew was at best only tremulous. His words pained her unaccountably, and feeling the force of a sudden wretchedness, she realised how she had been depending upon her interview with Lord Stinhurst's secretary to attenuate everyone's suspicion of Rhys. "No, it doesn't help Rhys. It doesn't do much of anything, I'm afraid."

"Tell us," St. James said.

There was, after all, so little to tell. Lord Stinhurst's secretary had been willing enough to talk about the telephone calls she had placed for her employer, once she realised how essential those calls might be in exonerating him of any complicity in the death of Joy Sinclair. So she had spoken openly to Lady Helen, going so far as to produce the notebook into which she had jotted down the message that Stinhurst had wished her to repeat for every call she made. It was straightforward enough. "Am unavoidably delayed in Scotland due to an accident. Will be in touch the moment I'm available."

Only one call differed from that repeated message, and although it was decidedly odd, it did not seem to wear the guise of guilt. "Resurfacing forces me to put you off a second time this month. Terribly sorry. Telephone me at Westerbrae if this presents a problem."

"Resurfacing?" St. James repeated. "Odd choice of words. Are you certain about that, Helen?"

"Completely. Stinhurst's secretary had written it down."

"Some theatre term?" Deborah suggested.

St. James eased himself awkwardly into the chair near her. She moved on the ottoman to give him room for his leg. "Who received that last, Helen?"

She referred to her notes. "Sir Kenneth Willingate."

"A friend? A colleague?"

"I'm not altogether sure." Lady Helen hesitated, trying to decide how to present her last piece of information in such a way that St. James would be drawn into its singularity. She knew how flimsy a detail it was, knew also how she was clinging to it in the hope that it would take them in any direction other than towards Rhys. "I'm probably grasping at straws, Simon," she continued ingenuously. "But there was one thing about that last call. All the others had been made to cancel appointments that Stinhurst had over the next few days. His secretary merely read the names to me right out of his

engagement book. But that last call to Willingate had nothing to do
with his engagement book at all. The name wasn't even written
there. So it was either an appointment that Stinhurst had arranged
on his own without telling his secretary . . ."

"Or it wasn't in reference to an appointment at all," Deborah
finished for her.

"There's only one way we're going to know," St. James remarked.
"And that's to bully the information from Stinhurst. Or to track
down Willingate ourselves. But we can't go any further without
involving Tommy, I'm afraid. We're going to have to give him what
little information we have and let him take it from there."

"But Tommy won't take it up! You know that!" Lady Helen
protested. "He's looking for a tie to Rhys. He's going to dog whatever
facts he believes will allow him to make an arrest. Nothing else
matters to Tommy right now! Or wasn't this past weekend enough
of a demonstration for you? Apart from that, if you involve him,
he's bound to discover that Barbara's gone her own way on the case
. . . with *our* help, Simon. You can't do that to her."

St. James sighed. "Helen, you simply can't have it both ways. You
can't protect them both. It's going to come down to a decision. Do
you take the chance of sacrificing Barbara Havers? Or do you
sacrifice Rhys?"

"I sacrifice neither."

He shook his head. "I know how you feel, but I'm afraid that
won't wash."

WHEN COTTER showed Barbara Havers into the study, she sensed
the tension at once. The room felt alive with it. An abrupt silence,
followed by a quick burst of welcoming conversation, revealed the
discomfort that the three others were feeling. The atmosphere
among them was charged and taut.

"What is it?" she asked.

They were, she had to admit, nothing if not an honest group.

"Simon feels we can't go further without Tommy." Lady Helen
went on to explain the peculiar telephone message that Stinhurst
had sent to Sir Kenneth Willingate.

"We have no authority to pop into these people's lives and
question them, Barbara," St. James put in when Lady Helen finished.
"And you know they don't have an obligation to talk to us. So unless
Tommy takes it on, I'm afraid we've met with a dead end."

Barbara reflected on this. She knew quite well that Lynley had no intention of turning away from the East Anglian lead. It was too enticing. He would brush off an abstruse telephone message to an unknown Londoner named Willingate as a waste of his time. Especially, she thought with resignation, since Lord Stinhurst was the man who had sent it. The others were right. They'd come to a dead end. But if she couldn't persuade them to go on without Lynley, Stinhurst would get away cleanly, without a scratch.

"Of course, we know that if Tommy discovers you've taken part of the case in another direction without his authorisation . . ."

"I don't care about that," Barbara said brusquely, surprised to find that it was the perfect truth.

"You may be suspended. Or sent back to uniform. Even sacked."

"That isn't important right now. This is. I've spent the whole filthy day chasing spectres in East Anglia without a hope of any of it coming to any good. But we're onto something here, and I've no intention of letting it die simply because someone might put me in uniform again. *Or* sack me. Or anything else. So if we have to tell him, we tell him. Everything." She faced them squarely. "Shall we do it now?"

In spite of her decision, the others hesitated. "You don't want to think about it?" Lady Helen asked.

"I don't need to think about it," Barbara replied. Her words were harsh, and she didn't temper them as she continued. "Look, I saw Gowan *die*. He'd pulled a knife out of his back and crawled across the scullery floor, trying to get help. His skin looked like boiled meat. His nose was broken. His lips were split. I want to find who did that to a sixteen-year-old boy. And if it costs me my job to track the killer down, that's a very minor cost as far as I'm concerned. Who's coming with me?"

Loud voices in the hallway precluded an answer. The door swung open and Jeremy Vinney pushed past Cotter. He was breathless, red-faced. His trouser legs were soaked up to his knees, and his ungloved hands looked raw from the cold.

"Couldn't get a taxi," he panted. "Ended up running all the way from Sloane Square. Was afraid I might miss you." He stripped off his coat and threw it down on the couch. "Found out who the fellow in the photograph was. Had to let you know at once. Name's Willingate."

"Kenneth?"

"The same." Vinney bent with his hands on his knees, trying to catch his breath. "Not all. Not *who* the bloke is that makes it so interesting. It's *what* he is." He flashed a quick smile. "Don't know what he was in 1963. But right now he's the head of MI5."

13

THERE WASN'T a person in the room who did not understand the full range of implications behind Jeremy Vinney's words. MI5: Military Intelligence, section five. The counterintelligence agency of the British government. It was suddenly clear why Vinney had come bursting in upon them, certain of his welcome, completely assured that he bore information vital to the case. If he had been a suspect before, surely this new twist took him out of the running entirely. As if convinced of this, he went on.

"There's more. I was intrigued by our conversation this morning about the Profumo–Keeler case in 1963, so I went through the morgue to see if there was any article alluding to a possible connection between their situation and Geoffrey Rintoul's death. I thought that perhaps Rintoul *had* been involved with a call girl and was trotting back to London to see her the night he was killed."

"But Profumo and Keeler seem like such ancient history," Deborah remarked. "Surely that sort of scandal wouldn't affect a family's reputation now."

Lady Helen agreed, but her comments were obviously reluctant. "There's truth to that, Simon. Murder Joy. Destroy the scripts. Murder Gowan. All because Geoffrey Rintoul was seeing a call girl twenty-five years ago? How can one argue that as a credible motive?"

"It depends on the level of importance attached to the man's position," St. James replied. "Consider Profumo's case as an example. He was secretary of state for war, carrying on a relationship with Christine Keeler, a call girl who also just happened to be seeing a man called Yevgeni Ivanov."

"Who was attached to the Soviet embassy but was reportedly a Soviet intelligence agent," Vinney added and smoothly continued. "In an interview with the police on an entirely different matter, Christine Keeler volunteered the information that she had been asked to discover from John Profumo the date on which certain atomic secrets were to be passed to West Germany by the Americans."

"A lovely person," Lady Helen commented.

"This leaked to the press—as perhaps she intended—and things heated up for Profumo."

"And for the government as well," Havers said.

Vinney nodded his agreement. "The Labour party demanded that Profumo's relationship with Keeler be debated before the House of Commons while the Liberal party demanded the prime minister's resignation because of it."

"Why?" Deborah asked.

"They claimed that as head of security services, the prime minister was either aware of all the facts on Profumo's relationship with the call girl and was hiding them or he was guilty of incompetence and neglect. However," Vinney finished, "the truth well might be that the prime minister merely felt he could not survive another serious case involving the resignation of one of his ministers, as would likely occur if Profumo's behaviour was examined closely. So he gambled that nothing against Profumo would come out. If the Profumo affair came to light so soon after the Vassall case, chances are the prime minister would have to resign."

"*Vassall?*" Lady Helen's body tensed. White-faced, she leaned forward in her chair.

Vinney looked at her, clearly perplexed by her reaction to his words. "William Vassall. He was sentenced to prison in October of sixty-two. He was an Admiralty clerk who was spying for the Soviets."

"My God. My *God!*" Lady Helen cried. She got to her feet, spun to St. James. "Simon! It's the line from the play that all the Rintouls reacted to. 'Another Vassall.' The character was running off with no time to return to London. He said he wouldn't become *another* Vassall. And they knew what it meant when they heard it. They knew! Francesca, Elizabeth, Lord and Lady Stinhurst! All of them knew! This was no call-girl relationship! It was nothing of the sort!"

St. James was already pushing himself out of his chair. "Tommy *will* move on this, Helen."

"On what?" Deborah cried.

"On Geoffrey Rintoul, my love. Another Vassall. It seems that Geoffrey Rintoul was a Soviet mole. And God help them, but every member of his family and a good part of the government appeared to know it."

LYNLEY HAD left the doors open between his dining and drawing rooms, largely so that he could hear the music from his stereo while he was eating dinner. For the past few days, food had held little attraction for him. Tonight was no different. Because of this, he pushed most of his lamb aside uneaten and instead gave himself over to the passion of a Beethoven symphony that swelled from the next room. He moved away from the table and leaned back in his chair with his legs stretched out before him.

In the last twenty-four hours, he had avoided thinking about what the case he was building against Rhys Davies-Jones was going to do to Helen Clyde. Steadfastly forcing himself to keep moving forward from fact to fact, he had managed to keep Helen out of his mind entirely. But she intruded now.

He understood her unwillingness to believe in Davies-Jones' guilt. She was, after all, involved with the man. But how would she react when she was faced with the knowledge—irrefutable and supported by a score of facts—that she had been cold-bloodedly used to facilitate a murder? And how could he possibly protect her from the devastation that knowledge was going to cause in her life? In thinking about this, Lynley found that he could no longer avoid looking directly at the truth of how damnably much he missed Helen and how irrevocably he might lose her if he continued his pursuit of Davies-Jones to its logical conclusion.

"My lord?" His valet was standing hesitantly in the doorway, rubbing the top of his left shoe against the back of his right leg as if in the need to make adjustments to his already immaculate appearance. He ran a hand over the top of his perfectly groomed hair.

Beau Brummel of Eaton Terrace, Lynley thought, and said encouragingly, "Denton?" when it appeared that the young man might go on with his grooming indefinitely.

"Lady Helen Clyde's just in the ante, my lord. With Mr. St. James and Sergeant Havers." Denton's expression was a model of nonchalance, something he no doubt considered suitable to the occasion. However, his tone conveyed some considerable surprise, and Lynley wondered how much Denton already knew—in that omniscient way of servants—about his rift with Lady Helen. He had, after all, been seeing Lady Helen's Caroline rather seriously for the past three years.

"Well, don't leave them standing in the hall," Lynley said.

"The drawing room, then?" Denton enquired solicitously. Much too solicitously for Lynley's liking.

He rose with a nod, irritably thinking, *I hardly expect they want to see me in the kitchen.*

The three of them were standing in a fairly tight knot at one end of the room when he joined them a moment later. They had chosen a position beneath the portrait of Lynley's father, and under the cover of the music, they were speaking to one another in hushed, urgent voices. But his entrance brought their conversation to an end. And then, as if his presence were a stimulus to do so, they began to shed their coats, hats, gloves, and mufflers. The action had the appearance of buying a bit of time. Lynley turned off the stereo, replaced the album in its jacket, and faced them curiously. They seemed unnaturally subdued.

"We've come across some information that you need to have, Tommy," St. James said, in very much the manner of a planned introduction.

"What sort of information?"

"It concerns Lord Stinhurst."

Lynley's eyes went at once to Sergeant Havers. She met them unflinchingly. "Are you part of this, Havers?"

"Yes, I am. Sir."

"It's my doing, Tommy," St. James said before Lynley could speak again. "Barbara found Geoffrey Rintoul's grave on the Westerbrae grounds, and she showed it to me. It seemed worth looking into."

Lynley maintained his calm with an effort. "Why?"

"Because of Phillip Gerrard's will," Lady Helen said impulsively. "Francesca's husband. He said he wouldn't allow himself to be buried on the grounds of Westerbrae. Because of the telephone calls Lord Stinhurst placed on the morning of the murder. They *weren't* only to cancel his appointments, Tommy. Because—"

Lynley looked at St. James, feeling the blow of treachery strike him from the single most unexpected quarter. "My God. You've told them about my conversation with Stinhurst."

St. James had the grace to drop his eyes. "I'm sorry. Truly. I felt I had no choice."

"No choice," Lynley repeated incredulously.

Lady Helen took a hesitant step towards him, her hand extended. "Please, Tommy. I know how you must feel. As if we're all against you. But that isn't it at all. Please. Listen."

Compassion from Helen was just about the last thing Lynley could bear at the moment. He struck out at her cruelly, without a thought. "I think we're all perfectly clear on where your interests lie, Helen. You can hardly be the most objective assessor of truth, considering your involvement in this case."

Lady Helen's hand fell. Her face was stricken with pain. St. James spoke, his voice cold with quick anger. "Nor can you, Tommy, if the truth be faced among us." He let a moment pass. Then he went on in a different tone, but as implacably as before. "Lord Stinhurst lied to you about his brother and his wife. First and last. A good possibility is that Scotland Yard knew he planned to do so and sanctioned it. The Yard chose you deliberately to handle this case because you were the most likely person to believe whatever Stinhurst told you. His brother and his wife never had an affair, Tommy. Now do you want to hear the facts, or shall we be on our way?"

Lynley felt as if ice were melting into his bones. "What in God's name are you talking about?"

St. James moved towards a chair. "That's what we've come to tell you. But I think we all could do with a brandy."

WHILE ST. JAMES outlined the information they had gathered on Geoffrey Rintoul, Barbara Havers watched Lynley, gauging his reaction. She knew how resistant he would be to the facts, considering Rintoul's privileged background and how closely it resembled Lynley's own. Everything in Lynley's upper-class constitution was going to act in concert, provoking him to disclaim each of their facts and conjectures. And the policewoman in Barbara knew exactly how insubstantial some of their facts were. The inescapable reality was that if Geoffrey Rintoul had indeed been a Soviet mole—working for years within that sensitive area of the Defence Ministry—the only way they would know for a certainty would be if his brother Stuart admitted it to them.

Ideally, they needed access to an MI5 computer. Even a file on Geoffrey Rintoul marked *inaccessible* would verify that the man had been under some sort of investigation by the counterintelligence agency. But they had no access to such a computer and no source within MI5 who could validate their story. Even Scotland Yard's Special Branch would be of no service to them if the Yard itself had sanctioned Lord Stinhurst's fabrication about his brother's death in Scotland in the first place. So it all came down to Lynley's ability to see past his tangle of prejudices against Rhys Davies-Jones. It all came down to his ability to look the truth squarely in the face. And the truth was that Lord Stinhurst, not Davies-Jones, had the strongest possible motive for wanting Joy Sinclair dead. Provided with the keys to Joy's room by his own sister, he had murdered the woman whose play—cleverly revised without his prior knowledge— had threatened to reveal his family's darkest secret.

"So when Stinhurst heard the name *Vassall* in Joy's play, he had to know what she was writing about," St. James concluded. "And consider how Geoffrey Rintoul's background supports his having been a spy for the Soviets, Tommy. He went to Cambridge in the thirties. We know that Soviet recruiting went on like the devil during that period. Rintoul read economics, which no doubt made him even more receptive to arguments in favour of the teachings of Marx. And then his behaviour during the war. Requesting reassignment to the Balkans gave him contact with the Russians. I shouldn't be at all surprised to discover that his control was in the Balkans as well. No doubt that's when he received his most important instructions: to work his way into the Ministry of Defence. God knows how much sensitive data he supplied the Soviets over the years."

No one said anything when St. James finished speaking. Their attention was on Lynley. They had taken their seats under the portrait of the seventh Earl of Asherton, and as they watched, Lynley lifted his eyes to his father's face as if in the need of counsel. His expression was unreadable.

"Tell me again what Stinhurst's message was to Willingate," he said at last.

St. James leaned forward. "He said that resurfacing forced him to put Willingate off a second time this month. And to telephone Westerbrae if that presented a problem."

"Once we discovered exactly who Willingate is, the message began to make more sense," Barbara continued. She felt a sense of urgency, a need to convince. "He seemed to be telling Willingate that the fact that Geoffrey Rintoul had been a mole had surfaced for the second time, the first time being on that New Year's Eve of 1962. So Willingate was to telephone Westerbrae to assist with a problem.

The problem being Joy Sinclair's death and the script she was writing that exposed all the details of Geoffrey's unsavoury past."

Lynley nodded.

Barbara went on. "Of course, Lord Stinhurst couldn't telephone Willingate himself, could he? Any research into the Westerbrae telephone records would have shown us that call. So he placed the one call to his secretary. She did the rest. And Willingate, understanding the message, *did* telephone him, sir. Twice, I should guess. Remember? Mary Agnes told me she heard *two* calls come in. They had to be from Willingate. One to find out what in God's name had happened. And the second to tell Stinhurst what he'd managed to set up with Scotland Yard."

"Remember as well," St. James said, "that according to Inspector Macaskin, Strathclyde CID never requested the Yard's assistance in the case at all. They were merely informed that the Yard would take over. It seems likely that Willingate arranged all that, telephoning someone in high command at the Yard to set the investigation up and then getting back to Stinhurst with the details of who the investigating officer would be. No doubt Stinhurst was more than ready for your appearance on the scene, Tommy. And he had all day to plan out a story that you, a fellow peer, would be likely to believe. It had to be a personal story, one that, as a gentleman, you would be unlikely to repeat. What better choice than his wife's allegedly illegitimate child? It was insidiously clever. He simply didn't take into account that you would confide in me. Nor that I—not very much of a gentleman myself, I'm afraid—would break your confidence. And I'm sorry I did that. Had there been any other way, I'd have said nothing. I hope you believe me."

St. James' last remark bore the sound of conclusion. But after it, Lynley merely reached for the brandy. He poured himself more and passed the decanter on to St. James. His hands did not shake, his face did not change. Outside, a horn honked twice on Eaton Terrace. An answering shout rose from a house nearby.

Feeling a rising need to force him into taking a position, Barbara spoke. "The question we were trying to answer on the way here, sir, is why the government would involve themselves in a case like this now. And the answer seems to be that in 1963 they engaged in a cover-up of Rintoul's activities—probably using the Official Secrets Act—in order to spare the prime minister the embarrassment of having a Soviet spy discovered in the high reaches of government so soon upon the heels of the Vassall situation and the Profumo scandal. Since Geoffrey Rintoul was dead, he could do the Defence

Ministry no further damage. He could only be of damage to the prime minister himself if the news of his activities leaked. So they kept that from happening. And now, they'd apparently prefer not to have that old cover-up exposed. I suppose it would be rather embarrassing for them. Or maybe they've debts to be paid to the Rintoul family and this is how they're paying them. At any rate, they've covered up again. Only . . ." Barbara paused, wondering how he would take the final bit of information, knowing only that in spite of their rows and the often insurmountable differences between them, she couldn't be the one to give him such pain.

Lynley took the opportunity himself. "I was to do it for them," he said hollowly. "And Webberly knew it. Right from the beginning."

In the devastation behind the words, Barbara recognised what Lynley was thinking—that this situation proved he was merely an expendable object to his superiors at the Met; that his was not a career with either value or distinction, so that if it were destroyed by the exposure of his even unconscious attempt to cover up the trail of Stinhurst's guilt in a murder investigation, there would be no real loss to anyone when he was dismissed. Never mind the fact that none of this was true. Barbara knew even a moment's belief in it would corrosively erode his pride.

In the past fifteen months, she had loved and hated and come to understand him. But never before had she perceived that his aristocratic background was a source of anguish to him, a burden of family and blood that he managed to carry with an unassuming dignity, even in the moments when he most longed to shrug it off.

"How could Joy Sinclair have known all this?" Lynley asked. His face was impeccably, painfully controlled.

"Lord Stinhurst told you that himself. She was *there* the night Geoffrey died."

"And I didn't even notice that there was nothing about Joy's play in her study." Lynley's voice was heavy with reproach. "Christ, what kind of police work is that?"

"The gentlemen from MI5 don't leave calling cards when they've searched a house, Tommy," St. James said. "There was no evidence of a search. You couldn't have known they had been there. And after all, you hadn't gone looking for information about the play."

"All the same, I shouldn't have been blind to its absence." He smiled grimly at Barbara. "Good work, Sergeant. I can't think where we'd be if I hadn't had you along."

Lynley's praise brought Barbara no joy. Never had she felt so completely wretched about having been in the right. "What shall we . . . ?" She hesitated, unwilling to take any more authority from him.

Lynley got to his feet. "We'll go for Stinhurst in the morning," he said. "I should like the rest of the night to think about what needs to be done."

Barbara knew what he really meant: to think about what he himself was going to do, faced with the knowledge of how Scotland Yard had used him. She wanted to say something to lighten the blow. She wanted to say that in spite of the plan to make him instrumental in a cover-up, it hadn't come off; they had proved themselves superior to it. But she knew that he would see through the words to the truth beneath them. *She* had proved herself superior to it. She had saved him from his own black folly.

With nothing more to be said, they began putting on their coats, pulling on gloves, adjusting hats and mufflers. The atmosphere was fraught with words needing to be spoken. Lynley took his time about replacing the brandy decanter, gathering the small crystal balloon glasses onto a tray, turning out the lights in the room. He followed them into the hall.

Lady Helen was standing in a pool of light near the door. She had said nothing for an hour, and now she spoke tentatively as he came to join them. "Tommy . . ."

"Meet me at the theatre at nine, Sergeant," Lynley said abruptly. "Have a constable with you to take Stinhurst in."

If she had not already realised how inconsequential her triumph really was in this game of detection, that brief exchange would have illustrated the point for Barbara with rare lucidity. She saw the gulf widen between Lynley and Lady Helen, felt its painful impassability like a physical wound. She said only, "Yes, sir," and reached for the door.

"Tommy, you *can't* ignore me any longer," Lady Helen insisted.

Lynley looked at her then for the first time since St. James had begun speaking in the drawing room. "I was wrong about him, Helen. But you need to know the worst of my sin. I wanted to be right."

He nodded good night and left them.

WEDNESDAY DAWNED under a leaden sky, the coldest day yet. The snow along the pavement had developed a hard, thin crust, grimy from soot and the exhaust of the city traffic.

When Lynley pulled up in front of the Agincourt Theatre at eight forty-five, Sergeant Havers was already waiting in front of it, bundled up to her eyebrows in her usual unbecoming brown wool, with a young police constable at her side. Lynley noted grimly that Havers had put some considerable thought into her selection of a constable, choosing the one least likely to be cowed by Stinhurst's title and wealth: Winston Nkata. Once a mainstay of the Brixton Warriors—one of the city's most violent black gangs—the twenty-five-year-old Nkata, through the patient intercession and continuing friendship of three hard-nosed officers in A7 Branch, was now an aspirant to the highest reaches of CID. Living proof, he liked to say, that if they can't arrest you, they'll damn well convert you.

He flashed Lynley one of his high-voltage smiles. " 'Spector," he called, "why you never drive that baby in *my* neighbourhood? We like to burn pieces *that* nice."

"The next riot, let me know," Lynley responded drily.

"Next riot, we send out invitations, man. Make sure everybody have a chance to be there."

"Ah. Yes. Bring your own brick."

The black man threw back his head and laughed unrestrainedly as Lynley joined them on the pavement. "I like you, 'Spector," he said. "Give me your home address. I think I got to marry your sister."

Lynley smiled. "You're too good for her, Nkata. Not to mention about sixteen years too young. But if you behave yourself this morning, I'm sure we can come to a suitable arrangement." He looked at Havers. "Has Stinhurst arrived yet?"

She nodded. "Ten minutes ago." In answer to his unasked question, she replied, "He didn't see us. We were having coffee across the way. He had his wife with him, Inspector."

"That," Lynley said, "is a stroke of luck. Let's go in."

Inside, the theatre buzzed with the activity attendant to a new production. The auditorium doors were open; conversation and laughter mixed with the noise of a crew at work, taking measurements for a set. Production assistants hurried by with clipboards in their hands and pencils behind their ears. In a corner by the bar, a publicist and a designer held a huddle over a large sheet of paper onto which the latter was sketching advertising draughts. It was altogether a place of creativity, humming with excitement, but this morning Lynley did not find himself at all regretful that he would be the instrument of bringing all these people's pleasure to an end. As would be the case once Stinhurst faced arrest.

They were walking towards the door to the production offices at the far side of the building when Lord Stinhurst came out of it, followed by his wife. Lady Stinhurst was speaking in an agitated rush, twisting a large diamond ring on her finger. She stopped everything—ring-twisting, speaking, walking—when she saw the police.

Stinhurst was cooperative enough when Lynley requested a private place to talk. "Come into my office," he said. "Shall my wife . . ." He hesitated meaningfully.

Lynley, however, had already decided exactly how Lady Stinhurst's presence could be turned to his advantage. Part of him—the better part, he thought—wanted to let her go in peace, and shrank from making her a chessman in the game of fact and fiction. But the other part of him needed her as a tool of blackmail. And he hated that part of himself, even as he knew he would use her.

"I'd like Lady Stinhurst there as well," he said briefly.

With Constable Nkata posted outside the door and instructions to Stinhurst's secretary to put no calls through that were not for the police, Lynley and Havers joined Lord Stinhurst and his wife in the producer's office. It was a room much like the man himself, coldly decorated in black and grey, fitted out with a compulsively neat hardwood desk and luxuriously upholstered wingback chairs, the air holding an almost imperceptible odour of pipe tobacco. The walls were hung with tastefully framed posters of former Stinhurst productions, proclamations of over thirty years of success: *Henry V*, London; *The Three Sisters*, Norwich; *Rosencrantz and Guildenstern Are Dead*, Keswick; *A Doll's House*, London; *Private Lives*, Exeter; *Equus*, Brighton; *Amadeus*, London. At one side of the room were grouped a conference table and chairs. Lynley directed them towards these, unwilling to allow Stinhurst the comfort and command of facing the police across the width of his polished desk.

As Havers rooted for her notebook, Lynley took out the photographs of the inquest as well as the enlargements which Deborah St. James had made. He laid them out on the table wordlessly. If everything St. James had said was true, Stinhurst had no doubt telephoned Sir Kenneth Willingate yesterday afternoon. He would be well fortified for this coming interview. Through a long, sleepless night Lynley had carefully reviewed the various ways he might head off another well-crafted set of lies. He had come to the realisation that Stinhurst did have at least one Achilles' heel. Lynley aimed his first remark in its direction.

"Jeremy Vinney knows the entire story, Lord Stinhurst. I don't know whether he'll write it since for the moment he has no hard evidence to back it up. But I have no doubt that he intends to start looking for that evidence." Lynley straightened the photographs with deliberate attention. "So you can tell me another lie. Or we can explore in detail the one you created for me this past weekend at Westerbrae. Or you can tell the truth. But let me point out to you that had you told me the truth about your brother in the first place, it would probably have gone no further than St. James, in whom I confided. But because you lied to me, and because that lie didn't fit in with your brother's grave in Scotland, Sergeant Havers knows about Geoffrey, as does St. James, as does Lady Helen Clyde, as does Jeremy Vinney. As will everyone with access to my report at Scotland Yard once I file it." Lynley saw Stinhurst's eyes go to his wife. "So what's it to be?" he asked, relaxing into his chair. "Shall we talk about that summer thirty-six years ago when your brother Geoffrey was in Somerset and you travelled the country in the regionals and your wife—"

"Enough," Stinhurst said. He smiled icily. "Hoist with my own petard, Inspector? Bravo."

Lady Stinhurst's hands writhed in her lap. "Stuart, what is all this? What have you told them?"

The question could not have come at a better time. Lynley waited for the man's response. After a long and thoughtful perusal of the police, Stinhurst turned to his wife and began to speak. However, when he did so, it was to prove beyond a doubt that he was a master player in the game of disarmament and surprise.

"I told him you and Geoffrey were lovers," he said. "I claimed that Elizabeth was your child, and that Joy Sinclair's play was about your affair. I told them that she had revised her play without my knowledge to revenge herself upon us for Alec's death. God forgive me, at least that last part was true enough. I'm sorry."

Lady Stinhurst sat in uncomprehending silence, her mouth contorting with words that would not emerge. One side of her face seemed to collapse with the effort. Finally she managed, *"Geoff? You never thought that Geoffrey and I . . . oh my God, Stuart!"*

Stinhurst started to reach towards his wife, but she cried out involuntarily and shrank from the gesture. He withdrew fractionally, leaving his hand lying on the table between them. The fingers curled, then tightened into the palm.

"No, of course not. But I needed to tell them something. I needed . . . I *had* to keep them away from Geoff."

"You needed to tell them . . . But he's *dead.*" Her face transformed with growing revulsion as she took in the enormity of what her husband had done. "Geoff's dead. And I'm not. Stuart, I'm not! You made a whore out of me to protect a dead man! You sacrificed me! My God! How *could* you have done that?"

Stinhurst shook his head. His words were laboured. "Not a dead man. Not dead at all. But alive and in this room. Forgive me if you can. I was a coward, first, last, and always. I was only trying to protect myself."

"From what? You've done nothing! Stuart, for God's sake. You did *nothing* that night! How can you say—"

"It isn't true. I couldn't tell you."

"Tell me what? Tell me *now!*"

Stinhurst stared long at his wife, as if he were trying to summon courage from an examination of her face. "I was the one who gave Geoff over to the government. All of you learned the worst about him on that New Year's Eve. But I . . . God help me, I'd known he was a Soviet agent since 1949."

STINHURST HELD himself perfectly still as he spoke, perhaps in the belief that a single movement would cause the floodgates to open and the accumulated anguish of thirty-nine years to come pouring out. His voice was matter-of-fact, and although his eyes became increasingly red-rimmed, he shed no tears. Lynley found himself wondering if Stinhurst was even capable of weeping after so many years of deceit.

"I knew that Geoff was a Marxist when we were at Cambridge. He made no secret of it, and frankly, I took it as a bit of a lark, something he would outgrow in time. And if he didn't, I thought what a laugh it would be to have the future Earl of Stinhurst committed to the workers' struggle to change the tide of history. What I didn't know was that his proclivities had been duly noted, and that he had been seduced into espionage while he was still a student."

"Seduced?" Lynley asked.

"It *is* a process of seduction," Stinhurst replied. "A combination of flattery and cajolery, making the student believe he plays an important role in the scheme of change."

"How did you come to know this?"

"I discovered it quite by chance, after the war when we were all in Somerset. It was the weekend my son Alec was born. I'd gone out looking for Geoff directly after I'd seen Marguerite and the baby. It was . . ." He smiled at his wife for the first and only time. Her face did not register a single response. "A *son*. I was so happy. I wanted Geoff to know. So I went out looking and found him in one of our boyhood haunts, an abandoned cottage in the Quantock Hills. Apparently he'd felt that Somerset was safe."

"He was meeting someone?"

Stinhurst nodded. "I probably would have thought it was only a farmer, but earlier that weekend I'd seen Geoff working in the study on some government papers, the sort that are stamped *confidential* in garish letters across the front. I thought nothing of it at the time, just that he'd brought work home. His briefcase was on the desk, and he was putting a document into a manila envelope. Not an estate envelope, nor a government one. I remember that distinctly. But I thought nothing of it until I came upon him in the cottage and saw him pass that same envelope to the man he was meeting. I've often thought that had I arrived a minute sooner—a minute later—I might well have assumed his companion was indeed a Somerset farmer. But as it was, once I saw the envelope change hands, I guessed the worst. Of course, for a moment I tried to tell myself that it was all a coincidence, that the envelope could not possibly be the same one I had seen in the study. But if it was only an innocent exchange of information that I'd witnessed—all legal and aboveboard—why arrange for it to take place in the Quantock Hills, in the middle of nowhere?"

"If you'd discovered them," Lady Stinhurst asked numbly, "why didn't they do . . . something to keep you from revealing what you knew?"

"They didn't know exactly what I'd seen. And even if they had, I was safe. In spite of everything, Geoff would have drawn the line at the elimination of his own brother. He was, after all, more of a man than I when it came right down to it."

Lady Stinhurst looked away. "Don't say that about yourself."

"It's true, I'm afraid."

"Did he admit to his activities?" Lynley asked.

"Once the other man was gone, I confronted him," Stinhurst said. "He admitted to it. He wasn't ashamed. He believed in the cause. And I . . . I don't know what I believed in. All I knew was that he was my brother. I loved him. I always had. Even though I was revolted by what he was doing, I couldn't bring myself to betray him. He would have *known*, you see, that I was the one to turn him in. So I did nothing. But it ate away at me for years."

"I should guess you finally saw your opportunity to take action in 1962."

"The government prosecuted William Vassall in October; they already had arrested and tried an Italian physicist—Giuseppe Martelli—for espionage in September. I thought that if Geoff's activities were uncovered then, so many years after I had come to know about them, he could hardly think I was the one to give him over to the government. So I . . . in November I handed my facts to the authorities. And surveillance began. In my heart, I hoped—I prayed—that Geoff would discover he was being watched and make his escape to the Soviets. He almost did."

"What prevented him?"

At the question, Stinhurst's clenched fist tightened. His hand shook with the pressure, knuckles and fingers white. In the outer office a telephone rang; an infectious burst of laughter sounded. Sergeant Havers stopped writing, cast a questioning look towards Lynley.

"What prevented him?" Lynley repeated.

"Tell them, Stuart," Lady Stinhurst murmured. "Tell the truth. This once. At last."

Her husband rubbed at his eyelids. His skin looked grey. "My father," he said. "He killed him."

STINHURST PACED the length of the room, his tall, lean figure like a rod save for his head, which was bent, his eyes on the floor.

"It happened much the way Joy's play depicted it the other night. There was a telephone call for Geoff, but my father and I came into the library without Geoff's knowledge and overheard part of it, heard him say that someone would have to get to his flat for the code book or the whole network would be blown. Father began to question him. Geoff—he was always so eloquent, such a master of the language—was frantic to get away at once. There was hardly time for an inquisition. He wasn't thinking straight, wasn't answering questions consistently, so Father guessed the truth. It wasn't really difficult after what we'd both heard of the telephone conversation. When Father saw that the very worst was true, something simply snapped. To him, it was more than treason. It was a betrayal of family, of an entire way of life. I think he was overcome in an instant with a need to obliterate. So . . ." From across the room, Stinhurst examined the lovely posters that lined his office walls. "My father went after him. He was like a bear. And I . . . God, I watched it all. Frozen. Useless. And every night since then, Thomas, I've relived that moment when I heard Geoff's neck crack like the branch of a tree."

"Was your sister's husband, Phillip Gerrard, involved?" Lynley asked.

"Yes. He wasn't in the library when Geoff's call came through, but he and Francesca and Marguerite heard my father shouting and came running from upstairs. They burst into the room just a moment after . . . it was done. Of course, Phillip immediately went for the phone, insisting that the authorities be sent for at once. But we . . . the rest of us pressured him out of it. The scandal. A trial. Perhaps Father going to prison. Francesca became hysterical at the thought. Phillip was obdurate enough at first, but ultimately, against all of us, especially Francie, what could he do? So he helped us take his—Geoffrey, the body—to where the road forks left to Hillview Farm and begins the descent right towards Kilparie village. We took only Geoff's car, to leave one set of tyre prints." He smiled in exquisite self-denigration. "We were careful about that sort of thing. There's a tremendous declivity that begins at the fork, with two switchbacks, one right after the other like a snake. We started the engine, sent the car off with Geoff in the driver's seat. The car built speed. At the first switchback it shot across the road, broke through the fence, made the drop to the second switchback below, and went over the embankment. It burst into flames." He pulled out a white handkerchief—a perfectly laundered linen square—and wiped at his eyes. He returned to the table but did not sit. "Afterwards, we walked home. The road was almost entirely ice, so we didn't even leave footprints. There was never really a question of its not being an accident." His fingers touched the photograph of his father, still lying where Lynley had placed it among the others on the table.

"Then why did Sir Andrew Higgins come from London to identify the body and testify at the inquest?"

"As insurance. Lest anyone notice anything peculiar about Geoff's injuries that might cause questions to arise about our story. Sir Andrew was my father's oldest friend. He could be trusted."

"And Willingate's involvement?"

"He arrived at Westerbrae within two hours of the accident. He'd been on his way to take Geoff back to London for questioning in the first place. A warning of his impending arrival was evidently the content of the telephone call my brother had received. Father told Willingate the truth. And a deal was struck between them. It would be an official secret. The government didn't want it known that a mole had been in place for years in the Ministry of Defence now that the mole was dead. My father didn't want it known that his son had been the mole. Nor did he want to stand trial for murder. So the accident story stood. And the rest of us vowed silence. We kept it as well. But Phillip Gerrard was a decent man. The knowledge that he'd allowed himself to be talked into covering up a murder consumed him for the rest of his life."

"Is that why he's not buried on Westerbrae land?"

"He felt he had cursed it."

"Why is your brother buried there?"

"Father wouldn't have his body in Somerset. It was all we could do to convince him to bury Geoff at all." Stinhurst finally looked at his wife. "We all broke on the wheel of Geoffrey's sedition, didn't we, Mag? But you and I worst of all. We lost Alec. We lost Elizabeth. We lost each other."

"It's always been Geoff between us, then," she said dully. "All these years. You've always acted as if *you* killed him, not your father. There were even times when I wondered if you had."

Stinhurst shook his head, refusing to accept exoneration. "I did. Of course I did. In the library that night, there was a split second of decision when I could have gone to them, when I could have stopped Father. They were on the floor and . . . Geoff *looked* at me. Maggie, I'm the last person he saw. And the last thing he knew was that his only brother was going to stand there and do nothing and watch him die. I may as well have killed him myself, you see. I'm responsible for it in the long run."

Treason, like the plague, doth take much in a blood. Lynley thought that Webster's line had never seemed so apt as it did now. For from the fountainhead of Geoffrey Rintoul's treachery had sprung the destruction of his entire family. And since the destruction would not sicken, it continued to feed upon the other lives that touched on the periphery of the Rintouls': on Joy Sinclair's and Gowan Kilbride's. But now it would stop.

There was just one more detail to be attended to. "Why did you involve MI5 this past weekend?"

"I didn't know what else to do. All I knew was that any investigation would inevitably centre itself round the script we were reading the night Joy died. And I thought—I *believed*—that a close scrutiny of the script would reveal everything my family and the government had been so careful to keep hidden for twenty-five years. When Willingate phoned me, he agreed that the scripts had to be destroyed. Then he got in touch with your people in Special Branch and they in turn contacted a Met commissioner, who agreed to send someone—someone special—to Westerbrae."

Those last words brought with them a renewed swelling of bitterness that Lynley fought against uselessly. He told himself that had it not been for Helen's presence at Westerbrae and the crushing revelation about her relationship with Rhys Davies-Jones, he would have seen through the web of lies that Stinhurst had woven, he would have found Geoffrey Rintoul's grave himself and drawn his own conclusions from it without the generous aid of his friends. At the moment, clinging to that belief was his only source of self-respect.

"I'm going to ask you to make a complete statement at the Yard," Lynley said to Stinhurst.

"Of course," he replied, and the denial that followed his acquiescence was as mechanical as it was immediate. "I didn't kill Joy Sinclair. Thomas, I swear it."

"He didn't." Lady Stinhurst's tone was more resigned than urgent. Lynley didn't respond. She went on. "I would have known had he left our room that night, Inspector."

Lady Stinhurst could not have chosen a single rationale less likely to meet with Lynley's belief. He turned to Havers. "Take Lord Stinhurst in for a preliminary statement, Sergeant. See that Lady Stinhurst goes home."

She nodded. "And you, Inspector?"

He thought about the question, about the time he still needed to come to terms with all that had happened. "I'll be along directly."

ONCE LADY STINHURST'S taxi was on its way to the family's Holland Park home and Sergeant Havers and Constable Nkata had escorted Lord Stinhurst from the Agincourt Theatre, Lynley went back into the building. He did not relish the idea of an accidental meeting with Rhys Davies-Jones, and there was no doubt at all that the man was somewhere on the premises today. Yet something prompted Lynley to linger, perhaps as a form of expiation for the sins he had committed in suspecting Davies-Jones of murder, in doing everything in his power to encourage Helen to suspect him of murder as well. Governed by the force of passion rather than by reason, he had scrambled for facts that would point the case in the Welshman's direction and had ignored those that wanted to lay the blame upon anyone else.

All this, he thought wryly, *because I was so stupidly ignorant of what Helen meant in my life until it was too late.*

"You needn't try to comfort me." It was a woman's faltering voice, coming from the far side of the bar, just out of the range of Lynley's vision. "I haven't come here on any but equal terms. You said, let's talk truthfully. Well, let's do! Unsparingly, truthfully, even shamelessly, then!"

"Jo—" David Sydeham responded.

"It's no longer a secret that I love you. It never was. I loved you as long ago as the time I asked you to read the stone angel's name with your fingers. Yes, it had begun that early, this affliction of love, and has never let go of me since. And that is my story—"

"Joanna, shut up. You've dropped at least ten lines!"

"I haven't!"

Sydeham and Ellacourt's words pounded their way into Lynley's skull. He crossed the lobby, reached the bar, unceremoniously grabbed the script out of Sydeham's hand, and without a word ran his eyes down the page to find Alma's speech in *Summer and Smoke*. He didn't use his spectacles, so the words were blurred. But legible enough. And absolutely indelible.

You needn't try to comfort me. I haven't come here on any but equal terms. You said, let's talk truthfully. Well, let's do! Unsparingly, truthfully, even shamelessly, then! It's no longer a secret that I love you. It never was. I loved you as long ago as the time I asked you to read the stone angel's name with your fingers. Yes, I remember the long afternoons of our childhood . . .

And yet, for a moment, Lynley had assumed Joanna Ellacourt had been speaking for herself, not using the words that Tennessee Williams had written. Just as young Constable Plater must have assumed when faced with Hannah Darrow's suicide note fifteen years earlier in Porthill Green.

14

BECAUSE OF a traffic snarl on the M11, he did not arrive in Porthill Green until after one o'clock, and by that time clouds humped along the horizon like enormous tufts of grey cotton wool. A storm was brewing. Wine's the Plough was not yet locked for its midafternoon closing, but rather than go into the pub at once for his confrontation with John Darrow, Lynley crunched across the snow on the green to a call box that leaned precariously in the direction of the sea. He placed a call to Scotland Yard. It was only a matter of moments before he heard Sergeant Havers' voice, and from the background noises of crockery and conversation, he guessed that she was taking the call from the officers' mess.

"Bloody hell, what happened to you?" she demanded. And then amended the question truculently with, "Sir. Where *are* you? You've had a phone call from Inspector Macaskin. They've done the complete autopsy on both Sinclair and Gowan. Macaskin said to tell you they've fixed Sinclair's time of death between two and a quarter past three. And, he said with a great deal of hemming and hawing that she hadn't been interfered with. I suppose that was his genteel way of telling me that there was no evidence of forcible rape or sexual intercourse. He said that the forensic team aren't through with everything they gathered from the room. He'll phone again as soon as they have it all done."

Lynley blessed Macaskin's thoroughness and his self-assured willingness to be of help, unthreatened by the involvement of Scotland Yard.

"We've taken Stinhurst's statement, and I've not been able to shake him into a single inconsistency about Saturday night at Westerbrae no matter how many times we've been through the story." Havers snorted scornfully. "His solicitor's just arrived—your typical old-boy, pinched-nostril type sent by the wife, no doubt, since his lordship hasn't lowered himself to request the use of a telephone from the likes of me or Nkata. We've got him in one of the interrogation rooms, but unless someone comes up with a piece of hard evidence or a witness in double time, we're in serious trouble. So where in God's name have you taken yourself?"

"Porthill Green." He cut off her protest with, "Listen to me. I'm not going to argue that Stinhurst isn't involved in Joy's death. But I'll not leave this Darrow situation unresolved. Let's not lose sight of the fact that Joy Sinclair's door was locked, Havers. So like it or not, our access route is still through Helen's room."

"But we've already agreed that Francesca Gerrard could well have given—"

"And Hannah Darrow's suicide note was copied from a play."

"A *play*? What play?"

Lynley looked across the green to the pub. Smoke curled from its chimney, like a snake against the sky. "I don't know. But I expect John Darrow does. And I think he's going to tell me."

"Where is that going to get us, Inspector? And *what* am I supposed to do with his precious lordship while you jolly about the Fens?"

"Take him through everything once again. With his solicitor present, if he insists. You know the routine, Havers. Plan it out with Nkata. Vary the questions."

"And then?"

"Then let him go for the day."

"Inspector—"

"You know as well as I that we have nothing substantial on him at the moment. Perhaps destruction of evidence in the burning of the scripts. But absolutely nothing else save the fact that his brother was a Soviet spy twenty-five years ago and he himself obstructed justice in Geoffrey's death. I hardly think it's productive to our case to arrest Stinhurst for that now. And you can't believe his solicitor isn't going to insist that we either charge him or release him to his family."

"We may get something more from the forensic team in Strathclyde," she argued.

"We may. And when that occurs, we'll pick him up again. For now, we've done all we can. Is that clear?"

He heard the exasperation that edged her reply. "And what will you have me do when I send Stinhurst toddling on his way?"

"Go to my office. Shut the door. Don't see anyone. Wait to hear from me."

"And if Webberly wants a report on our progress?"

"Tell him to rot," Lynley replied, "right after you tell him we're wise to Special Branch and MI5's involvement in the case."

He could hear Havers' smile—in spite of herself—across the telephone line. "A pleasure, sir. As I've always said, when the ship is sinking, one may as well bash a few holes in the bow."

WHEN LYNLEY asked for a ploughman's lunch and a pint of Guinness, John Darrow looked as if he would much rather refuse the business. However, the presence of three dour-looking men at the bar and an elderly woman dozing over gin and bitters by the crackling fire seemed to discourage him from doing so. Therefore, within five minutes, Lynley was occupying one of the tables near the window, tucking into a large plate of Stilton and Cheddar, pickled onions, and crusty bread.

He ate calmly enough, not bothered by the curiosity evidenced in the ill-hushed questions of the other customers. Local farmers, no doubt, they would soon be off to see to the rest of their day's work, leaving John Darrow with no choice but to face another interview that he appeared to be doing his best to avoid.

Indeed, Darrow had become decidedly congenial towards the men at the bar within moments of Lynley's arrival, as if an unaccustomed infusion of bonhomie into his behaviour would encourage them to linger long after they would otherwise have departed. They were talking of sports at the moment, a loud conversation about Newcastle football that was interrupted when the pub door opened and a young boy—perhaps sixteen years old—hurried in from the cold.

Lynley had seen him coming from the direction of Mildenhall, on an ancient motorbike whose predominant colour was mud. Wearing heavy work boots, blue jeans, and an antique leather jacket—all stained liberally with what appeared to be grease—the boy had parked in front of the pub and had spent several minutes across the street, admiring Lynley's car and running his hand along the sleek line of its roof. He had the sturdy build of John Darrow, but his colouring was as light as his mother's had been.

"Whose boat?" he called out cheerfully as he entered.

"Mine," Lynley replied.

The boy sauntered over, tossing fair hair off his forehead in that self-conscious way of the young. "Dead nice, that." He gazed out the window longingly. "Set you back a few quid."

"*And* continues to do so. It guzzles petrol as if I were the sole support of British Petroleum. Most of the time, frankly, I think about taking on your mode of transportation."

"Sorry?"

Lynley nodded towards the street. "Your motorbike."

"Oh that!" The boy laughed. "Quite a piece, that. Got in a smash with it last week and it didn't even take a dent. Not that you'd notice if it had. It's so old that—"

"You've chores to do, Teddy," John Darrow interrupted sharply. "See to them."

While his words effectively ended the conversation between his son and the London policeman, they also served to remind the others of the time. The farmers dropped coins and notes onto the bar, the old woman by the fire gave a loud snort and awoke, and within moments only Lynley and John Darrow were left in the pub. The muted sound of rock and roll and a banging of cupboards in the flat above them spoke of Teddy seeing to his chores.

"He's not in school," Lynley noted.

Darrow shook his head. "He's finished. Like his mum in that. Didn't hold much with books."

"Your wife didn't read?"

"Hannah? Girl never opened a book that I saw. Didn't even own one."

Lynley felt in his pocket for his cigarettes, lit one thoughtfully, opened the file on Hannah Darrow's death. He removed her suicide note. "That's odd, then, isn't it? Where do you suppose she copied this from?"

Darrow pressed his lips together as he recognised the paper Lynley had shown him once before. "I've nothing more to say on't."

"You do, I'm afraid." Lynley joined the man at the bar, Hannah's note in his hand. "Because she was murdered, Mr. Darrow, and I think you've known that for fifteen years. Frankly, up until this morning, I was certain you'd done the murdering yourself. Now I'm not so sure. But I have no intention of leaving today until you tell me the truth. Joy Sinclair died because she came too close to understanding what happened to your wife. So if you think her death is going to be swept aside because you'd rather not talk about what happened in this village in 1973, I suggest you reconsider. Or we can all go into Mildenhall and chat with Chief Constable Plater. The three of us. You and Teddy and I. For if you won't cooperate, I've no doubt your son has some pertinent memory of his mother."

"You leave the lad out of it! He's nothing to do with this! He's never known! He *can't* know!"

"Know what?" Lynley asked. The publican played with the porcelain pulls on the ale and the lager, but his face was wary. Lynley continued. "Listen to me, Darrow. I don't know what happened. But a sixteen-year-old boy—just like your son—was brutally murdered because he came too close to a killer. The same killer—I swear it, I feel it—who murdered your wife. And I *know* she was murdered. So for God's sake, help me before someone else dies."

Darrow stared at him dully. "A boy, you say?"

Lynley heard rather than saw the initial crumbling of Darrow's defences. He pressed the advantage mercilessly. "A boy called Gowan Kilbride. All he wanted in life was to go to London to be another James Bond. A boy's dream, wasn't it? But he died on the steps of a scullery in Scotland, with his face and chest scalded like cooked meat and a butcher knife in his back. And if the killer comes here next, wondering how much Joy Sinclair managed to learn from you . . . How in God's name will you protect your son's life or your own from a man or woman you don't even know!"

Darrow openly struggled with the weight of what Lynley was asking him to do: to go back into the past, to resurrect, to relive. This, in the hope that he and his son might be secure from a killer who had touched their lives with devastating cruelty so many years ago.

His tongue flicked across his dry lips. "It was a man."

DARROW LOCKED the pub door, and they moved to a table by the fire. He brought an unopened bottle of Old Bushmill's with him, twisted off the seal, and poured himself a tumbler. For at least a minute, he drank without speaking, fortifying himself for what he would ultimately have to say.

"You followed Hannah when she left the flat that night," Lynley guessed.

Darrow wiped his mouth on the back of his wrist. "Aye. She was to help me and one of the local lasses in the pub, so I'd gone upstairs to fetch her, and I found a note on the kitchen table. Only, wasn't the same note as you've there in the file. Was one telling me she was leaving. Going with some fancy nob to London. To be in a play."

Lynley felt a stirring of affirmation and with it a nascent vindication that told him that, in spite of everything he had heard from St. James and Helen, Barbara Havers and Stinhurst, his instincts had not led him wrong after all. "That's all the note said?"

Darrow shook his head darkly and looked down into his glass. The whisky gave off a heady smell of malt. "No. She took me to task . . . as a man. And did a bit of comparing so I'd know for certain what she'd been up to and what'd made her decide to leave. She wanted a *real* man, she said, one who knew how to love a woman proper, please a woman in bed. I'd never pleased her, she said. Never. But this bloke . . . She described how he did it to her so, she said, if I ever fancied having a woman in the future, I'd know how to do it right, for once. Like she was doing me a favour."

"How did you know where to find her?"

"Saw her. When I read the note, I went to the window. She must've only just left a minute or two before I went up to the flat because I saw her down at the edge of the village, carrying a big case, setting off on the path to the canal that runs through Mildenhall Fen."

"Did you think of the mill at once?"

"I thought of nothing but getting my hands on the bloody little bitch and beating her silly. But after a moment, I thought how much tastier it would be to follow her, catch her with him, and have at them both. So I kept my distance."

"She didn't see you following her?"

"It was dark. I kept to the far edge of the path where the growth is thickest. She turned round two or three times. I thought she knew I was there. But she just kept walking. She got a bit ahead of me where there's a bend in the canal, so I missed the turn to the mill and kept going for . . . perhaps three hundred yards. When I finally saw I'd lost her, I figured where she must be heading—there was little else out there—so I doubled back quick and made my way along the track to the mill. Her case was lying some thirty yards down the way."

"She'd gone on without it?"

"It was dead heavy. I thought she'd gone on to the mill to have that bloke come back for it. So I decided to wait and have at him right there on the path. Then I'd go on and see to her in the mill."

Darrow poured himself another drink and shoved the bottle towards

Lynley, who demurred. "But no one came back for the case," he went on. "I waited some five minutes. Then I crept up along the path to have a better look. Hadn't got as far as the clearing when this bloke come out of the mill at a run. He tore round the side. I heard a car start and take off. That was it."

"Did you get a look at him?"

"Too dark. I was too far away. I went on to the mill after a moment. And I found her." He set his glass on the table. "Hanging."

"Was she exactly as the police pictures show her?"

"Aye. Except there was a bit of paper sticking from her coat pocket, so I pulled that out. It was the note I gave to the police. When I read it, I saw how it was meant to look like a suicide."

"Yes. But it wouldn't have looked like suicide had you left her suitcase there. So you brought it home with you."

"I did. I took it upstairs. Then I raised a cry, using the note from her pocket. The other note I burned."

In spite of what the man had been through, Lynley found himself feeling a sore spot of anger. A life had been taken, callously, cold-bloodedly. And for fifteen years the death had gone unavenged. "But why did you do all that?" he asked. "Surely you wanted her murderer brought to justice."

Darrow's look betrayed a derisive weariness. "You've no idea what it's like in a village like this, do you, pommy boy? You've no idea how it'd feel to a man, having his neighbours all know that his randy little wife'd been snuffed while she was trying to leave him for some ponce she thought'd make her feel better between her legs. And not snuffed by her husband, mind you, which everyone in the village would have understood, but by the very bastard who was poking her behind her husband's back. Are you trying to tell me that, had I let Hannah stand as murdered, none of that would have come out?" Although his voice rose incredulously, Darrow contin-ued, as if to shun a response. "At least this way, Teddy's never had to know what his mum was really like. As far as I was concerned, Hannah was dead. And Teddy's peace of mind was worth letting her murderer go free."

"Better his mother should be a suicide than his father a cuck-old?" Lynley enquired.

Darrow pounded a fist hard onto the stained table between them. "Aye! For it's me he's been living with these fifteen years. It's me he's to look in the eye every day. And when he does, he sees a *man*, by God. Not some puling fairy who couldn't hold a woman to her marriage vows. And do you think that bloke could have held on to her any better?" He poured more liquor, spilling it carelessly when the bottle slipped against the glass. "He promised her acting coaches, lessons, a part in some play. But when that all fell through, how much flaming—"

"A part in a play? Coaches? Lessons? How do you know that? Was it in her note?"

Jerking himself towards the fire, Darrow didn't answer. But Lynley suddenly saw a sure reason why Joy Sinclair must have made ten telephone calls to him, what she had been insistently seeking in her conversation with the man. No doubt in his anger he had inadvertently revealed to her the existence of a source of information she desperately needed to write her book.

"Is there a record, Darrow? Are there diaries? A journal?"

There was no response.

"Good God, man, you've come this far! Do you know her killer's name?"

"No."

"Then what *do* you know? How do you know it?"

Still Darrow watched the fire impassively. But his chest heaved with repressed emotion. "Diaries," he said. "Girl was always too bloody full of herself. She wrote everything down. They were in her valise. With all her other things."

Lynley took a desperate shot, knowing that if he phrased it as a question the man would claim he had destroyed them years ago. "Give the diaries to me, Darrow. I can't promise that Teddy will never learn the truth about his mother. But I swear to you that he won't learn it from me."

Darrow's chin lowered to his chest. "How can I?" he muttered.

Lynley pressed further. "I know Joy Sinclair brought everything back to you. I know she caused you grief. But for God's sake, did she deserve to die alone, with an eighteen-inch dagger plunged through her neck? Who of us deserves that kind of death? What crime committed in life is worth that kind of punishment? And Gowan. What about the boy? He'd done absolutely nothing, yet he died as well. Darrow! Think, man! You can't let their deaths count for nothing!"

And then there were no more words to be said. There was only waiting for the man to decide. The fire popped once. A large ember dislodged and fell from the grate to roll against the fender. Above them, Darrow's son continued with his chores. After an agonising pause, the man raised his heavy head.

"Come up to the flat," he said tonelessly.

*   *   *

THE FLAT was reached by an outer rather than an inner stairway, running up the rear of the building. Below it, a gravel-strewn path led through the tangled mass of a forlorn garden to a gate, beyond which the endless stretch of fields lay, broken only by an occasional tree, a canal, the hulking shape of a windmill on the horizon. Everything was colourless under the melancholy sky, and the air carried upon its rich peaty scent an acknowledgement of the generations of flooding and decay that had gone into the composition of this desolate part of the country. In the distance, drainage pumps rhythmically *tuh-tumped*.

Opening the door, John Darrow admitted Lynley into the kitchen where Teddy was on his hands and knees with scouring pads, rags, and a pail of water, seeing to the interior of a grimy oven well past its youth. The floor surrounding him was damp and dirty. From the radio on a counter, a male singer squawked in a catarrhal voice. At their entrance, Teddy looked up from his toil, grimacing disarmingly.

"Waited too long on this mess, Dad. I'd do a sight better with a chisel, I'm afraid." He grinned, wiping his hand on his face and laying a streak of something sludgy from cheekbone to jaw.

Darrow spoke to him with gruff affection. "Get below with you, lad. See to the pub. The oven can wait."

The boy was more than agreeable. He hopped to his feet and flicked off the radio. "I'll take a few rubs at it every day, shall I? That way," again the grin, "we might have it cleaned by next Christmas." He sketched a light-hearted salute in the air and left them.

When the door closed on the boy, Darrow spoke to Lynley. "I've her things in the attic. I'll thank you to look through them up there so Teddy won't come upon you and want to have a look for himself. It's cold. You'll want your coat. But at least there's a light."

He led the way through a meagrely furnished sitting room and down a shadowy hall off of which the flat's two bedrooms opened. At the end of this, a recessed trapdoor in the ceiling gave them access to the attic. Darrow shoved the door upwards and pulled down a collapsible metal stairway, fairly new by the look of it.

As if reading Lynley's mind, he said, "I come up here time and again. Whenever I need reminding."

"Reminding?"

Darrow responded to the question drily. "When I feel the urge for a woman. Then I have a look through Hannah's diaries. That cures the itch like nothing else." He heaved himself up the stairs.

The attic bore qualities not entirely unlike those of a tomb. It was eerily still, airless, and only slightly less cold than the out-of-doors. Dust hung thickly upon cartons and trunks, and sudden movements sent clouds of it flying upwards in suffocating bursts. It was a small room, filled with the scent of age: those vague odours of camphor, of musty clothing, of damp and rotting wood. A weak shaft of afternoon light sifted its way through a single, heavily streaked window near the roof.

Darrow pulled on a cord hanging from the ceiling, and a bulb cast a cone of light onto the floor beneath it. He nodded towards two trunks that sat on either side of a single wooden chair. Lynley noted that neither chair nor trunks were dusty. He wondered how often Darrow paid visits to this sepulchre of his marriage.

"Her things're in no sort of order," the man said, "as I wasn't much concerned with what I did with everything. The night she died I just dumped the case out into her chest of drawers as fast as I could before getting the village up to search. Then later, after the funeral, I packed everything up in those two trunks."

"Why did she wear two coats and two sweaters that night?"

"Greed, Inspector. She couldn't fit anything more into her case. So if she wanted to take them, she had to wear or carry them. I suppose wearing seemed easier. It was cold enough." Darrow took a set of keys from his pocket and unlocked the trunks on either side of the chair. He shoved the top off each and then said, "I'll leave you to it. The diary you want's on the top of the stack."

When Darrow was gone, Lynley put on his reading spectacles. But he did not reach at once for the five bound journals that lay on top of the clothes. Rather, he began by examining her other belongings, developing an idea of what Hannah Darrow had been like.

Her clothes were of the sort that are cheaply made with the hope of passing themselves off as expensive. They were showy—beaded sweaters, clingy skirts, short gauzy dresses cut very low, trousers with narrow legs and flared bottoms and zips in the front. When he examined these, he saw how the material stretched and pulled away from the metal teeth. She had worn her clothes tight, moulded to her body.

A large plastic case gave off the strange odour of animal fat. It held a variety of inexpensive cosmetics and creams—a painter's box of eyeshadows, half a dozen tubes of very dark lipstick, an eyelash curler, mascara, three or four kinds of lotion, a package of cotton

wool. Tucked into a pocket was a five months' supply of birth
control pills. One set of the pills was partially used.

A shopping bag from Norwich contained a collection of new
lingerie. But here again, her selections were tawdry, an uneducated
girl's idea of what a man might find seductive. Insubstantial bikini
panties of scarlet, black, or purple lace, overhung with garter belts
of the same material and colour; diaphanous brassieres, cut low to
the nipple and decorated with strategically placed, coy little bows;
slithering petticoats slit to the waist; two nightgowns designed
identically, without bodices and merely concocted with two wide
satin straps that crisscrossed from waist to shoulders, covering
nothing much at all.

Underneath this was a stack of photographs. Looking through
them, Lynley saw that they were all of Hannah herself: each one
showing her off at her best, whether she was posing on a stile,
laughing down from horseback, or sitting on the beach with the
wind in her hair. Perhaps they were to be publicity photographs. Or
perhaps she had needed reassurance that she was pretty or validation
that she existed at all.

Lynley picked up the journal on top of the stack. Its cover was
cracked with age, several of the pages were stuck together and a
number of others had become swollen with the damp. He leafed
through them carefully until he found the final entry, one-third of
the way through. Written on March 25, 1973, it was the same
childish handwriting that was on the suicide note, but unlike that
note, this work was rich with misspellings and other errors.

Its settled. Im leaving tommorrow night. Im so glad its finally
decided between us. We talked and talked tonight for hours
to get it all planned out. When it was decided for good and
all, I wanted to love him but he said no weve not enough
time, Han, and for a moment I thought praps he was angry
becouse he even pushed my hand away but then he smiled
that melty smile of his and said darling love we'll have plenty
of time for that every night of the week once we get to
London. London!!! LONDON!!! This time tommorrow! He
said his flats ready and that hes taken care of everything. I
cann't think how Im going to get threw tommorrow thinking
about him. Darling love. Darling love!

Lynley looked up, his eyes on the attic's single window and on
the dust motes that floated in its weak oblong of light. He had not

considered the possibility that he might feel even slightly moved by the words of a woman so long dead, a woman who painted herself with a garish array of colours, dressed herself with an eye for lubricity, and still managed to become caught up with excitement at the idea of a new life in a city that was for her a place of promise and dreams. Yet her words had indeed touched him somehow. With her buoyant confidence, she was like a water-starved plant, thriving for the very first time under someone's skill and attention. Even in addressing herself awkwardly to sensuality, she wrote with an unconscious innocence. Unschooled in the world, Hannah Darrow had ultimately made herself the perfect victim.

He began to flip forward through the journal, skimming the entries, looking for the point at which her relationship with the unidentified man began. He found it on January 15, 1973, and as he read, he felt the fire of certainty begin its slow burn through his veins.

Had the best time ever in Norwich today which is fair hard to beleive after the row with John. Me and Mum went to shop there as she said that should cheer me up proper. We stopped in for Aunt Pammy and took her along as well. (She'd been tippling again since the morning and smelled of gin—it was awful.) At lunch we saw a playbill and Pammy said we owed ourselfs a treat so she took us to the play mostly, I think, becouse she wanted to sleep it off which she did with proper snoring till the man behind her kicked her seat. I was never at a play befor, can you credit that? It was about some dutchess who gets passed a dead mans hand and then ends up getting strangled and then everyone stabs each other. And one man kept talking about being a wolf. Quite a piece, I say. But the customes were real pretty Ive never seen nothing like them all these long gowns and head pieces. The ladys so pretty and the men wearing funny tights with little pouches in front. And in the end they gave the dutchess lady flowers and people stood and clapped. I read in the programe whear they travel all round the country doing plays. Fancy that. Made me want to do somthing as well. I hate being stuck in PGreen. Somtimes the pub makes me want to scream. And John wants to do it to me all the time and I just dont want it anymore. Ive not been right since the baby but he wont beleive me.

There followed a week in which she wearily catalogued her life in the village: a round of doing laundry, seeing to the baby's needs, talking to her mother on the telephone daily, cleaning the flat, working in the pub. She seemed to have no female friends. Nothing other than work and television occupied her time. On January 25, Lynley found the next pertinent entry.

Somthing happened. I can harly beleive it even when I think about it. I lied and told John I was bleeding again and had to see the doctor. A new doctor in Norwich, a specalist, I said. Said I'd stop by Aunt Pammy's for supper as well so he was not to worry if I was late. I cant think why I was clever enough to say that! I just wanted to see that play again and those customes! I didnt get a very good seat I was way in the back without my specs and it was a different play. Dead boring with lots of people talking about getting married or moving away and these three ladys hating the woman there brother married. Funny thing is that it was the same actors! And they were all so diffrent from the other play. I cant think how they dont get mixed up. After it was over, I went round to the back. I just thought praps I could say a word to one or two of them or have them sign my programe. I waited for an hour. But everyone came out in couples or groups. Only 1 bloke was alone. I dont know who he played becouse like I said my seat was too far back but I wanted him to sign my programe only I got nervous. So I followed him!!! I cant think what made me do it. But he went to a pub and got himself a meal and drank and I watched him and finally I just walked up and said your in that play arent you? Will you sign my programe? Just like that. Cor he was hansome. He was real suprised so he asked me to sit down and we got to talking about the theatre and he said hes been involved in it for lots of years. I told him how much I liked the dutchess play and how pretty the customes were. And he said did I want to come back to the theatre and have a real look at them. He said they werent much to look at up close. He said I could probaly even try a custome on if no one was about. So we went back there! Its so big behind the stage! I didnt know what to think. All these dressing rooms and waiting areas and tables filled with props. And the sets! There made of wood and they look just like stones!!! We went into a dressing room and he showed me this row of customes. They were velvet! I never touched nothing so soft ever. So he said do you want to try it on. No one will know. And I did!!! Only when I took it off, my hair got caught in it and he worked it loose and then he started kissing my neck and running his hands all over me. And there was this couch thing in the corner but he said no, no right now on the floor and he pulled down all the gowns and we made love in the middle of them! Afterwards we heard a womans voice in the theatre and I was real scared and he said I dont bloody care who it is, Oh God I dont care, I dont care, and he laughed so happy and started in on me again! And it didnt even hurt!!! I was hot and cold and things happened inside and he laughed again and said silly girl thats how its sposed to be! He asked me will I come to him next week. Will I!!! I got home after midnight but John was still down in the pub so he didnt know. I hope he dosent want it. I cant think but it'll still hurt with him.

The next five days in the journal were reflections on the Norwich lovemaking, the sort of dramatic nonsense that lives in a young girl's head the first time a man fully awakens her to the joys—rather than the duties—of the flesh. The sixth day took her thoughts in another direction. It was dated January 31.

He wont be there forever. Its a touring company and there off in March! I cant bear the thought. I shall see him tommorrow. I shall try to get his home address. John asks why Im off to Norwich again and I said I have to see the doctor. I said I have a bad pain inside and the doctor said he was not to touch me for a while till it goes away. How long, he wanted to know. What kind of pain? I said when you do it to me it hurts and the doctor said thats not right so your not to do it to me until the pain stops. Ive not been right since Teddys birth, I told him. I dont know if he beleives me but hes not touched me thank God.

On the next page she reported her meeting with her lover.

He took me to his rooms!!! Well, there not much. Just a grotty bed-sit in an old house near the cathedral. He dosent have harly anything in it becouse his real digs are in London. And I cant think why hes taken a place so far from the theatre. He says he likes to walk. Besides, he said with that smile of his, we dont need much, do we? He undressed me right by the door and we did it first standing!!! Then after I told him I knew he was leaving in March with the theatre group. I said I thought I could be an actress. It dosent look hard. I could do as well as those ladys I've seen. He said yes, that I ought to think about it, that he could see to it I got acting lessons and a coach. And then I said I was hungry and could we go out for somthing to eat. And he said he was hungry as well . . . but not for food!!!!

Apparently, for the next week, Hannah had no contact with the man. But she spent most of her time planning out a future with him. It centred itself on the theatre, which was to be the way she tied herself to him and escaped Porthill Green. She wrote briefly about her plans on February 10.

He cares for me. He said as much. Mum would say all men say that when there having a grind and you just as well not trust them till there trousers are up. But this is different. I know he means it. So Ive thought it out and it seems the best way is to join the company. I wouldent expect a big part at first. I dont know much about what to do but I could memerise easy enough. And if Im in the company we wont have to worry about being apart. I dont want to lose him. I gave him the number so he could ring me here in the flat but he hasent yet. I know hes busy. But if he dosent ring me by tommorrow Im going back to Norwich to see him. I'll wait by the theatre.

Her visit to Norwich was not recorded until February 13.

LOTS has happened. I did go into Norwich. I waited and waited outside the theatre. Then he came out. But he wasnt alone. He was with one of the ladys in the play and another man. They were talking together like it was some sort of argument. I said his name. At first he didnt here me so I went up to him and touched him on the arm. They went all just sort of dead when I did that. Then he smiled and said, hello I didnt see you there. Have you been waiting long? Excuse me for a moment. And he and the lady and the other man went to a car. The lady and man got in and left but he came back to me. He was mad, I could tell. But I said why didnt you interduce me to them? And he said what are you doing here without letting me know your coming? And I said why should I are you embrassed of me? And he said dont be a little fool. Dont you know Im trying to get you into the company? But I cann't make a move too soon before your ready. These are professonals and they wont accept anyone whos not a professonal as well so start acting like one. So I started to cry. And he said oh damn, Han, dont do that. Come on. So we went to his rooms. Lord I was there till 2 a.m. I went back the day before yesterday and he said he was working on an awdition for me but I would have to learn a very hard scene from a play. I was hoping it would be the dutchess play but it was the other one. He said to copy the part down and then to memerise it. It seemed awfully long and I asked why I had to write it why couldent he just give me a script. But he said there arent enough and it would be missed and then they would know and my awdition wouldent be a surprise. So I copied. But I didnt get it done and will have to go back tommorrow. We made love. He didnt seem to want to at first but he was happy enough after we did it!!

Lynley did not miss the perfunctory quality of the girl's final statements, and he wondered that she did not notice it herself. But apparently she had been too intent upon joining the theatrical company and starting life with a new man to notice the moment that lovemaking became simply an expected routine.

Her next entry was on February 23.

Teddy was ill for 5 days. Bad. John went on and on about it till I thought I would scream. But I got away 2x to finish copying that old script. I dont know why I just cant have one but he says they would know. He says just to memerise my part and not to worry about how to act it. He says hell show me how to act it. Of course he should know!!! Thats what hes good at. Anyway its only 8 pages. So what Im going to do is suprise him. I'll act it for him! Then he wont have any douts about me. Sometimes I think he dose have douts. Except when we go to bed. He knows how mad I am for him. I can harly be round him without wanting to take off his close. He likes that. He says oh God Hannah you know what I like dont you? You really know how, better than anyone. Your better than anything. Then he forgets what were talking about and we do it.

Hannah had devoted her next several entries to a detailed description of their lovemaking. These pages were heavily thumbed, no
doubt the section that John Darrow turned to whenever he wanted
to remember his wife in the worst possible light. For she was
meticulous in description, omitting nothing, and at the last comparing her husband's endowments and his performance with those of
her lover. It was a brutal evaluation, nothing that a man would get
over very quickly. It gave Lynley an idea of what her farewell note to
John Darrow must have been like.

The penultimate entry was on March 23.

Ive been practicing all week when Johns down in the pub.
Teddy watches me from his cot and laughs something wicked
to see his mum prancing round like a russion lady. But Ive
got it down. Was dead easy, that. And in 2 nights Im off to
Norwich so we can decide what to do and when Im to have
my awdition. I can harly wait. Im lonely for him right now.
John was on me like a pig this morning. He said its been 2
months since the doctor said he couldent and he was threw
with waiting for him to say he could. It almost made me sick
when he put his tong in my mouth. He tasted like shit I swear
it. He said thats better now isnt it Han and he did me so hard
I tried not to cry. When I think that till 2 months ago I
thought thats what it was sposed to be like and I was just
sposed to put up with it. I have to laugh now. I know better.
And Ive decided to tell John befor I leave. He deserves it after
this morning. He thinks hes such a MAN. If he only knew
what a real man and I do to each other in bed hed probaly
faint. God, I dont know if I can wait 2 more days to see him
again. I miss him so. I DO LOVE HIM.

Lynley snapped the journal closed as Hannah Darrow's comments came together in his mind, like a puzzle finally completed.
Prancing around like a Russian lady. A play about a man who gets
married, whose sisters hate his wife. People talking endlessly about
moving away or marrying. And the poster itself—as big as life—on
Lord Stinhurst's office wall. *The Three Sisters*, Norwich. The life
and death of Hannah Darrow.

He began searching through the rest of her belongings, digging
past clothes and handbags and gloves and jewellery. But he did not
find what he was looking for until he turned to the second trunk.
There at the bottom, past sweaters and shoes, beneath a girlhood

scrapbook filled with clippings and mementoes, was the old theatre programme he had prayed to find, Hannah's wire-rimmed spectacles hooked onto its cover. Designed with a diagonal stripe across the front to serve as division between the two pieces that the company were doing in repertory, the programme was fashioned with stark letters, white upon black on the top half and the reverse on the bottom: *The Duchess of Malfi* and *The Three Sisters*.

Impatiently, Lynley skimmed through the pages, looking for the cast. But when he came to it, he stared incredulously, scarcely believing the obscene twist of mocking chance that had governed the casting of the performances. For with the exception of Irene Sinclair and the addition of actors and actresses in whom he had no interest, everyone else was absolutely the same. Joanna Ellacourt, Robert Gabriel, Rhys Davies-Jones, and, to complicate matters further, Jeremy Vinney in a minor role, no doubt the swan song of a brief career on the stage.

Lynley tossed the programme to one side. He got up from the chair and paced across the little room, rubbing his forehead. There had to be something that he had not noticed in the few entries Hannah had made about her lover. Something that revealed his identity in even an oblique fashion, something Lynley himself had already read without realising what it meant. He returned to his chair, picked up the journal, and began it all again.

It was not until the fourth time through that he found it: *He says hell show me how to act it. Of course he should know!!! Thats what hes good at.* The words implied only two possibilities: the director of the production or the actor who was in the scene from which Hannah's "suicide note" had been drawn. The director would be skilled in showing an untutored girl the rudiments of a performance. An actor from the same scene would be able to show her how to play the role with ease, since he had been performing opposite an actress doing it for several weeks.

A quick survey of the programme told Lynley that Lord Stinhurst had been the director. He scored a point for Sergeant Havers' intuition. Now all that was left was to find out where in *The Three Sisters* the "suicide note" belonged and who played the roles in that scene. For he could visualise it now—Hannah going to the mill to meet her lover, in her pocket the eight pages of script that she had meticulously copied by hand for her audition. And the man who killed her, who took those eight pages, tore off the single part that would look like a suicide note, and took the rest with him, leaving her body hanging from the ceiling.

Lynley closed the trunks, turned off the light, and grabbed the stack of journals and the programme. Downstairs in the flat, he found Teddy in the sitting room with his feet propped up on a cheap, food-splattered coffee table, eating fish fingers from a blue tin plate. A pint of ale stood on the floor, half drunk. A small colour television was tuned in to a sports programme, downhill skiing by the look of it. Seeing Lynley, the boy hopped to his feet and turned off the television.

"Have you any books of plays in the flat?" Lynley asked, although he was fairly certain what the reply would be.

"Books of plays?" the boy repeated with a shake of his head. "Not a one. You're *sure* you want a book? We've records and such. Magazines as well." He seemed to realise as he spoke that Lynley was not looking for sources of entertainment. "Dad says you're a cop. Says I'm not to talk to you."

"Something you appear to be disregarding for the moment."

The boy made a wry face and nodded towards the journals under Lynley's arm. "About Mum, isn't it? I've read 'm, you see. Dad left the keys one night. I've been through 'm all." He rolled onto the balls of his feet awkwardly, driving one hand into the pocket of his blue jeans. "We don't talk about it. Don't think Dad could. But if you catch this bloke, will you let me know?"

Lynley hesitated. The boy spoke again.

"She was my mum, you know. She wasn't perfect, wasn't no la-de-da type. But she was my mum all the same. She didn't do bad to me. And she didn't kill herself."

"No. She didn't that." Lynley headed for the door. He paused there and thought of a way he might answer the boy's need. "You watch the papers, Teddy. When we've got the man who killed Joy Sinclair, that'll be the man you want."

"Will you get him for my mum as well, Inspector?"

Lynley considered lying to save the boy from facing yet another harsh reality. But as he studied his friendly, anxious face, he knew he couldn't do so. "Not unless he confesses."

The boy nodded with childish sophistication, although his jaw tightened whitely. He said with deliberate and painful carelessness, "No evidence, I suppose."

"No evidence. But it's the same man, Teddy. Believe me."

The boy turned back to the television. "I remember her a bit, is all." He fiddled with a knob without turning on the set. "Do get him," he said in a low voice.

*   *   *

RATHER THAN stop in Mildenhall and run the risk of wasting time finding no public library, Lynley drove on to Newmarket where he knew there would be one. Once there, however, he spent twenty minutes fighting his way through the late afternoon traffic until he found the building he was looking for at a quarter past five. He parked illegally, left his police identification in plain sight propped against the steering wheel, and hoped for the best. Concerned that it had begun to snow, knowing that every moment was precious as a result of this, he dashed up the steps into the library, with the Norwich theatre programme folded into a pocket of his overcoat.

The building smelled powerfully of beeswax, old paper, and a central heating system that was sadly overworked. It was a place of high windows, dark bookcases, brass table lamps fitted out with tiny white shades, and an enormous U-shaped circulation desk behind which a well-tailored man in large spectacles pumped information into a computer. This last looked gratingly out-of-place in the otherwise antique environment. But at least it made no noise.

Lynley strode to the card catalogue and hunted through it for Chekhov. Within five minutes he was sitting down at one of the long, battle-worn tables with a copy of *The Three Sisters* opened in front of him. He began scanning it, at first reading only the first line of each speech. Midway through the play, however, he realised that, from the length of the speeches and the way the suicide note had been torn, what Hannah had written might well have come from the middle of a speech. He began again, more slowly, yet all the while anxiously aware of the bad weather outside that would impede the flow of traffic to London, aware of the time that was passing and what might be happening in the city while he was gone. It took him nearly thirty minutes to find the speech, ten pages into act 4. He read the words once, then a second time to make sure.

What trifles, what silly little things in life will suddenly for no reason at all, take on meaning. You laugh at them just as you've always done, consider them trivial, and yet you go on, and you feel that you haven't the power to stop. Oh, let's not talk about that! I feel elated, I see these fir trees, these maples and birches, as if for the first time, and they all gaze at me with curiosity and expectation. What beautiful trees and, in fact, how beautiful life ought to be with them! I must go, it's time . . . There's a tree that's dead, but it goes on swaying in the wind with the others. So it seems to me that if I die, I'll still have a part in life, one way or another. Good-bye my darling . . . The papers you gave me are on my table under the calendar.

The speaker had not been one of the women, as Lynley had originally supposed, but one of the men. Baron Tuzenbach, speaking to Irina in the final moments of the play. Lynley pulled the Norwich programme out of his pocket, opened it to the cast, ran his finger down the page and found what he had dreaded—and hoped—to see. Rhys Davies-Jones had indeed played Tuzenbach to Joanna Ella-court's Irina, Jeremy Vinney's Ferapont, and Robert Gabriel's Andrei in that winter of 1973.

It was, at last, the verification he had sought. For what better man to know how a set of lines could be used than the man who had said them night after night? The man Helen trusted. The man she loved and believed to be innocent.

Lynley shelved the book and went in search of a telephone.

15

FOR THE ENTIRE DAY, Lady Helen had known that she should have felt exultant. After all, they had done what she had been determined they should do. They had proven Tommy wrong. Through their explorations into Lord Stinhurst's background, they had proven nearly every suspicion against Rhys Davies-Jones in the deaths of Joy Sinclair and Gowan Kilbride to be without merit. They had, in doing so, altered the entire direction of the case. So when Sergeant Havers telephoned St. James at noon with the information that Stinhurst had been brought in for interrogation, that he had admitted to the truth about his brother's involvement with the Soviets, Lady Helen knew that she should have been swept up in a tide of jubilation.

Shortly after two, she had left St. James' house, had spent the remainder of the day in preparation for her evening with Rhys, an evening that would be one of loving celebration. She had prowled the streets of Knightsbridge for hours, in search of the perfect sartorial accompaniment to her mood. Except that soon enough she found that she wasn't at all sure of her mood. She wasn't sure of anything.

She told herself at first that the welter she was in arose from the fact that Stinhurst had admitted to nothing in the deaths of Joy Sinclair and Gowan Kilbride. But she knew she could not hold on to that lie for long. For if Strathclyde CID were able to turn up a hair, a spot of blood, or a latent fingerprint to tie the Scotland deaths to Stinhurst, she would then have to face what was really at the centre

251

of her turmoil today. And at the centre was not an argument over one man's guilt and another man's innocence. At the centre was Tommy, his despairing face, his final words to her last night.

Yet she knew quite distinctly that whatever pain Tommy felt couldn't be allowed to matter to her now. For Rhys was innocent. *Innocent.* And she had clung so tenaciously to that belief for the past four days that she could not let it go long enough to think of anything else, could not let herself be turned in any other direction but his. She wanted Rhys cleared completely in everyone's eyes, wanted him to be seen for what he truly was—and seen by everyone, not just by her.

It was after seven when her taxi drew up to her flat on Onslow Square. Snow was falling heavily, wave after silent wave of it drifting from the east into soft piles along the iron fence that bordered the green at the centre of the square. When Lady Helen stepped into the frosty air and felt the sweet sting of flakes against her cheeks and eyelashes, she spent a moment admiring the change that fresh snow always brought to the city. Then, shivering, she scooped up her packages and ran up the tiled front steps of the building that housed her flat. She fumbled in her handbag for her keys, but before she could find them the door was swung open by her maid, who drew her inside hastily.

Caroline Shepherd had been with Lady Helen for the past three years, and although she was five years younger than her employer, she was passionately devoted to Lady Helen's every interest, so she minced no words when the cold night air caught at her cloud of black hair as she slammed the door home. "Thank God! I've been that worried about you. Do you know it's gone seven and Lord Asherton's been ringing again and again and again this past hour? And Mr. St. James as well. *And* that lady sergeant from Scotland Yard. And Mr. Davies-Jones has been here these last forty minutes waiting for you in the drawing room."

Lady Helen dimly heard it all but acknowledged only the last. She handed her packages over to the younger woman as they hurried up the stairs. "Lord, am I really as late as that? Rhys must wonder what's become of me. And it's your evening off, isn't it? I *am* sorry, Caroline. Have I made you dreadfully late? Are you seeing Denton tonight? Will he forgive me?"

Caroline smiled. "He'll see his way to that if I encourage him proper. I'll just pop these in your room and be on my way."

Lady Helen and Caroline occupied the largest flat in the building, seven rooms on the first floor with a large drawing room that overlooked the square below. Here, the curtains were undrawn, and Rhys Davies-Jones stood at the French doors that spilled light onto a small balcony crusted with snow. He turned when Lady Helen entered.

"They've had Stinhurst at Scotland Yard for most of the day," he said, his brow furrowed.

She hesitated at the door. "Yes. I know."

"Do they actually think . . . I can't believe that, Helen. I've known Stuart for years. He couldn't have . . ."

She swiftly crossed the room to him. "You've known *all* these people for years, haven't you, Rhys? Yet one of them did kill her. One of them killed Gowan."

"But Stuart? No. I can't . . . Good God, *why?*" he asked fiercely.

The room's lighting placed part of his body in shadow, so she could not see him distinctly, but she could hear in his voice the insistent plea for trust. And she did indeed trust him—she knew that without a doubt. But even so, she couldn't bring herself to delineate for him all the details of Stinhurst's family and background. For doing that would ultimately reveal Lynley's humiliation, all the errors in judgement he had made over the past few days, and for the sake of the long friendship she had shared with Lynley—no matter that it might well be dead between them now—she found that she could not bear to expose him to the possibility of anyone's derision, deserved or not.

"I've thought about you all day," she answered simply, laying her hand on his arm. "Tommy knows you're innocent. I've always known that. And we're here together now. What else really matters at the heart of it?"

She felt the change in his body even as she spoke. His tension dissolved. He reached for her, his face melting, warming with his lovely smile. "Oh God, nothing. Nothing at all, Helen. Only you and I." He pulled her to him, kissing her, whispering only the single word *love*. No matter the horrors of the past few days. They were over now. It was time for going on. He drew her away from the windows to the couch that sat in front of a low fire at the opposite end of the room. Pulling her down next to him, he kissed her again, with more assurance, with a rising passion that kindled her own. After a long while, he lifted his head and ran his fingers in a feather-like touch along the line of her jaw and across her neck.

"This is madness, Helen. I've come to take you to dinner and I find that all I can manage to think about is taking you to bed. At once, I'm rather ashamed to admit. We'd best be off before I lose interest in dinner altogether."

She lifted a hand to his cheek, smiling fondly when she felt its heat.

At her gesture, he murmured, bent to her again, his fingers working loose the buttons of her blouse. Then his mouth moved warmly against her bare throat and shoulders. His fingers brushed against her breasts. "I love you," he whispered and sought her mouth again.

The telephone rang shrilly.

They jumped apart as if an intruder were present, staring at each other guiltily as the telephone went unanswered. It made its way through four jarring double rings before Lady Helen realised that Caroline, already two hours behind schedule on her free evening, had left the flat. They were entirely alone.

Her heart still pounding, she went into the hallway and lifted the receiver on its ninth ring.

"Helen. Thank God. Thank *God.* Is Davies-Jones with you?"

It was Lynley.

HIS VOICE was tightly strung with such unmistakable anxiety that Lady Helen froze. Her mind felt numb. "What is it? Where are you?" She knew she was whispering without even intending to do so.

"In a call box near Bishop's Stortford. There's a bloody great wreck on the M11 and every back road I've tried has been done in by the snow. I can't think how long it's going to take me to get back to London. Has Havers spoken to you yet? Have you heard from St. James? Damn it all, you've not answered me. Is Davies-Jones with you?"

"I've only just got home. What is it? What's wrong?"

"Just answer me. Is he with you?"

In the drawing room, Rhys was still on the couch, but leaning towards the fire, watching the last of the flames. Lady Helen could see the play of light and shadow on the planes of his face and in his curly hair. But she couldn't speak. Something in Lynley's voice warned her off.

He began to talk rapidly, driving the words home to her with the strength of a terrifying, passionate conviction.

"Listen to me, Helen. There was a girl. Hannah Darrow. He met her when he was in *The Three Sisters* in Norwich in late January of 1973. They had an affair. She was married, with a baby. She planned to leave her husband and child to take up a life with Davies-Jones. He convinced her that she was going to audition for the stage and she practised a part he chose for her, believing that after her audition she would run off with him to London. But the night they were to leave, he murdered her, Helen. And then he hanged her from a hook in the ceiling of a mill. It looked like a suicide."

She managed only a whisper. "No. Stinhurst—"

"Joy's death had nothing at all to do with Stinhurst! She was planning to write about Hannah Darrow. It was to be her new book. But she made the mistake of telling Davies-Jones about it. She phoned him in Wales. The tape recorder in her purse even had a message to herself, Helen, reminding her to ask Davies-Jones how to handle John Darrow, Hannah's husband. So don't you see? He knew all *along* that Joy was writing this book. He knew as early as last month. So he suggested to Joy that you be given the room right next to her, to make sure he had access. Now for the love of God, I've had men out looking for him since six o'clock. *Tell* me if he's with you, Helen!"

Every force within her joined in conjunction to prevent her from speaking. Her eyes burned, her throat closed, her stomach tightened like a vise. And although she fought against the vivid memory, she heard Rhys' voice clearly, those words of condemnation spoken so easily to her at Westerbrae. *I'd been doing a winter's season round Norfolk and Suffolk . . . when I got back to London she was gone.*

"Hannah Darrow left a diary," Lynley was saying desperately. "She left the programme from the play. I've seen them both. I've read it all. Helen, please, darling, I'm telling you the truth!"

Dimly, Lady Helen saw Rhys get up, saw him go to the fire, saw him pick up the poker. He glanced in her direction. His face was grave. No! It was impossible, absurd. She was in no danger. Not from Rhys, never from Rhys. He wasn't a murderer. He had *not* killed his cousin. He couldn't kill anyone. But Tommy was still speaking. Even as Rhys began to move.

"He arranged for her to copy a scene from the play in her own writing and then he used part of what she'd copied as the suicide note. But the words . . . they were from one of his own speeches in the play. It was Tuzenbach. *He* was Tuzenbach. He's killed three people, Helen. Gowan died in my arms. For the love of God, answer me! Tell me! Now!"

Her lips formed the hateful word in spite of her resolve. She heard herself say it. "Yes."

"He's there?"

Again. "Yes."

"Are you alone?"

"Yes."

"Oh God. Caroline's out?"

It was easy, so easy. Such a simple word. "Yes."

And as Lynley continued to speak, Rhys turned back to the fire, poked at it, added another log, returned to the couch. Watching him, understanding the implications of what she had just done, of the choice she had made, Lady Helen felt tears sting at the back of her eyes, felt the constriction in her throat, and knew that she was lost.

"Listen to me carefully, Helen. I want to put a tail on him until we get the final forensic report from Strathclyde CID. I could bring him in before then, but all it would amount to is another go-round with nothing to show. So I shall phone the Met now. They'll send a constable, but it may take as long as twenty minutes. Can you keep him with you for a while? Do you feel safe enough with him to do that?"

She battled against despair. She could not speak.

Lynley's own voice was torn. "Helen! Answer me! Can you manage twenty minutes with him? Can you? For God's sake—"

Her lips were stiff, dry. "I can manage that. Easily."

For a moment, she heard nothing more, as if Lynley were evaluating the exact nature of her response. Then he asked sharply: "What does he expect from you tonight?"

She didn't reply.

"Answer me! Has he come to take you to bed?" When still she said nothing, he cried, "Helen! Please!"

She heard herself whisper hopelessly, "Well, that should take up your twenty minutes nicely, shouldn't it?"

He was shouting, "No! Helen! Don't—" when she hung up the phone.

SHE STOOD with her head bent, struggling for composure. Even now, he was placing his call to Scotland Yard. Even now the twenty minutes had begun.

Odd, she thought, that she felt no fear. Her heart throbbed in her ears, her throat was dry. But she was not afraid. She was alone in the flat with a killer, with Tommy miles away, with a snowstorm sealing off easy escape. But she was not at all afraid. And it came to her, as hot tears seared and demanded release, that she was not afraid because she no longer cared. Nothing mattered any longer, least of all whether she lived or died.

BARBARA HAVERS picked up the telephone in Lynley's office on the second ring. It was a quarter past seven, and she had been sitting at his desk for over two hours, smoking so steadily that her throat was raw and her nerves strung to breaking. She was so relieved to hear Lynley's voice at last that her release of tension gave way to hot anger. But her imprecations were interrupted by the intensity of his voice.

"Havers, where's Constable Nkata?"

"Nkata?" she repeated stupidly. "Gone home."

"Get him. I want him at Onslow Square. Now."

She stubbed out her cigarette and reached for a piece of paper. "You've found Davies-Jones?"

"He's in Helen's flat. I want a tail on him, Havers. But if it comes to it, we're going to have to bring him in."

"How? Why?" she demanded incredulously. "We've virtually nothing to work with in spite of this Hannah Darrow angle which God knows is about as thin as what we have on Stinhurst. You told me yourself that every single one of them save Irene Sinclair was involved in that Norwich production in seventy-three. That *still* includes Stinhurst. And besides, Macaskin—"

"No arguments, Havers. I've no time at the moment. Just do as I say. And once you've done it, telephone Helen. Keep her talking to you for at least thirty minutes. More if you can. Do you understand?"

"Thirty minutes? What am I supposed to do? Tell her the flipping story of my life?"

Lynley made a sound of furious exasperation. "God damn it, do as I say for once! Now! And wait for me at the Yard!"

The line went dead.

Havers placed the call to Constable Nkata, sent him on his way, slammed down the receiver, and stared moodily at the papers on Lynley's desk. They comprised the final information from Strathclyde CID—the report on fingerprints, the results of having used the fibre-optic lamp, the analysis of blood stains, the study of four hairs found near the bed, the analysis of the cognac Rhys Davies-Jones had taken to Helen's room. And all of it amounted to a single nothing. Not one shred of evidence existed that could not be argued away by the least skilled barrister.

Barbara faced the fact that Lynley was as yet unaware of. If they were going to bring Davies-Jones—or anyone else—to justice, it was not going to be on the strength of anything they could get from Inspector Macaskin in Scotland.

HER NAME was Lynette. But as she sprawled beneath him, writhing hotly and moaning appreciatively at his every thrust, Robert Gabriel had to school himself to remember that, had to discipline himself not to call her something else. After all, there had been so many over the past few months. Who could possibly be expected to keep them all straight? But at the appropriate moment, he recalled who she was: the Agincourt's nineteen-year-old apprentice set designer whose skin-tight jeans and thin yellow jersey now lay in the darkness on the floor of his dressing room. He had discovered soon enough—and with considerable joy—that she wore absolutely nothing beneath them.

He felt her fingernails clawing at his back and made a sound of delight although he would have vastly preferred some other method of her signalling her mounting pleasure. Still, he continued to ride her in the manner she seemed to prefer—roughly—and tried his best not to breathe in the heavy perfume she wore or the vaguely oleaginous odour that emanated from her hair. He murmured subtle encouragement, keeping his mind occupied with other things until she had taken satisfaction and he might then seek his own. He liked to think he was considerate that way, better at it than most men, more willing to show women a good time.

"Ohhhh, don't stop! I can't stand it! I *can't!*" Lynette moaned.

Nor can I, Gabriel thought as her nails danced abrasively down his spine. He was three-quarters of the way through a mental recitation of Hamlet's third soliloquy when her ecstatic sobbing reached its crescendo. Her body arched. She shrieked wildly. Her nails sank into his buttocks. And Gabriel made a mental note to avoid teenagers henceforth.

That decision was affirmed by Lynette's subsequent behaviour. Having taken her pleasure, she became an inert object, passively and not so patiently waiting for him to finish with his own. Which he did quickly, groaning out her name with feigned rapture at the appropriate moment and all the time as eager to bring this encounter to an end as she seemed to be. Perhaps the costume designer would be a likelier possibility for tomorrow, he thought.

"Ohhh, tha' was a bit all right, wasn't it?" Lynette said with a yawn when it was over. She sat up, swung her legs off the couch, and groped on the floor for her clothes. " 'Ave you the time?"

Gabriel glanced at the luminous dial of his watch. "A quarter past nine," he replied, and in spite of his desire that she be on her way so that he could have a thorough wash, he ran his hand up her back and murmured, "Let's have another go tomorrow night, Lyn. You drive me mad," just in case the costume designer proved unattainable.

She giggled, took his hand, and placed it on her melon-sized breast. Even at her age, it was beginning to sag, the result of her eschewing undergarments. "Can't, luv. Me 'usband's on the road tonight. But 'e'll be back tomorrow."

Gabriel sat up with a jerk. "Your *husband*? Christ! Why didn't you tell me you were married?"

Lynette giggled again, squirming into her jeans. "Didn't ask, did you? 'E drives a lorry, gone at least three nights a week. So . . ."

God, a lorry driver! Twelve or thirteen stone of muscle with the IQ of a good-sized vegetable marrow.

"Listen, Lynette," Gabriel said hastily, "let's cool this thing off, shall we? I don't want to come between you and your husband."

He felt rather than saw her careless shrug. She pulled on her jersey and shook back her hair. Again, he caught its odour. Again, he tried not to breathe.

" 'E's a bit thick," she confided. " 'E'll never know. There's nothing to worry about as long as I'm there when 'e wants me."

"Still and all," Gabriel said, unconvinced.

She patted his cheek. "Well, you jus' let me know if you want another tumble. You aren't 'alf bad. A bit slow, is all, but I s'pose that's due to your age, isn't it?"

"My age," he repeated.

"Sure," she said cheerfully. "When a bloke gets along in years, things take a bit of time to heat up, don't they? *I* understand." She scrambled on the floor. "Seen my 'andbag? Oh, 'ere it is. I'm off then. P'raps we'll 'ave a go on Sunday? My Jim'll be back on the road by then." That being her sole form of farewell, she made her way to the door and left him in the dark.

My age, he thought, and he could hear his mother's cackle of ironic laughter. She would light one of her foul Turkish cigarettes, regard him speculatively, and try to keep her face vacant. It was her analyst's expression. He hated her when she wore it, cursing himself for having been born to a Freudian. What we're dealing with, she would say, is typical in a man your age, Robert. Midlife crisis, the sudden realisation of impending old age, the questioning of life's purpose, the search for renewal. Coupled with your over-active libido, this propels you to seek new ways of defining yourself. Always sexual, I'm afraid. That appears to be your dilemma. Which is unfortunate for your wife, as she seems to be the only steadying influence available to you. But you *are* afraid of Irene, aren't you? She's always been too much woman for you to cope with. She made demands on you, didn't she? Demands of adulthood that you simply couldn't face. So you sought out her sister—to punish Irene and to keep yourself feeling young. But you couldn't have everything, lad. People who want everything generally end up with nothing.

And the most painful fact was that it was true. All of it. Gabriel groaned, sat up, began the search for his clothes. The dressing-room door opened.

He had only time to look in that direction, to see a thick shape against the additional darkness of the hallway outside his door. He had only a moment to think, *Someone's shut off all the corridor lights*, before a figure stormed across the room.

Gabriel smelled whisky, cigarettes, the acrid stench of perspiration. And then a rain of blows fell, on his face, against his chest, savagely pounding into his ribs. He heard, rather than felt, the cracking of bones. He tasted blood and ate the torn tissue in his mouth where his cheek was driven into his teeth.

His assailant grunted with effort, spewed spittle with rage, and finally rasped on the fourth vicious blow between Gabriel's legs, "Keep your soddin' piece in your trousers from now on, man."

Gabriel thought only, *Absolutely no teenagers next time*, before he lost consciousness.

LYNLEY REPLACED the telephone and looked at Barbara. "No answer," he said. Barbara saw the muscle in his cheek contract. "What time did Nkata first phone in?"

"A quarter past eight," she replied.

"Where was Davies-Jones?"

"He'd gone into an off-licence near Kensington Station. Nkata was in a call box outside."

"And he *was* alone? He hadn't taken Helen with him? You're certain of that?"

"He was alone, sir."

"But you spoke to her, Havers? You did speak to Helen *after* Davies-Jones left her flat?"

Barbara nodded, feeling a growing concern for him that she would have rather lived without. He looked completely worn out. "She phoned me, sir. Right after he'd left."

"Saying?"

Barbara patiently repeated what she had told him once already. "Only that he'd gone. I did try to keep her on the line for thirty minutes when I first phoned, just as you asked. But she wouldn't have it, Inspector. She only said that she'd got company and could she telephone me later. And that was it. I don't think she wanted my help, frankly." Barbara watched the play of anxiety cross Lynley's face. She finished by saying: "I think she wanted to handle it alone, sir. Perhaps . . . well, perhaps she doesn't see him as a killer yet."

Lynley cleared his throat. "No. She understands." He pulled Barbara's notes across his desk towards him. They contained two sets of data, the results of her interrogation of Stinhurst and the final information from Inspector Macaskin at Strathclyde CID. He put on his spectacles and gave himself over to reading. Outside his office, night subdued the normal jangle of noises in the department. Only the occasional ringing of a telephone, the quick raising of a voice, the congenial burst of laughter told them that they were not alone. Beyond, snow muffled the sounds of the city.

Barbara sat opposite him, holding Hannah Darrow's diary in one hand and the playbill from *The Three Sisters* in the other. She had read them both, but she was waiting for his reaction to the material she had prepared for him during his absence in East Anglia and his entanglement in traffic on the way back to London.

He was, she saw, frowning as he read and looking as if the past few days had made demands upon him that were scarring their way into his very flesh. She averted her eyes and made an exercise out of considering his office, pondering the ways it reflected the dichotomy of his character. Its shelves of books bowed to the proprieties of his job. There were legal volumes, forensic texts, commentaries upon the judges' rules, and several works from the Policy Studies Institute, evaluating the effectiveness of the Metropolitan Police. They composed a fairly standard collection for a man whose interest was well focussed on his career. But the office walls inadvertently cut through this persona of professionalism and revealed a second Lynley, one whose nature was filled with convolutions. Little enough hung there: two lithographs from America's Southwest that spoke of an abiding love of tranquillity, and a single photograph that disclosed what had lain long at the heart of the man.

It was of St. James, an old picture taken prior to the accident that had cost him the use of his leg. Barbara noticed the overtly innocuous details: how St. James stood, his arms crossed, leaning against a cricket bat; how the left knee of his white flannels bore a large, jagged tear; how a grass stain made a cumulous shadow on his hip; how he laughed unrestrainedly and with perfect joy. Summer past, Barbara thought. Summer dead forever. She knew quite well why the photograph hung there. She moved her eyes away from it.

Lynley's head was bent, supported by his hand. He rubbed three fingers across his brow. It was some minutes before he looked up, removed his spectacles, and met her gaze. "We've nothing here for an arrest," he said, gesturing at the information from Macaskin.

Barbara hesitated. His passion on the telephone earlier that evening had so nearly convinced her of her own error in seeking an arrest of Lord Stinhurst that even now she thought twice before pointing out the obvious. But there was no need to do so, for he went on to speak of it himself.

"And God knows we can't take Davies-Jones on the strength of his name in a fifteen-year-old playbill. We may as well arrest any one of them if that's all the evidence we have."

"But Lord Stinhurst burnt the scripts at Westerbrae," Barbara pointed out. "There's still that."

"If you want to argue that he killed Joy to keep her silent about his brother, yes. There *is* still that," Lynley agreed. "But I don't see it that way, Havers. The worst Stinhurst really faced was familial humiliation if the entire story about Geoffrey Rintoul became known through Joy's play. But Hannah Darrow's killer faced exposure, trial, imprisonment if she wrote her book. Now, which motive seems more logical to you?"

"Perhaps . . ." Barbara knew she had to suggest this carefully, "we've a double motive. But a single killer."

"Stinhurst again?"

"He did direct *The Three Sisters* in Norwich, Inspector. He could be the man Hannah Darrow met. And he could have gotten the key to Joy's bedroom door from Francesca."

"Look at the facts that you've forgotten, Havers. Everything about Geoffrey Rintoul had been removed from Joy's study. But everything related to Hannah Darrow—everything that led us right to her death in 1973—was left in plain sight."

"Of course, sir. But Stinhurst could hardly have asked the boys at MI5 to collect everything about Hannah Darrow as well. That hardly applied to the government's concern, did it? It wasn't exactly an Official Secret. And besides, how could he have known what she had gathered on Hannah Darrow? She merely mentioned John Darrow at dinner that night. Unless Stinhurst—all right, unless the killer—had actually been inside Joy's study prior to the weekend, how would he know for sure what material she had managed to gather? Or managed not to gather, for that matter."

Lynley stared past her, his face telling her that he was caught up in a sudden thought. "You've given me an idea, Havers." He tapped his fingers against the top of his desk. His eyes dropped to the journal in Barbara's hand. "I think we've a way to manage it all without a single thing from Strathclyde CID," he said at last. "But we'll need Irene Sinclair."

"Irene Sinclair?"

He nodded thoughtfully. "She's our best hope. She was the only one of them not in *The Three Sisters* in 1973."

DIRECTED BY a neighbour who had been drawn into staying with and calming her children, they found Irene Sinclair not at her home in Bloomsbury but in the waiting area of the emergency room at the nearby University College Hospital. When they walked in, she jumped to her feet.

"He asked for no police!" she cried out frantically. "How did you . . . what are you . . . ? Did the doctor phone you?"

"We've been to your home." Lynley drew her to one of the couches that lined the walls. The room was inordinately crowded, filled with an assortment of illnesses and accidents manifesting themselves in selected cries and groans and wretchings. That pharmaceutical smell so typical of hospitals hung heavily in the air. "What's happened?"

Irene shook her head blindly, sinking onto the couch, cradling her cheek with her hand. "Robert's been beaten. At the theatre."

"At this time of night? What was he doing there?"

"Going over his lines. We've a second reading tomorrow morning and he said that he wanted a feeling for how he sounded on the stage."

Lynley saw that she didn't believe the story herself. "Was he on the stage when he was attacked?"

"No, he'd gone to his dressing room for something to drink. Someone switched off the lights and came upon him there. Afterwards, he managed to get to a phone. Mine was the only number he could remember." This last statement had the ring of excusing her presence.

"Not the emergency number?"

"He didn't want the police." She looked at them anxiously. "But *I'm* glad you've come. Perhaps you can talk some sense into him. It's only too clear that he was meant to be the next victim!"

Lynley drew up an uncomfortable plastic chair to shield her from the stares of the curious. Havers did likewise. "Why?" Lynley asked.

Irene's face looked strained, as if the question confused her. But something told Lynley it was part of a performance designed specifically and spontaneously for him. "What do you mean? What else could it be? He's been beaten bloody. Two of his ribs are cracked, his eyes are blackened, he's lost a tooth. Who else could be responsible?"

"It's not the way our killer's been working, though, is it?" Lynley pointed out. "We've a man, perhaps a woman, who uses a knife, not fists. It doesn't really look as if anyone intended to kill him."

"Then what else could it be? What are you saying?" She drew her body straight to ask the question, as if an offence had been given and would not be brooked without some form of protest.

"I think you know the answer to that. I imagine you've not told me everything about tonight. You're protecting him. Why? What on earth has he done to deserve this kind of devotion? He's hurt you in every possible way. He's treated you with a contempt that he hasn't bothered to hide from anyone. Irene, listen to me—"

She held up a hand and her agonised voice told him her brief performance was at an end. "Please. All right. That's more than enough. He'd had a woman. I don't know who she was. He wouldn't say. When I got there, he was still . . . he hadn't . . ." She stumbled for the words. "He couldn't manage his clothes."

Lynley heard the admission with disbelief. What had it been like for her, going to him, soothing his fear, smelling those unmistakable odours of intercourse, dressing him in the very same clothes he had torn from his body in haste to make love to another woman? "I'm trying to understand why you still feel loyalty to a man like this, a man who went so far as to deceive you with your very own sister." Even as he spoke, he considered his words, considered how Irene had attempted to spare Robert Gabriel tonight, and thought back to what had been said about the night Joy Sinclair died. He saw the pattern clearly enough. "You've not told me everything about the night your sister died either. Even in that, you're protecting him. *Why*, Irene?"

Her eyes closed briefly. "He's the father of my children," she replied with simple dignity.

"Protecting him protects them?"

"Ultimately. Yes."

John Darrow himself could not have said it better. But Lynley knew how to direct the conversation. Teddy Darrow had shown him.

"Children generally discover the worst there is to know about their parents, no matter how one longs to protect them. Your silence now does nothing but serve to protect your sister's killer."

"He *didn't*. He couldn't! I can't believe that of Robert. Nearly anything else, God knows. But not that."

Lynley leaned towards her and covered her cold hands with his own. "You've been thinking he killed your sister. And saying nothing about your suspicions has been your way of protecting your children, sparing them the public humiliation of having a murderer for a father."

"He *couldn't*. Not that."

"Yet you think he did. *Why?*"

Sergeant Havers spoke. "If Gabriel didn't kill your sister, what you tell us can only help him."

Irene shook her head. Her eyes were hollows of terrible fear. "Not this. It *can't*." She looked at each one of them, her fingers digging into the worn surface of her handbag. She was like a fugitive, determined to escape but recognising the futility of further flight. When she began to speak at last, her body shuddered as if an illness had taken her. As, in a way, it had. "My sister was with Robert that night in his room. I heard them. I'd gone to him. Like a fool . . . God, why am I such a pathetic fool? He and I had been in the library together earlier, after the read-through, and there was a moment then when I thought that we might really go back to the way things had been between us. We'd been talking about our children, about . . . our lives in the past. So later, I went to Robert's room, meaning to . . . Oh God, I don't know *what* I meant to do." She ran a hand back through her dark hair, gripping it hard at the scalp as if she wanted the pain. "How much more of a fool can I possibly be in one lifetime? I almost walked in on my sister and Robert for a *second* time. And the funny part—it's almost hysterical when one really thinks about it—is that he was saying exactly the same thing that he had been saying to Joy that day in Hampstead when I found them together. 'Come on, baby. Come on, Joy. Come on! Come *on!*' And grunting and grunting and grunting like a bull."

Lynley heard her words, recognising the kaleidoscopic effect they had on the case. They threw everything into a new perspective. "What time was this?"

"Late. Long after one. Perhaps nearly two. I don't actually know."

"But you heard him? You're certain of that?"

"Oh, yes. I heard him." She bent her head in shame.

Yet after that, Lynley thought, she would still seek to protect the man. That kind of undeserved, selfless devotion was beyond his comprehension. He avoided trying to deal with it by asking her something altogether different. "Do you remember where you were in March of 1973?"

She did not seem to take in the question at once. "In 1973? I was . . . surely I was at home in London. Caring for James. Our son. He was born that January, and I'd taken some time off."

"But Gabriel wasn't home?"

She pondered this. "No, I don't think he was. I think he was appearing in the regionals then. Why? What does that have to do with all this?"

Everything, Lynley thought. He put all his resources into compelling her to listen and understand his next words. "Your sister was getting ready to write a book about a murder that occurred in March of 1973. Whoever committed that murder also killed Joy and Gowan Kilbride. The evidence we have is virtually useless, Irene. And I'm afraid we need you if we're to bring this creature to any kind of justice."

Her eyes begged him for the truth. "Is it Robert?"

"I don't think so. In spite of everything you've told us, I simply don't see how he could have managed to get the key to her room."

"But if he was *with* her that night, she could have given it to him!"

That was a possibility, Lynley acknowledged. How to explain it? And then how to align it with what the forensic report revealed about Joy Sinclair? And how to tell Irene that even if, by helping the police, she proved her husband innocent, she would only be proving her own cousin Rhys guilty?

"Will you help us?" he asked.

Lynley saw her struggle with the decision and knew exactly the dilemma she faced. It all came down to a simple choice: her continued protection of Robert Gabriel for the sake of their children, or her active involvement in a scheme that might bring her sister's killer to justice. To choose the former, she faced the uncertainty of never knowing whether she was protecting a man who was truly innocent or guilty. To choose the latter, however, she in effect committed herself to an act of forgiveness, a posthumous absolution of her sister's sin against her.

Thus, it was a choice between the living and the dead wherein the living promised only a continuation of lies and the dead promised the peace of mind that comes from a dissolution of rancour and a getting on with life. On the surface, it appeared to be no choice at all. But Lynley knew too well that decisions governed by the heart could be wildly irrational. He only hoped Irene had grown to see that her marriage to Gabriel had been infected with the disease of his infidelities, and that her sister had played only a small and unhappy role in a drama of demise that had been grinding itself out for years.

Irene moved. Her fingers left damp marks on her leather handbag. Her voice caught, then held. "I'll help you. What do I have to do?"

"Spend tonight at your sister's home in Hampstead. Sergeant Havers will go with you."

16

WHEN DEBORAH ST. JAMES answered the door to Lynley's knock the next morning at half past ten, her unruly hair and the stained apron she wore over her threadbare jeans and plaid shirt told him he had interrupted her in the midst of her work. Still, her face lit when she saw him.

"A diversion," she said. "Thank God! I've spent the last two hours working in the darkroom with nothing but Peach and Alaska for company. They're sweet as far as dogs and cats go, but not much for conversation. Simon's right there in the lab, of course, but his entertainment value plunges to nothing when he's concentrating on science. I'm so glad you've come. Perhaps you can rout him out for morning coffee." She waited until he had removed overcoat and muffler before she touched his shoulder lightly and said, "Are you quite all right, Tommy? Is there anything . . . ? You see, they've told me a bit about it and . . . You don't look well. Are you sleeping at all? Have you eaten? Should I ask Dad . . . ? Would you like . . . ?" She bit her lip. "Why do I always babble like an idiot?"

Lynley smiled affectionately at her jumble of words, gently pushed one of her fallen curls back behind her ear, and followed her to the stairs. She was continuing to speak.

"Simon's had a phone call from Jeremy Vinney. It's put him into one of those long, mysterious contemplations of his. And then Helen rang not five minutes later."

Below her, Lynley hesitated. "Helen's not here today?" In spite

269

of his tone, which he had endeavoured to keep guarded, he saw that Deborah read through the question easily. Her green eyes softened.

"No. She's not here, Tommy. That's why you've come, isn't it?" Without waiting for his answer, she said kindly, "Do come up and talk to Simon. He knows Helen better than anyone, after all."

St. James met them at the door to his laboratory, an old copy of Simpson's *Forensic Medicine* in one hand and a particularly grisly-looking anatomical specimen in the other: a human finger preserved in formaldehyde.

"Are you rehearsing a production of *Titus Andronicus*?" Deborah asked with a laugh. She took the jar and the book from her husband, brushed a kiss against his cheek, and said, "Here's Tommy, my love."

Lynley spoke to St. James without preamble. He wanted his questions to sound purely professional, a natural extension of the case. He knew he failed miserably. "St. James, where's Helen? I've been phoning her since last night. I stopped by her flat this morning. What's happened to her? What's she told you?"

He followed his friend into the lab and waited impatiently for a response. St. James typed a quick notation into his word processor, saying nothing. Lynley knew the other man well enough not to push for an answer when none was forthcoming. He bit back his misgivings, waited, and let his eyes roam round the room in which Helen spent so much of her time.

The laboratory had been St. James' sanctuary for years, a scientific haven of computers, laser printers, microscopes, culture ovens, shelves of specimens, walls of graphs and charts, and in one corner a video screen on which microscopic samples of blood or hair or skin or fibre could be enlarged. This last modernity was a recent addition to the lab, and Lynley recalled the laughter with which Helen had described St. James' attempts to teach her how it worked just three weeks past. *Hopeless, Tommy darling. A video camera hooked into a microscope! Can you imagine my dismay? My God, all this computer-age wizardry! I've only just recently come to understand how to boil a cup of water in a microwave oven.* Untrue, of course. But he'd laughed all the same, immediately freed of whatever cares the day had heaped upon him. That was Helen's special gift.

He had to know. "What's happened to her? What's she told you?"

St. James added another notation to the word processor, examined the consequent changes in a graph on the screen, and shut down the unit. "Only what you told her," he replied in a voice that was perfectly detached. "Nothing more, I'm afraid."

Lynley knew how to interpret that careful tone, but for the moment he refused to engage in the discussion that St. James' words encouraged. Instead he temporised with, "Deborah's told me Vinney phoned you."

"Indeed." St. James swung around on his stool, pushed himself off it awkwardly, and walked to a well-ordered counter where five microscopes were lined up, three in use. "Apparently, no newspapers are picking up the story of the Sinclair death. According to Vinney, he turned in an article about it this morning only to have it rejected by his editor."

"Vinney's the drama critic, after all," Lynley noted.

"Yes, but when he phoned round to see if any of his colleagues were working on the murder, he discovered that not one had been assigned to the story. It's been killed from higher up. For the time being, according to what he's been told. Until there's an arrest. He was in a fair state, to say the least." St. James looked up from a pile of slides he was organising. "He's after the Geoffrey Rintoul story, Tommy. And a connection between that and Joy Sinclair's death. I don't think he plans to rest until he has something in print."

"He'll never see it happen. In the first place, there's not one accessible shred of evidence against Geoffrey Rintoul. In the second place, the principals are dead. And without damned solid evidence, no newspaper in the country is going to take on so potentially libelous a story against so distinguished a family as Stinhurst's." Lynley felt suddenly restless, needing movement, so he walked the length of the room to the windows and looked down at the garden far below. Like everything else, it was covered with last night's snow, but he saw that all the plants had been wrapped in burlap and that breadcrumbs were spread out neatly on the top of the garden wall. *Deborah's loving hand*, he thought.

"Irene Sinclair believes that Joy went to Robert Gabriel's room the night she died," he said and sketched out the story that Irene had related to him. "She told me last night. She'd been holding it back, hoping to protect Gabriel."

"Then Joy saw *both* Gabriel and Vinney during the night?"

Lynley shook his head. "I don't see how it's possible. She can't have been with Gabriel. At least not in bed with him." He related the autopsy information from Strathclyde CID.

"Perhaps the Strathclyde team have made a mistake," St. James noted.

Lynley smiled at the idea. "With Macaskin as their DI? What do you think the likelihood of that is? Certainly nothing I'd want to make a book on. Last night when Irene told me, I thought at first that she had been mistaken in what she heard."

"Gabriel with someone else?"

"That's what I thought. That Irene had only assumed it was Joy. Or perhaps assumed the worst about what was going on between Joy and Gabriel in the room. But then I thought that she might very well have been lying to me, to implicate Gabriel in Joy's death, all the time protesting that she wants to protect him for her children's sake."

"A fine revenge, that," Deborah noted from the doorway of her darkroom where she stood listening, with a string of negatives in one hand and a magnifying glass in the other.

St. James crisscrossed the stack of slides absently. "It is indeed. Clever as well. We know from Elizabeth Rintoul that Joy Sinclair was in Vinney's room. So there's corroboration, if Elizabeth's to be trusted. But who's to corroborate Irene's claim that Joy was also with her husband? Gabriel? Of course not. He'll deny it hotly. And no one else heard it. So it's left to us to decide whether to believe the philandering husband or the long-suffering wife." He looked at Lynley. "Are you still certain about Davies-Jones?"

Lynley turned back to the window. St. James' question brought back with stinging clarity the report he had received from Constable Nkata just three hours before, immediately after the constable's night of trailing Davies-Jones. The information had been simple enough. After leaving Helen's flat, he had gone into the off-licence, where he purchased four bottles of liquor. Nkata was completely certain of the number, for following the purchase, Davies-Jones had begun to walk. Although the temperature had been well below freezing, he appeared to notice neither that nor the snow that continued to fall. Instead, he had kept up a brutal pace along the Brompton Road, circling Hyde Park, making his way up to Baker Street, and ultimately ending at his own flat in St. John's Wood. It had taken over two hours. And as Davies-Jones walked, he twisted off the cap of one bottle after another. But in lieu of a swig of the liquid inside, he had rhythmically, savagely, dashed the contents out into the street. Until he'd gone through all four bottles, Nkata had said, shaking his head at the waste of fine liquor.

Now Lynley thought again about Davies-Jones' behaviour and concentrated on what it implied: a man who had overcome alcoholism, who was fighting for a chance to put his career and his life back together. A man rigidly determined not to be defeated by anything, least of all by his past.

"He's the killer," Lynley said.

IRENE SINCLAIR knew it had to be the performance of her career, knew she had to gauge the proper moment without a single cue from anyone to tell her when it had arrived. There would be neither an entrance nor an instance of supreme drama when every eye was focussed on her. She would have to forego both of those pleasures for the theatre of the real. And it began after the company's lunch break when she and Jeremy Vinney arrived at the Agincourt Theatre simultaneously.

She was alighting from a cab just as Vinney dodged through the heavy traffic to cross the street from the café. A horn sounded its warning, and Irene looked up. Vinney was carrying his overcoat rather than wearing it, and seeing this, she wondered if his departure from the café had been prompted hastily by her own arrival. The journalist verified this himself with his first words. They were tinged with what sounded like malicious excitement.

"Someone got to Gabriel last night, I understand."

Irene stopped, her hand on the theatre door. Her fingers were curled tightly round its handle, and even through her gloves she could feel the sharp stab of icy metal. There didn't seem to be a point to questioning how Vinney had come upon the news. Robert had managed to get himself to the theatre this morning for the second reading, in spite of taped ribs, a black eye, and five stitches in his jaw. The news of his beating had travelled through the building within minutes of his arrival. And although cast members, crew, designers, and production assistants had smote the air with their hot exclamations of outrage, any one of them could have surreptitiously phoned Vinney with the story. Especially if any of them felt the need to engineer a spate of embarrassing public notoriety that would enable them to settle a private score or two with Robert Gabriel.

"Are you asking me about this for publication?" Irene asked. Hugging herself against the cold, she entered the theatre. Vinney followed. No one appeared to be about. The building was hushed. Only the persistent odour of burnt tobacco gave evidence that the actors and staff had been meeting all that morning.

"What did he tell you about it? And no, this isn't for publication."

"Then why are you here?" She kept her brisk pace towards the auditorium with Vinney dogging her stubbornly. He caught her arm and stopped her just short of the heavy, oak doors.

"Because your sister was my friend. Because I can't get a single word from anyone at the Met in spite of their long afternoon with our melancholy Lord Stinhurst. Because I couldn't get Stinhurst on the phone last night and I've an editor who says I can't write a syllable about any of this until we've some sort of miraculous clearance from above to do so. Everything about the mess stinks to heaven. Or doesn't that concern you, Irene?" His fingers dug into her arm.

"What a filthy thing to say."

"I come by it naturally. I get particularly filthy when people I care for are murdered and life just cranks on with merely a nod of acknowledgement to mark it."

Sudden anger choked her. "And you think I don't care about what happened to my sister?"

"I think you're delighted as hell," he replied. "The crowning glory would have been to be the one to plunge the knife yourself."

Irene felt the cruel shock of his words, felt the colour drain from her face. "My God, that's not true and you know it," she said, hearing how close her voice was to breaking. She jerked away from him and dashed into the auditorium, only imperfectly aware of the fact that he followed her, that he took a seat in the darkness of the last row, like a lurking Nemesis, champion of the dead.

The confrontation with Vinney was exactly what she had not needed prior to meeting with the cast members again. She had hoped to use all of her lunch hour to reflect upon how she would perform the role that Sergeant Havers had schooled her for last night. Now, however, she felt her heart pounding, her palms sweating, and her mind taken up with a violent denial of Vinney's final accusation. It was not true. She swore that to herself again and again as she approached the empty stage. Yet the turmoil she felt would not be stilled by such a simple expedient as denial, and knowing how much rested on her ability to perform today, she fell back upon an old technique from drama school. She took her place at the single table in the centre of the stage, brought her folded hands to her forehead, and closed her eyes. Thus, it proved nothing at all for her to move into character a few moments later when she heard approaching footsteps and her cousin's voice.

"Are you all right, Irene?" Rhys Davies-Jones asked.

She looked up, managing a weary smile. "Yes. Fine. A bit tired, I'm afraid." That would be enough for now.

Others began to arrive. Irene heard rather than saw them, mentally ticking off each person's entrance as she listened for signs of strain in their voices, signs of guilt, signs of increased anxiety. Robert Gabriel gingerly took his place next to her. He fingered his swollen face with a rueful smile.

"I've not had a chance to say thank you for last night," he said in a tender voice. "I'm . . . well, I'm sorry about it, Renie. I'm most wretchedly sorry about everything, in fact. I would have said something when the doctors had finished with me, but you'd already gone. I rang you up, but James said you were at Joy's in Hampstead." He paused for a reflective moment. "Renie. I thought . . . I did hope we might—"

She cut him off. "No. There was a great deal of time for me to think last night, Robert. And I did that. Clearly. At last."

Gabriel took in her tone and turned his head away. "I can guess what kind of thinking you accomplished at your sister's," he said with aggrieved finality.

The arrival of Joanna Ellacourt allowed Irene to avoid an answer. She swept up the aisle between her husband and Lord Stinhurst as David Sydeham was saying, "We want final approval of *all* the costumes, Stuart. It's not part of the original contract, I know. But considering everything that's already happened, I think we're within our rights to negotiate a new clause. Joanna feels—"

Joanna did not wait for her husband to argue the merits of their case. "I'd like the costumes to reflect who the starring role belongs to," she said pointedly, with a cool glance at Irene.

Stinhurst did not reply to either of them. He looked and moved like a man ageing rapidly. Managing the stairs seemed to drain him of energy. He appeared to be wearing the very same suit, shirt, and tie that he'd had on yesterday, the charcoal jacket rumpled, its sleeves badly creased. As if he'd given up interest in his appearance entirely. Watching him, Irene wondered, with a chill, if he would even live to see this production open. When he took his chair, with a nod of acknowledgement towards Rhys Davies-Jones, the new reading began.

They were midway through the play when Irene allowed herself to drop off to sleep. The theatre was so warm, the atmosphere on the stage was so close, their voices rose and fell with such hypnotic rhythm that she found it easier than she had supposed it would be to let herself go. She stopped worrying about their willingness to believe in the role she was playing and became the actress she had been years ago, before Robert Gabriel had entered her life and undermined her confidence with year after year of public and private humiliation.

She even felt herself beginning to dream when Joanna Ellacourt's voice snapped angrily, "For God's sake, would someone wake her up? I've no intention of trying to work my way through this with her sitting there like a drooling grandmother snoring at a kitchen fire."

"Renie?"

"Irene!"

She opened her eyes with a start, pleased to feel the rush of embarrassment sweep over her. "Did I drop off? I'm terribly sorry."

"Late night, sweetie?" Joanna asked tartly.

"Yes, I'm afraid . . . I . . ." Irene swallowed, smiled flickeringly to mask pain, and said, "I spent most of the night going through Joy's things in Hampstead."

Stunned astonishment met this announcement. Irene felt pleased to see the effect her words had upon them, and for a moment she understood Jeremy Vinney's anger. How easily indeed they had forgotten her sister, how conveniently their lives had moved on. But not without a stumbling block for someone, she thought, and began to construct it with every power available to her. She brought tears into her eyes.

"There were diaries, you see," she said hollowly.

As if instinct alone told her that she was in the presence of a performance capable of upstaging her own, Joanna Ellacourt sought their attention again. "No doubt an account of Joy's life makes absolutely fascinating reading," she said. "But if you're awake now, perhaps this play will be fascinating as well."

Irene shook her head. She allowed her voice to raise a degree. "No, no, that isn't it. You see, they weren't hers. They had come by express yesterday and when I opened them and found the note from the husband of that wretched woman who had written them—"

"For God's sake, is this really necessary?" Joanna's face was white with anger.

"—I started to read. I didn't get very far, but I saw that they were what Joy had been waiting for to do her next book. The one she talked about just the other night in Scotland. And suddenly . . . I seemed to realise that she was really dead, that she wouldn't ever be back." Irene's tears began to fall, becoming suddenly copious as she felt the first swelling of genuine grief. Her next words only marginally touched upon the script that she and Sergeant Havers had so painstakingly prepared. She was rambling, she knew it, but the words had to be said. And nothing else mattered but saying them. "So she'll never write it now. And I felt as if . . . with Hannah Darrow's diaries sitting there in her house . . . I ought to write the book for her if only I could. As a means of saying that . . . in the end, I understood how it happened between them. I *did* understand. Oh, it hurt. God, it was agony all the same. But I understood. And I don't think . . . She was *always* my sister. I never told her that. Oh God, I can't go back there now that she's dead!"

And then, having done it, she let herself weep, understanding at last the source of her tears, mourning the sister she had loved but forgiven too late, mourning the youth she had wasted in devotion to a man who finally meant nothing to her. She sobbed despairingly, for the years gone and the words unspoken, caring for nothing at last but this act of grief.

Across from her, Joanna Ellacourt spoke again. "This cuts it. Can't any of you do something with her, or is she going to blubber for the rest of the day?" She turned to her husband. "David," she insisted.

But Sydeham was gazing out into the theatre. "We've a visitor," he said.

Their eyes followed his. Marguerite Rintoul, Countess of Stinhurst, was standing midway down the centre aisle.

SHE WAITED only as long as it took to close the door to her husband's office. "Where were you last night, Stuart?" she demanded, doing nothing to hide the asperity in her voice as she pulled off her coat and gloves and threw them down on a chair.

It was a question which Lady Stinhurst knew quite well she would not have asked twenty-four hours ago. Then she would have accepted his absence in her usual, pathetically cringing fashion, hurt and wondering and afraid to know the truth. But now she was beyond that. Yesterday's revelations in this room had combined with a long night of soul-searching to produce an anger so finely honed that it could not be blunted by any stony wall of protective and deliberate inattention.

Stinhurst went to his desk, sat behind it in the heavy leather chair.

"Sit down," he said. His wife didn't move.

"I asked you a question. I want an answer. Where were you last night? And please don't ask me to believe that Scotland Yard kept you until nine this morning. I like to think I'm not that much of a fool."

"I went to an hotel," Stinhurst said.

"Not your club?"

"No. I wanted anonymity."

"Something you couldn't have at home, of course."

For a moment, Stinhurst said nothing, fingering a letter opener that lay on his desk. Long and silver, it caught the light. "I found I couldn't face you."

Perhaps more than anything else, her reaction to that single sentence signalled the manner in which their relationship had changed. His voice was even, but brittle, as if the slightest provocation might cause him to break down. His skin was pallid, his eyes bloodshot and, when he placed the letter opener back on his desk, his wife saw that his hands trembled. And yet, she felt herself unmoved by all this, knowing perfectly well that its cause was not his concern for her welfare or the welfare of their daughter or even for himself, but concern over how he was going to keep the story about Geoffrey Rintoul's despicable life and his violent death out of the newspapers. She had seen Jeremy Vinney herself in the back of the theatre. She knew why he was there. Her anger swelled anew.

"There I was at home, Stuart, patiently waiting as I always have done, worrying about you and what was happening at Scotland Yard. Hour after hour. I thought—I realised only later how foolish I was being—that somehow this tragedy might serve to bring us closer to each other. Imagine my thinking that, in spite of the story you produced about my 'affair' with your brother, we might still put this marriage of ours back together. But then you never even phoned, did you? And, like a fool, I waited and waited obediently. Until I finally saw that things are quite dead between us. They have been for years, of course, but I was far too afraid to face that. Until last night."

Lord Stinhurst raised a hand as if in the hope of forestalling further words. "You do choose your moments, don't you? This isn't the time to discuss our marriage. I should think you'd see that if nothing else."

Always, it was his voice of dismissal. So cold and final. So rigid with restraint. Odd, how it didn't affect her one way or the other now. She smiled politely. "You've misunderstood. We aren't discussing our marriage, Stuart. There's nothing to discuss."

"Then why—"

"I've told Elizabeth about her grandfather. I thought we might do it together last night. But when you didn't come home, I told her myself." She walked across the room to stand in front of his desk. She rested her knuckles against its pristine surface. Her fingers were newly bare of rings. He watched her but did not speak. "And do you know what she said when I told her that her beloved grandfather had killed her uncle Geoffrey, had snapped his handsome neck in two?"

Stinhurst shook his head. He lowered his eyes.

"She said, 'Mummy, you're standing in the way of the telly. Would you move, please?' And I thought, isn't that rich? All these years, dedicated to protecting the sacred memory of a grandfather she adored, have come down to this. Of course, I stepped out of her way at once. I'm like that, aren't I? Always cooperative, eager to please. Always hoping things will turn out for the best if I ignore them long enough. I'm a shell of a person in a shell of a marriage, wandering round a fine house in Holland Park with every advantage save the one I've wanted so desperately all these years. Love." Lady Stinhurst watched for a reaction on her husband's face. There was nothing. She continued. "I knew then that I can't save Elizabeth. She's lived in a house of lies and half-truths for too many years. She can only save herself. As can I."

"What's that supposed to mean?"

"That I'm leaving you," she said. "I don't know if it's permanent. I don't have the bravado to claim that, I'm afraid. But I'm going to Somerset until I have everything sorted out in my mind, until I know what I want to do. And if it does become permanent, you're not to worry. I don't require much. Just a few rooms somewhere and a bit of peace and quiet. No doubt we can work out an equitable settlement. But if not, our respective solicitors—"

Stinhurst swung his chair to one side. "Don't *do* this to me. Not today. Please. Not on top of everything else."

She gave a regretful laugh. "That's really what it is, isn't it? I'm about to cause you one more headache, just another inconvenience. Something else to have to explain away to Inspector Lynley, if it comes down to that. Well, I would have waited, but as I needed to talk to you anyway, now seemed as good a time as any to tell you everything."

"Everything?" he asked dully.

"Yes. There's one thing more before I'm on my way. Francesca telephoned this morning. She couldn't bear it any longer, she said. Not after Gowan. She thought she would be able to. But Gowan was dear to her, and she couldn't bear to think that she had made less of his life and his death by what she had done. She was willing to at first, for your sake, of course. But she found that she couldn't keep up the pretence. So she plans to speak to Inspector Macaskin this afternoon."

"What are you talking about?"

Lady Stinhurst pulled on her gloves, picked up her coat, preparatory to leaving. She took brief, hostile pleasure in her final remarks. "Francesca lied to the police about what she did, and what she saw, the night Joy Sinclair died."

"I'VE BROUGHT Chinese food, Dad." Barbara Havers popped her head into the sitting room. "But I shall have to ask you not to fight with Mum over the shrimp this time. Where is she?"

Her father sat before the television set, which was tuned deafeningly into BBC-1. The horizontal hold was slipping, and people's heads were being cut off right at the eyebrows so that it looked a bit like a science fiction show.

"Dad?" Barbara repeated. He gave no answer. She walked into the room, lowered the volume, and turned to him. He was asleep, his jaw slack, the tubes that fed him oxygen askew in his nostrils. Racing magazines covered the floor near his chair and a newspaper was opened over his knees. It was too hot in the room, in the entire house for that matter, and the musty smell of her parents' ageing seemed to seep from the walls and the floor and the furniture. This mixed with a stronger, more recent scent of food overcooked and inedible.

Barbara's movement made sufficient noise to waken her father, and, seeing her, he smiled, showing teeth that were blackened, crooked, and in places altogether missing. "Barbie. Mussa dozed off."

"Where's Mum?"

Jimmy Havers blinked, adjusting the tubes in his nostrils and reaching for a handkerchief into which he coughed heavily. His breathing sounded like the bubbling of water. "Just next door. Mrs. Gustafson's come down with flu again and Mum's taken her some soup."

Knowing her mother's questionable culinary talents, Barbara wondered briefly if Mrs. Gustafson's condition would improve or worsen under her ministrations. Nonetheless, she was encouraged by the fact that her mother had ventured out of the house. It was the first time she had done so in years.

"I've brought Chinese," she told her father, indicating the sack she cradled in one arm. "I'm off again tonight, though. I've only half an hour to eat."

Her father frowned. "Mum won't like that, Barbie. Not one bit."

"That's why I've brought the food. Peace offering." She went on to the kitchen at the back of the house.

Her heart sank at the sight of it. A dozen tins of soup were lined up near the sink with their lids gaping open and spoons stuck in them as if her mother had sampled each one before deciding which to offer their neighbour. Three had actually been heated, in separate pans which still stood on the stove with the fire left carelessly on beneath them and their contents burnt to nothing, sending up a scent of scalded vegetables and milk. Perilously near the flame, a package of biscuits lay open, spilling out its contents, its wrapper hastily torn away and part of it discarded on the floor.

"Oh hell," Barbara said wearily, turning off the stove. She put her package down onto the kitchen table, next to her mother's newest album of travel information. A glance told her that Brazil was this week's destination, but she wasn't interested in looking at the collection of brochures and photographs clipped from magazines. She rummaged beneath the sink for a rubbish sack and was dropping the tins of soup into it when the front door opened, hesitant steps teetered down the uncarpeted hall, and her mother appeared at the kitchen door, a badly scored plastic tray in her hands. Soup, biscuits, and a withered apple were all in place upon it.

"It went cold," Mrs. Havers said, her colourless eyes trying to focus past her own confusion. She was wearing only an irregularly buttoned cardigan over her shabby housedress. "I didn't think to cover the soup, lovey. And when I got there, her daughter had come to stay and said that Mrs. Gustafson didn't want it."

Barbara looked at the curious mixture and blessed Mrs. Gustafson's daughter for her wisdom if not for her tact. The soup was a blend of everything on the stove, an unappealing concoction of split pea, clam chowder, and tomato with rice. Rapidly cooling in the night air, it had formed a puckered skin on the top so that it vaguely resembled coagulating blood. Her stomach churned uneasily at the sight.

"Well, no matter, Mum," she said. "You thought about her, didn't you? And Mrs. Gustafson will be sure to learn of that. You were neighbourly, weren't you?"

Her mother smiled vacantly. "Yes. I was, wasn't I?" She set the tray down on the very edge of the table. Barbara lunged forward to catch it before it toppled to the floor. "Have you seen Brazil, lovey?" Affectionately, Mrs. Havers fingered the tattered artificial leather cover of her album. "I did some more work on it today."

"Yes. I had a quick glance." Barbara continued sweeping things off the work top into the rubbish. The sink was piled with unwashed crockery. A faint odour of rot emanated from it, telling her that uneaten food was also buried somewhere beneath the mess. "I've brought Chinese," she told her mother. "I'm off again in a bit, though."

"Oh, lovey, no," her mother responded. "In this cold? In the dark? I don't think that's wise, do you? Young ladies should not be on the streets alone at night."

"Police business, Mum," Barbara replied. She went to the cupboard and saw that only two clean plates were left. No matter, she thought. She would eat out of the cartons once her parents had taken their share.

She was setting the table as her mother puttered uselessly in her wake when the front doorbell rang. They looked at each other.

Her mother's face clouded. "You don't suppose that's . . . No, I know. Tony won't come back, will he? He's dead, isn't he?"

"He's dead, Mum," Barbara replied firmly. "Put the kettle on for tea. I'll get the door."

The bell rang a second time before she had a chance to answer it. Muttering impatiently, flipping on the exterior light, she pulled the door open to see, unbelievably, Lady Helen Clyde standing on the front step. She was dressed completely in black from head to toe, and that should have served as warning enough for Barbara. But at the moment, all she could contemplate was the horrifying thought that, unless this was a nightmare from which she could mercifully awaken, she was going to have to ask the other woman into the house.

The youngest daughter of the tenth Earl of Hesfield, child of a Surrey great house, denizen of one of the most fashionable districts in London. Come to this netherworld of Acton's worst neighbourhood . . . for what? Barbara gaped at her wordlessly, looked for a car in the street, and saw Lady Helen's red Mini parked several doors down. She heard her mother's nervous whimper some distance behind her.

"Lovey? Who is it? It's not . . ."

"No, Mum. It's fine. Don't worry," she called back over her shoulder.

"Forgive me, Barbara," Lady Helen said. "If there had been any other way, I would have taken it."

The words brought Barbara back to herself. She held the door open. "Come in."

When Lady Helen passed her and stood in the hall, Barbara felt herself looking at her home involuntarily, seeing it as the other woman must see it, as a place where lunacy and poverty whirled wildly hand in hand. The worn linoleum on the floor unwashed for months at a time, tracked with footprints and puddles of melted snow; the faded wallpaper peeling away at the corners with a damp patch growing mouldy near the door; the battered stairway with hooks along the wall on which ragged coats hung carelessly, some unworn for years; the old rattan umbrella rack, with great gaping holes in its sides where wet umbrellas had eaten through the palm over time; the odours of burnt food and age and neglect.

My bedroom's not like this! she wanted to shout. *But I can't keep up with them and pay the bills and cook the meals and see that they clean themselves!*

But she said nothing. She merely waited for Lady Helen to speak, feeling a hot tide of shame wash over her when her father shambled to the door of the sitting room in his baggy trousers and stained grey shirt, pulling his oxygen along behind him in its trolley.

"This is my father," Barbara said and, when her mother peeped out of the kitchen like a frightened mouse, "and my mother."

Lady Helen went to Jimmy Havers, extending her hand. "I'm Helen Clyde," she said, and looking into the kitchen, "I've interrupted your dinner, haven't I, Mrs. Havers?"

Jimmy Havers smiled expansively. "Chinese tonight," he said. "We've enough if you want a bite, don't we, Barbie?"

At another time, Barbara might have taken grim amusement from the thought of Lady Helen Clyde eating Chinese food out of cartons, sitting at the kitchen table and chatting with her mother about the trips to Brazil and Turkey and Greece that occupied the inner reaches of her madness. But now she only felt weak with the humiliation of discovery, with the knowledge that Lady Helen might somehow betray her circumstances to Lynley.

"Thank you," Lady Helen was replying graciously. "But I'm not at all hungry." She smiled at Barbara, but it was at best only an unsteady effort.

Seeing this, Barbara realised that whatever her own state was in the face of this visit, Lady Helen's was worse. Thus, she spoke kindly. "Let me just get them started eating, Helen. The sitting room's over there if you don't mind a rather large sort of mess."

Without waiting to see how Lady Helen might react to her first sight of the sitting room, with its ancient creaking furniture and general air of decay, Barbara ushered her father into the kitchen. She took a moment to soothe her mother's querulous fears about their unexpected visitor, dishing out rice, fried shrimp, sesame chicken, and oyster beef as she considered why the other woman had appeared on her doorstep. She didn't want to think that Lady Helen might already be aware of the machinery set in progress for tonight's arrest. She didn't want to think that the potential arrest might be the reason for this visit in the first place. Yet, all the time she knew in her heart that there could be no other reason. She and Lady Helen Clyde did not exactly travel in the same circle of friends. This was hardly an impulsive social call.

When Barbara joined her in the sitting room a few minutes later, Lady Helen did not leave her long in suspense. She was sitting on the edge of the sagging, artificial horsehair couch, her eyes on the wall opposite where a single photograph of Barbara's younger brother hung among ten rectangles of darker wallpaper, remnants of a previous collection of memorabilia devoted to his passing. As soon as Barbara entered the room, Lady Helen got to her feet.

"I'm coming with you tonight." She made a small, embarrassed movement with her hands. "I'd have liked to put that more politely, but there doesn't seem to be a point, does there?"

There also seemed to be no point to lying. "How did you find out?" Barbara asked.

"I telephoned Tommy about an hour ago. Denton told me he was on a surveillance tonight. Tommy generally doesn't do surveillance, does he? So I assumed the rest." She gestured again, with an unhappy smile. "Had I known where the surveillance was to be, I simply would have gone there myself. But I didn't know. Denton didn't know. There was no one at the Yard who could or would tell me. So I came to you. And I *will* follow you there if you don't let me come with you." She lowered her voice. "I'm terribly sorry. I know what kind of position this puts you in. I know how angry Tommy will be. With both of us."

"Then why are you doing this?"

Lady Helen's eyes moved back to the photograph of Barbara's brother. It was an old school picture, not very well taken, but it depicted Tony the way Barbara liked to remember him, laughing, showing a missing front tooth, a face freckled and elfish, a mop of hair.

"After . . . everything that's happened, I *must* be there," Lady Helen said. "It's a conclusion. I need it. And it seems that the only way I can bring it to an end for myself—the only way I can forgive myself for having been such a blundering fool—is to be there when you take him." Lady Helen looked back at her. She was, Barbara saw, terribly pale. She looked frail and unwell. "How can I tell you how it feels to know that he used me? To know how I turned on Tommy when all he wanted to do was to show me the truth?"

"We phoned you last night. The inspector has been trying to reach you all day. He's half-mad with worry."

"I'm sorry. I didn't . . . I couldn't face him."

"Forgive me for saying so," Barbara said hesitantly, "but I don't think the inspector's taken any pleasure at all from being in the right in this case. Not at your expense."

She did not go on to mention her afternoon meeting with Lynley, his restless pacing as he set up the surveillance team, his continuous telephone calls to Lady Helen's flat, to her family's home in Surrey, to the St. James house. She did not go on to mention his black brooding as the afternoon wore on, or how he jumped for the telephone each time it rang, or how his voice maintained an indifference that was contravened by the tension in his face.

"Will you let me come with you?" Lady Helen asked.

Barbara knew the question was a mere formality. "I don't see how I can stop you," she replied.

LYNLEY HAD BEEN at Joy Sinclair's home in Hampstead since half past four. The members of the surveillance team had arrived not long after, establishing themselves in prearranged locations, two in a dirty van with a flat tyre parked midway down Flask Walk, another above the bookstore on the corner of Back Lane, another in an herb store, still another on the high street with a view towards the underground station. Lynley himself was in the house, not far from the most logical means of access: the dining-room doors that faced the back garden. He sat in one of the low chairs in the unlit sitting room, monitoring the conversation that came spitting through the radio from his men on the outside.

It was just after eight when the van team announced, "Havers on the lower end of Flask Walk, sir. She's not alone."

Perplexed, Lynley got to his feet, went to the front door, and cracked it open just as Sergeant Havers and Lady Helen passed under a street lamp, their faces exposed in its eerie amber glow. After a quick survey of the street, they hurried into the front garden and through the door.

"What in God's name—" Lynley began hotly once he'd shut the door behind him and they stood in a circle of darkness within the hall.

"I gave her no choice, Tommy," Lady Helen said. "Denton told me you were on a surveillance. I put the rest together and went to Sergeant Havers' house."

"I won't have you here. Damn it all, anything could happen." Lynley walked into the sitting room where the radio was, picked it up, and began to speak. "I'm going to need a man here to—"

"No! Don't do this to me!" Lady Helen reached out desperately but did not touch him. "I did just what you asked of me last night. I did everything you asked. So let me be here now. I need to be, Tommy. I won't get in your way. I promise. I swear it. Just let me end this the way I need to. Please." He felt suddenly torn by irrational indecision. He knew what he had to do. He knew what was right. She no more belonged here than caught up in the middle of a public brawl. Words came to his lips—appropriate and dutiful— but before he could say them, she spoke in a manner that struck him to the quick. "Let me get over Rhys the best way I know how. I beg it of you, Tommy."

"Inspector?" a voice crackled from the radio.

Lynley's own voice was harsh. "It's all right. Maintain your positions."

"Thank you," Lady Helen whispered.

He couldn't reply. All he could think of was the single most telling remark she had made. *I did everything you asked.* Remembering her final words to him last night, he couldn't bear the thought of what that meant. Unable to respond, he moved past her into a dim corner of the dining room, flicked the curtains a scant inch to view Back Lane, saw nothing, and returned. Their long waiting together began.

FOR THE NEXT six hours, Lady Helen was as good as her word. She did not move from the chair she had taken in the sitting room. She did not speak. There were times when Lynley thought she was asleep, but he could not see her face clearly. It was merely a ghostly blur under the black bandana she wore.

A trick of lighting made her seem insubstantial, as if she were fading from him, the way an image on a photograph does over time. The soft brown eyes, the arch of brow, the gentle curve of cheek and lips, the frankly stubborn chin—all these became less definite as the hours passed. And as he sat opposite her, with Sergeant Havers making a third of their triangle of anticipation, he felt a yearning for her that he had never known before, having nothing at all to do with sex and everything to do with the soul's calling out to a spirit kindred and essential to the completion of one's own. He felt as if he had been travelling a great distance, only to arrive where he had started, only to know the place truly and for the very first time.

Yet all along he had the distinct sensation of being too late.

The radio crackled to life at ten past two. "Company, Inspector. Coming down Flask Walk . . . Keeping hard to the shadows . . . Oh, very nice technique, that . . . An eye out for coppers . . . Dark clothes, dark knit cap, collar on the coat pulled up . . . Stopped now. Three doors down from the nest." There was a pause of several minutes' duration. Then the whispered monologue began again. "Crossed the street for another look . . . Continuing the approach . . . Crossing over again towards Back Lane . . . This is our baby, Inspector. No one walks this way down a street at two in the morning in this kind of weather. . . . Giving it over. I've lost sight. . . . Turned down Back Lane."

Another voice picked it up, said only, "Suspect approaching the garden wall . . . pulling something down over the face . . . running a hand along the bricks . . ."

Lynley switched off the radio. He moved noiselessly into the deepest shadows of the dining room. Sergeant Havers followed. Behind them, Lady Helen stood.

At first Lynley saw nothing beyond the dining room doors. And then a black shape appeared against the inky sky as the intruder's body rose to the top of the garden wall. A leg swung to the inside, then another. Then a soft thud as he hit the ground. No face was visible, which at first seemed impossible since there was light enough from both stars and the street lamps on Back Lane to illuminate the snow, the sketching of the tree against it, the contrast of mortar against the brick wall, even to a certain extent the interior of the house. But then Lynley saw that the man was wearing a ski mask. And suddenly he was so much less of an intruder, so much more of a killer.

"Helen, go back in the sitting room," Lynley breathed. But she did not move. He looked over his shoulder to see that her wide eyes were fixed upon the figure in the garden, upon his stealthy progress to the door. Her fist was raised, clenched to her lips.

And then the unbelievable happened.

As he mounted the four steps, reached a hand out to try the door, Lady Helen cried frantically, "No! Oh God, Rhys!"

And chaos erupted.

Outside, the figure froze only for an instant before he bolted for the wall and took it in a single leap.

"Jesus Christ!" Sergeant Havers shouted and headed for the dining room doors, flinging them open, letting in a rush of freezing night air.

Lynley felt immobilised by the force of disbelief at what Helen had done. She *couldn't* have . . . She hadn't meant . . . She would never . . . She was coming towards him in the darkness.

"Tommy, *please* . . ."

Her shattered voice brought him to his senses abruptly. Shoving her to one side, he dashed for the radio and said tersely, "We've lost him." That done, he ran for the front door, raced outside, insensible to the sound of pursuit behind him.

"Up towards the high street!" a voice shouted from above the bookstore across the street as Lynley tore past.

He did not need to hear it. Ahead of him, he saw the black shape running, heard the frantic pounding of his footsteps on the pavement, saw him slip on a patch of ice, right himself, and run on. He was not bothering to seek the safety of the shadows. Instead he dashed down the middle of the street, flashing in and out of the light from the street lamps. The sound of his flight thundered on the night air.

A few steps behind him, Lynley heard Sergeant Havers. She was running at full speed, cursing Lady Helen violently with every foul word she knew.

"Police!" The two constables from the van had exploded round the corner, coming up quickly behind them.

Ahead, their quarry burst onto Heath Street, one of the larger arteries of Hampstead Village. The headlamps of an oncoming car trapped him like an animal. Tyres screeched, a horn honked wildly. A large Mercedes skidded to a stop inches from his thighs. But he did not run on. Instead, he whirled, lunging for the door. Even at the distance of half a block, Lynley could hear the terrified screaming from inside the car.

"You! Stop!" Another constable charged round the corner from the high street, less than thirty yards from the Mercedes. At the shout, however, the black-garbed figure spun to the right and continued his flight up the hill.

But the pause at the car had cost him time and distance, and Lynley was gaining on him, was close enough to hear the roaring of his lungs as he surged towards a narrow stone stairway that led to the hillside and the neighbourhood above. He took the steps three at a time, stopping at the top where a metal basket of empty milk bottles stood outside the shadowed arch of a front door. Grabbing this, he hurled it down the steps in his wake before running on, but the shattering glass served only to frighten several neighbourhood dogs who set up a tremendous howling. Lights went on in the buildings that lined the stairs, making Lynley's going easier and the broken glass nothing to contend with at all.

At the top of the stairs, the street was sided by enormous beech and sycamore trees that filled it with looming shadows. Lynley paused there, listening against the night wind and the howling animals for the sound of flight, looking for movement in the darkness. Havers came up next to him, still cursing as she gasped for breath.

"Where's he—"

Lynley heard it first, coming from his left. The dull thud against metal as the runner—his vision impaired by the ski mask—fell against a dustbin. It was all Lynley needed.

"He's heading for the church!" He spun Havers back to the stairs. "Go for the others," he ordered. "Tell them to head him off at St. John's! Now!"

Lynley didn't wait to see if she would obey. The pounding footsteps ahead of him drew him back into the chase, across Holly Hill to a narrow street where he saw in a moment of triumph that every advantage was going to be his. A series of high walls along one side, an open green on the other. The street offered absolutely no protection. In an instant he saw his man some forty yards ahead, turning into a gateway that was open in the wall. When he reached the gate himself, he saw that the snow had gone uncleared in the drive, that elongated footprints led across a broad lawn into a garden. There, a struggling form battled a hedge of holly, his clothes snagging on the spiny leaves. He gave a raw cry of pain. A dog began to bark furiously. Floodlights switched on. On the high street below, the sirens started, grew maddeningly loud as the police cars approached.

This last seemed to give the man the rush of adrenaline he needed to free himself from the bushes. As Lynley closed in, he cast a wild glance towards him, gauged his proximity, and tore himself from the plants' painful embrace. He fell to his knees—free—on the other side of the hedge, scrambled back up, ran on. Lynley spun in the other direction, saw a second gate in the wall, and ploughed his way to it through the snow at the cost of at least thirty seconds. He threw himself into the street.

To his right, St. John's Church loomed beyond a low brick wall. There, a shadow moved, crouched, leaped, and was over it. Lynley ran on.

He took the wall easily himself, landing in the snow. In an instant he saw a figure moving swiftly to his left, heading for the graveyard. The sound of sirens grew nearer, the sound of tyres against wet pavement echoed and shrieked.

Lynley fought his way through a snowdrift up to his knees, gained hold on a spot of cleared pavement. Ahead, the dark shape began dodging through the graves.

It was the kind of mistake Lynley had been waiting for. The snow was deeper in the graveyard, some tombstones were buried completely. Within moments, he heard the other man thrashing frantically as he crashed into markers, trying to make his way across to the far wall and the street beyond it.

Nearby, the sirens stopped, the blue lights flashed and twirled, and police began to swarm over the wall. They were carrying torches which they shone on the snow, white light arcing out to catch the runner in its glare. But it also served to illuminate the graves distinctly, and he picked up his pace, dodging sarcophagi and monuments, as he headed for the wall.

Lynley stuck to the cleared path which wound through the trees, thickly planted pines that spread their needles on the pavement, providing a rough surface for his shoes against the ice. He gained time from ease of movement here, precious seconds that he used to locate his man.

He was perhaps twenty feet from the wall. To his left two constables were fighting their way through the snow. Behind him, Havers was on his path through the graves. To his right was Lynley, on a dead run. There was no escape. Yet, with a savage cry that seemed to signal a final surge of strength, he made a leap upwards. But Lynley was on him too quickly.

The man whirled, swung wildly. Lynley loosened his grasp to dodge the punch, giving the other a second's opportunity to climb the wall. He made his vault, caught at the top, gripped fiercely, lifted his body, began to go over.

But Lynley countered. Grabbing at his black sweater, he pulled him back, locked his arm round the man's neck, and flung him into the snow. He stood panting above him as Havers arrived at his side, wheezing like a distance runner. The two constables ploughed their way up and one of them managed to say, "You're done for, son," before he gave way to a fit of coughing.

Lynley reached forward, yanked the man to his feet, pulled off his ski mask, jerked him into the torchlight.

It was David Sydeham.

17

"JOY'S DOOR wasn't locked," Sydeham said.

They sat at a metal-legged table in one of the interrogation rooms at New Scotland Yard. It was a room designed to allow no escape, bearing not a single decorative appointment that might give flight even to imagination. Sydeham did not look at any of them as he spoke, not at Lynley, who sat across from him and worked to draw together all the details of the case; not at Sergeant Havers, who for once took no notes but merely interjected questions to add to their body of knowledge; not at the yawning shorthand typist—a twenty-two-year veteran of police work who recorded everything with an expression of boredom that suggested she had already heard every entanglement possible in the kinds of human relationships that end in violence. Faced with the three of them, Sydeham had turned his body to give them the benefit of his profile. His eyes were on a corner of the room where a dead moth lay, and he stared at it as if seeing there a recreation of the past days of violence.

His voice sounded nothing more than monumentally weary. It was half past three. "I'd got the dirk earlier when I went down to the library for the whisky. It was easy enough to pull it off the dining room wall, go through the kitchen, up the back stairs, and along to my room. And then, of course, all I had to do was wait."

"Did you know that your wife was with Robert Gabriel?"

Sydeham moved his eyes to the Rolex whose gold casing glittered in a half-crescent beneath his black sweater. Caressingly, he rotated a finger round its face. His hands were quite large, but without callosity, unexposed to labour. They didn't look at all like the hands of a killer.

"It didn't take long to work it out, Inspector," he finally replied. "As Joanna herself would no doubt point out, I had wanted her together with Gabriel, and she was just giving me what I wanted. Theatre of the real in spades. It was an expert revenge, wasn't it? Of course, I wasn't sure at first that she was actually with him. I thought—perhaps I hoped—she'd gone somewhere else in the house to sulk. But I suppose I really knew that's not at all her style. And at any rate, Gabriel was fairly forthright about his conquest of my wife the other day at the Agincourt. But then, it isn't the kind of thing he'd be likely to keep quiet about, is it?"

"You assaulted him in his dressing room the other night?"

Sydeham smiled bleakly. "It was the only part of this bloody mess that I truly enjoyed. I don't like other men stuffing my wife, Inspector, whether she's a willing participant or not."

"But you're more than willing to have another man's wife, if it comes down to it."

"Ah. Hannah Darrow. I had a feeling that little minx would do me in, in the end." Sydeham reached for a Styrofoam cup of coffee on the table before him. His nails made crescent patterns upon it. "When Joy talked at dinner about her new book, she mentioned the diaries she was trying to get off John Darrow, and I could see fairly well how everything was going to come down. She didn't seem the sort to give up just because Darrow said no once. She hadn't got to where she was in her career by shrinking away from a challenge, had she? So when she talked about the diaries, I knew it was just a matter of time before she had them. And I didn't know what Hannah had written so I couldn't take the chance."

"What happened that night with Hannah Darrow?"

Sydeham brought his eyes to Lynley. "We met at the mill. She was some forty minutes late, and I'd begun to think—to hope, actually—that she wasn't coming. But she showed up at the last in her usual fashion, hot to make love right there on the floor. But I . . . I put her off. I'd brought her a scarf she'd seen in a boutique in Norwich. And I insisted she let me put it on her right then." He watched his hands continue their play on the white cup, fingers pressing upon its rim. "It was easy enough. I was kissing her when I tightened the knot."

Lynley thought about the innocent references he had been too blind to see earlier in Hannah's diary and took a calculated gamble with, "I'm surprised you didn't have her one last time right there in the mill, if that's what she wanted."

The payoff he was looking for came without a pause. "I'd lost the touch with her. Each time we met, it was becoming more difficult." Sydeham laughed shortly, an expression of contempt that was self-directed. "It was going to be Joanna all over again."

"The beautiful woman who rises to fame, who's the object of every man's steamy fantasy, whose own husband can't service her the way she wants."

"I'd say you've got the picture, Inspector. Nicely put."

"Yet you've stayed with Joanna all these years."

"She's the one thing in my life that I did completely right. My unmitigated success. One doesn't let something like that go easily, and as for me, I'd never have considered it. I couldn't let her go. Hannah merely came along at a bad time for Jo and me. Things had been . . . off between us for about three weeks. She'd been thinking of signing on with a London agent and I felt a bit left out in the cold. Useless. That must have been what started my . . . trouble. Then when Hannah came along, I felt like a new man for a month or two. Every time I saw her, I had her. Sometimes two or three times in a single evening. Christ. It was like being reborn."

"Until she wanted to become an actress like your wife?"

"And then it was history repeating itself. Yes."

"But why on earth kill her? Why not just break it off?"

"She'd found my London address. It was bad enough when she showed up at the theatre one evening when Jo and I were setting off with the London agent. After that happened, I knew if I left her behind in the Fens, she'd show up one day at our flat. I would have lost Joanna. There simply didn't seem to be another choice."

"And Gowan Kilbride? Where did he fit in?"

Sydeham placed his coffee cup back onto the table, its rim caved in all around, entirely useless now. "He knew about the gloves, Inspector."

THEY COMPLETED their preliminary interview with David Sydeham at five-fifteen in the morning and staggered, red-eyed, out into the corridor where Sydeham was led to a telephone to make a call to his wife. Lynley watched him go, feeling caught in a flood of pity for the man. This surprised him, for justice *was* being served by the arrest. Yet he knew that the effect of the murders—that stone thrown into a pond whose surface cannot remain unchanged by the intrusion—had only just begun for everyone. He turned away.

There were other things to contend with, among them the press, finally eager for a statement, materialising from nowhere, shouting questions, demanding interviews.

He pushed past them, crumpled into nothing a message from Superintendent Webberly that was pressed into his hand. Nearly blind with exhaustion, he made his way towards the lift, caught up at last in only one conscious thought: to find Helen. In only one conscious need: to sleep.

He found his way home like an automaton and fell onto his bed fully clothed. He did not awaken when Denton came in, removed his shoes, and covered him with a blanket. He did not awaken until the afternoon.

"IT WAS HER EYESIGHT," Lynley said. "I noticed nearly everything else in Hannah Darrow's diaries save the reference to the fact that she hadn't worn her spectacles to that second play, so she couldn't see the stage clearly. She only *thought* Sydeham was one of the actors because he came out the stage door at the end of the performance. And of course, I was too blinded by Davies-Jones' role in *The Three Sisters* to realise what it meant that Joanna Ellacourt had been in the same scene from which the suicide note was drawn. Sydeham would know any scene Joanna was in, probably better than the actors themselves. He helped her with her lines. I heard him doing that myself at the Agincourt."

"Did Joanna Ellacourt know her husband was the killer?" St. James asked.

Lynley shook his head, taking the proffered cup of tea from Deborah with a faint smile. The three of them sat in St. James' study, dividing their attention among cakes and sandwiches, tarts and tea. A misty shaft of late afternoon sunlight struck the window and reflected against a mound of snow on the ledge outside. Some distance away, rush-hour traffic on the Embankment began its noisy crawl towards the suburbs.

"She'd been told by Mary Agnes Campbell—as had they all—that Joy's bedroom door was locked," he responded. "Like me, she thought Davies-Jones was the killer. What she didn't know—what no one knew until late yesterday afternoon—was that Joy's door hadn't been locked all night. It was only locked once Francesca Gerrard went into the room to look for her necklace at three-fifteen, found Joy dead, and, assuming her brother had done it, went down to her office for the keys and locked the door in an attempt to protect him. I should have heard the lie when she told me the pearls were on the chest of drawers by the door. Why would Joy have put them there when the rest of her jewellery was on the dressing table on the other side of the room? I'd seen that myself."

St. James selected another sandwich. "Would it have made a difference had Macaskin managed to reach you before you left for Hampstead yesterday?"

"What could he have told me? Only that Francesca Gerrard had confessed to him that she lied to us at Westerbrae about the door being locked. I don't know whether I would have had the common sense to put that together with a number of facts that I had been choosing to ignore. The fact that Robert Gabriel had a woman with him in his bedroom; the fact that Sydeham *admitted* that Joanna had not been with him for some hours the night Joy died; the fact that *Jo* and *Joy* are two easy names to confuse, especially for a man like Gabriel, who pursued women tirelessly and took as many to bed as he could manage."

"So that's what Irene Sinclair heard." St. James moved in his chair to a more comfortable position, grimacing as the lower part of his leg brace caught against the piping on the ottoman's edge. He disengaged it with an irritable grunt. "But why Joanna Ellacourt? She's not made it a secret that she loathes Gabriel. Or was that dramatic loathing, part of the ploy?"

"She loathed Sydeham more than Gabriel that night, because he'd got her into Joy's play in the first place. She felt he'd betrayed her. She wanted to hurt him. So she went to Gabriel's bedroom at half past eleven and waited there, to take her revenge on her husband in coin that he would well understand. But what she didn't realise was that, in going to Gabriel, she'd given Sydeham the opportunity he had been looking for ever since Joy made the remark about John Darrow at dinner."

"I suppose Hannah Darrow didn't know that Sydeham was married."

Lynley shook his head. "Evidently not. She'd only seen them once together and even then another man was with them. All she knew was that Sydeham had access to drama coaches and voice coaches and everything else that went into success. As far as Hannah was concerned, Sydeham was the key to her new life. And for a time, she was *his* key to a sexual prowess he had been lacking."

"Do you suppose Joy Sinclair knew about Sydeham's involvement with Hannah Darrow?" St. James asked.

"She hadn't got that far in her research. And John Darrow was determined she never would. She merely made an innocent remark at dinner. But Sydeham couldn't afford to take a chance. So he killed her. And of course, Irene's references to the diaries at the theatre yesterday were what took him to Hampstead last night."

Deborah had been listening quietly, but now she spoke, perplexed. "Didn't he take a terrible chance when he killed Joy Sinclair, Tommy? Couldn't his wife have returned to their room at any moment and found him gone? Couldn't he have run into someone in the hall?"

Lynley shrugged. "He was fairly sure where Joanna was after all, Deb. And he knew Robert Gabriel well enough to believe that Gabriel would keep her with him as long as he could possibly continue to demonstrate his virility. Everyone else in the house was easily accounted for. So once he heard Joy return from Vinney's room shortly before one, all he had to do was wait a bit for her to fall asleep."

Deborah was caught on an earlier thought. "But his own *wife* . . ." she murmured, looking pained.

"I should guess that Sydeham was willing to let Gabriel have his wife once or twice if he could get away with murder. But he wasn't willing to let the man boast about it in front of the company. So he waited until Gabriel was alone at the theatre. Then he caught him in his dressing room."

"I wonder if Gabriel knew who was beating him," St. James mused.

"As far as Gabriel was concerned, it probably could have been any number of men. And he was lucky it wasn't. Anyone else might have killed him. Sydeham didn't want to do that."

"Why not?" Deborah asked. "After what happened between Gabriel and Joanna, I should think Sydeham would be more than happy to see him dead."

"Sydeham was nobody's fool. The last thing he wanted to do was narrow my field of suspects." Lynley shook his head. His next words reflected the shame he felt. "Of course, what he didn't know was that I had sufficiently narrowed it myself already. A field of one. Havers said it best. Police work to be proud of."

The other two did not respond. Deborah twisted the lid on the porcelain teapot, slowly tracing the petal of a delicate pink rose. St.

James moved a bit of sandwich here and there on his plate. Neither of them looked at Lynley.

He knew they were avoiding the question he had come to ask, knew they were doing it out of loyalty and love. Still, undeserving as he was, Lynley found himself hoping that the bond between them all was strong enough to allow them to see that he needed to find her in spite of her desire not to be found. So he asked the question.

"St. James, where's Helen? When I got back to Joy's house last night, she'd vanished. Where is she?"

He saw Deborah's hand drop from the teapot, saw it tighten on the pleats of her russet wool skirt. St. James lifted his head.

"That's too much to ask," he responded.

It was the answer Lynley had expected, the answer he knew was owed to him. Yet, in spite of this, he pressed them. "I can't change what happened. I can't change the fact that I was a fool. But at least I can apologise. At least I can tell her—"

"It's not time. She's not ready."

Lynley felt a surge of anger at such implacable resolution. "Damn you, St. James. She tried to warn him off! Did she tell you that as well? When he came over the wall, she gave a cry that he heard, and we nearly lost him. Because of Helen. So if she's not ready to see me, she can tell me that herself. Let *her* make the decision."

"She's decided, Tommy."

The words were spoken so coolly that his anger died. He felt his throat tighten in quick reaction. "She's gone with him, then. Where? To Wales?"

Nothing. Deborah moved, casting a long look at her husband, who had turned his head to the unlit fire.

Lynley felt rising desperation at their refusal to speak. He'd met with the same kind of refusal from Caroline Shepherd at Helen's flat earlier, the same kind of refusal on the telephone when he spoke to Helen's parents and three of her sisters. He knew it was a punishment richly due him, and yet in spite of that knowledge, he railed against it, refused to accept it as just and true.

"For God's sake, Simon." He felt riven by despair. "I love her. You, above all people, know what it means to be separated like this from someone you love. Without a word. Without a chance. Please. Tell me."

Unexpectedly then, he saw Deborah reach out quickly. She grasped her husband's thin hand. Lynley barely heard her voice as she spoke to St. James.

"My love, I'm sorry. Forgive me. I simply can't do this." She turned to Lynley. Her eyes were bright with tears. "She's gone to Skye, Tommy. She's alone."

HE FACED only one last task before heading north to Helen, and that was to see Superintendent Webberly and, through seeing him, to put a period to the case. To other things as well. He had ignored the early-morning message from his superior, with its official congratulations for a job well done and its request for a meeting as soon as possible. Filled with the realisation of how blind jealousy had governed every step of his investigation, Lynley had hardly wanted to hear anyone's praise. Much less the praise of a man who had been perfectly willing to use him as an unwitting tool in the master game of deceit.

For beyond Sydeham's guilt and Davies-Jones' innocence, there still remained Lord Stinhurst. And Scotland Yard's dance of attendance upon the commitment of the government to keeping a twenty-five-year-old secret out of the public eye.

This remained to be dealt with. Lynley had not felt himself ready for the confrontation earlier in the day. But he was ready now.

He found Webberly at the circular table in his office. There, as usual, open files, books, photographs, reports, and used crockery abounded. Bent over a street map which was outlined heavily in yellow marking pen, the superintendent held a cigar clenched between his teeth, filling the already claustrophobic room with a malodorous pall of smoke. He was talking to his secretary, who sat behind his desk, cooperatively nodding and note-taking and all the time waving her hand in front of her face in a useless attempt to keep the cigar smoke from permeating her well-tailored suit and smooth blonde hair. She was, as usual, as close a replica of the Princess of Wales as she could make herself.

She rolled her eyes at Lynley, wrinkled her nose delicately in distaste at the smell and the clutter, and said, "Here's Detective Inspector Lynley, Superintendent."

Lynley waited expectantly for Webberly to correct her. It was a game the two of them played. Webberly preferred *mister* to the use of titles. Dorothea Harriman ("call me Dee, *please*") vastly preferred titles to anything else.

This afternoon, however, the superintendent merely growled and looked up from his map, saying, "Did you get everything, Harriman?"

His secretary consulted her notes, adjusting the high scalloped collar of her Edwardian blouse. She wore a pert bow tie beneath it. "Everything. Shall I type this lot up?"

"If you will. And run thirty copies. The usual routing."

Harriman sighed. "Before I leave, Superintendent? . . . No, don't say it. I know, I know. 'Put it on the tick, Harriman.' " She shot Lynley a meaningful look. "I've so much time on the tick right now that I could take my honeymoon on it. *If* someone would be so good as to pop the question."

Lynley smiled. "Blimey. And to think I'm busy tonight."

Harriman laughed at the answer, gathered up her notes, and brushed three paper cups from Webberly's desk into the rubbish. "See if you can get him to do something about this pit," she requested as she left.

Webberly said nothing until they were alone. Then he folded the map, slid it onto one of his filing cabinets, and went to his desk. But he did not sit. Rather, puffing on his cigar contentedly, he looked at the London skyline beyond the window.

"Some people think it's lack of ambition that makes me avoid promotion," Webberly confided without turning. "But actually it's the view. If I had to change offices, I'd lose the sight of the city coming to light as darkness falls. And I can't tell you what pleasure that's given me through the years." His freckled hands played with the watch fob on his waistcoat. Cigar ash fluttered, ignored, to the floor.

Lynley thought about how he had once liked this man, how he had respected the fine mind inside the dishevelled exterior. It was a mind that brought out the best in those under his command, conscientiously using each one to his personal strength, never to his weakness. That quality of being able to see people as they really were had always been what Lynley admired most in his superior. Now, however, he saw that it was double-edged, that it could be used—indeed, *had* been used in his case—to probe a man's weakness and use that weakness to meet an end not of his own devising.

Webberly had known without a doubt that Lynley would believe in the given word of a peer. That kind of belief was part and parcel of Lynley's upbringing, a precious clinging to "my word as a gentleman" that had governed people of his class for centuries. Like the laws of primogeniture, it could not be sloughed off easily. And that is what Webberly had depended upon, sending Lynley to hear Lord Stinhurst's manufactured tale of his wife's infidelity. Not Mac-Pherson, Stewart, or Hale, or any other DI who would have listened sceptically, called in Lady Stinhurst to hear the story herself and then moved on to uncover the truth about Geoffrey Rintoul without a second thought.

Neither the government nor the Yard had wanted that to happen. So they had sent in the one man they believed could be depended upon to take the word of a gentleman and hence to sweep all connections to Lord Stinhurst right under the carpet. That, to Lynley, was the unpardonable offence. He couldn't forgive Webberly for having done it to him. He couldn't forgive himself for having mindlessly lived up to their every expectation.

It didn't matter that Stinhurst had been innocent of Joy Sinclair's death. For the Yard had not known that, had not even cared, had desired only that key information in the man's past not come to light. Had Stinhurst been the killer, had he escaped justice, Lynley knew that neither the government nor the Yard would have felt a moment's compunction as long as the secret of Geoffrey Rintoul was safe.

He felt ugly, unclean. He reached into his pocket for his police identification and tossed it onto Webberly's desk.

The superintendent's eyes dropped to the warrant card, raised back to Lynley. He squinted against the smoke from his cigar. "What's this?"

"I'm done with it."

Webberly's face looked frozen. "I'm trying to misunderstand you, Inspector."

"There's no need for that, is there? You've all got what you wanted. Stinhurst is safe. The whole story is safe."

Webberly took the cigar from his mouth and crushed it among the stubs in his ashtray, spattering ash. "Don't do this, lad. There's no need."

"I don't like being used. It's a funny quirk of mine." Lynley moved to the door. "I'll clean out my things—"

Webberly's hand slammed down against the top of his desk, sending papers flying. A pencil holder toppled to the floor. "And you think I *like* being used, Inspector? Just what's your fantasy about all this? What role have you assigned me?"

"You knew about Stinhurst. About his brother. About his father. That's why I was sent to Scotland and not someone else."

"I knew only what I was *told*. The order to send you north came from the commissioner, through Hillier. Not from me. I didn't like it any better than you did. But I had no choice in the matter."

"Indeed," Lynley replied. "Well, at least I can be grateful that I do have choices. I'm exerting one of them now."

Webberly's face flooded with angry colour. But his voice stayed calm. "You're not thinking straight, lad. Consider a few things before your righteous indignation carries you nobly towards professional martyrdom. I didn't know a thing about Stinhurst. I still don't know, so if you care to tell me, I'd be delighted to hear it. All I can tell you is that once Hillier came to me with the order that you were to have the case and no one else, I smelled a dead rat floating in somebody's soup."

"Yet you assigned me anyway."

"Damn you for a fool! I wasn't given a choice in the matter! But see it for what it was, at least. I assigned Havers as well. You didn't want her, did you? You fought me on it, didn't you? So why the hell do you think I *insisted* she be on the case? Because of all people, I *knew* Havers would stick to Stinhurst like a tick on a dog if it came down to it. And it came to that, didn't it? Blast you, answer me! Didn't it?"

"It did."

Webberly drove a thick fist into his open palm. "Those sods! I *knew* they were trying to protect him. I just didn't know from what." He fired Lynley a dark look. "But you don't believe me, I dare say."

"You're right. I don't. You're not that powerless, sir. You never have been."

"You're wrong, lad. I am, when it comes to my job. I do as I'm told. It's easy to be a man of inflexible rectitude when you've the freedom to walk out of here anytime you smell something a little unpleasant. But I don't have that kind of freedom. No independent source of wealth, no country estate. This job isn't a lark. It's my bread and butter. And when I'm given an order, I follow it. As unpleasant as that may seem to you."

"And if Stinhurst had been the killer? If I'd closed the case without making an arrest?"

"You didn't do that, did you? I trusted Havers to see that you wouldn't. And I trusted you. I knew that your instincts would take you to the killer eventually."

"But they didn't," Lynley said. The words cost him dearly in pride, and he wondered why it mattered so much to him that he had been such a fool.

Webberly studied his face. When he spoke, his voice was kind yet still keen with perception. "And that's why you're tossing it in, isn't it, laddie? Not because of me and not because of Stinhurst. And not because some higher-ups saw you as a man they could use to meet their own ends. You're tossing it in because you made a mistake. You lost your objectivity on this one, didn't you? You went after the wrong man. So. Welcome to the club, Inspector. You're not perfect any longer."

Webberly reached for the warrant card, fingered it for a moment before taking it to Lynley. Without formality, he shoved it into the breast pocket of his coat.

"I'm sorry the Stinhurst situation happened," he said. "I can't tell you it won't happen again. But if it does, I should guess you won't need Sergeant Havers there to remind you that you're more of a policeman than you ever were a bloody peer." He turned back to his desk and surveyed its mess. "You're due time off, Lynley. So take it. Don't report in till Tuesday." And then, having said that, he looked up. His words were quiet. "Learning to forgive yourself is part of the job, lad. It's the only part you've never quite mastered."

HE HEARD the muted shout as he drove up the ramp from the underground car park and pulled onto Broadway. It was fast growing dark. Braking, he looked in the direction of St. James's Park Station, and among the pedestrians he saw Jeremy Vinney loping down the pavement, topcoat flapping round his knees like the wings of an ungainly bird. As he ran, he waved a spiral notebook. Pages, covered with writing, fluttered in the wind. Lynley lowered the window as Vinney reached the car.

"I've done the story on Geoffrey Rintoul," the journalist panted, managing a smile. "Jesus, what a piece of luck to catch you! I need you to be the source. Off the record. Just to confirm. That's all."

Lynley watched a flurry of snow blow across the street. He recognised a group of secretaries making their end-of-day dash from the Yard to the train, their laughter like music rising into the air.

"There's no story," he said.

Vinney's expression altered. That momentary sharing of confidence was gone. "But you've spoken to Stinhurst! You can't tell me he didn't confirm every detail of his brother's past! How could he deny it? With Willingate in the inquest pictures and Joy's play alluding to everything else? You can't tell me he talked his way out of that!"

"There's no story, Mr. Vinney. I'm sorry." Lynley began to raise the window but stopped when Vinney hooked his fingers over the glass.

"She wanted it!" His voice was a plea. "You know Joy wanted me to follow the story. You know that's why I was there. She wanted everything about the Rintouls to come to light."

The case was closed. Her murderer had been found. Yet Vinney pursued his original quest. There was no possibility of a journalistic coup involved for him since the government would quash his story without a thought. Here was loyalty far beyond the call of friendship. Once again, Lynley wondered what lay at its heart, what debt of honour Vinney owed Joy Sinclair.

"Jer! Jerry! For God's sake, hurry up! Paulie's waiting and you know he'll get himself all hot and bothered if we're late again."

The second voice drifted from across the street. Delicate, petulant, very nearly feminine. Lynley tracked it down. A young man— no more than twenty years old—stood in the archway leading into the station. He was stamping his feet, shoulders hunched against the cold, and one of the passageway lights illuminated his face. It was achingly handsome, possessing a Renaissance beauty, perfect in feature, in colour, in form. And a Renaissance assessment of such beauty rose in Lynley's mind, Marlowe's assessment, as apt now as it had been in the sixteenth century. *To hazard more than for the Golden Fleece.*

Finally, then, that last puzzle piece clicked into position, so obvious a piece that Lynley wondered what had kept him from placing it before. Joy hadn't been talking *about* Vinney on her tape recorder. She had been talking *to* him, reminding herself of a point she wanted to make in a future conversation with her friend. And here across the street was the source of her concern: *"Why be in such a lather over him? It's hardly a lifetime proposition."*

"Jerry! Jemmy!" the voice wheedled again. The boy spun on one heel, an impatient puppy. He laughed when his overcoat billowed out round his body like a circus clown's garb.

Lynley moved his eyes back to the journalist. Vinney looked away, not towards the boy but towards Victoria Street.

"Wasn't it Freud who said there are no accidents?" Vinney's voice sounded resigned. "I must have wanted you to know, so you'd understand what I meant when I said that Joy and I were always— and only—friends. Call it absolution, I suppose. Perhaps vindication. It makes no difference now."

"She did know?"

"I had no secrets from her. I don't think I could have had one if I tried." Vinney looked deliberately back at the boy. His expression softened. His lips curved in a smile of remarkable tenderness. "We are cursed by love, aren't we, Inspector? It gives us no peace. We seek it endlessly in a thousand different ways, and if we're lucky, we do have it for a shuddering instant. And we feel like free men then, don't we? Even when we bear its most terrible burden."

"Joy would have understood that, I dare say."

"God knows. She was the only one in my life who ever did." His hand dropped from the window. "So I owe her this about the Rintouls, you see. It's what she would have wanted. The story. The truth."

Lynley shook his head. "Revenge is what she wanted, Mr. Vinney. And I do think she got that. After a fashion."

"So that's the way it's to be? Can you really let it end this way, Inspector? After what these people have done to you?" He waved in the direction of the building behind them.

"We do things to ourselves," Lynley replied. He nodded, raised the window, and drove on.

HE WOULD LATER SEE the trip to Skye as a phantasmagorical blur of continually changing countryside that he was only dimly aware of as he flew towards the north. Stopping merely for food and petrol and once for a few hours of rest at an inn somewhere between Carlisle and Glasgow, he arrived at Kyle of Lochalsh, a small village on the mainland across from the Isle of Skye, in the late afternoon the following day.

He pulled into the car park of an hotel on the waterfront and sat gazing at the strait, its rippled surface the colour of old coins. The sun was setting, and on the island the majestic peak of Sgurr na Coinnich looked covered in silver. Far below it, the car ferry pulled away from the dock and began its slow movement towards the mainland, carrying only a lorry, two hikers who hugged one another against the bitter cold, and a slender solitary figure whose smooth chestnut hair blew round her face, which was lifted, as if for blessing, to the last rays of the winter sun.

Seeing Helen, Lynley all at once perceived the sheer lunacy of his coming to her now. He knew he was the last person she wanted to see. He knew that she wanted this isolation. Yet none of that mattered as the ferry drew nearer to the mainland and he saw her eyes fall upon the Bentley in the car park above her. He got out, pulled on his overcoat, and walked down to the landing. The wind blew frigidly against him, buffeting his cheeks, whipping through his hair. He tasted the salt of the distant North Atlantic.

When the ferry docked, the lorry started up with a foul emission of smoke, and trundled down the Invergarry road. Arm in arm, the hikers passed him, laughing, a man and a woman who stopped to kiss, then to ponder the opposite shore of Skye. It was hung with clouds, dove grey turning to the lavish hues of sunset.

The drive north from London had given Lynley long hours in which to contemplate what he would say to Helen when he finally saw her. But as she stepped from the ferry, brushing her hair from her cheeks, words were lost to him. He wanted only to hold her in his arms and knew beyond a doubt that he did not have that right. Instead, he walked wordlessly at her side up the rise towards the hotel.

They went inside. The lounge was empty, its vast front windows offering a panorama of water and mountains and the sunset-shot clouds of the island. Lady Helen walked to these and stood before them, and although her posture—the slightly bent head, the small curved shoulders—spoke volumes of her desire for solitude, Lynley could not bring himself to leave her with so much left unsaid between them. He joined her and saw the shadows under her eyes, smudges of both sorrow and fatigue. Her arms were crossed in front of her, as if in the need of warmth or protection.

"Why on earth did he kill Gowan? More than anything else, Tommy, that seems so senseless to me."

Lynley wondered why he had ever given a moment to thinking that Helen, of all people, would greet him with the score of recriminations that he had so steadfastly earned. He had been prepared to hear them, to admit to their truth. Somehow in the confusion of the last few days, he had forgotten the basic human decency that was the central core of Helen's character. She *would* put Gowan before herself.

"At Westerbrae, David Sydeham claimed that he'd left his gloves at the reception desk," he replied, watching her eyes lower thoughtfully, the lashes dark against her creamy skin. "He said he'd left them there when he and Joanna first arrived."

She nodded in comprehension. "But when Francesca Gerrard ran into Gowan and spilled all those liqueurs that night after the reading, Gowan had to clean the entire area. And he saw that David Sydeham's gloves weren't there at all, didn't he? But he must not have remembered it at once."

"Yes, I think that's what happened. At any rate, once Gowan

remembered, he would have realised what it meant. The single glove that Sergeant Havers found at the reception desk the next day—and the one that you found in the boot—could have got there only one way: through Sydeham's putting them there himself, after he killed Joy. I think that's what Gowan tried to tell me. Just before he died. That he hadn't seen the gloves at the reception desk. But I . . . I thought he was talking about Rhys."

Lynley saw her eyes close painfully upon the name, knew she hadn't expected to hear it from him.

"How did Sydeham manage it?"

"He was still in the sitting room when Macaskin and the Wester-brae cook came to me and asked if everyone could be allowed out of the library. He slipped into the kitchen then and got the knife."

"But with everyone in the house? Especially with the police?"

"They'd been packing up to leave. Everyone was wandering here and there. And besides, it was only the work of a minute or two. After that, he went up the back stairs and along to his room."

Without thinking, Lynley raised his hand, grazed it gently along the length of her hair, following its curve to touch her shoulder. She did not move away from him. He felt his heart beat heavily against his chest.

"I'm so sorry about everything," he said. "I had to see you to say at least that much, Helen."

She didn't look at him. It seemed as if the effort to do so was monumental, as if she found herself unequal to the task. When she spoke, her voice was low and her eyes were fixed on the distant ruin of Caisteal Maol as the sun struck its crumbling walls for the final time that day.

"You were right, Tommy. You said I was trying to replay Simon to a different ending, and I discovered that I was. But it wasn't a different ending after all, was it? I repeated myself admirably when it came down to it. The only thing missing from the wretched scenario was a hospital room for me to walk out of, leaving him lying there entirely alone."

No acrimony underscored her tone. But Lynley didn't need to hear it to know how each word carried its full weight of searing self-loathing. "No," he said miserably.

"Yes. Rhys knew it was you on the telephone. Was that just two nights ago? It seems like forever. And when I rang off, he asked me if it was you. I said no, I said it was my father. But he *knew*. And he saw that you'd convinced me that he was the killer. I kept denying it, of course, denying everything. When he asked me if I'd told you he was with me, I even denied that as well. But he knew I was lying. And he saw that I'd chosen, just as he'd told me I'd choose." She lifted a hand as if to touch her cheek, but again it seemed that it required too much effort. She dropped it to her side. "I didn't even need to hear a cock crow three times. I knew what I'd done. To both of us."

Whatever his own desires in coming to her here, Lynley knew he had to convince Lady Helen of his culpability in the sin she believed she had committed. He had to give her that much, if nothing else.

"It isn't your fault, Helen. You wouldn't have done any of that had I not forced you into it. What were you to think when I told you about Hannah Darrow? What were you to believe? *Whom* were you to believe?"

"That's just it. I could have chosen Rhys in spite of what you said. I knew that then, I know it now. But instead, I chose you. When Rhys saw that, he left me. And who could blame him? Believing one's lover is a murderer does rather irreparable damage to a relationship, after all." She finally looked at him, turning, so near that he could smell the pure, fresh scent of her hair. "And until Hampstead, I did think Rhys was the killer."

"Then why did you warn him off? Was it to punish me?"

"Warn him . . . ? Is that what you thought? No. When he came over the wall, I saw at once it wasn't Rhys. I . . . I'd grown to know Rhys' body, you see. And that man was too big. So without thinking, I reacted. It was horror, I think, the realisation of what I'd done to him, the knowledge that I'd lost him." Her head turned back to the window, but only for a moment. When she went on, her eyes once again sought his. "At Westerbrae, I'd come to see myself as his saviour, the fine, upright woman who was going to make him whole again after he'd been in ruins. I saw myself as his reason for never drinking again. So you see, you were really right at the heart of it, weren't you? It was just like Simon after all."

"No. Helen, I didn't know what I was talking about. I was half-mad with jealousy."

"You were right, all the same."

As they spoke, shadows lengthened in the lounge, and the barman walked through, turning on lights, opening the bar at the far end of the room for its evening business. Voices drifted to them from the reception desk: a crucial decision to be reached about postcards, a good-humoured debate about the next day's activities. Lynley listened, longing for that sweet normality of a holiday from home with someone he loved.

Lady Helen stirred. "I must change for dinner." She began to move towards the lift.

"Why did you come here?" Lynley asked abruptly.

She paused but did not look at him. "I wanted to see Skye in the dead of winter. I needed to see what it was like to be here alone."

He put his hand on her arm. Her warmth was like an infusion of life. "And have you seen enough of it? Alone, I mean."

Both of them knew what he was really asking. But instead of replying, she walked to the lift and pressed the button, watching its light single-mindedly, as if she were observing an amazing act of creative genius. He followed and barely heard her when she finally spoke.

"Please. I can't bear to cause either of us any more pain."

Somewhere above them, the machinery whirred. And he knew then that she would go on to her room, seeking the solitude she had come for, leaving him behind. But he saw that she intended this to be no few minutes' separation between them. Instead, this was something indeterminate, endless, something not to be borne. He knew it was the worst possible time to speak. But there would probably not be another opportunity.

"Helen." When she looked at him, he saw that her eyes were liquid with tears. "Marry me."

A small bubble of laughter escaped her, not a sound of humour but one of despair. She made a tiny gesture, eloquent in its futility.

"You know how I love you," he said. "Don't tell me it's too late."

She bowed her head. In front of her the lift doors opened. As if they beckoned her to do so, she put into words what he had been afraid—and had known—she might say. "I don't want to see you, Tommy. Not for a while."

He felt wrenched by the words, managed only, "How long?"

"A few months. Perhaps longer."

"That feels like a sentence of death."

"I'm sorry. It's what I need." She walked into the lift, pushed the button for her floor. "Even after this, I still can't bear to hurt you. I never could, Tommy."

"I love you," he said. And then again, as if each word could serve as its own painful act of contrition. "Helen. Helen. I love you."

He saw her lips part, saw her fleeting, sweet smile before the lift doors closed and she was gone.

*   *   *

BARBARA HAVERS was in the public bar of the King's Arms not far from New Scotland Yard, moping into her weekly pint of ale. She'd been nursing it along for the past thirty minutes. It was an hour before closing, long after the time when she should have made her way back to her parents and Acton, but she hadn't been able to bring herself to that yet. The paperwork was filed, the reports completed, the conversations with Macaskin at an end for now. But as always, at the conclusion of a case, she had a sense of her own uselessness. People would go on brutalising one another, despite her meagre efforts to stop them.

"Buy a bloke a drink?"

At Lynley's voice, she looked up. "I thought you'd gone to Skye! Holy God, you look done in."

He did indeed. Unshaven, his clothes rumpled, he looked like last year's Christmas wish.

"I *am* done in," he admitted, making a pathetically visible effort to smile. "I've lost count of the hours I've spent in the car over the last few days. What're you drinking? Not tonic water tonight, I take it?"

"Not tonight. I've moved up to Bass. But now you're here, I may change my poison. Depends on who's paying."

"I see." He took off his overcoat, threw it down carelessly on the next table, and sank into a chair. Feeling in his pocket, he produced cigarette case and lighter. As always she helped herself, regarding him over the flame that he held for her.

"What's up?" she asked him.

He lit a cigarette. "Nothing."

"Ah."

They smoked companionably. He made no move to get himself a drink. She waited.

Then with his eyes on the opposite wall he said, "I've asked her to marry me, Barbara."

It was as she expected. "You don't exactly look like the bearer of glad tidings."

"No. I'm not." Lynley cleared his throat, studying the tip of his cigarette.

Barbara sighed, felt the weighty, sore blanket of his unhappiness, and found to her surprise that she wore it as her own. At the nearby bar Evelyn, the blowsy barmaid, was fingering her way, bleary-eyed, through the night's receipts and doing her best to ignore the leering advances of two of the establishment's regular patrons. Barbara called out her name.

"Aye?" Evelyn responded with a yawn.

"Bring on two Glenlivets. Neat." Barbara eyed Lynley and added, "And keep them coming, will you?"

"Sure, luv."

When they were delivered to the table and Lynley reached for his wallet, Barbara spoke again.

"It's on me tonight, sir."

"A celebration, Sergeant?"

"No. A wake." She tossed back her whisky. It lit her blood like a flame. "Drink up, Inspector. Let's get ourselves soused."